MOONCHASERS

&

OTHER STORIES

Books by Ed Gorman

The Autumn Dead
Blood Moon
Cold Blue Midnight
A Cry of Shadows
The First Lady
The Marilyn Tapes
Night Kills
Night of Shadows
The Night Remembers
Shadow Games

STORY COLLECTIONS
Cages
The Face and Other Stories
Moonchasers and Other Stories
Prisoners

MOONCHASERS

&

OTHER STORIES

ED GORMAN

A TOM DOHERTY ASSOCIATES BOOK
NEW YORK

MOONCHASERS AND OTHER STORIES

Copyright © 1996 by Ed Gorman

A Forge Book
Published by Tom Doherty Associates, Inc.
175 Fifth Avenue
New York, N.Y. 10010

Forge® is a registered trademark of Tom Doherty Associates, Inc.

Library of Congress Cataloging-in-Publication Data

Gorman, Edward.
    Moonchasers and other stories / by Ed Gorman.
        p.   cm.
    "A Tom Doherty Associates book."
    ISBN 0–312–86010–2
    1. United States—Social life and customs—20th century—Fiction. I. Title.
PS3557.O759M66   1996
813'.54—dc20   95–40770

First edition: January 1996

Printed in the United States of America

0 9 8 7 6 5 4 3 2 1

This book is a belated thank-you to four professors whose wisdom and kindness helped me become a writer: Charles Cannon, Burton Kendle, Robert Renk, and Todd Zeiss.

TABLE OF CONTENTS

INTRODUCTION

These stories are, at least in an oblique way, a record of my time on the planet.

A lot of the people you'll meet here, I've known in life.

The dwarf woman of "The Wind from Midnight," for instance, is a dwarf woman I used to work with in a hotel. At day's end we frequently pushed a pint of cheap bourbon back and forth, a forlorn pair of scared drunks. She died long ago, when we were young. I still occasionally visit her grave and talk to her. She was a lovely, endearing woman.

The hero of "Moonchasers" is a kid I grew up with, one who, at fifteen, knew more about honor and wisdom than I know today.

The old man in "Render unto Caesar" did in life what he does in my story—walk around the neighborhood looking for dead cats, which he then gave decent burials. A strange old guy, to be sure, but a profoundly decent soul for all his oddness. And, yes, the young woman existed, too, and her husband really was that violent with her.

What happens to the married couple in "Stalker" happened to friends of mine. Their daughter was murdered. The couple never recovered. That happens a lot, as people in the victims' rights movement will tell you. Look at the face of Ron Goldman's father sometime. I hope that someday he'll find peace again.

"The Ugly File" is based on a woman I did a documentary film about. She gave birth to a terribly deformed baby. She felt estranged from the entire human race. She didn't think even her husband could understand what she was going through, as perhaps he couldn't.

The woman in "Prisoners" is based on a bright, elegant, talented young woman who used to work with me—and who spent several long sad years visiting her husband in prison.

And so on.

None of these stories is literally autobiographical, of course. I'm a storyteller, not a diarist.

But in choosing the tales for this collection, I tended to select those pieces that had personal meaning for me. I didn't choose any that relied strictly on plot. The older I get, the less those stories interest me as either reader or writer.

A number of editors should be thanked here. Janet Hutchings, of *Ellery Queen,* who is not only an astute editor but one of the gentlest people I've ever known; Kris Rusch, of *The Magazine of Fantasy & Science Fiction,* who knows how to get the best from me; Rich Chizmar, of *Cemetery Dance,* who helps me push against the constraints of the predictable; and Greg Cox, of Forge, who is a past master at handling writers. He makes you think that all those great ideas were yours, not his. Thanks for everything, Greg.

Finally, I'd like to thank my beautiful wife, Carol, for her patience, support and encouragement; and my beautiful mother for driving me to the library all those years ago when she probably had much better things to do.

I had a good time writing these stories. I hope you have a good time reading them.

MOONCHASERS

"There are men who can lust with parts of themselves.
Only their brain or their hearts burn and then not completely. There are others, still more fortunate, who
are like the filaments of an incandescent lamp. They
burn fiercely, yet nothing is destroyed."
—Nathanael West, *The Day of the Locust*

*For my son Joe from the old man with love and pride
And for Robert Mitchum*

i

Yes, sir, it was just about the best sort of summer you could ask
for, when you were fifteen, that is, and it was 1958 and you
were living in Somerton, Iowa, which is forty miles due east of
Waterloo, where just a month earlier I'd seen Buddy Holly, Little
Richard and Gene Vincent and his Blue Caps all perform at the
Electric Light Ballroom.

Of course, neither Barney nor I let on that it was a good summer because if there is one thing that Barney and I liked to do it was
bitch about living our lives out in Somerton. Pop. 16,438. There
were maybe five pretty girls our age, none of whom would have a
darn thing to do with us, and one mean and muscular seventeen-
year-old named Maynard whom Barney and I had in some way of-
fended (if Maynard wanted to be pissed at anybody, it should have
been his parents for giving him that name). Fortunately for us,
Hamblin's Rexall had a good supply of science fiction magazines
and Gold Medal suspense novels and Ace Double Books. And the
Garden Theater likewise had the usual good supply of movies with
monsters in them. And Robert Mitchum.

That was the big thing Barney and I had in common. Sure we

liked *Amazing* and *Fantastic* with all those nifty Valigursky covers, and sure we liked all those teen monster movies with all those Southern California bikini girls, and sure we thought that Marlon Brando and Montgomery Clift and the late James Dean were really cool, but the coolest guy of all was Robert Mitchum. The Garden brought back *Thunder Road* for a week and Barney and I went four days running. And the same for when the Garden brought back *Night of the Hunter* and *Blood on the Moon*. We were there because Mitch was there.

Anyway, that's sort of the picture of how things were in our lives before that hot August night when Barney and I walked along the railroad tracks out on the east edge of town, smoking on a fresh contraband package of Lucky Strikes, and sipping at two ice-dripping eight-cent bottles of Pepsi.

We'd pretty much decided that this was going to be the night we broke into the abandoned warehouse and found out just what was in there. According to most of the little kids in Somerton, the warehouse was home to various kinds of spooks. Older kids, who didn't just have driver's ed learner permits like ours, took a different slant. They said that the migrant workers from the next town over snuck their daughters in there at night and ran a whorehouse that put all others to shame.

In the moonlight, the railroad tracks shone silver for a quarter of a mile. The air smelled of hot creosote from the railroad ties that had baked all day in the sun. Between tracks and warehouse was a winding creek, along the dark banks of which you could smell summer mud and hear throaty frogs and see the silhouette of the willow tree bent and weeping.

"We're gonna get our butts kicked," Barney said, "if they catch us."

Of course that's what Barney said before just about everything we ever did. Everything that was any fun, anyway.

But I didn't like to think uncharitable thoughts about Barney because he had it rough. His father had tried and failed in business several times. The family was pretty poor. And whenever his father quit going to his Alcoholics Anonymous meetings, he always got drunk for two or three days and beat up Barney's mom pretty bad.

A couple of times somebody had to call the chief of police and have him come over.

The warehouse was this big corrugated steel building with loading docks on both the west and east sides. There was a large window on the north end revealing the shadowy space where the office had been.

The window had long ago been smashed out, of course, and most of the exterior warehouse walls bore the chalk scrawlings of various kids—Class of '58, BG + FH, I Luv Judy! The kind of stuff, I'm told by my army corporal and former Eagle Scout brother, Gerald, is proof positive of immature minds.

So there it sat like a big monument left behind by some alien species. When the warehouse was first closed down, back in '56, kids of every age trooped out there to smash windows and hurl rocks at the steel walls, which were pretty obliging about making neat sounds when the rocks struck. But then the kids got sort of bored with the place and quit coming. Now they mostly spent time at the abandoned grain elevator on the west edge of town. The elevator was more fun because it was more dangerous. One kid had already fallen off the interior ladder and broken a leg and an arm. It was only a matter of time till some poor overenthusiastic kid got killed in there and so the place had developed a certain dark aura that the warehouse could never match.

As we were climbing through the office window, Barney said, "You don't really think there are ghosts and stuff in here, do ya?"

I just shook my head. Barney just kept moving.

We spent the first ten minutes inside walking around the front of the place and stepping on crunchy little rat droppings. It was pretty neat, actually, sort of like in those movies where they drop the atomic bomb and the few survivors walk around inside empty grocery stores and places like that and take everything they want.

Of course, there wasn't much to take inside this warehouse.

I remember my dad, who owned the haberdashery in town, saying once that the two guys who built this warehouse had no head for business, which was why they went broke so fast. And their creditors must have cleaned them out because when we went through the door leading to the back, all we saw was this huge empty concrete floor with moonlight splashing through six dirty, broken windows.

"This is where I'm going to bring Janie Mills," Barney said, "and screw her brains out."

"Good idea," I said, "and I'll double with you and bring Sharon Waggoner."

Barney had the grace to laugh. Janie Mills and Sharon Waggoner were the two most stuck-up girls in our class. They wouldn't come out here with us if we had them at gunpoint.

The place smelled of dust and heat and rain-soaked wood and truck oil and a turd-clogged toilet somewhere that hadn't been flushed in a long time.

"Hey!" Barney shouted suddenly.

And then laughed his ass off when the word echoed back to us through the moonlight and shadows.

"Hey!" I shouted, too, and listened as my own sound likewise began repeating itself.

This was another Somerton bust and we both knew it, which was why we'd both been shouting. Because there was nothing else to do. Because, as usual in Somerton, nothing was as it had been advertised. There were no spooks, no ghosts; and there were most definitely no voluptuous whores eager to free us from the prison of our virginity.

Barney took the Lucky Strike pack from the pocket of my short-sleeved shirt (we traded off the privilege of carrying the pack) and took a book of matches from his own shirt and lit up and that was when I saw the door move.

The door was way at the other end of the wide, empty warehouse floor, some kind of closet, I guessed. Barney's match had pointed my eye in that direction and that was how I came to notice the partially open door move a few inches closer to the frame.

Or I thought I had, anyway. Maybe, because I was so bored, I just wanted to think that something like that had happened.

"Let's go," Barney said. "We still got time to hit Rexall for a cherry Coke."

I nudged him in the ribs and nodded toward the end of the moonpainted floor.

"Huh?" he said out loud.

I whispered to him, "Somebody's in the closet up there."

He whispered back. "Bullshit."

"Bullshit yourself. I saw that door move."

Barney squinted his eyes and looked down the length of floor. He stared a long time and then whispered. "I didn't see it move."

"Somebody's in that closet."

And this time when he looked at me, I saw the beginnings of fear in his eyes.

You're in a shadowy, empty building on the edge of nowhere and you suddenly realize that not too far away is somebody or something lurking in a dark closet. Probably watching every move you make.

"Let's go," Barney whispered.

I shook my head. "I want to find out who's in there."

Barney gulped. "You're crazy."

"No, I'm just bored."

"You really gonna walk up there?"

I nodded and started walking.

At first it was sort of a lark. I could sense Barney behind me, watching with a kind of awe. That crazy sumbitch Tom was going to walk right up to that closet door, just the way Mitch would, and back here stood that A-1 chicken Barney. He would positively be ashamed of himself.

It was a great feeling, it really was. For the first twenty steps or so anyway.

Then I felt this sickening feeling in my stomach and bowels and a cold shudder went through me.

Hell, I wasn't brave. I was just some dumb-ass fifteen-year-old from Somerton, Iowa, and if I really believed that somebody was in that closet then I should turn around and get the hell out of here.

"I'll tell you, you're one ballsy guy and I mean that," Barney said.

And then I knew I would go over and open that closet door because Barney's admiration was just too much to lose.

Besides, I was starting to convince myself that I had just imagined the door moving anyway.

We reached the metal door and I put my hand out and took the knob.

"God, Tom, you really gonna open it?"

For an answer, I yanked the door open.

And there, in the middle of the chill deep closet darkness, sitting with his back against the far wall, was a man holding in his left hand a big cop-style flashlight and in his right a big criminal-style pistol.

"God," Barney said.

"Anybody else with you?" the man said. And right away he looked sort of familiar but I wasn't sure why. He was a tall guy, a little on the beefy side, with a kind of handsome face and dark hair and the saddest eyes I'd ever seen on a man except for maybe my Uncle Pete when Doc Anderson told him that Aunt Clarice had only two months to live.

The guy was pointing the gun directly at me. Or so it seemed. "N-no, sir."

"How'd you boys find out about me?"

"We didn't find out about you, sir," I said. "I mean not till we got in the warehouse here."

He asked our names and we told him.

And then for the first time I saw him get all seized up and heard him give out with a hard little grunt, the way you do when somebody hits you in the stomach. Or when you're in an awful lot of pain.

He tried to sit up and still keep both his gun and his flashlight on us but he wasn't having an easy time of it. I knew right away it was because of the blood all over the side of his dirty white shirt, and the green pussy stuff that was all mixed up in it.

I'd seen enough gangster movies to know what was going on here, especially when I let my eyes wander over to the big canvas bag sitting maybe half a foot from him, just on the edge of the light.

"You going to kill us?" Barney said.

Which was just like something Barney *would* say.

The guy just looked at Barney and said, "You got any candy bars or anything like that on you?"

"No, sir."

"How about you?"

I shook my head.

The guy grimaced again. The pain must have been pretty bad. The smell sure was.

"Sir," Barney said. "I don't mean to be nosey or anything, but you look like you should see a doctor."

For the first time the guy smiled. And when he did, and just in the way he did, I realized who he looked like. "You know any doctors who'd be willing to come out here?"

"No, but we could help you into town to see Doctor Anderson. He's real nice."

Barney was just jabbering, terrified.

"You boys know who I am?"

"I don't think so," I said.

"Danton's my name. Roy Danton. Yesterday in Des Moines there was a bank robbery. That was me and my brother. He set the whole thing up. We were careful not to hurt anybody but one of the guards there thought he saw a chance to stop us so he opened fire as we were leaving. He killed my brother and wounded me." The grimace again. "The whole state's looking for me by now." He let his eyes drift over to the money satchel. "Hell, I don't even know how much we got. And now I don't even care. With Mike dead, I mean."

There was this real long dusty silence in the closet with the guy just staring off and all and you could feel how sad he was about his brother.

"I'm sorry," Barney said. "About Mike, I mean. I've got a kid brother named Glenn and I'd sure feel bad if somebody shot him."

I didn't think it was the right time to point out that a lot of people in Somerton wanted the pleasure of shooting his obnoxious little brother, Glenn.

Danton looked us over again. You had the sense his mind was always working hard, always trying to figure things out. "You boys have probably never met anybody like me, have you?"

"No, sir," Barney said.

"Your folks are probably real respectable, aren't they?"

"Yessir," Barney said.

"And nobody in the family's ever been in any serious trouble, have they?"

"Except for my older brother Kenny," Barney said. "He got arrested for shooting off firecrackers the night before it was legal."

Danton laughed softly. "They give him the electric chair?"

"No, sir."

"I envy the hell out of you boys."

"Us?"

"That's right, Barney. You. It's summer and you don't have anything to think about except how you're going to spend all these long, lazy days, and what movie you're going to see downtown, and maybe what girl you hope you run into out at the swimming pool." His gaze was faraway now, as if what he was describing was more real than him being in this closet with a bullet in his side and a satchel of cash near his hand and two smalltown hayseeds standing in front of him.

"I never had that," he said. "But nobody's to blame for how I turned out except me. I don't hold with all the blame people put on each other. When you do something wrong, there's only one person to blame and that's yourself."

"Your folks still alive?" Barney said.

But Danton didn't say any more. He just grimaced once from the pain and then sat there and took a few deep shuddering breaths.

I could see how weak he was. The flashlight was shaking a little and the gun looked as if it was about to fall from his hand.

"How far from town are we?" Danton said.

"Mile and a half or so," I said.

"You boys interested in making a few dollars?"

Barney said, "Huh?"

"Getting me some things. A little food and a little medicine."

Barney looked over at me and I looked over at him right back. Him being my best friend and all it was easy to tell that he was thinking the same thing I was. This guy had to be really crazy, letting us walk right out of here with the understanding that we'd get him some stuff and bring it back.

What we'd do, of course, was race back to town and run up the four wide steps of the one-story redbrick police station and tell McCorkindale, the night-duty desk cop, just where he could find himself a bank robber.

"Sure, we'd be glad to do that," I said. "And you wouldn't even have to pay us."

Danton laughed. "You must really think I'm dumb."

We didn't say anything.

"I let you boys walk out of here and you go right to the cops. And then the cops come back here with shotguns and surround this place and then tomorrow morning, I find myself in jail. Where I'll be for the rest of my life probably."

Danton raised his eyes. "How old are you boys?"

"Fifteen and a half," Barney said. "I am, anyway. Tom is fifteen and a quarter."

"You two ever known anybody who killed himself?"

Barney gulped. "No, sir."

"How about you, Tom?"

"I guess not."

Danton stared at me with those sad eyes of his and all I could think of was Uncle Pete and how he came over late one night to tell Dad, who is his brother, about Aunt Clarice, and how he just sat in the recliner in the living room and cried like a baby.

"Well, I'm going to leave it up to you boys. How I'm going to handle things, I mean." He nodded to the bank satchel. "Barney, you come over here and dig out some money."

"Yessir."

Barney went over and knelt down. Being out of flashlight range, he worked mostly in the dark but a minute or so later he shoved his hand into the range of the flashlight. His tight fist was crammed full of green cash, bills sticking out every which way there were so many.

"That should do it," Danton said.

Barney stood up, real unsteady on his feet, and came back over next to me.

"You have a good memory, Tom?"

"Pretty good."

"See if you can remember this, then." And he sailed right into this long list of stuff like gauze and boric acid and bandages, things to take care of his wound, and food, a lot of stuff with sugar in it and then hot dogs because, he said, he could eat them cold. And at the end, he added, "And get me some kind of writing tablets and some envelopes." Pain tightened his face again. "I want to write my brother's, wife, Peg, a letter. They've got a six-month-old kid and I figure Peg could use some money." He nodded to the satchel.

"We'll take this money and get what you want and then come right back."

And then Danton laughed again and it was spooky, crazy laughter really, like the kind madmen always laugh in science fiction movies after they've created a monster or something, except in Danton's case it was real.

"Kid, I wish you could see how obvious you are. You just can't wait to get your ass out of here and go to the cops, can you?"

Barney gulped but didn't say anything.

"And you know what? I'd probably do the same thing if I was you. In fact, I'm sure I would." Then he quit smiling. "But you're going to have to make a real adult decision, both of you boys. I don't want to go to prison. I really don't. I'd never survive in there and I know it. I want to get up to Alaska where I've got a cousin and try living the way regular people do, the way I've never been able to before. That's why I need those medical supplies and that food. It'll at least get me going again."

He stopped talking. He just stared at us a long dusty sad time and then he raised the gun and put the barrel of it right to his temple and said, "If you bring the cops back, I'll end it right here. And that isn't a bluff. And I'm sorry to put it on you like this but I don't have any choices left in my life. I'm leaving it up to you to decide."

Then there was just the dust and shadow and quiet of the closet and the sad (and I saw now) sort of crazy blue eyes of Roy Danton.

"You mean we can go?" Barney said.

"You can go."

"Just like that?"

"Just like that."

"Just walk right out of here?"

"Just walk right out of here."

"And you won't shoot us in the back?"

"And I won't shoot you in the back."

"Jeez," Barney said.

We turned around and left the closet and walked the moonlit length of warehouse floor, rat droppings crunching beneath our feet, without saying a word.

And then we started running like hell.

Five minutes later we were on the railroad ties and smoking Lucky Strikes and hurrying back to town. There was an owl on the night, and phantom clouds across the quarter moon, and a far rumbling train we could feel trembling in the tracks themselves.

"You think we'll get a reward?" Barney said.

"Probably."

"What'll you do with yours?"

"Save up for a car."

"You think Clarence will let you have your own car when you're sixteen?"

We always referred to our fathers by their first names. Clarence and George.

"Sure. Wouldn't George let you have one?"

"Not since Kenny knocked up his girlfriend in the backseat of that old Plymouth George bought him for his birthday."

"But Kenny and Donna are married."

"Now they're married. But they weren't then. And that's what George got so pissed about. Kenny was supposed to go on to college. But now he's working at the factory and he's got two kids and he isn't even twenty-one yet."

"Well, I'm pretty sure Clarence'll let me have a car."

We walked a little more, both of us tossing rocks still warm from sunlight down the silver beams of tracks.

"You know who he looks like?" Barney said.

"Who who looks like?"

"Roy Danton. Who he looks like?"

And then we stopped. We were just at the junction where the

tracks swung eastward and went around Somerton.

By now my clothes were stuck to me because it was not only a hot summer, it was a humid summer.

"Yeah," I said. "I know."

"Robert Mitchum."

I nodded.

"That's the only thing that sort of bothers me about turning him in," Barney said. "It's kind of like turning in Mitch."

We just stared at each other for awhile, just a couple of small-town teenagers, neither one of us wanting to say what we felt, and consequently not saying anything at all.

We left the tracks and walked into town. The houses started right away, neat little blocks of them, living rooms all aglow with black-and-white picture tubes, an occasional Elvis record on the air from an upstairs bedroom window, a few front porch swings squeaking in the darkness.

"You see the way he made those faces when the pain got him?" Barney said.

"Yeah."

"We're doing him a favor, turning him in."

By now we reached the town square. The shops and stores that surrounded it stayed open till nine because it was Friday night and night was about the only time farmers in the nearby towns could get in here.

The Dairy Queen was open, and so was Hamblin's Pharmacy, and Henry's Hawkeye Supermarket, and the big Shell station where they had four bays and where most of the dragstrip guys took their cars, and Seldon's International TV (he took a lot of kidding about that "International" bit believe me) and the Western Auto store and the Earle's Cigars and Billiards and four taverns so noisy they sounded like they were having jukebox wars inside or something.

People sat everywhere, on park benches and car hoods and curbsides, fanning themselves with paper fans of the sort that the funeral home gives you at wakes, with Jesus on one side and a message (plus the address and phone number) from the funeral parlor on the other.

The night smelled of cigar smoke and beer and heat and summer lightning and perfume. And there were old people and young people and pretty people and ugly people and rich people and poor people and people who loved each other and people who hated each other all caught up in those smells.

And Barney and I just stood on the corner across from the red brick building with the big Police sign over the double-wide front door . . . just stood and stared in through the front windows at the uniformed men on night duty.

"You really think he looks like Mitch?" Barney said.

"A little. Not a lot. But a little."

"We'd really get our butts kicked if we didn't turn him in."

"I know."

"You really think he'll kill himself if the cops come?"

"What am I, a swami? How would I know?"

But right away Barney got that patented hangdog look in his eyes, the one that makes you feel bad even when Barney's at fault, and I said, in a lot more friendly way, "I guess I'm afraid he would. Kill himself, I mean."

"Mitch would kill himself."

"You think so?"

"I know so. No prison bars for him. I think he said that in one of his movies."

"In several of his movies, actually."

"Mitch would definitely do it. Definitely."

I sighed. "I wish he'd killed somebody."

"Huh?"

"Roy Danton. I wish he'd killed somebody."

"Why?"

" 'Cause then it'd be easier to turn him in."

"Yeah?"

"Sure. Robbery's pretty bad but it's not like killing anybody."

"I never thought of it that way, I guess."

"So even though he's a bad guy he isn't a *real* bad guy. You know?" Barney shook his head. "I don't want to turn him in either, Tom, but we gotta. We just gotta."

"I know."

"So let's get it over with."

The police station was real bright inside. And noisy. Phones were ringing and there was some kind of teletype deal in the corner and it was clacking away and three uniformed men were rushing around, their rubber heels squeaking on the tile floors the way nurse's shoes do in hospitals.

It was so cold from the air-conditioning that I nearly froze on the spot.

We walked up to the front desk where Sergeant McCorkindale normally sits only it wasn't Sergeant McCorkindale, it was the new recruit named Meeks who wore glasses and was pudgy and was already getting bald.

"Hi, boys."

"Hi," I said.

"Help you with something?"

"We need to talk to Sergeant McCorkindale."

"You don't look like fishes to me."

"Huh?" Barney said.

"Onliest people talking to Sergeant McCorkindale right about now would be the carp or the blue gill. He's up to Kahler's Lake fishing for two days."

And right then I saw Cushing coming out of his office down the hall.

"Well," he said, "look who's here. My two favorite little girls."

I suppose every town has a cop like Cushing, a real slick operator that all the ladies think is cute, and the kind of cruel and cunning man that other men are always sucking up to out of plain undignified fear.

Clarence always said that he used to feel sorry for Cushing, the way Cushing's parents were both killed in that automobile accident when Cushing was just ten. But Clarence had long ago forgotten all about the accident and concentrated on what a jerk Cushing had grown up into.

Cushing was a decorated marine in Korea. He got home late from the war because of an injury to his leg and they had a parade just for him because not only was he a wounded war hero he'd also been the best high school quarterback this valley has ever seen.

He went six foot easy and if his gut was a little loose now and there was a little fleshy pad beneath the line of chin and jaw, he was still an impressive man, always dressed nattily in one of the many suits Bruce Harcourt over at Harcourt's Men Shop gave him a discount on, and always cracking his chewing gum with a certain malicious delight. He had black black eyes that shone with a very strange light.

The summer previous Barney and I had broken into the deserted high school out near the highway. Assistant Police Chief (which generally meant the man who was in charge at night) Stephen B. Cushing happened to be cruising by at the very same time we were crawling in one of the windows.

And parked his car. And came in after us.

There are a lot of stories going around about what happened that night, some of them pretty juicy of course, but our version, and after all we were there, is pretty simple: he came in after us and we ran away. He called for us to stop but, given what we knew about Cushing we were afraid to stop, and so we climbed out of the building again and took off running.

Cushing hadn't been so lucky. He'd crawled out the window after us but instead of hitting the ground running, he'd simply hit the ground, falling one story to hard hard pavement and breaking his arm in the process.

I don't need to tell you how bad it looks for a cop to chase two punk teenagers and have those punk teenagers get away. But for a tough marine and former football hero to break his arm in the process—

My father, the respectable haberdasher, was not happy that his son had gotten into trouble with the law. I was grounded for two weeks, shorn of allowance, and ordered to leave the living room every time something good came on TV (I even had to miss the *Maverick* show where they made fun of *Gunsmoke*).

But even given his embarrassment about his son having to appear in juvenile court, my father at dinner one night broke into a grin and said, "You should see Cushing these days, dear. He won't look any of us merchants in the eye, and he's cut out his swaggering entirely. I'm not saying I think what Tom here did was right but

maybe this was the only way to cut Cushing down a peg or two."
Cushing used to come in all the stores and let it be known in various
ways that as assistant police chief, he expected favors and discounts
from the men he was sworn to protect. The merchants didn't like it
but you didn't say anything against Cushing in this town. Not without Cushing getting even, anyway.

So now here we stood one year later and Cushing was still refer-
ring to us as "girls," which he did loudly whenever he saw us on the
street. He couldn't get real mean with us, the way he got mean with
that Negro who ended up in the hospital a few years back—I mean,
haberdasher may not sound like much to you but in a town the size
of Somerton, a haberdasher has some influence and Cushing had to
be careful—but he could and did harass us whenever he got the
chance.

Cushing watched us with his strange black eyes as Meeks said,
"These boys were asking for Sergeant McCorkindale."

"They were?" Cushing grinned. "You girls come in to confess to
something?"

Meeks looked uncomfortable when Cushing called us girls. He
kind of wriggled and waggled around in his desk chair.

"They were real polite," he said. "I mean, they weren't causing
any trouble or anything."

"That's the nice thing about little girls," Cushing said. "They're
usually well-behaved."

He took out a pack of Cavaliers and tamped one down on the
pack and then put it to his mouth and took out this really nice silver
Zippo.

"So how can I help you two?" He apparently had other things to
do. Now he sounded as if he just wanted to rush us out of here.

Barney's gaze strayed over to mine. We had the same thought.
We couldn't tell Cushing about Roy Danton because if Danton
didn't kill himself, Cushing would be glad to do it for him.

"He said he'd help us with this term paper we're gonna write
next year," I said.

"Yeah, about the police."

Cushing grinned. He couldn't let an opportunity like this go by.
"So you nice little girls are also A students, huh?"

A students? God, Barney and I together barely got passing grades. If they'd given courses in Ray Bradbury, Edgar Rice Burroughs and Robert Mitchum, we would have been hailed as geniuses. But unfortunately our school board was hopelessly square.

Cushing lit his cigarette. He was still looking us over. You got the impression that he'd have liked to start beating on us right then and there.

But all he said was, "Why don't you girls go on home? We're busy."

And with that, he turned around and went back to his office.

Meeks said, kind of sheepish, "He just gets in a bad mood sometimes."

And right then I liked the hell out of Meeks because he was the same kind of geek we were, fist fodder for all the Cushings in the world.

"Thanks, Meeks," I said.

"Yeah," Barney said. "Thanks."

When we were outside in the steaming night again, Barney said, "You know, if God gave me permission to kill three people you know who I'd name?"

"Cushing and who else?"

"Cushing, Cushing and Cushing."

I laughed. "Me, too."

Barney nodded to Hamblin's Pharmacy down the block. "We'd better hurry up if we're going to get Danton that stuff."

"I was thinking," I said.

"Yeah?"

"I'll bet if Danton didn't have that bullet in him, he could kick the living shit right out of Cushing."

"With one hand tied behind his back."

"And blindfolded."

"Let's go," Barney said, "and get that stuff."

"Yeah," I laughed. "Like good little girls."

Hamblin's was where I first read Ray Bradbury and Theodore Sturgeon and Robert Bloch and John D. MacDonald and Mickey Spillane so even given the fact that Mr. Hamblin, the shriveled-up little guy who owns it is something of a grouch, I'll always like the place. There's a soda fountain with twelve stools where one day Patty Lake accidentally leaned against my arm with one of her breasts and I fell in love with her for the whole school year; and the magazine stand where *Popular Photography* once had a nude shot of a very pretty young woman, and she wasn't even African; and the sacred wire paperback rack that kind of creaks when you turn it around; and the sandwich board where Ina makes the most incredible tuna salad sandwiches I've ever had, no offense Mom.

I was hoping Becky Martin would be working, Becky being not only the tallest girl in junior class but the most beautiful, too, reminding me a lot of Dana Wynter in *Invasion of the Body Snatchers,* who even two years later I still had a sort of crush on.

But Becky wasn't working, Hamblin himself was.

He was up on a stepladder putting boxes of storage away. I guess it was a sign of our growing maturity that neither Barney nor I smirked or poked each other when we saw it was boxes of Kotex he was putting away.

"Help you, boys?"

"Need some things, Mr. Hamblin," I said.

"Be right down."

A few minutes later he was behind the counter, this rabbity bald little guy who always reminded me of Andy Clyde who was Hopalong Cassidy's sidekick in the movies, and he got the first two items, bandages and gauze, and set them up but then he stopped all of a sudden, wiping his hands on his clean white apron and said, "Boric acid?"

"Yes, Mr. Hamblin."

"This for your folks?"

"Huh?" Barney said.

"Your folks. Is this stuff for your folks?"

"Yeah," I lied. "Yeah. My dad fell down and—"

"—broke his leg," Barney said.

Barney could sometimes be real dumb. My dad Clarence came into Hamblin's at least once a day. And when he wasn't sporting a broken leg—

"At least we think it's broken," I said. "You never can tell with a broken leg. One minute it's broken and the next it's—"

"And the next it's what?" Hamblin said.

"Huh?" Barney said.

By now Hamblin was watching us very carefully. "You're up to something, aren't you?"

"Huh?"

"Your pop don't have a broken leg any more than I do, does he?"

"Huh?"

"I ain't talkin' to you, Barney. I'm talkin' to Tom."

"No, sir," I said, "he doesn't have a broken leg. We're just getting this stuff so we can learn first aid."

"You two troublemakers learn first aid? For what? So you can patch up all the people you play jokes on?"

"We don't do that anymore, Mr. Hamblin."

"No, sir, we don't," Barney said.

"We want to join the Civil Air Patrol and one of the requirements is that you learn first aid."

"Civil Air Patrol, huh?"

"Yessir," I said. Actually, I had a cousin over in Cedar Rapids who was in the Civil Air Patrol, and he got up before dawn three mornings a week and went out to this little office on top of the broadcast booth at the football stadium and scanned the sky with his binoculars. He was supposed to be looking for Russian bombers that had somehow gotten through our radar but what he mostly saw was UFOs. According to him there were a lot more UFOs than most people realized.

"I'm going to give you boys this stuff but if I find out that you pulled any practical jokes on anybody tonight—"

"We don't do stuff like that anymore," I said. "We're in high school now."

We ordered six more items, all medical-type stuff, and Hamblin slammed each one down as he set it on the glass top of the display case.

He put it all in a paper bag and then without thinking I opened my fist, the one I had all the new green money inside of, and then the money all fluttered to the ground.

"God!" Barney said. And we were both on the floor picking it up.

I kept looking up at Hamblin. He kept staring at all the fifties and twenties in disbelief.

"Where'd you boys get money like that?"

"Huh?" Barney said.

"Savings," I said. "I've been saving my Christmas money for the past five years and here it is."

Which he didn't believe at all, of course. Not at all.

I took a twenty and paid him but he took it without looking at it, his eyes still fixed on all the other bills fanned out in my hand.

I stuffed the bills in my pocket and watched Hamblin go down to the cash register and punch the amounts up. The register bell dinged when the cash drawer opened. Barney started to say something but I shook my head.

Hamblin came back with my change, counted it out and handed over the bag.

"Your pop at home, Tom?"

"Yes, sir."

And that was all he said. But of course he didn't have to say any more at all.

I picked up the bag and Barney and I walked out.

Barney said, "Old man Hamblin's gonna call Clarence."

"I know."

"And Clarence is gonna have a lot of questions for you when you get home tonight."

"I know."

"And then the cops are gonna find out about Roy."

"I know."

"Sonofabitch," Barney said, "I don't want to see the cops get Roy, do you?"

"I sure don't," I said.

We went inside Henry's Hawkeye Supermarket and did the grocery shopping fast, getting stuff Roy could eat without cooking, cold cuts and Roman Meal bread and Hostess cupcakes and freezing Pepsis from the cooler and then Barney said, "You go ask the checkout girl to help you find something."

"Huh?" I said, sounding just like Barney.

"Go on."

So I did. She was the only employee I could see anywhere in the store. She helped me find paper lunch sacks, which I made a big fuss about needing desperately. I kept wondering what Barney was doing.

Then he was back and said, "Well, I'd better be going, Tom. George wants me home early tonight."

So we all went up to the lanes and she checked us out and Barney kept giving me this look I'd never seen before and without knowing quite why, I knew I wanted to get the hell out of there and fast.

On the street, Barney said, "I got 'em."

"Got what?"

"Cigarettes. Three packs. Chesterfields. I couldn't reach anything else. That's why I had you distract her."

There's this older kid, Lem, who usually buys cigarettes for Barney and me. He's real poor and sort of ugly and everybody laughs at him but he's actually a good guy and he has a six-year run of *Amazing Stories* and we pay him a dime every time he buys us a pack. But we didn't have time for Lem tonight.

We walked fast going back to the warehouse. And we walked a little scared.

The warehouse was just as dark as we'd left it. We climbed in through the window and went over to the closet. "Roy, Roy, we're back."

The door was still open but there was no answer from the darkness inside. No flashlight clicked on, and there wasn't any noise, either, that cramped pained noise Roy made every time he breathed.

"Roy?" Barney said.

No answer.

"Here," I said, handing Barney the sack of groceries.

"What're you gonna do?"

"Go in there. See what's wrong."

We both stared at the dark, dark closet.

I took two, three steps into the closet. I couldn't see anything.

The dust made me sneeze. What I didn't need now was an allergy attack.

And then I tripped over something and fell forward, putting my hands up flat against the back wall.

I stood there panting, sweating.

And then I heard him. It was real faint but I knew right away it was him because of the labored, reedy sound of his breathing.

"You OK?" Barney said.

"Get in here," I said.

By the time Barney made it into the closet, I was on the floor picking up the flashlight and getting it clicked on and shining the beam in Roy's face.

If he hadn't been breathing, I would have thought he was dead. One afternoon a few years back Barney and I snuck into the back of the Devlin Mortuary and peeked at two corpses old man Devlin had laid out on gurneys. It was pretty gross, the pasty fish-belly color of the flesh, that is, and the way they didn't move at all. But then I guess when you think about it, that's what being dead means, that you don't move. Never again.

"Hold this," I said to Barney and gave him the flashlight.

He kept the beam on Roy. I grabbed one of the Pepsis and got it open and put the bottle to Roy's lips and forced a little into his mouth.

It took him maybe a full minute but his eyes finally came open. And then it was maybe another twenty seconds before he showed any signs of recognizing us. His wound was starting to take its toll. He looked real pale and there was a kind of crust on his lips and his sweat was cold-looking and greasy and, to be honest, he kind of smelled pretty bad. That's one thing movies can't give you—smell. When John Dillinger and Pretty Boy Floyd and Al Capone die up there on the screen, the audience doesn't have any idea of how bad they smell.

"Hey, slugger," Roy said to me.

"We got your stuff," Barney said.

Roy raised his eyes to Barney. Even that seemed to take a lot of effort. "Thanks, kid."

So we fed him. Barney propped the light up on top of the

money sack and sat on one side of Roy and I sat on the other. We put the grocery sack between us and took turns feeding him, the way we once fed a hawk. We were out in the woods one bright fall morning and we heard this big booming gun go off and it was this hunter of course and then we heard something fall into the bushes beside us and it was this hawk. He was all covered with blood and his dark eyes were frantic and wild and we were scared for him and scared for us because we didn't know what to do. And so we just grabbed all these colorful autumn leaves and made him this little bed and he just sat there staring up at us and we tried feeding him grass and we tried feeding him leaves and Barney even dug up some nightcrawlers with his fingers but the hawk wouldn't eat any of them and so all we could do was pet him and say soft little things to him like the soft little things you say to sick kitties and we knew he was dying and he knew he was dying and then he started twitching and shuddering and making these tiny scared noises and so Barney picked him up and put him in his lap, not caring about the blood or anything, and sort of started rocking him, back and forth, back and forth, back and forth till I had to say, very softly, "Barney, I think he's dead" and Barney looked down at the unmoving bird and said "You're a fucking liar, Tom, he isn't dead!" but he was dead, of course, the poor bastard, and so I took him from Barney's hands, lifted him real gentle, and all the time I did Barney just kept screaming at me "You're a fucking liar, Tom! That's what your fucking problem is, buddy-boy! You're a fucking liar!" And I took the hawk down to the river bank where the earth was softer and I scooped out this grave with my hands and I put him in it and even all the way down to the blue run of river, even above the jays and the owls and the ravens, I could hear Barney crying.

So it was sort of like that now, feeding Roy. I mean, because he was so weak he couldn't even hold a piece of cold meat in his fingers.

"It's so goddamned cold in here," he said.

On the bank Time and Temperature sign downtown about twenty minutes earlier the Temp had been 89.

Barney fed him the Twinkies and the Pepsi and I fed him the Oscar Mayer sliced bologna and dutch loaf. And then we both took turns feeding him the Cracker Jacks which Barney had said would be a good way to finish off the meal.

When he was finished eating, Roy said, "You boys bring the bandages and stuff?"

"Yessir," I said. "We sure wouldn't forget something like that."

And right then, just the way he gave me this almost imperceptible nod of thanks, he looked a whole lot like Mitch.

"You boys think you can clean a wound?"

"Sure," Barney said.

I looked over at him and frowned. What the hell did we know about cleaning a wound?

"You just take the hydrogen peroxide and let it soak into some of those cotton balls I told you to get and then you just kind of clean the wound," Roy said.

We cleaned the wound.

I'll tell you, it was unlikely either Barney or I were ever going to get scholarships to medical school, the way we poured too much peroxide on the cotton balls and spilled the stuff all over, and the way we grimaced when we had to tear the blood-soaked part of his shirt away from the wound.

"Oh, God," Barney said when we finally got a good look at the wound. So much for a quiet, steady manner.

I wanted to say oh, God, too, but I just bit down real hard on my lip and took one of the soaked cotton balls and put it up to the wound.

Where the bullet had gone in everything was kind of scabby and you could see green pus leaking from the hole.

In all, we went through eleven cotton balls. I got rid of as much of the scabbing as I found, and at least temporarily I stopped the pus from seeping.

And then we were done and Roy sat back against the wall and felt in his shirt pocket for a cigarette but he was all out so Barney handed over the Chesterfields he'd taken from the supermarket and said, "This was the only brand I could steal."

"They're fine. I appreciate it." He got a cigarette in his mouth, looking a whole lot like Mitch just then, and then he took his Zippo out and thumbed it into lighting. He set the lighter down on the floor and I looked at it. Somebody had carved a skull and crossbones into it, with two little fake red diamonds for the eyes. It was the coolest lighter I'd ever seen.

"There's one Twinkie left, Roy," Barney said. "You want it?"

"You eat it, kid," Roy said.

I laughed. "He was hoping you'd say that."

Barney gulped it down in two bites.

Roy kept dragging on his cigarette but he did it with his eyes closed. His breathing was starting to get real noisy again and you could tell he was exhausted.

"You think you could bring me some more food tomorrow night?" Roy said. He kept his eyes closed.

"Sure," I said. "But we can do better than that. We can bring you some rolls for breakfast."

"Yeah," Barney said. "From Emma's Cafe. She makes 'em fresh every morning."

Eyes closed, he shook his head very gently. "Somebody might see you in the daylight. You don't want to make anybody suspicious. Wait till night to come out here."

When he used the word "suspicious" my stomach knotted up. I kept thinking of old man Hamblin at the pharmacy just staring at all the money I had.

"Roy," Barney said.

"Yeah?"

"Could I use your lighter?"

"Sure."

"I really appreciate it," he said, leaning forward and taking the lighter from where it sat on top of the pack of Chesterfields on the floor.

The way the three of us sat, we might have been around a campfire.

Barney picked up the lighter and stared at the skull and crossbones and a low whistle came from his lips. "Cool."

Barney got a cigarette going and I got a cigarette going and then Barney said, "Roy?"

"Yeah." Eyes still closed.

"Would you really have killed yourself if we'd brought the law back?"

Roy thought a long moment. "You want an honest answer?"

"Uh-huh."

"I don't know if I got the guts to kill myself. I've thought about it all my life off and on, and one night when I caught my girlfriend in bed with this guy, I put a gun in my mouth but I couldn't pull the trigger. I wanted to and I think in a strange way she wanted me to, too, but I couldn't. I just couldn't."

And then he made a little grunting sound again and he took the cigarette from his mouth and jabbed it out on the floor. And then he gave out with this deep sigh that made his chest shudder.

"I don't think I can talk anymore, boys. I need some sleep."

"We'll be back tomorrow night, Roy," I said. "We'll bring you better food, too."

We left him, left the warehouse, and went back to town.

"You think he's gonna die?" Barney said, just as we started down the tracks.

"I don't know."

"Maybe we should turn him in. Maybe that really would be doing him a favor."

"What if he killed himself?"

"You heard him. He said he didn't have the guts."

"No, he said maybe he didn't have the guts. There's a difference."

We came to Spring Street, my street.

"Night," Barney said.

"Night," I said, and started to walk away.

When I was out of the streetlight and walking in the shadows, I heard Barney say, "You really think he looks like Mitch?" and I called back, "Yeah, I think he looks a lot like Mitch," and then we were both lost to our respective blocks, just footsteps now in the summer night.

Our house has a lot of gables and gingerbreading which should make it a Victorian, I guess, but my mom says it's not really a Victorian, at least not a regular one anyway. She always says this whenever somebody visits us for the first time and says "I just love Victorian houses." Most of us in the family just close our ears when she starts in.

Mom and Dad were in the living room with my eight-year-old sister, Debbie, watching the Late News with Earle Rochester who my dad says is a) a Democrat and b) a funny-looking gink who can't keep his opinions to himself ("See how he sneers whenever he says the name Eisenhower?" he always says to my mom, by which you can guess that Clarence is a Republican).

Dad was sitting in the leather recliner, which is his sacred chair, and wearing his Purple Passion (as Mom calls them) Bermuda shorts and a sport shirt.

The first thing he said to me was, "How come you were buying hydrogen peroxide and boric acid and gauze and stuff like that at Hamblin's tonight?"

He kept staring right at the TV, as if he wasn't missing a word, but asking me his question and then waiting for an answer.

I was ready for him. On the walk home I'd thought up a good one. "Barney and I were going to fix up this tackling dummy like it got all beaten up and then hang a sign on it that said 'This is what happens to bullies, Maynard' but Barney got scared and chickened out."

"You're just begging Maynard to come after you again," Clarence said.

I said good night to everybody and went upstairs. Things had gone much easier than I thought they would with Dad, I thought, as I went in the bathroom and peed and brushed my teeth and washed my face.

Mom had turned the fan on in my bedroom so it was going to be pretty good for sleeping.

I got the light on and stripped down to my underwear and picked up a new issue of *Imagination,* which had a lead novel by one of my favorite writers, Dwight V. Swain. I started to lie down when the door eased open and Dad stuck his head in.

"All right if I come in and talk a minute?"

"Sure." So it wasn't over. And I knew what was coming.

He sat on the edge of the bed and looked at me. He's not a very big guy but boy can he scowl.

"I'm going to ask you one question, one time only and if you ever told the truth in your life, it had better be this time. You understand?"

"I understand."

"Hamblin said you had a lot of money on you. Twenties and fifties. Is that true?"

"Yessir."

"Care to tell me just where the hell you found that kind of money?"

"Out by the old fairgrounds." I'd been ready for that one, too.

"The fairgrounds?"

"Down by the crick. In a paper bag. Nearly three hundred dollars."

"Is that the truth?"

I didn't feel good about lying to Clarence but I didn't have any choice. "That's the truth."

"That money should have been turned over to the police."

"We tried. We went to the police station and asked for Sergeant McCorkindale but he went fishing for a couple of days."

"There are other policemen there."

"Yeah but then Cushing came in and started calling us girls and insulting us the way he usually does."

"Cushing's a jerk. You shouldn't pay any attention to him."

I shrugged. "I get tired of being insulted."

"I'm going to speak to the chief about that. I'll tell him I want Cushing to keep his tongue off my son."

I shook my head. "That'll just make it worse, Dad. Cushing'll get me alone somewhere and then make fun of me for siccing you on the chief."

He nodded. "I suppose you're right." He glanced around the room. "Where's the rest of the money?"

"In my jeans pocket."

"How much did you spend?"

"Fourteen bucks."

"I'll take the rest of it over to the chief in the morning."

"Fine."

He thought a minute and said, "I wish I could tell you that the next time Cushing says something to you I'd clean his clock for him."

"I know, Dad."

"I'm just not very tough."

"Neither am I, Dad. I guess it runs in the family."

"But guys like that usually get theirs in the end. One way or another, they get it."

ii

The next morning around ten, I met Barney by the water fountain in the town square. As usual, a lot of the old men who play checkers all day long had pulled their green park benches up so they could be closer to the fountain. I've never figured that out. All these old-timers must have had a bad drought when they were kids because they sure do treat the fountain like somebody was going to sneak up and take it away.

The first thing Barney asked, his red hair brilliant in the hot August sun, his blue-and-white striped polo shirt already showing little patches of sweat here and there, was "Clarence ask you about the money?"

"Uh-huh."

"You tell him what we talked about?"

"He was pretty cool about it, actually. I'm going to get a paper bag and stuff the rest of the money in it and give it to him. Roy won't need it. He's got plenty more."

"So old man Hamblin called him then?" Barney said.

"Sure. Did you think he wouldn't?"

"I wish we could go out there. To see Roy, I mean."

"So do I."

"I woke up in the middle of the night. I had this dream that Roy was dead."

"He's pretty tough. Did you read the newspaper this morning?" My dad subscribes to the *Des Moines Register*. Even though it's pretty much a "Democratic rag" as he frequently calls it, it's the only daily we can get in this part of the state.

"Yeah," Barney said. "He really is a tough guy."

Right there on the front page, in a big black blaring headline, it had said: State Police Seek Fugitive and just below this was a picture of Roy looking more like Mitch than ever. The story told of how Roy had been a war hero in Korea but that he'd drifted into crime with his older brother and how authorities suspected that they'd been responsible for at least ten bank robberies in the past six months.

"He's a pretty cool guy, no doubt about it," Barney said.

"Very cool guy," I said.

"What're we gonna do all day?"

"You wanna see a flick?"

"Which one?"

"*Blackboard Jungle* is back at the Rialto."

"And there's another one," Barney said.

"What's the other one?" In those days, the Rialto always played two and sometimes three movies. Of course, when they had three of them, you could bet that two of them were real dogs, usually something with Bing Crosby and a lot of nuns.

"It's a western with Rory Calhoun."

"I still say," I said, "that Rory is a fake name."

"You wanna go or not?"

I shrugged. "Guess there isn't much else to do."

So we killed two hours before going to the movies by riding our bikes all over town and seeing who was out and around. We saw Maynard the bully unloading peat moss at his uncle's hardware store and just as we were passing him, Barney said, "I'll give you a buck if you give him the finger."

"I'll give you two bucks if you give him the finger."

But of course, wanting to live till sundown, neither one of us gave him the finger.

The Blackboard Jungle was still a pretty cool movie. The only problem was that I couldn't see myself as any of those kids. They were really kind of whiny and immature. I mean I'd much rather be Glenn Ford than any of the kids. (For one thing, Glenn had made two movies with Rita Hayworth, who I still think is the most beautiful and sexy and in some strange way saddest woman I've ever seen, her sadness being a part of her beauty.)

And Rory Calhoun was pitiful as usual. He looks like a decent guy and I'm sure he is a decent guy but he sure can't act. And when a fifteen-year-old kid from Somerton, Iowa, knows you can't act then you really can't act.

But it was air-conditioned and three rows ahead of us sat two really cute girls from Catholic school (Dad has never liked Catholics much but Mom says except for the Pope they're very fine people) and there were some especially neat coming attractions for two new monster movies. (Later on, I'd learn that coming attractions are a lot like life—the buildup is usually better than the payoff.)

When we got out, the sunlight was blinding and my body felt like some invisible demon had taken this huge paint roller and covered me with glue.

We got on our bikes and started down the block. We stopped at the corner for a red light and that was when the black Plymouth sedan pulled up to the curb. The window was rolled down on the passenger side. Cushing had to lean way over. "Afternoon, ladies."

Neither of us said anything.

"I want you to ride those bikes of yours over to the square and wait for me there. I'll meet you by the drinking fountain."

Even Cushing was fixated on the drinking fountain. "You girls understand me?"

We didn't nod or anything but obviously we were going to do what he told us.

When he pulled away, Barney said, "I think we're in trouble."

"I think you're right."

"That jerk."

We rode over to the square.

Since it was nearing suppertime, the square was pretty quiet, except for a couple of squirrels running around the edges of the wading pool where I used to go when I was five or so. But one day I saw some little kid's turd floating in there and I got out of the water and I never got back in again. I mean never.

We sat on the bench next to the fountain. Cushing parked down by the railroad tracks so it took him a few minutes to get up here.

He had on a straw fedora and a baby blue–colored summer-weight suit and his usual big mean grin.

He went over to the fountain and had himself a drink and then flicked some water from his hand (everybody gets wet at that fountain) and then he took out this long pack of Viceroys and knocked one out on the edge of his fist and then he put it in his mouth and lit it and said, "Where'd you girls get all that money?"

"Huh?" Barney said.

"Last night at Hamblin's. Hamblin told me all about it."

"Found it," I said.

"Found it where?"

"Laying near the crick."

"What crick?"

"Out by the fairgrounds."

"It was just laying there?"

"In a sack."

"What kind of sack?"

"Paper sack."

"How much was in it?"

"About three hundred dollars."

"Where is it now?"

"At my house. My dad made me make up the money I spent from this savings account he keeps for me. He's gonna take it to the chief tonight."

"You could be in a lot of trouble."

"I know," I said.

But I knew better than that and so did Cushing. The Chief and Dad are in Rotary and Lions and Odd Fellows and the Masons together and twice a year they go hunting and fishing and they're real good friends and so I'd practically have to kill somebody before the chief did anything to me. I guess that's what Roy meant when he said I was respectable.

Cushing dragged on his cigarette a few times and swatted flies with his big hand a few times and just kept staring at us.

"You know what I think?" he said.

"What?" I said.

"That there's more money somewhere and that you're just not telling your dad about it."

The shadows were getting longer and a yellow passenger train was just pulling into the depot, furious with August heat and oil and power, and the people sat in the windows looking out at our little town, city people most likely, wondering how folks could live in such a small place. Once in a while I'd see really pretty girls in those windows and I'd have dreams about them for long days after the train had pulled out.

Cushing looked at Barney now. "How about *you*?"

"Huh?"

"You gonna tell me?"

"Tell you what?"

"About the rest of the money."

"About the rest of what money?"

"About the rest of the money by the crick."

"He wasn't lying, Tom wasn't, Detective Cushing. We gave everything back except what we spent at Hamblin's."

"How about what you spent at Henry's supermarket?"

"How'd you know about that?" Barney said.

"When old man Hamblin told me about you being in there with all that crisp, green cash I just naturally got curious. I went to every store in town that was open last night and asked if you girls had been in there."

I guess that while he was one real big loud-mouthed showboat, Cushing was also a pretty good detective.

"So how about it?" Cushing said.

He was back to looking at me.

"How about what?" I said.

"How about telling me where the rest of the money is."

I don't know why but something about the way he said that— the words he chose, I mean—seemed odd to me but right then I didn't have time to think about it. I just had time to say, "There isn't any rest of the money. There's nearly three hundred dollars in a sack at my house that my dad is taking over to the chief's tonight."

"So that's how it's gonna be, huh, girls?"

"Honest, Detective Cushing," Barney said, getting that kind of whiny tone in his voice. "Tom's telling the truth."

Cushing held his cigarette up high and then dropped it straight down to the wet ground around the drinking fountain. Like he was dropping a bomb or something. And then he ground it out with the toe of his snappy black-and-white wingtips.

And then he stared at us.

"This is gonna get real bad, girls. Real bad."

"What is?" Barney said.

"This whole thing. With the money."

"But—"

Cushing held up his hand. "The last time I had a run-in with you little girls, everything went your way. The chief wouldn't press charges and the juvenile officers didn't see your breaking into that place as any big deal. It's going to be different this time. And I think you know what I'm talking about."

And then he left. No more words. Just left.

When Cushing had vanished on the other side of the bandstand, Barney said, "You think he knows about Roy?"

"I don't know. But I think he thinks there's a lot more money and that we have it."

"You gonna tell Clarence about Cushing?"

"No, because if I tell Clarence he'll start asking me a lot more questions."

We sat quiet for quite awhile, just watching the town at suppertime, merchants closing down, rolling up their striped awnings and turning out the display lights in the windows. Every summer seemed to get shorter the older I got, and at warm day's end there's a melancholy about everything, long purple shadows and mothers calling their kids in for dinner, and I felt this kind of sadness I can't explain, even though I was only fifteen I felt real old and I sensed that in just a few summers more all of us would be gone, I mean everybody I passed on the street young and old alike and all the people I loved including Mom and Dad and Gram and Debbie, all gone to ground and utterly forgotten with nobody to remember how beautiful the wine-colored dusk was on a snow-covered January night or how people laughed at Jack Benny on the radio or how neat it was to get a brand-new Ace Double Book or how the bonfire glowed on Homecoming night out at the football stadium or how lonely I felt the night Emmy Chambers told me that she liked Bobby Criker better than me or how much fun it was to chase fireflies with a jar on a July night with your aunt and uncle from Minneapolis sitting on the screened-in porch watching or how one spring night walking by the river I was so overwhelmed by the moonsilver water and the scent of appleblossoms and the friendly yips and yaps of neighborhood dogs that I knew absolutely positively that there was a God or how I sometimes had really corny dreams about saving some girl I loved from a burning house or how beautiful and neat and clean Main Street looked after a night rain— All those people and thoughts and memories would be dead. Mom and Dad would likely go first, and then all their friends and relatives, and then me and all my friends and relatives, and then Debbie and all her friends and relatives, generations born and generations dying until there was absolutely no trace of us left, almost as if we hadn't existed, absolutely nobody who could remember us at all, the people of Somerton with all their wishes and dreams and desires and fears would be at best a rotted skeleton or two to be dug up three thousand years hence and looked at and shrugged over and then forgotten utterly once again.

"You all right?"

Barney brought me back. "I'm fine," I said. But I wasn't. I never am when I start thinking of eternity that way.

"What time we going out to see Roy?"

"How about seven?"

"Meet you by the tracks?"

"Fine. But let's walk."

"OK by me."

"I'll stop by Henry's and pick up Roy's stuff and meet you then." I rode home. Douglas Edwards and the CBS News was on. Mom was serving the first sweet corn of the year along with broccoli and Jello. Usually Mom doesn't let us eat in front of the TV— she'd read a piece in *Parents* magazine about how the American family was going to hell in a handbasket largely because of TV and rock and roll—but the heat evidently changed her mind for tonight at least, the living room being a lot cooler than the family room.

I sat beside Debbie on the couch. We both had metal TV trays which were kind of wobbly. She said, "It's hard to eat this corn with that tooth gone, Mom."

Which was when I figured out why she'd looked so strange when I'd come in. One of her front teeth was missing. In case I forgot to mention it, she's eight.

"Just do your best, honey," which is what Mom usually said to stuff like that.

"Let's see," I said.

Debbie put her little face with the big thick glasses she had to wear up for me to see. There was a hole in the top row.

"You still have the tooth?"

"Upstairs."

"Be sure and put it under your pillow."

"How much do you think he'll leave this time?"

"Maybe fifty cents."

"Boy!"

Last time she lost a tooth, Dad put a quarter under her pillow while she was asleep, then I went in my room and took a quarter from my Roy Rogers savings bank (I never got around to throwing things away, I guess) and then slipped it under her pillow, too.

We went back to eating. After Douglas Edwards the local news came on which of course set Dad off griping about how every single person in the news business was a Democrat if not a Communist. Dad had never forgiven the press for what they did—or what he said they did, anyway—to his idol Robert Taft. You know, when Ike "stole" the Republican nomination from him.

The phone rang. Mom, who was on her way to the kitchen, got it and said, "For you, Tom."

"Guess who's been cruising past my house?" Barney said.

"Who?"

"Who do you think? Cushing."

"Cushing? You sure?"

"Positive."

"When you leave, go out the back door. And then go down the alley. I'll meet you at our old clubhouse."

"Maybe he'll start cruising past your house, too."

"I'll see you in twenty minutes."

When I went back into the living room, a commercial was on so Dad was talking to everybody. "I took that money over to the chief and told him how you found it out by the crick and all. He wants you to stop in in the next couple days and talk to him."

"Is he mad?"

"Not mad but kinda disappointed, I think. That you didn't turn it in as soon as you found it. He said something I didn't even think about."

"Like what?"

"Like about that bank robber. The FBI thinks he's up in the northern part of the state but now the chief thinks maybe he's around here somewhere, the way you found that money and all. Anyway, if you'd brought the money in right away, the chief could've put some men on looking for the robber. Now the guy's probably long gone."

I made a quick pit stop upstairs and in five minutes was ready to go.

In the kitchen, I worked fast. I grabbed a paper sack from a drawer and dropped an apple in it, and then followed the apple with two slices of wheat bread, three slices of summer sausage, two bottles of Pepsi, a slice of Mom's chocolate cake with white frosting that I wrapped in wax paper, and some carrot sticks that Mom always kept in this plastic bowl. I didn't have to worry about them hearing me because the window air-conditioner sounded like a B-52 but I didn't want Mom to wander out in the kitchen and see me loading up and then start asking all these questions.

I went out the back way, down the three back porch steps, under the clotheslines, past the dog house, along the row of garbage cans next to the small white garage whose shingles smelled as if they'd melted some in the heat, and out into the narrow gravel chalk-dust alley where I used to be Roy Rogers, Gene Autry, Allan "Rocky" Lane and Lash LaRue, sometimes all on the same day.

It took me twenty minutes to get to the clubhouse, which was this long-abandoned garage on the downwind side of the city dump which, as you might think, did not smell exactly wonderful during a windless sundown of eighty-six degrees. I'd smoked my first cigarette in this garage, and then got so sick that I couldn't get out of bed for a day, and got my first glimpse of a *Playboy* foldout which Barney's sixteen-year-old cousin Stan had copped from his dad's bureau drawer.

The clubhouse resembled this old sagging weatherworn outhouse in this small field of burned grass and empty tin cans and jagged broken pop bottles.

Barney was inside, squatted over in a shadowy corner with a bottle of Pepsi and a Lucky Strike. The last of the dusty sunlight peeped through the spaces between the boards. I'd brought along my old Boy Scout flashlight, which is the color a baby shits when he's got the trots, and I shined it all over the dirt floor. About the only thing to see were a couple of squirming nightcrawlers who looked like my light had just woken them up.

"You see Cushing?" Barney said.

"Huh-uh."

"I didn't, either."

I asked him for a cigarette and when I got it going, I told him what the chief had said, about the found money maybe belonging to the bank robber.

"No wonder Cushing's following us," Barney said.

"He probably thinks we can lead him to the robbery money."

"And to the robber. Wouldn't he get some kind of award?"

"Reward, Barney. You always say that. It's reward."

"Up yours."

"Spoken like a truly mature person."

Barney said, "How we gonna get to Roy without Cushing finding out?"

"We'll just have to be careful."

He poked the sack. "You swipe him some pretty good stuff?"

"He's probably so hungry he'd eat shoe leather."

"You wanna go?"

"Let's look for Cushing first."

One nice thing about the clubhouse, you've got spy holes all over the place. I wish my house had a few spy holes, too. You never know when they'll come in handy.

Barney took one wall and I took the other. We both looked for any sign of Cushing's car. But there was just blanched prairie and the burning malodorous city dump and small frame houses on this particular edge of town.

So we went. We cut wide around the dump, Barney saying what he always said ("I'll bet there's a lot of valuable stuff in there if you just had the time to look through it all") and then saw the railroad tracks gleaming in the last few minutes of fiery sunlight.

All that separated us from the tracks was a wide area of dusty gravel. We were just walking over to it when Barney said, "Oh, God! Look!"

And there, maybe three hundred yards behind us, came Cushing's unmarked police car.

"What'll we do?" Barney said.

"Just calm down."

"Huh?"

"Just calm down, Barney, or he'll know something's wrong for sure. Just keep walking. But instead of turning up toward the tracks, we'll turn the other way to the crick."

Cushing's tires made a lot of slow crunching noise on the gravel.

He got alongside us, doing maybe five, six miles an hour, and said, "How're my little girl friends doing tonight?" He had on dark shades and he grinned like a killer.

We didn't say anything. We just kept walking toward the hill that would eventually slope down to the crick. There was a pussy willow tree there that gave a lot of shade during the day.

"You girls stop right there. I want to talk to you."

I heard him jerk on his emergency brake and then get out of the car. You could smell the gas and oil and heat of the motor.

He walked over in front of us. We'd stopped walking, just like he'd told us to.

"The sack. What's in it?"

"Nothing special," I said. Then, "We're going hiking tonight so we brought some food for a snack." I was getting so good at this lying business that I was starting to scare myself.

He took the sack, opened it and then shoved his hand way down inside it. I thought of the time Johnny Worchester did that with this old sack he'd found near the crick one day and this giant milk snake was coiled up inside. Legend has it that Johnny filled his pants right on the spot.

Cushing found the piece of chocolate cake. "Look here what I found." He grinned. "I always heard that your mom was a real fine cook, Tom."

"She is."

"Why don't I find out for myself and try this piece of cake?"

"That isn't yours, Cushing, it's mine."

"That's right, darling, it is your cake, isn't it?" At which point he took the cake and squeezed it in his fist, squishing and scrunching till there would be no way to separate the cake from the waxed paper. Now it was just this little brown ball.

He threw the cake back into the sack and then dropped the sack at my feet. "That story of yours is bullshit," he said.

"What story?" I said.

"About finding that money by the crick."

"That's where we found it," I said.

"You know where the rest of that money is, don't you?"

"Rest of what money?" Barney said.

"Rest of the bank robbery money, that's what money," Cushing said. "That's where you little girls are going tonight, isn't it? To get some more of that money?"

"We're going for a hike," Barney said.

"To Hampton Hill," I said.

"Watch the stars," Barney said.

"Have a little snack," I said.

We were pissing him off and it was great. He just stood there, this bully-boy cop with his bully-boy gun and his bully-boy Hollywood shades, and he knew we were lying to him and there wasn't a goddamn thing he could do about it.

"You girls have yourselves a real nice time tonight," he said.

And right away I knew something was wrong, the sly way he said it.

"I'll see you later."

And then he turned around and walked back to his car and got in and drove away.

I watched his tail lights flare as he turned the corner, then go out of sight behind the Solar Oil Company depot.

Gone. Cushing was gone. And he shouldn't have been. Not that fast anyway. Not without ragging us a lot more than he did.

"Pretty cool the way you stood up to him," Barney said. "Maybe he'll leave us alone now."

"Barney, he's up to something."

"Up to what?"

"I don't know and that's what scares me."

"Maybe he'll go talk to Clarence."

"Nah. He wouldn't do that. He's up to something else."

We walked and night lifted us up gently in the palm of its dark hand. The tracks thrummed again with the energy of distant trains and the jays and wrens and ravens sang their birdy asses off. It was cooler now, and so the night smelled not just of heat but of flowers and mown grass and fast chill creek water.

We crossed the tracks and jumped over the water and went up the slope to the warehouse that sat silent all in deep shadow and moonlight.

I felt nervous about everything but I couldn't exactly say why so I just kept walking to the warehouse, gripping the sack tighter.

We went in through the front window the way we had last night and then walked the length of the floor to the closet.

Roy wasn't there. I shined my Boy Scout flashlight all over the inside. There was no sign of him. Everything was gone except for two stubbed-out cigarette butts and dried red spots on the dirty, tiled floor. No doubt what the red spots were. Everything else he'd taken with him. Leaving no traces made sense, I thought. That way the cops would never know he'd even been here.

But it all bothered me. Roy hadn't looked too good last night, certainly not good enough to travel. Not very far anyway.

And then Barney said, "Listen."

I didn't hear it at first, not with all the electricity humming in the power lines above us and the frogs by the creek and an airplane somewhere up by the round golden moon.

But then I heard it.

Some faint noise at the front of the building.

Barney wasn't quite inside the closet. Now he peeked his head out the door.

"See anything?" I whispered.

He shook his head.

We were getting spooked was all, I thought. Came in here and found Roy gone. No wonder we were getting spooked.

And then I heard it again. Some faint scuffing sound somewhere at the front of the building.

"In here," I whispered, pulling him into the closet.

We waited in the darkness. Our breaths came in huge ragged gasps. We smelled of night and heat and sweat. Faintly, I could smell the food we'd brought Roy last night.

The scuffing sound came closer.

By now I knew what it was. Somebody walking across the floor, trying to be quiet.

Then somebody said, voice echoing in the darkness of the empty warehouse, "You girls having fun in there?"

"Shit," I said to myself.

Cushing had followed us.

We didn't make a big deal of it. I mean we didn't put our hands up or anything. We just walked out and stood in this little patch of moonlight with all the rat droppings crunching beneath our feet and then Cushing just came out of the shadows and said, "You girls are pretty easy to track. All I had to do was park my car on the other side of the oil depot and give you a few minutes and then start following you."

He pointed to the left cuff of his buff blue summer suit. The cuff was all muddy. "Except I took a wrong step when I got to the crick." He smiled. "I should send you little ladies the cleaning bill."

"How come you followed us?" Barney said.

"No more of your bullshit, OK?" Cushing said. "I'm sick and fucking tired of your bullshit. When I ask you a question this time, I want a straight fucking answer or there'll be hell to pay. You two little girls understand me?"

He'd just exploded like that, no warning at all. He was a scary guy, no doubt about it.

"Now," he said, "where's Roy Danton?"

"Who's Roy Danton?" I said.

He took one step forward and slapped me so hard I couldn't see for maybe a minute.

The whole side of my face felt hot and numb and I couldn't get rid of the stars flashing in my eyes.

"Where is Roy Danton?"

I wasn't sure I could do it but I wanted to try. I opened my mouth, eager to see what I'd say next. "I don't know any Roy Danton."

Before he could slap me again, Barney jumped in between us. "Leave him alone!"

This time he grabbed Barney and shoved him all the way back into the closet where he bounced off the back wall and dropped to the floor. Then he grabbed me and started slapping again. Two, three times, hard vicious slaps. I saw more stars. I tried hitting back and kicking back but he was too big and too skilled, like some mutant older brother.

"That's what this bag was for, wasn't it?" he said. "You were bringing Danton some food."

He'd let me go now and I started backing up to the closet.

Cushing took a flashlight from his jacket, a small silver one like Doc Anderson uses when he wants you to say Ahhh and look at your tonsils, and then he pushed past me and went into the closet.

All I kept thinking of were the dried drops of blood on the floor.

Cushing looked up and down, his flashlight like a giant firefly in the darkness, and Barney just sat on the floor and watched him and rubbed the back of his head where it had collided with the wall.

I stood inside the door, to the right of Cushing, and that was how I saw the water drop from the ceiling to the top of Barney's head. Barney reached up and patted his head and then brought his finger away. There was a dark smear on the back of his fingers.

I looked up. It wasn't water dripping from the ceiling. It was blood. And I had a pretty good idea whose blood it was, too.

A few seconds later, Cushing found the blood from yesterday. He kept his light pointed down to the floor, right on it.

He got down on his haunches for a closer look.

"How bad was his wound?" he said.

"Whose wound?" Barney said.

For a moment, Cushing looked as if he was going to hit Barney again.

"Do you little girls have any idea how much trouble you're in?"

We didn't say anything.

"This means Wayland, the juvenile detention home. You know the kind of boys you'll meet in that home? Did you hear about the stabbing they had there last year? Two kids just about your age stabbed to death in their sleep? And Wayland's just where you'll be going once I tell the chief that you've been helping that bank robber hide out."

And right then another drop of blood fell. I saw Barney's head jerk up and his eyes scan the ceiling and his hand go up and touch his scalp again.

Cushing had been watching me, not Barney.

"Your old man won't be able to help you out of this one, believe me," he said. "And neither will the chief, even if he wants to, which he probably won't."

Barney was staring at me and pointing to his head.

"You've only got one choice," Cushing droned on. "And that's to tell me the truth. Tell me everything that happened. And then tell me where he was going when he left here."

"Milwaukee," I said.

"Milwaukee?"

"He knows people there and when he left this morning, that's where he was headed."

"He left this morning?"

"Right."

"What time?"

"Just about dawn. That's what he said he'd do anyway."

The lies were coming so good and so quick I was scaring myself again.

"If he left this morning, how come you came out here tonight?"

"He said he'd leave some money for us," Barney said.

He was getting good at it, too.

"Did he?"

"No," Barney said, making himself look real dejected.

Cushing smiled. "That's where you girls are naive. Trusting a bank robber like that."

We were silent.

"Milwaukee," Cushing said again. "He say who he knew there?"

"Some name. I don't remember exactly," I said.

"Try."

"John," I said.

"I thought it was Don," Barney said.

"John or Don or something like that," I said.

"John or Don or something like that, huh?" Cushing said, and then backhanded me hard enough to push me all the way across the closet floor. I banged my head against the back wall just the way Barney had.

He turned off the light. "You little girls have yourselves a real nice hike."

And then he left.

He went out of the closet and back across the wide, moonlit floor and out the front window.

We just sat there, frozen, listening to his footsteps recede, listening to him become just one more faint noise in the night.

"Shit," Barney said.

I got my Boy Scout flashlight out and aimed it up at one of the ceiling tiles, which were very wide and very dark, which was why the dripping blood hadn't shown.

"Roy?"

"Yeah," he said. "Be careful. This may be a trick. He may be right outside. One of you boys go watch for him, all right?"

"I'll go watch," Barney said.

It took Roy several minutes to get down. He was dirty and sweaty and he looked even weaker than he had yesterday. He clutched his satchel of bank money tight against his wound. Some of his blood was smeared on the satchel.

In case you're wondering how he got up and down, he had a rope tied to a paint-splattered aluminum stepladder he'd found. After he used the ladder to climb up to the beams above the ceiling panels, he pulled the ladder up behind him.

"I wondered if you boys could keep our little secret so I thought I'd better get up there in case the law came looking for me," he said, as he started in on the food.

He didn't eat much and that's one way I knew he was worse than he'd been last night. When you're real sick, you lose your appetite. He was in a lot of pain. Every few seconds a spasm would come and make him groan.

When he was done trying to eat, he took the pack of Chesterfields Barney had stolen and put one in his mouth.

He took out his Zippo. He got the lighter to his cigarette but when he tried to flick the spark up—

The lighter tumbled from his hands, a dim flash of metal in the weak dusty beam of my flashlight. The lighter made a metallic chinking sound when it hit the floor.

I picked it up right away and lit his Chesterfield for him.

"Thanks," he said, weakly.

Pretty soon, he was unconscious again and as I sat there staring at him in the beam of my flashlight, I saw that even when he was sleeping he looked a lot like Mitch.

I picked up the flashlight and moved the beam real close to his wound and got a good look at it. The pussy stuff covered the blood now like an oil slick. His whole body trembled. The smell was awful.

I knew what I was seeing, of course. I was seeing a man in the final stages of his life. I felt sorry as hell for him.

"Barney?" I said.

A moment later he was in the doorway. "Look at him."

"God, he looks terrible."

"You know what we have to do?"

"Yeah. How long you think he's got?"

"I don't know," I said. "But not long if we don't get an ambulance and a doctor real soon."

We took a last look at Roy. He just sat there. His body was still twitching, his right leg especially. Even his eyelids, closed in sleep, twitched a little.

Then we got out of there.

We were going to get Roy some help and right then we didn't

think of him having to stand trial or going to prison or anything. We just wanted him to live.

We were a few hundred yards from the warehouse when the two shots rang out somewhere behind us in the prairie night.

And then I was running, running faster than I ever had in my life, down to the creek and across the grassy flat to the warehouse, and then straight up to the warehouse window. Barney was right behind me.

By the time I reached the closet, my lungs were heaving so hard I thought I might throw up.

Then I knelt next to Roy and played the flashlight over his face and chest. Touched the artery on his neck. Touched the artery in his wrist.

"He's dead, isn't he?" Barney said.

"Yeah."

"Sonofabitch. Money's gone, too."

I looked. He was right. The money satchel was gone.

I brought the light down Roy's torso, to see where he'd been shot. The first wound had been in his side. This one was right in his chest. There was a tiny black hole right in the center of this huge blooming flower of blood.

I shone the light to the floor where his right hand lay turned up, his gun grasped in his fingers.

I thought of him being unconscious when we left, of him being so weak that he couldn't hold his lighter up.

There was no way he'd come to and grabbed his gun. Even a dumb teenager like me could figure out what had happened here.

"Cushing killed him in cold blood and then put that gun in Roy's hand," I said.

"And took the money."

"And took the money."

I guess until then the whole thing had been an adventure. When you grow up in a small town like Somerton, you keep hoping that something really remarkable will happen to you. And it sure did for us, finding Roy and all, and bringing him food and helping him hide out.

But now it was different. Now it was scary. One day outside one

of the downtown taverns I saw two drunks get into it so viciously
that one bit a piece of an ear off the other. Nobody could seem to
get them apart. Finally, the tavern owner had to get out a hose and
spray them down the way he would have two angry dogs. I remember thinking that for all the movie violence I'd seen, I really didn't
know much about the real thing—the way men beat on each other
with a frenzy and a relish that makes me sick inside.

The way Roy had been killed made me sick inside. The way
Cushing made me sick inside.

"What're we gonna do?" Barney said.

"Tell the chief."

"Everything?"

"Everything."

Barney and I took one last look at Roy, bloody and waxen and
dead, propped up sad and awkward against the wall. There was just
this silence, a deeper silence than I'd ever heard before, and then I
figured out what I was listening to—eternity. That's what I was
hearing, something I'd always heard about but never heard for myself before. Eternity.

iii

On the way in, Barney and I decided to tell our dads first—and let
them tell the chief. It would be better that way, at least for us, even
though telling Clarence and George wasn't going to be easy.

There was a fight on TV when I reached the front porch. Clarence was a boxing fanatic. He sat there in those purple Bermudas of
his and whaled away at empty air just like he was Marciano whaling
away at an opponent. He liked Negro boxers fine, especially if they
reminded him in any way of Joe Louis, whom he inevitably called
"poor Joe Louis," but for some reason he hated Mexican fighters.
Maybe a Mexican beat him up once or something.

Anyway, that was the scene when I got home that night, Clarence alone in the living room in his purple Bermudas throwing lefts
and rights and jumping up and down in his recliner and grunting
and groaning loud enough to make the family cat look real spooked.

Mom and Debbie were long gone, of course. They knew better than to watch Clarence at the fights.

Anyway, Clarence in his purple Bermuda shorts and throwing punches with great and noisy abandon—he turned and looked at me and said—

"Somethin' wrong, son?"

"I need to talk to you, Dad."

"Son, there's a fight on."

"I know there's a fight on."

"It's Hurricane Jackson. He's getting ready to throw his bolo punch."

"Dad—"

His attention roamed back to the screen where two Negroes were pounding on each other.

"Dad—"

Glancing over at me desperately: "Son, is it anything that can wait?"

"No, Dad, I'm sorry but it can't."

"Is this real serious or something?"

"Real serious, Dad."

"You want me to get your mom?"

"No, Dad. I just want to talk to you. Alone."

"Then let's go out to the kitchen. I need a beer."

So we went out to the kitchen and sat down and—

He had a beer and I had a Pepsi.

"So, son, what is it?" Clarence said as we sat in the kitchen where it was at least ten degrees hotter than the living room. The kitchen was great in the winter but in the summer it was a sweat box with only one tiny window for a breeze.

"You know that money I told you I found?" I said.

"Uh-huh."

"I didn't find it. Somebody gave it to me."

"Gave it to you? Who gave it to you?"

So I told him. Every single bit of it, right up to tonight where we left Roy dead in the warehouse.

"And Cushing killed him?"

"Yessir."

"And it wasn't self-defense, you don't think?"

"Nosir, Roy couldn't even hold up his lighter a few minutes earlier."

"So Cushing murdered him in cold blood?"

"Yessir."

"And then took the money?"

"Yessir."

"You don't have any doubt about that?"

"Nosir."

He pawed sweat from his face. "You're going to be in a lot of trouble, son."

"Yessir."

"Why the hell'd you help out a bank robber, anyway? And don't tell me it was because he looked like Robert Mitchum. That's the craziest goddamn thing I've ever heard of." He shook his head. "Jesus, Mary and Joseph, because he looked like fucking 'Mitch?' "

Until that very moment in my young life, I had never heard Clarence use the F word. And issuing from his lips, it sounded both more vile and more silly than it ever had before.

"Chief Pike'll probably bring charges against both you and Barney."

"I know."

"This is going to be pretty embarrassing at the Rotary."

"I'm sorry, Dad."

"A goddamn bank robber. Haven't I raised you better than that?"

"Yessir."

And then we heard the first sirens, loud and near on the hot dark night.

"They're probably going to get the body."

"Yessir."

He swigged more beer. "You let me go talk to Pike first. I'll tell him everything and then I'll call and have you come down."

"All right."

"He won't be happy when I tell him about Cushing. He's got a blind spot for that guy. Thinks he walks on water. I guess it's because his own son died in that tractor accident awhile back and Cushing sort of fills the void. And Cushing's own folks died in that car accident when he was ten."

"Yessir."

He stood up. "I'm going to go get ready. Put on a clean shirt and all."

"Yessir."

"I'm also going to tell your mother."

I nodded.

He stood looking at me for a long time in silence then he shook his head and left the kitchen.

I went into the living room. I could feel this awful sadness come over me. I just kept thinking of Roy and how sad and frail he looked when he dropped the lighter because he'd been too sick to hold it up—

And right then I became aware of the lighter in my pocket. I dug it out and then turned on the floor lamp and held the lighter up to the round yellow bulb.

It was Roy's, the Zippo with the skull and crossbones designed into the silver surface. I must have stuck it in my pocket after I lit his cigarette. I shoved it back in my pocket. I wasn't going to mention it to anybody. It was something I intended to keep.

Clarence came down with Mom right behind him. They looked the way they usually do at funerals, grim in a very formal way. Clarence had on a short-sleeved white shirt and a dark pair of pants. He reeked of Old Spice. He walked over to me and said, "I'll call you in a little while."

I nodded.

Clarence went over and gave Mom a quick small peck on the cheek and then went out, the screen door banging behind him.

Mom went over and sat primly on the edge of the couch. I could tell she wanted to talk. I could also tell she didn't know what to say.

After a time, she cleared her throat and said, "You've hurt your father very deeply."

"I know."

"He has to maintain a certain reputation in this town."

"I know."

"And he's worried that you might—"

"I know what he's worried about, Mom. That I might have to go to reform school."

And then she broke into tears and in the light from the floor lamp she looked suddenly old and haggard and even more frail than Roy had there at the last, and so I went over to her and took her in my arms and held her and just let her cry the way Clarence would have in this circumstance. There really wasn't much else I could do.

Every few minutes while we waited, I'd touch the lighter and think of Roy dying and I'd get sad all over again. I'd never see him or hear him again. That's the strange part. How people just vanish from your life like that. Forever.

Just after eleven, the phone rang. Mom insisted on getting it.

After she spoke a few words standing next to the stairway, I knew she was talking to Clarence.

She still looked pretty old, as if some kind of age transformation had taken place just in the last hour and a half.

Then she said, "Your father wants to speak with you," and held the phone out to me.

Clarence said, "You'd better get your butt over here fast. This isn't turning out the way I thought."

"I'm not sure what that means."

"I can't explain right now, son. But you get over here to the police station right now."

"How about Barney?"

"You let Barney's folks worry about Barney. Right now my only concern is you."

"Yessir."

This late at night, the old town was pretty neat. Almost nothing moved, all the cars were parked, all the people were inside, and the streetlight shadows gave everything the texture and depth of a very gentle painting of a small town all asleep.

I rode my bike through the empty town square and down the block past all the storefronts where the mannequins watched me go. Only the taverns were open, big hot smoky machines grinding out chilly neon light and jukebox wisdom and hard desperate laughter. As I went by I smelled yeasty beer and dirty cigars.

There was a Channel 3 station wagon parked in the No Parking space in front of the police station. Up on the top of the steps stood Chief Pike and Detective Cushing being interviewed by a whole gaggle of reporters. Everything was a blaze of light and a click and clack of still cameras and motion picture cameras. The mayor was there and all the city council and maybe six local gendarmes in uniform and—

And Barney.

He stood right between Pike and Cushing.

And as I dropped my bike on the sidewalk and started walking toward the front of the station, Barney started talking into this microphone this reporter had put in his face.

"How does it feel to be a hero, Barney?"

A hero? What the hell was going on here? All I could think of was how strange Clarence had sounded on the telephone, how he'd said, "This isn't turning out the way I thought."

And then Chief Pike saw me and shouted, "Look! There's our other hero now!"

Fifty faces turned to look at me. Me—the most self-conscious guy I knew. Even walking up in front of a class to read a paper makes me sick to my stomach. All those eyes staring, staring—and right at me.

And the reporters deserted Pike and Cushing and Barney and came running down the stairs toward me.

I wasn't sure what to do. I wanted to run but I knew I'd better not do that.

"How does it feel to be a hero?" asked this guy in a bow tie and straw hat.

"I'm afraid I—" I started to say.

Flashbulbs went nova in my face. I was blinded.

"No need to be modest," another reporter said. "Detective Cushing told us all about it. How you and Barney called him and told him where to find Roy Danton. You boys are heroes!"

"Too bad Detective Cushing didn't find the money, though," said a third reporter.

"Danton hid it somewhere around here, you can be sure of that," an auxiliary cop named Michaelson said. He was one of Cushing's friends, or liked to pretend he was anyway. But mostly he was a fat, pushy jerk.

My sight was starting to come back.

I raised my eyes and looked up the stairs to Barney. He just shrugged, seeming just as confused about all this as I was.

"Even without the money, though," the reporter with the bow tie said, "you boys'll get some kind of reward. You just wait and see."

And then I felt an arm slide around my shoulder and when I turned my head I saw Clarence.

"How does that boy of yours make you feel?" asked a reporter.

"Proud. Darned proud."

"Let's get a picture of you two just like that," said a photographer.

Then they all started snapping pictures.

And then somebody had the notion of me and Clarence going up the steps for a group shot. And after the group shot—

"How about you two boys standing over there on either side of Detective Cushing? We'll get a good shot of just you three."

It was all kind of like a movie, real and unreal at the same time, especially the part where Barney and I stood on the step beneath Cushing so he could put his hands on our shoulders.

"That's great! Just great!" cried the photographer. "Now if I could just get you boys to smile a little!"

Cushing dug his hands into our shoulders and leaned down and whispered, "I saved you two little assholes from going to reform school. So smile!"

So we smiled. Or tried to, anyway, but right now all I could think about was what a clever sonofabitch Cushing was, one hell of a lot cleverer than I ever would have thought.

And when the reporters were through with us they concentrated on Cushing alone. They sounded like high school girls cooing over Elvis.

"Were you scared going into that dark warehouse when you knew somebody like Roy Danton was in there?"

"Well, scared, sure, but that's what the folks in this community pay me to do."

"How'd you finally bag him, Detective Cushing?"

Another self-effacing shrug. "Just kind of snuck up on the closet where my two good friends Tom and Barney told me he'd be. Then I just told him that I was giving him twenty-five seconds to come out with his hands above his head or I'd be coming in."

"He say anything to that?"

Boyish grin. "Well, yes, he did say something to that but it sure isn't something I could repeat here."

"Then what happened?"

"Well, a policeman's only as good as his word. I'd warned him that I'd be coming in and that's just what I did. I kicked the door open and went in."

"Is that when he shot at you?"

He nodded. "One shot was all he had time to get off. That's when I killed him."

Barney and Clarence and I stood there and watched this Academy Award performance and I'm sure we were all thinking the same thing. Good ol' Cushing was going to have it every which way he wanted it. He'd killed a man in cold blood and he'd stolen nearly $50,000 in cash yet he was being treated as a hero.

And the only two people who could testify against him couldn't say a word because by now nobody would believe them. They were all running after Cushing like kids after a Fourth of July float.

I couldn't take any more. I just kept thinking of Roy and how eternity had talked back to me. I said to Clarence, "I'm going home."

I was about to say something else when people started turning their heads to the old white Buick ambulance slowly making its way around the far edge of the town square.

It was headed to the hospital. With Roy inside.

If Cushing saw it, he didn't let on. He still stood at the top of the stairs, showing his gun to reporters and letting them get closeups of it. The chief just walked around shaking everybody's hand as if Cushing had given birth to a fifteen-pound baby or something. Just then Cushing did look up. He stared right at me. Ordinarily, what I saw in his eyes would have frightened me. But right now I didn't care. Right now all I could think about was Roy.

He held my gaze for a long time, giving me a full dose of his threatening look. Then he went back to a reporter who was snapping yet another picture.

More people kept coming. By now all the parking spaces around the square had been taken up. Some people didn't even seem to know what was going on. They'd just heard the noise and seen the lights and drifted over from their humid summer beds. It all reminded me of the scene in *Invasion of the Body Snatchers* where all the people in town come to the square so they can be made into pod people. I guess I was pissed off enough at the moment to think of Somerton that way—exulting in Detective Cushing's bravery without questioning it for a moment. Or wondering how it was that an already badly wounded man had needed to be shot to death. No, they didn't know these things but in their frenzy to have a hero, they wouldn't listen to them, either, even if I'd brought them up.

I went down to my bike and rode home.

Mom and Debbie were up in the living room. I went over and kissed them good night and started up the stairs. "Aren't you going to tell me what happened?" Mom asked.

"Dad'll tell you," I said. "I just really don't want to talk."

In my room, I turned off the lights and sat next to the window and smoked a Lucky. This way I could blow the smoke out the screen. Mom was less likely to notice the smell.

I used Roy's lighter to get my cigarette going and then I just sat there a long time, three or four cigarettes long, and thought of how much I hated Cushing. I could still see him smiling for the cameras. I could still see him pointing the gun dramatically for the reporters.

I Shot Jesse James. There was a film made with that title once, a good film as I remembered it, and Cushing was just as much of a fink as Bob Ford—the man who shot Jesse in the back—had ever been.

Roy hadn't needed to die. Hell, he'd been unconscious. But if he'd lived, he would have been able to tell Chief Pike that Detective Cushing had stolen the money.

Finally, I went to bed. I tried to stop thinking about Cushing by thinking about the new girl everybody said was coming to school this fall. I'd always had this dream that this really elegant girl, like Audrey Hepburn say, would come to our school from some real sheltered background, a convent or something like that, and she wouldn't judge boys by the standards the other girls used—good looks or money or status or muscles—she'd just judge them by what was in their hearts. And so guess who the new girl, at least in my dreams, always fell madly in love with? Right.

I lay there a long time that night thinking about the new girl.

A long time later, the three of them came up and went to sleep. I waited until I thought it was safe and then I went into Debbie's room and put a silver dollar beneath her pillow. She snored in a cute little way and muttered something far below my ability to hear. I kissed her on the forehead and went back to my room, done with my job as Tooth Fairy.

When I got up in the morning, Clarence was there.

Usually, Clarence would have been at work by now but this morning he'd waited for me.

I had Wheaties and wheat toast and orange juice (or "OJ" as Debbie called it) and a vitamin and half a cup of coffee. I felt exhausted. Coffee helped sometimes.

"The governor's coming next Tuesday."

"The governor?" I said.

"The governor," Clarence said. "There's going to be a picnic for you and Barney and Cushing in the square and then the governor's going to give you each some kind of award."

"You know Cushing's got the money?"

"I know."

"And you know he killed Roy in cold blood?"

"I know."

"And you're not mad?"

"Son," he said, glancing up at Mom. "Son, your mother and I had a good long talk last night."

Whenever Clarence and Mom had a "good long talk" about anything, it always meant that I would have to do something I didn't want to.

"More Wheaties, hon?" Mom said.

I shook my head.

"We think you should go along with everything, Tom," Clarence said.

Mom came over and put her hands on my shoulders. "If Cushing had told the truth, you'd be in a lot of trouble, dear. A lot of trouble. This way—"

"This way, Cushing gets away with murder and gets to keep all the money!" I pushed back from the table and stood up, looking at them in disbelief and disgust.

"You aren't any better than Cushing! You're willing to go along with lies, too!"

"Tom, listen—" Clarence started to say.

But I was already on the far side of the banging screen door off the kitchen.

I got on my bike and rode over to Barney's. About halfway there I started feeling badly about yelling at my folks the way I had. They weren't perfect, true, but then I'd heard rumors to the effect that I wasn't perfect, either. Hard as that was to believe.

People always call Barney's area "the poor section" but I actually like it better than where we live. I guess it's the bluffs, all the woodsy hills that run right up to the backyards of most of the houses. Of course, the houses themselves aren't the best—old frame jobbies long in need of paint and roof shingles and uncracked window glass. But I would happily have traded our fancy new carport for just one of those bluffs.

Barney sat on the porch. He wasn't reading or eating. He was just staring.

When he saw me, he said, "You hear about the governor?"

"Yeah."

"God."

"Yeah."

"I'll bet Cushing buys a new suit."

"I'll bet he does, too."

I went up and sat next to him on the porch.

"You tell George the truth yet?" I said. Obviously, he hadn't told his father the truth last night.

"Not yet."

"When you going to?"

Barney didn't say anything for a long time. We just watched the traffic.

"I've been thinking," Barney said.

"About what?"

"About maybe not telling George the truth."

"What?"

He looked over at me. "Who'd believe us, anyway?"

"That's not the point."

"Sure it's the point. My mom says the governor's probably going to give us a reward or something. Wouldn't you like to get a reward?"

"Not this way. God, Barney, we owe it to Roy."

"I've also been thinking about Roy."

"What about him?"

"Now, don't go getting pissed."

"I'm going to sock you right in the mouth, Barney. You wait and see."

"All I mean is—"

"All you mean is that you're a chickenshit little bastard with no principles at all."

And then I hit him, and hard enough to bring forth some blood from his nose.

And right away I was sorry. And said so: "I'm sorry, Barney."

"Fuck yourself." He sat there dabbing at his nose with a finger. He looked like he wanted to cry.

"Maybe I'd better go," I said.

"Yeah. Maybe you'd better."

"You wanna go to a movie this afternoon?"

"No."

"You wanna—"

"I don't wanna anything, Tom. You're a spoiled prick is what you are. Maybe you don't need the reward but I do. I don't live in any fancy-ass house the way you do."

"Our house isn't fancy. It's plain."

"Plain hell."

Every time we got in a fight, no matter what it was about, it ended up about where I lived and where he lived. I tried to understand but I couldn't. Where I lived didn't make any difference to me; and I sure didn't care where Barney lived.

I went down the stairs and got on my bike. "I'm sorry I hit you."

"Yeah."

"I am."

"Just go, Tom. Just go."

"OK. And if you change your mind about going to the pool tonight—"

"I won't."

Everywhere I went that day, people kept stopping me on the street and congratulating me for helping brave Detective Cushing capture the notorious bank robber.

When I couldn't stand it anymore, I went home and sat on the screened-in porch reading *Double Star* and thinking about how Barney looked just after I'd slugged him.

A couple times I got up and went inside and called Barney but his mom very carefully told me that he was out somewhere, which meant that he was hanging around the house but that he didn't want to talk to me.

After I finished Heinlein, I picked up a Rex Stout novel. I really liked Nero Wolfe, which is to say that like a lot of mystery readers I really hated Nero Wolfe . . . but I thanked Rex Stout for giving me so many opportunities to hate the fat man in such a pleasant way. I hoped I could be just like Archie when I grew up—acid-tongued and really successful with women.

The Stout novel gave me the idea for the letter. Nero Wolfe was looking into some poison pen letters and I started thinking . . . what if somebody left the governor an anonymous letter on the podium next Tuesday? And what if the letter told the truth, the whole truth and nothing but the truth about Roy Danton and how he'd come to be shot and where the money really was right now?

Wouldn't such a letter force the governor to look into the case more closely?

Around four that afternoon, the sunlight just starting to cool, I got up and mowed the lawn. Mom had been after Dad for two years to buy a power mower. Western Auto always has them on sale, she'd say. But Clarence could be real stubborn about some things and power mowers was one of them. I don't want to see any of Tom's fingers or toes getting ground up in those blades, he'd say. And when he put it that way, I wasn't sure I wanted a power mower, either.

That night I called Barney three times. He still wouldn't come to the phone. The next day I called him six times and the day after that I called him four—and he still wouldn't come to the phone. He was still mad at me for hitting him.

I spent most of Sunday cruising around on my bike and about two in the afternoon, I ended up at the Dairy Queen.

And who should be sitting on one of the benches, surrounded like two teenage rock-and-roll stars, but Barney and Cushing?

They each had tall twenty-five-cent cones and they each had their own little gaggle of admirers. Barney's were girls our age . . . and Cushing's were older women in their early twenties.

That's when I decided I wanted to punch Barney all over again. The way he was looking over at Cushing, it was easy to see they'd become friends.

Didn't Barney remember what Cushing had done to Roy?

Didn't Barney care anymore?

Monday, the day before Labor Day, I didn't do much. I didn't call Barney because I was afraid that if he did come on the phone I'd start yelling at him. I went down to the drugstore and bought a Lionel White Gold Medal novel called *Murder Takes the Bus* and went home and read it. At the time, I had just started reading Gold Medals and this one was very, very good. Not as good as Shell Scott, who managed to be tough and funny and sexy, but good nonetheless.

I guess I should tell you that people were still stopping me on the street and pumping my hand and saying how proud they were and wasn't it neat that the governor was coming—and what else could I say? I said I was glad they were proud and I pumped their hands right back and I said it was indeed neat that the governor was coming.

Monday night, I wrote the letter. Four times I wrote the letter. I knew it had to be short and to the point but I also knew that it had to shake him up when he read it.

Now all I had to do was figure out how I was going to get it up on the podium without anybody seeing me.

As I was sealing it, there was a tiny, soft knock on my door. I said come in and Debbie appeared. She wore her old faded WinkyDink T-shirt (remember the TV show where you drew on this plastic sheet you put over the TV screen?) and a pair of jeans and no shoes. Her hair was done in pigtails.

"I've been thinking," she said.

"About what?"

"The Tooth Fairy."

"What about him?"

"Well, on Christmas Eve Santa Claus gets around on a sleigh and on Halloween witches get around on brooms—but how does the Tooth Fairy get around?"

"He takes the bus."

She giggled.

"Really," I said. "He's got one of those twenty-trip passes you can buy for two bucks."

She giggled some more.

"I think you left that dollar under my pillow."

"Me? Nah. Where would I get a dollar?"

"I just wanted to thank you."

"Thank him. Not me."

"The Tooth Fairy? The one who rides the bus all the time?"

"That's the guy."

She smiled. And then she said it: "Mrs. Kelvin at the church is having me carry some flowers up and set them on the platform just before the governor gets there."

"God."

"What?"

"You suppose you could do me a favor?"

So I told her about the letter and how I needed to get it up there.

"You'd have to be fast."

"I will be," she said.

"And you'll have to be crafty."

"I will be," she said.

"And you could get in some trouble if you get caught."

"It'll be neat," she said.

So we went through it a couple of times, how she'd set the flowers down and then look around to see if anybody was watching her, and then how she'd set the letter down on the podium and get out of there, fast.

"You scared?"

"A little bit," she said.

"You won't tell Mom?"

"Huh-uh."

"Or Clarence?"

"Huh-uh."

"Promise?"

She held up her fingers in the Bluebird pledge. "I promise."

That night, I actually got some sleep. When I woke up, the letter was the first thing I thought of.

Today it was all going to come tumbling down for Cushing. I couldn't wait.

The event was right at noon. The only problem I had was passing the hours till that time came.

I rode over town and watched the city hall people put the final touches on the town square. There was so much red-white-and-blue it was almost blinding. The bandstand was draped in bunting and already a couple of chubby guys in red sportcoats from the Dixieland band were there sliding their trombones and walking around as if they were pretty hot stuff, butch wax on their hair and real loud heel clips on their shoes. I guess I don't like them because the time Clarence tried to get in with his clarinet they wouldn't take him. Clarence acted like it didn't bother him but I knew it did. Clarence is too nice a guy to get his feelings hurt like that. Anyway, they have a lousy band—every other song seems to be "Muskrat Ramble" and Clarence sure couldn't have made it any worse, even though, I have to admit, his clarinet playing is pretty lousy.

Then I heard somebody say, "Hey! Here comes the heroes!"

And when I turned to look over by the birdshit-speckled Civil War statue, there was Barney and his new best friend Detective Cushing.

Barney saw me but he pretended he didn't. He just kept walking right up to the bandstand with Cushing.

I went home and lay down on my bed.

Debbie came in wearing a white blouse and red shorts and blue
Keds. "Red, white and blue. Get it?"

I nodded.

"Where's the letter?"

"On top of the desk."

"You OK?"

"Not really," I said. "But I'd rather not talk about it."

She went over and picked up the letter. "You ever going to tell
me what it says?"

"Maybe someday."

"Boy, everybody sure is excited about the governor coming to
town." She smiled. "Everybody except Pop."

Governor Hamling was a Democrat, a fact that Clarence wasn't
exactly crazy about.

She came over and stood above me. "You ever going to be all
right again?"

"Someday."

"It's been a long time."

"Just a couple days."

"Well, that's a long time, isn't it?"

"I guess."

"Come on."

"What?"

"You can walk me over to the square. It's about time, anyway."

And so it was.

I went into the bathroom and got ready and then we went out to
the garage and got my bike and Debbie got on the handlebars and
we took off.

"Boy, look," Debbie said when we were two blocks from the
square.

The highway runs right through town. Right now an entire
block of traffic was crawling along with motorcycle cops at the front
and back and this long black limousine right in the middle. Emer-

gency lights—but no sirens—flashed. The motorcycle cops wore sunglasses and looked real mean.

I'd never seen—or felt—this kind of fervor before, not even for Little Richard.

Women stood on street corners waving handkerchiefs at the governor. Grumpy old men waved wrinkled old arms. And little kids jumped up and down and laughed and shouted and pointed.

And it was all for a lie, a damnable lie.

For the next half hour, people came to the square. They came from in town and the small villages surrounding the town and they came from the farms and they came from places as distant as Des Moines. The Dixieland band was already whooping it up and a guy with a torpedo-like tank of oxygen sold red and yellow and green balloons and Harvey at his little white popcorn shack didn't have enough arms to keep up with all the business and up on the bandstand itself the mayor was showing off his familiar pot belly and his brand-new Panama hat. It was just like the county fair only there wasn't any cowshit smell floating on the breeze from the livestock barns.

I'd gotten there early enough to get a front row seat. I wanted to get a real good view of the governor opening that envelope, reading the letter and then announcing to everybody that he would have to call off the ceremonies—"And why?" he'd thunder. "Because this man—" And here he'd point like God with a lightning bolt shooting from his finger—"Because this man Cushing is a liar and a thief and a murderer!" And the crowd would ooooo and aaaaa and the chief would take out his gun and arrest Cushing and—

"You belong on the stage, son."

An older, male voice brought me out of my fantasy.

It was the mayor. "You hear me, Tom?"

"Uh, yeah, I guess."

The mayor led me up the steps to the stage of the bandstand. The Dixieland band—"The Hellcats" was what they called themselves though in the newspaper letters column one day, Mrs. J. D. Bing, who was always writing letters, suggested for the sake of propriety that they rename themselves the "Heckcats"—the band was rolling out on "When the Saints Go Marching in." The noise was deafening. And I'm a guy who plays "Summertime Blues" by Eddie Cochran so loud even our cats go down to the basement to hide.

Cushing and Barney sat to the right of the podium. The governor, who looked vaguely like the mayor with his big belly and his Panama hat, stood on the edge of the steps shaking hands and waggling his pudgy fingers at little babies and saying over and over and over what a fine lovely day it was for a festivity like this. That's what he called it. A "festivity."

The mayor led me to the front row. Cushing and Barney sat in folding chairs near the podium. Cushing was talking. Barney was laughing. The best of buddies. Didn't Barney remember Roy at all?

The mayor had me sit next to Barney. I started to object—but what was the use?

I could feel Barney and Cushing staring at me as I sat down. They'd quit talking and laughing. They just sat there now.

People came over and shook our hands and clapped us on the shoulders. A newspaper guy snapped several pictures. Aunts, uncles and cousins in the crowd out there would spot me and wave and I'd wave back, feeling self-conscious and awkward but not wanting them to think that being a "hero" had gone to my head, the way it had to my second cousin Larry's head the time he saved that dog from a burning building, and then had his friend in a country western band write a song about him. Larry had that damned thing recorded and pressed and four years later was still handing out copies of "Larry Baines, A Roy Rogers Kinda Guy." And his wife, at every single family gathering I'd attended ever since, always talked about Larry's "political plans" which he'd be announcing any day she always breathlessly confided. Larry pumped gas out at the Clark station on Highway 2.

Then the mayor brought the governor over to meet the three of us. The governor seemed like a real nice guy but shaking hands with him was like picking up a real fatty, greasy patty of sausage.

"This is a real thrill for me," he said to the three of us. "Our country needs more people like you."

I glared over at Cushing. Yeah, he was just what the country needed more of, all right.

And then I saw Debbie, half hidden behind this huge vase of yellow and blue and amber summer flowers. She brought them right up to the podium, setting them down on the railing of the bandstand.

Then she looked over at me and gave a little nod and then leaned up and set the white envelope down on the podium itself.

And then she was gone, half running, back down the steps and into the crowd.

I was starting to sit down again—you had to stand up to meet a governor, I guess—and that's when I saw him watching me . . . Cushing.

His eyes strayed over to the podium and then back to me.

He'd obviously seen me watching Debbie and had gotten curious . . . and now he wanted to know about the envelope.

Just then the band, which had given us all a blessed break, sailed into the "Chattanooga Choo-Choo" and then there was just the confusion that results from nobody being able to hear anything. The band guys were puffing their cheeks out and bugging their eyes and spitting all over the place and making everybody on the bandstand silently plead for mercy.

Barney still wouldn't look at me but I saw him frown as soon as the music exploded. He hated Dixieland even more than I did.

Then the mayor stepped over to the center of the bandstand.

And then I saw Cushing get up and kind of edge over to the podium and I knew right away what he was going to do.

He was going to snatch the letter I'd written the governor and make sure that the governor never got to see it.

I got up, too. I had to stop him.

Cushing did it the right way. He didn't make any bold play for the podium, he just eased his way over by shaking a few hands, patting a few backs, grinning a few grins. Even before becoming a "hero," he'd been a popular guy with many of the townspeople. War heroes never went out of fashion.

I got as close to him as I could without stepping on the backs of his shoes.

I knew now that I was going to have to take the envelope myself. I'd just hold on to it till I had the chance to slip it back up there.

Cushing was now maybe a foot from the podium. He was trying to inch his hand behind the broad back of the mayor, who was waving his hands at the band to wrap things up—inch it behind the mayor's back and pick off the white envelope Debbie had just set on the podium.

That was when I moved, moved so fast that I bumped into Cushing.

He looked down at me and scowled. He knew what I was trying to do. The same thing he was trying to do.

His eyes raised and settled on the envelope.

The bandstand was crowded. It was hard to move past all the bodies.

But he took a final step forward, put his hand out, his fingers started to close on the edge of the envelope.

I lunged—and snapped the letter from his fingers. I'd moved quickly enough that he hadn't been able to stop me.

But just as I turned to go back to my seat, he reached down and locked his hand around my wrist.

The odd thing was, the stage was so packed with people standing around gabbing that nobody could see how he was twisting my wrist. We stood in the middle of maybe twenty people. It was like smothering to death inside this tiny hot sweaty box.

Nobody had ever twisted my wrist like that.

"You little bastard," he whispered in my ear. I could hear him even above the band. "Give that to me."

His face was pure rage—but controlled rage—he couldn't afford to lose his poise in front of everybody.

He twisted my wrist harder.

And then the band stopped abruptly.

And the sweaty, important dignitaries made for their seats again.

And there we were, suddenly exposed so everybody could see us.

And Cushing let go immediately. What choice did he have? Here was this supposed hero and he was twisting the hell out of some poor kid's arm.

He let go.

And then I let go, too, my entire hand and wrist so numb from pain that I didn't feel the letter flutter from my grasp.

There it was on the floor—

And I was bending to pick it up—

And Cushing was bending to pick it up—

But before either of us got to it, the mayor stooped—no small feat, given his gut—and retrieved it from the floor.

He held it up and read aloud, "To the Governor."

Cushing glared at me and I glared right back.

"Your honor," the mayor said, "somebody wrote you a letter."

And the mayor of this fair city personally hand-delivered my letter to the governor for me.

"What's this?" the governor said.

But the mayor was already stepping to the podium and giving a little 1-2-3 test to the public address system.

Cushing stared at the letter in the governor's hand. For a second, I had the sense that he was going to jump the governor and rip the letter from him. Cushing looked highly pissed and at least a little bit crazy.

With the mayor already going into his introduction of the governor—"One of the favorite sons in this land of plenty of ours"—all Cushing and I could do was go back to our seats.

Which we did.

When I looked at the governor again, he was opening the envelope.

He took out the letter—

Unfolded it—

Scanned it quickly—

And just then the mayor said, "Ladies and Gentlemen, I give you our own beloved governor!"

The band played. And grown-ups applauded. And teenagers tried to make it look as if they were applauding. And babies cried because all the hoopla was scaring the hell out of them. And a cop turned on a siren. And several of the town dogs standing on the edge of the square started barking.

And the governor just kept reading and rereading the letter.

Just the way I'd wanted him to.

Everything died down, finally.

The governor stepped up to the podium, adjusted the microphone to his own height, the entire PA system ringing with the adjustment, and then he leaned forward and held the letter up for all the crowd to see and then he said—

"Over the years, I've noted that no matter what the occasion or what the event, there's always somebody who tries to spoil it. Out of envy or spite or plain mendacity, they want to ruin a splendid event that everybody else is enjoying. A few minutes ago somebody handed me this letter—and I'll tell you, I've never read such a pack of lies in my life. And if you don't mind, I'm going to take care of this matter right now."

And right then and right there, our own beloved governor of our own beloved state ripped the shit out of the letter I'd sent him.

White pieces of paper fluttered to the ground and our own beloved governor said, "Now I want to thank you for inviting me here and letting me have the honor of handing out these awards to these fine citizens of yours."

To be honest, I didn't pay a lot of attention to the rest of the ceremony. I only knew that the few times I looked at Cushing, he was smirking.

And when the governor went to shake my hand, Cushing, who was right behind me, kicked me so hard in the ankle I could barely stand up.

iv

Autumn came and with it all the pleasures of that season—the smoky air, the Indian summer sunlight, the ring of the schoolbell in the crisp morning, the snap and crackle and glow of the bonfire on the prairie night at the Homecoming ceremony behind the stadium, and all the quick excited laughter of the little kids scurrying along the street on Halloween night, tripping on their too-long costumes and hoping that Mrs. Grundy was still giving out shiny new quarters, and shoving Tootsie Rolls and Clark bars and sticky sweet popcorn balls into their mouths—my favorite season.

The new girl came to school and she was almost painfully pretty and just as painfully stuck-up. I went up to her twice and tried to introduce myself but she saw me coming and then pretended to fall into deep conversation with the other stuck-up girl she was walking down the hall with. Stuck-up girls have this secret club they all belong to, and it runs coast-to-coast.

Then in the mornings on the way to school, you'd suddenly see skins of ice on the creek water, and the wraith of your breath as you spoke. Dad had his two best months ever at the store in September and October, Mom finally got the wall-to-wall carpeting she'd always wanted (a combined birthday-anniversary-Christmas gift, Dad explained) and Debbie got her first boyfriend, this very shy chunky kid who walked her home from school every night and then took off like an arrow whenever he saw me or Mom.

Somerton itself changed, too. The town square, for instance, had a naked and lonely look, shorn as it was of blooming trees and growing foliage. Litter skittered across the dead, brown grass and the bandstand took on the look of a home that had been mysteriously (and perhaps violently) abandoned. Even a little Dixieland music was preferable to this.

A few store-owners started putting up Christmas decorations in early November, with the expected number of old ladies complaining about it—"Show some proper respect. The Lord's birthday is in December, not November"— and there was the expected number of letters in the local paper about how crass Christmas had become.

Hunting season opened and while I could never kill an animal that way, I had to admit there was something thrilling about the stalking part of it, all dressed up in red-and-black checkered caps and jackets and armed with a long rifle and creeping through the fallen cornstalks and along the frozen creek and up the red clay hills, the air pure and fine and chill, and the chestnut roans beautiful as they ran the pasture land nearby.

And you're no doubt wondering about Barney and Cushing.

As of November 10, Barney still hadn't spoken to me. We had several classes a day together, we had the same lunch period, we took the same route home, but Barney always managed to avoid me.

His friendship with Cushing ended right after the governor's appearance. At least I think it did. At any rate, you never saw him with Cushing anywhere. About the only person you ever did see Barney with was a country kid that everybody was always pretty cruel to, a cross-eyed boy who wore Big Mac bib overalls and who had a bad stutter. Jennings, his name was.

As for Cushing, he got himself a snazzy new aqua Plymouth two-door and gave the gossips some very good news by dating the town's only femme fatale, a very dramatic divorcee named Babe Holkup, who had once been the exclusive property of one R.K. "Buddy" Holkup, former high school football great and now resident of Ft. Madison Penitentiary because he kept taking home samples from the bank where he worked. Babe, whose real name was actually Elberta, divorced Buddy when he still had five years to go on his sentence. About this same time, at least according to the gossips I mentioned above, Elberta also started wearing falsies and hose without seams. And getting threatening letters from Buddy. It all sounded like one of those old George Raft movies they play on late-night TV. The times Cushing saw me, he just smirked a bit. He didn't call me a girl anymore and he didn't try to look scary. He just moved on. Apparently he didn't think I was any kind of threat to him.

And I guess I wasn't, not until I had the dream, the strangest dream of my life.

Here was Mitch and here was Roy and damned if they didn't look more alike than I'd even thought.

And Mitch said, "It's time you grow up, Tom. It's time you do right by Roy."

Well, first of all, I'd never had a movie star in my dreams before, so that part of it was startling enough, especially since it was Robert Mitchum himself.

And second of all, Roy looked kind of pissed off. Like maybe I really *hadn't* done right by him.

"I'm sorry, Roy."

And Roy said, "He's got the money."

"I know."

And then Mitch said, "You can get the money, Tom. You're a young man now. You're not a boy anymore."

And what was I going to do? Argue with Robert Mitchum, than whom there was no cooler guy in the entire known universe?

And then Roy said, "It's in his house somewhere. That's where you'll find it."

And then the dream was over and it was November 13 of a gray and frosty morning and I was just waking up and needing very badly to urinate and Mom was calling upstairs for breakfast and Debbie was in the bathroom gargling, which she always did very, very loudly.

—It's in his house somewhere, Tom.

—You're a young man now, Tom. You're not a boy anymore.

in his house somewhere in his house somewhere in his house somewhere kept echoing through my mind the way it does in the movies sometimes.

And all the time I peed and all the time I showered and all the time I dressed and all the time I teased Debbie about her insistence on taking the first bowl of Sugar Frosted Flakes and all the time I walked along to school and all the time I played basketball in gym class during first period—

—all that time I just kept hearing it over and over and over and over again—

in his house somewhere in his house somewhere in his house somewhere

After school, I went home and got out my bike. Strictly speaking, it was a little late in the year for the old Schwinn. People were bundled up inside parkas already. And the Offenberger kids had already built their first snowman of the year—they built them so tall that sometimes the *Des Moines Register* put them in the paper— and the streets were so icy in spots they were dangerous.

Cushing lived on the east edge of town where the houses grew much farther apart, and where the yards looked more like acreages because most of them had scrawny white chickens and grunting quick little hogs running around enclosed areas.

Cushing's place was an old two-story white clapboard house with a big red barn in the back. It sat on four acres of farmland which somebody down the road owned and farmed. There was a fat oak tree across from it, so I pulled in over there so I could look more closely at the house.

A screened-in porch covered the front. On the right side of the place was another door. The windows were all dark in the drab gray November afternoon. Smoke curled from the chimney. There was no garage nor a driveway as such but there were two strips of concrete that the tires of a car would fit. The strips ran along the left side of the house. A lost and lonely-looking stray mutt ran around in frantic circles in the winter-flat cornfield.

Unless Cushing had his car out back or something, nobody was home. His night shift would start in another twenty minutes, just at four. He was probably already at the station.

I wanted to walk over to that side door, jimmy it open, go in and find the cash and then carry it straight to the chief's office, drop it on his desk and then tell him where I got it.

Then I saw a black-and-white patrol car coming from a block and a half away so I quick ran my bike down a slanting hill under a small bridge nearby. I waited there until I heard and felt the patrol car rumble over the ties overhead.

I didn't want a patrolman telling Cushing that he'd seen me standing across the street from Cushing's house.

It was completely dark and no more than twenty-five degrees when I left the house on foot that night.

It was a long walk to Cushing's. I smoked three cigarettes on the way.

With no nearby streetlight, and no cars washing their headlight beams over the place, Cushing's house was lost in shadow. There was only a quarter moon and a few stars bright above the flat fallen cornfield.

I went up to the front door. I had expected to find it securely locked and it was. I also expected to find the side door securely locked and, you guessed it, it was, too.

I went around back where against the left side of the small, enclosed back porch there was a latticework ensnarled with dead, spiky vines of some kind.

I was a good climber. At Scout camp I took merit badges in climbing—of course I also took merit badges, of the unofficial sort,

in leading the most snipe hunts, using the most unique dirty words
(a lot of which, to be honest, I more or less made up) and armpit
farting, which is not necessarily something I'm proud of these days
but I sure was at the time.

I went right up the latticework. I stood on the porch roof which
was high enough so I could walk right over to the second-story window. I gave it a try. It was unlocked. I raised the bottom pane with
no trouble at all.

One minute later, I stood in Cushing's bedroom.

It smelled of: gas heat, sleep, cigarette smoke, minty aftershave, Wildroot hair oil and the same kind of bunion medicine
Clarence used.

What I saw was: a well-made double bed, a large crucifix hanging above the headboard, a five-drawer bureau, two framed photographs of Cushing 1) in his marine uniform 2) in his Somerton
police uniform. There was a shaggy throw rug on the floor, a tightly
packed closet that smelled of mothballs, and a box filled with magazines and paperbacks, the former mostly *Cavalier* and the latter
running to Gold Medals by people like David Goodis and Peter
Rabe. It was tough to admit but Cushing and I liked the same kind
of reading material.

I saw all these things in the narrow beam of my flashlight.

I spent twenty minutes in the room and found nothing spectacular except an extra handgun he kept in one drawer of the bureau
and a can of lighter fluid and some underwear and socks and things
in another. I then proceeded to go through the rest of the house.

I was there about an hour and a half. I learned that Cushing a)
kept a tidy house b) was the proud owner of six fifths of Old Grandad bourbon c) used Trojans.

What I didn't learn was where he kept the money he'd stolen
from Roy. I looked in all the obvious places—cupboards, closets,
the bottom of his clothes hamper—and then in all the not-so-
obvious places . . . behind the couch . . . and under the three throw
rugs on the living-room floor (in the Hardy Boys books, there were
always lots of trapdoors sitting around).

And—nothing.

I stood in his dark living room, my beam off. I'd been going at it hard enough to work up a sweat. My heart pounded.

I still had the dream of taking the money to the chief and throwing it on his desk and—

The phone rang and scared the hell out of me.

I stood there trembling and feeling foolish for jumping up the way I had. It was loud and alien-sounding in the darkness of somebody else's house. . . .

It rang ten times and then was quiet. I decided now was the time to go. Maybe I hadn't found the money but I hadn't been caught, either.

I went back upstairs and out the window. Half a minute later, I stood on the porch roof looking at the barn out back. Talk about a perfect place to hide bank robbery loot.

Next time, I'd concentrate on the barn.

I climbed down the latticework and started around the side of the house and ran straight into Barney.

"What the hell're you doing here?" I said.

"I followed you."

"Followed me? For what?"

"I walk by your place just about every night after dinner but I'm always scared to come up to the door."

"I shouldn't have hit you that time, Barney. I'm sorry."

"No, you should've hit me. You should've beat the shit out of me. The way I let Roy down, I mean. I'm the one who should be sorry."

We didn't say anything then, just stood in shadow and moonlight and kind of slugged each other on the arm. Good old Barney. He was a pain in the ass sometimes but he was the only kid in town who knew who Ed Emsh the magazine cover artist was—so how could you turn your back on him?

I took out a cigarette and lit it and Barney looked at the lighter and said, "Roy's lighter, huh?"

He took it and held it up to the moonlight. "Pretty cool. Those little red jewels for eyes and all." He handed it back. "I spent my hundred bucks already. Did you?"

The governor had given us both one-hundred-dollar US savings bonds last summer.

"Nah. I gave mine to Debbie. I didn't feel right about spending it—" I knew this would make Barney feel bad and I wanted it to—then I thought about how poor his family was and how Barney always wore pretty old clothes and how Clarence always called Barney's father "luckless" and I said, "But I don't blame you for spending yours, Barney."

"You really don't?"

"No, Barney, I really don't." I socked him on the arm a few more times, like it was some kind of Olympic event I was training for, good old all-American armsocking, and then we left.

We took a back road home, one that ran along the tracks, one that wouldn't get us seen by any wandering cop cars, one that shone with frost.

"You didn't find the money, huh?" he said.

"Huh-uh."

"You going back?"

"Yeah. Tomorrow I'm gonna try the barn."

"You mind if I come?"

"I'll be pissed if you don't."

The next afternoon I got chewed out when the teacher found out that I had *Halo for Satan* by John Evans, which is a very good mystery, tucked down behind my history textbook.

Mrs. Morrissey, hoping to humiliate me, said, "And just what does Mr. Evans have to say about Napoleon?"

I just sat there and squirmed, the way she wanted me to.

"Or what does Mr. Evans have to say about Mozart?"

More squirming.

"Or Woodrow Wilson?"

You get the point. She threw out several more historical names and asked me what Mr. Evans had to say about each one of them and all I could do was sit there and take it, all the while wanting to tell her that he was actually a good writer and that she should try reading him sometime but of course you don't talk to teachers that way.

Finally the bell rang and when I went up to the door, she said, "Tom, come here, please, and bring that so-called book of yours."

That's what she always called paperbacks: so-called books.

I went over to her desk. Five years ago, I would have known what to do. Put my hands out, palms down, so she could beat them with a ruler. But we were both too old for that.

"This is the third time this semester I've caught you reading these so-called books in class. They're trash."

I knew I was getting red and hot, the way I do when I get mad and can't do anything about it.

She grabbed the book from my hands and tore it in two and then dropped the two halves in her wastebasket. "Just where it belongs."

Last year, she'd taught us George Orwell's *1984*, and how the thought police worked. Mrs. Morrissey apparently didn't know that she'd become one of them.

I told Barney about this at lunch. Barney looked sort of depressed today, the way he usually does when something bad happened at home, usually meaning that George had quit going to his AA meetings and was drinking again.

On the way home, a gray and frozen afternoon, Barney said, "You scared?"

"About tonight?"

"Uh-huh."

"Huh-uh."

"Really?"

"Really. Just pissed."

"Because Cushing's getting away with it?"

"Uh-huh."

"You know those two days when he was taking me for rides and stuff?"

"Uh-huh."

"He wasn't that bad a guy."

"Yeah, he only killed Roy in cold blood and stole all that money."

"My mom says that's my problem."

"What is?"

"That I feel sorry for too many people."

"I feel sorry for a lot of people, too, Barney, but Cushing sure isn't one of them."

"When you watch him up close sometimes there's this kind of sadness about him. You know that book by Cain that I liked so much?"

Barney couldn't ever remember titles. *"Double Indemnity?"*

"Yeah. That's who Cushing reminds me of. The guy in that. He's real angry and tough but he's kind of sad, too, in a strange way. You know, how George gets when he gets drunk and cries sometimes about WWII and how his buddies died and all that stuff. You ever notice how there's something sad about real mean guys, even like Maynard? Like they get so pissed that they don't know what to do with themselves?"

And I had to admit that I had noticed that.

When we got to the corner where he went east and I went west, I said, "I'll meet you here right at six-fifteen."

"OK." He looked at me then and said, "George went after Mom again last night."

"Beat her up?"

"Yeah."

"Bad?"

"Pretty bad. Black eye. Got a bruise on her cheek. Chipped tooth."

I could see he wanted to cry.

"I'm sorry, Barney."

"My little brother saw it and he really got scared."

"God, Barney."

"You know the worst thing?"

"What?"

"I feel sorry for him, too."

"For your old man?"

"Yeah."

I smiled bleakly and said, "Your mom's right, Barney, you feel sorry for too many people."

☙   ☙   ☙

Barney called just as we were finishing dinner.

He was whispering and that usually meant only one thing. George was still drunk and on a rampage. I heard Barney's mom crying softly in the background. Barney sounded like he was crying, too. "I better not go out tonight, Tom. I better stay with my mom."

"She gonna be OK?"

"Long as I'm here to protect her," he said. Then, "I better go." I went up to my room and did my homework. A couple hours later I heard the phone ring and Mom called from downstairs and said it was for me.

Barney said, "Sorry I had to whisper when I called."

"Is everything all right?"

"He passed out. That's when everything gets back to normal. He sleeps it off for a day and then he's real sorry. You know how it goes."

"Did he hurt your mom?"

"He slapped her a couple of times is all."

That would sound funny to anybody who didn't know Barney and his family—how George had slapped her a couple of times "is all" but given the fact that he'd put her in the hospital a few times, "is all" was pretty modest.

"You up for tomorrow night?" Barney said.

"Yeah. Are you?"

"Can't wait. I need some excitement."

That was the only time Barney really liked to get into trouble, after a bout with George. It was like the only way Barney could forget it all was to lose it in doing something risky.

The next night, Barney was at the right corner at the right time. We took alleys and back roads out to Cushing's, not wanting anybody to see us, liking the idea that we were skulking even when we didn't necessarily have to.

We stood behind the oak tree across the street from Cushing's. All the windows were dark.

The wind in the chimney made a neat moaning sound.

"You ready?"

"Yeah," Barney said.

So we stepped out from behind the oak tree and started to cross the street and just then the car turned the corner several yards away, and shone its headlights on us.

"Just keep walking," I said.

And so we did. Across the street. Onto Cushing's lawn.

And then the car stopped even with us and somebody rolled down the passenger window—you could hear a radio play low and smell cigarette smoke—and then a voice said, "You boys up to anything in particular?"

I couldn't make out a face inside the car. "Who is it?"

"It's Michaelson, is who is it. And I'm curious what you boys are doing out here at this time of night."

And then he hit us right in the face with the spotlight he had mounted on his driver's door.

Michaelson was this fat slob who sold appliances during the day and was an auxiliary policeman on the side. Now everybody in Somerton knew that the most an auxiliary policeman ever did was direct traffic at the county fair and things like that. What they got was a uniform and a badge and a billy club. What they didn't get was a gun or a car or any respect. Michaelson had been on the steps of the police department the night Roy was killed—hanging around his supposed friend Cushing. Even Cushing didn't seem to like him all that much.

Of course, Michaelson pretended he was a pretty big deal strutting around the fair city of Somerton. He had a whip antenna on his '53 Ford fastback and he wore his uniform just to go buy a loaf of bread and the way he walked around with his gut hanging over his hand-tooled western belt, he gave the impression that he was one tough guy.

"You boys hear me?"

"Huh?" Barney said.

"I asked you what you was doing out here?"

I dug in my pocket and took out my Lucky pack and held it up in the beam of the spotlight.

"This is what we're doing out here. Smoking. We don't want our folks to find out."

"Oh," he said. Then, "You're too young to smoke."

"That's why we're sneaking around."

"I could run you two in."

Michaelson always said that. About running people in.

Then he did just what you'd expect somebody like Michaelson to do. He killed the spotlight, rolled up the passenger window, and then took off—laying a strip of rubber that must have run thirty feet.

"What a dink," I said.

We were in the dark again.

"I don't think we'd better go down to the barn tonight."

"Neither do I," I said.

"He's gonna tell Cushing he saw us out here sure as hell."

I agreed.

We walked back home.

On the way, he said, "Mom said she's gonna get a divorce."

"She always says that after something happens."

"He knocked her down and kicked her this time. Then I jumped him. This was the other night."

He sounded confused, and like he wanted to cry again. "I wish I was like Mitch. I wouldn't take shit from anybody. Not from anybody."

When we reached the corner where we always said good-bye, I said, "You're a good guy, Barney, you know that?"

"If I was a good guy, I'd help my mom better."

"You're doing all you can."

"Yeah but when I see her down there on the floor with blood all over her face—"

And this time he took off running, vanished in the darkness outside the small circle of streetlight, loping slapping footsteps in the winter gloom.

Because of Michaelson telling Cushing about us, we decided to wait for another week before going back out to the barn.

The night was somewhere in the low teens. Barney was in a better mood, anyway. George was deep into his penitent role now, begging his wife to forgive him and not toss him out. This was the only time the family really had any peace, when George was like this.

We got to Cushing's about 7:30. There was a frosty half moon and a sky low and bright with midwestern stars. No lights shone in the house. No car was parked in the driveway. We checked the corner. We didn't see Michaelson parked there waiting for us to make our move.

"Ready?"

"Yeah," Barney said.

We ran across the street and along the walk that paralleled the house and then Barney stopped.

"I'm freezing my ass off."

"You'll be fine. You got the whistle?"

"Yeah."

We'd agreed that Barney would scout—if he saw anything strange, he'd take this basketball whistle that belonged to my older brother, the right honorable Corporal Gerald, and blow the hell out of it.

"Hurry up," he said.

He was starting to irritate me, the way only somebody you really like can irritate you.

I took off running. The ground was winter-hard between house and barn.

I pushed the big sliding barn door back only far enough so I could slip in. The place smelled of hay and kerosene and sweet horseshit and winter. I got my flashlight on and moved the beam around the place.

It was pretty well empty, actually. From the ancient horsecollars on the walls and the hay rakes and manure shovels stuck in the corners, you could see that somebody had probably kept animals here at one time. Probably had farmed it, too. But that was long ago. Everything was now dusty and stiff and faded.

I'll skip over the next half hour. It was a bitch but it was also pretty boring. I must have covered every single inch of that barn, as well as the haymow. I had no idea what I was looking for, just something that looked like it would be a good hiding place. I remembered the tarpaulin sack Roy had had the money in. A guy could hide that without too much trouble.

I went up and down the haymow ladder twice, making sure that I hadn't overlooked anything up there. I went into each stall with the rake and cleared the floor of hay and looked for any kind of trapdoor. A lot of the older barns in this area had them. About half-way through all this, my flashlight started flickering on and off, which reminded me of a pretty neat way the Hardy Boys had sent signals in one of their books. At least it had seemed pretty neat to me when I was a little kid.

I found a lot of dead stuff, too: a cat, two rats, a sparrow and this really obese possum. Poor bastard probably ate himself to death.

And then I was walking straight down the center of the barn and I turned my ankle and I acted real mature about it—I stood right there, pain traveling up my ankle and calf and thigh like thunderbolts—and I must have strung somewhere between fifty and sixty swearwords together. I didn't know who to be pissed off at, but I was sure pissed off at somebody.

And then I tried to put pressure on my foot and ankle again and I realized that the reason I tripped was that below all the hay, there was a slight indentation in the ground.

I dropped to my knees and started digging up the hay like a dog searching for a lost bone.

I dug up hay and then I dug up earth with the help of the rake tines and then I felt a piece of cold unyielding wood below the level of dirt.

Among all the long-deserted gardening tools, I found a shovel and I went right to work. I was so excited I forgot all about my ankle.

I dug for about ten minutes. The hole grew wide, wide enough that I could reach down and feel the shape of a wooden box.

I set the shovel down. I started to bend over to raise the box from the hole when Barney said, "Tom."

I turned around.

Barney stood in the door of the barn.

"What're you doing in here?" I said.

And then a second silhouette stepped up behind Barney. "He

didn't have any choice. Neither of you little girls have any choice now."

"Aw, shit," I said. "Aw, shit."

"Get in there," Cushing said to Barney and pushed him into the barn.

"Michaelson cruised by and saw me, I guess. He musta gone and got Cushing," Barney said.

The three of us stood around the hole in the middle of the barn. Wind slammed the hay doors against the barn.

Cushing stepped into the light, such as it was, the flashlight lying on its side on the ground. He wore a nice new overcoat. He always looked spiffy. He also had a gun in his gloved hand.

"Get that box up from there," he said. "And hurry up."

"Why?"

He kicked me. There was no warning, there was no threat. He just kicked me. Right in the mouth, and so hard that my mouth filled up immediately with hot, thick blood.

"Leave him alone!" Barney said.

"You get down there and help him," Cushing said, and shoved Barney down next to me.

I didn't want to get kicked again, so I got to work. I worked fast and I worked good and in less than five minutes, I had the long, square box sitting up on the ground. There was a padlock on it the size of a catcher's mitt.

Cushing threw me a key. "Open it up, girls."

We got it open. Inside was the bag filled with cash.

"Take it out of there."

We took it out.

"Set it on the ground."

We set it on the ground.

"This time when I hide it, you little girls'll never find it. Believe me. Now stand up."

We stood up.

"Next time I see you little girls around here, you're really gonna get hurt. You understand me?"

I couldn't talk real well. I just sort of nodded. Barney just sort of nodded, too.

All I could think of was how much I hated Cushing, how smug and violent he was, and how he'd killed Roy when Roy had no chance of defending himself—

And that was when I remembered the lighter, Roy's lighter, in my pocket.

"Now you two little girls get the hell out of here and never set foot on my property again."

He waved his gun at us.

We got.

My ankle hurt and my mouth hurt and my head hurt. I felt angry and humiliated and terrified.

We went maybe a quarter mile and I said, and it wasn't any too easy for me to speak, "I'm going back, Barney."

"Huh?"

"Back into his house."

"For what?"

I told him.

"You're crazy, Tom."

"Maybe so but I'm goin' back."

I turned around and started back in the darkness toward the house. Cushing wouldn't have had time to hide it yet.

A minute or two later Barney was right alongside of me.

"I know you'd be pissed if I didn't go along."

He was right.

Cushing's police car was parked along the side of his house. The kitchen light was on. I could see him, more shadow than substance, moving around in there.

We went to the back of the house and got on the latticework and went up real quiet. It wasn't difficult at all, not even with my ankle in the condition it was.

We got in his bedroom and then stood very still. All I could hear was our ragged breathing; all I could smell was our sweat.

I remembered right where it was, what drawer it was in, and where he kept the bullets, too.

Barney stood by the door watching and listening while I got Cushing's extra gun and loaded it up. My brother, Gerald, had taught me how to shoot, even if I didn't want to kill animals, which he said I'd "grow out of someday." Then I grabbed the small yellow can of Zippo lighter fluid, which Cushing kept in the drawer below.

When I got the gun all loaded up we crept down the hallway and then crept down the stairs and then crept across the darkened living room and crept out to the kitchen.

Cushing's back was to us. In the bright light, he sat at the table. He poured Old Grandad straight from the bottle into a small water glass. His gun was on the table. So was the bag of money.

"You make one move, Cushing, and I'm going to blow your fucking head off. You understand me?"

I thought I sounded pretty good for a guy with a mouthful of blood.

I moved into the kitchen fast, so that he could see that I held a gun on him.

Barney came in right behind me.

"Well," Cushing said, smirking, "if it isn't my two little girl-friends."

"Get the money, Barney, and put it over in the sink."

Mention of the money ended Cushing's smirk.

"What the hell do you think you're doing?"

He started to get up from his chair but I eased the hammer back on the pistol.

"I'm not real good with firearms, Cushing. I might just blow your head off by accident."

He saw the wisdom of that.

Barney took the sack over to the big white sink. He unzipped the top of the sack and started filling the sink with small bundles of cash.

"What the hell're you two doing?" Cushing said.

"Douse it, Barney," I said.

Barney took the can of Zippo lighter fluid I'd given him and squirted clear fluid all over the money.

"You crazy bastard," Cushing said to me, now that he'd figured out what we were going to do.

From my pocket I took Roy's lighter and held it up for Cushing to see.

And then I set the money on fire.

It went up in this huge whoof of flame and smoke.

Cushing jumped up and tried to get past me at the money.

But he was already too late. Barney had done a good job of soaking all the bills.

"You stupid little bastard," he said.

And that's when he made his lunge for his gun and that's when I shot him.

He screamed and dropped immediately to the floor, his gun falling away from his grasp.

I'd shot him somewhere in the shoulder, apparently in a place that was pretty painful judging by the way he kept rolling around and moaning.

"You little prick," he said when he saw me walk around the table and stand over him. "All that money—wasted."

"We better call somebody," Barney said.

I nodded, looked down with great disgust at Cushing and then remembered what Barney had said the other night—about feeling sorry for him.

And I did, too, just then because his face was different now— instead of rage and arrogance, there was this terrible sorrow.

I thought of the hawk that day, and how the hunters had brought him down.

"You had it coming, Cushing. You killed Roy."

I started to walk back to where Barney stood in the kitchen doorway, setting the gun down on the counter on my way.

I started to go call the chief but then Barney saw something behind me and shouted, "Watch out, Tom! He's got his gun!"

Cushing had inched his fingers to his gun and had tightened his hand around it.

I looked over to the gun I'd just set on the counter. And realized that I'd never be able to reach it before Cushing killed us.

"The chief's gonna know about you, Cushing," I said. "He's gonna know you killed us and know you killed Roy, too."

And then something pretty strange happened. Cushing tried to pull himself to an upright position, the way Roy had right before he died . . . and when he did this, just for a second, he looked just like Roy. And even a little bit like Mitch.

And then something even stranger happened.

Cushing raised his gun and started to point it straight at my heart but then stopped and pointed it right at—

He was—

putting it—

tight against his—

forehead—

and pulling the—

trigger and—

And I heard Barney scream. And then I heard myself scream, too, and I heard the boom of the weapon discharging and heard the splat and splatter of his brains splash against the bottom of the wall like dishwater being emptied—

Then there was just this silence.

I'd only heard this silence one other time, those moments right after I realized Roy was dead and I was trying to call him back from eternity, shouting down this long dark endless corridor—

"God," Barney said. "God."

Because there really wasn't anything else to say. There really wasn't.

Here Roy hadn't had nerve enough to kill himself and was killed by Cushing who, in the end, did have nerve enough—

I tried not to think of how Cushing's folks had both been killed when Cushing was only ten. I didn't want to be like Barney. I didn't want to feel sorry for people I should hate. . . .

V

Well, it took several long weeks to learn what the county attorney had in mind, but finally he told Clarence that he wasn't going to press any charges after all, and that given how it had all ended, we'd probably learned our lessons, Barney and I.

We were celebrities of sorts at school again. The new girl even asked if she could interview me for the school paper. Of course when I asked her if she'd like to stop at Hamblin's some time for a soda, she said, (very politely) No Thank You.

In the spring, Barney's mom did finally divorce George, and

then Barney and all of his family except George moved to Pennsylvania. For the first two months, he wrote every other week. Then I didn't hear much from him anymore until, eight years later, he was killed in fighting in Vietnam. His wife, a very nice woman named Diedre, called to tell me how much I'd meant to him and to say that she hoped we'd meet some day. Four years after that, Clarence died of liver cancer. Mom went to move in with Debbie, whose husband was a professor at the state university where Debbie was a junior. The professor had left his wife and two daughters for Debbie and Mom wasn't exactly what you called thrilled about it all.

I was the only one to stay in Somerton. I became Clarence's business partner in the haberdashery and when he died, I took over completely. I have one son who was born with spina bifida and another son who, I am happy to say, was born in perfect health. My wife, Myrna, is the sweetest, most gentle person I have ever known.

About every five or six years, whenever there's turnover at the local paper, some twenty-four-year-old reporter comes over to the store and says he'd like to talk to me about the Roy Danton incident. The folks of Somerton never seem to tire of hearing about it. I always agree. My sons, who always like to hear about it, too, would give me hell if I didn't.

On those occasions when I go to the cemetery to speak with my dead father and my dead friend Barney, I sometimes stop and look at the grave of Stephen B. Cushing. I'm not sure why. Perhaps because I've never quite been able to forget how Barney felt sorry for him—and how I, too, felt sorry for him right there at the very end—this man I so despised.

I see his desperate eyes right there at the last—and hear the lone gunshot. . . .

It's a lot less trouble sometimes, when you just plain and simple hate somebody.

I still go for walks along the tracks sometimes, out where the warehouse is now a small manufacturing plant, and I think of that long-ago summer and it is like a dream somehow—lived out by somebody who was not exactly me, not the me in the mirror today anyway. . . .

And I think of Roy, too, of course. But it's funny, you know. A few years ago I saw an old Robert Mitchum picture on the tube . . . and the truth is, Roy hadn't looked a damn thing like him. Not a damn thing like him at all . . .

TURN AWAY

On Thursday she was there again. (This was on a soap opera he'd picked up by accident looking for a western movie to watch since he was all caught up on his work.) Parnell had seen her Monday but not Tuesday then not Wednesday either. But Thursday she was there again. He didn't know her name, hell it didn't matter, she was just this maybe twenty-two twenty-three-year-old who looked a lot like a nurse from Enid, Oklahoma, he'd dated a couple of times (Les Elgart had been playing on the Loop) six seven months after returning from WWII.

Now this young look-alike was on a soap opera and he was watching.

A frigging soap opera.

He was getting all dazzled up by her, just as he had on Monday, when the knock came sharp and three times, almost like a code.

He wasn't wearing the slippers he'd gotten recently at Kmart so he had to find them, and he was drinking straight from a quart of Hamms so he had to put it down. When you were the manager of an apartment building, even one as marginal as the Alma, you had to go to the door with at least a little "decorousness," the word Sgt.

Meister, his boss, had always used back in Parnell's cop days.

It was 11:23 A.M. and most of the Alma's tenants were at work. Except for the ADC mothers who had plenty of work of their own kind what with some of the assholes down at social services (Parnell had once gone down there with the Jamaican woman in 201 and threatened to punch out the little bastard who was holding up her check), not to mention the sheer simple burden of knowing the sweet innocent little child you loved was someday going to end up just as blown-out and bitter and useless as yourself.

He went to the door, shuffling in his new slippers which he'd bought two sizes too big because of his bunions.

The guy who stood there was no resident of the Alma. Not with his razor-cut black hair and his three-piece banker's suit and the kind of melancholy in his pale blue eyes that was almost sweet and not at all violent. He had a fancy mustache spoiled by the fact that his pink lips were a woman's.

"Mr. Parnell?"

Parnell nodded.

The man, who was maybe thirty-five, put out a hand. Parnell took it, all the while thinking of the soap opera behind him and the girl who looked like the one from Enid, Oklahoma. (Occasionally he bought whack-off magazines but the girls either looked too easy or too arrogant so he always had to close his eyes anyway and think of somebody he'd known in the past.) He wanted to see her, fuck this guy. Saturday he would be sixty-one and about all he had to look forward to was a phone call from his kid up the Oregon coast. His kid, who, God rest her soul, was his mother's son and not Parnell's, always ran a stopwatch while they talked so as to save on the phone bill. Hi Dad Happy Birthday and It's Been Really Nice Talking To You. I-Love-You-Bye.

"What can I do for you?" Parnell said. Then as he stood there watching the traffic go up and down Cortland Boulevard in baking July sunlight, Parnell realized that the guy was somehow familiar to him.

The guy said, "You know my father."

"Jesus H. Christ—"

"—Bud Garrett—"

"—Bud. I'll be goddamned." He'd already shaken the kid's hand and he couldn't do that again so he kind of patted him on the shoulder and said, "Come on in."

"I'm Richard Garrett."

"I'm glad to meet you, Richard."

He took the guy inside. Richard looked around at the odds and ends of furniture that didn't match and at all the pictures of dead people and immediately put a smile on his face as if he just couldn't remember when he'd been so enchanted with a place before, which meant of course that he saw the place for the dump Parnell knew it to be.

"How about a beer?" Parnell said, hoping he had something besides the generic stuff he'd bought at the 7-Eleven a few months ago.

"I'm fine, thanks."

Richard sat on the edge of the couch with the air of somebody waiting for his flight to be announced. He was all ready to jump up. He kept his eyes downcast and he kept fiddling with his wedding ring. Parnell watched him. Sometimes it turned out that way. Richard's old man had been on the force with Parnell. They'd been best friends. Garrett Sr. was a big man, six-three and fleshy but strong, a brawler and occasionally a mean one when the hootch didn't settle in him quite right. But his son . . . Sometimes it turned out that way. He was manly enough, Parnell supposed, but there was an air of being trapped in himself, of petulance, that put Parnell off.

Three or four minutes of silence went by. The soap opera ended with Parnell getting another glance of the young lady. Then a "CBS Newsbreak" came on. Then some commercials. Richard didn't seem to notice that neither of them had said anything for a long time. Sunlight made bars through the venetian blinds. The refrigerator thrummed. Upstairs but distantly a kid bawled.

Parnell didn't realize it at first, not until Richard sniffed, that Bud Garrett's son was either crying or doing something damn close to it.

"Hey, Richard, what's the problem?" Parnell said, making sure to keep his voice soft.

"My, my Dad."

"Is something wrong?"

"Yes."

"What?"

Richard looked up with his pale blue eyes. "He's dying."

"Jesus."

Richard cleared his throat. "It's how he's dying that's so bad."

"Cancer?"

Richard said, "Yes. Liver. He's dying by inches."

"Shit."

Richard nodded. Then he fell once more into his own thoughts. Parnell let him stay there a while, thinking about Bud Garrett. Bud had left the force on a whim that all the cops said would fail. He started a rent-a-car business with a small inheritance he'd come into. That was twenty years ago. Now Bud Garrett lived up in Woodland Hills and drove the big Mercedes and went to Europe once a year. Bud and Parnell had tried to remain friends but beer and champagne didn't mix. When the Mrs. had died Bud had sent a lavish display of flowers to the funeral and a note that Parnell knew to be sincere but they hadn't had any real contact in years.

"Shit," Parnell said again.

Richard looked up, shaking his head as if trying to escape the aftereffects of drugs. "I want to hire you."

"Hire me? As what?"

"You're a personal investigator aren't you?"

"Not anymore. I mean I kept my ticket—it doesn't cost that much to renew it—but hell I haven't had a job in five years." He waved a beefy hand around the apartment. "I manage these apartments."

From inside his blue pin-striped suit Richard took a sleek wallet. He quickly counted out five one-hundred-dollar bills and put them on the blond coffee table next to the stack of Luke Short paperbacks. "I really want you to help me."

"Help you do what?"

"Kill my father."

Now Parnell shook his head. "Jesus, kid, are you nuts or what?"

Richard stood up. "Are you busy right now?"

Parnell looked around the room again. "I guess not."

"Then why don't you come with me?"

"Where?"

When the elevator doors opened to let them out on the sixth floor of the hospital, Parnell said, "I want to be sure that you understand me."

He took Richard by the sleeve and held him and stared into his pale blue eyes. "You know why I'm coming here, right?"

"Right."

"I'm coming to see your father because we're old friends. Because I cared about him a great deal and because I still do. But that's the only reason."

"Right."

Parnell frowned. "You still think I'm going to help you, don't you?"

"I just want you to see him."

On the way to Bud Garrett's room they passed an especially good-looking nurse. Parnell felt guilty about recognizing her beauty. His old friend was dying just down the hall and here Parnell was worrying about some nurse.

Parnell went around the corner of the door. The room was dark. It smelled sweet from flowers and fetid from flesh literally rotting.

Then he looked at the frail yellow man in the bed. Even in the shadows you could see his skin was yellow.

"I'll be damned," the man said.

It was like watching a skeleton talk by some trick of magic.

Parnell went over and tried to smile his ass off but all he could muster was just a little one. He wanted to cry until he collapsed. You sonofabitch, Parnell thought, enraged. He just wasn't sure who he was enraged with. Death or God or himself—or maybe even Bud himself for reminding Parnell of just how terrible and scary it could get near the end.

"I'll be damned," Bud Garrett said again.

He put out his hand and Parnell took it. Held it for a long time.

"He's a good boy, isn't he?" Garrett said, nodding to Richard.

"He sure is."

"I had to raise him after his mother died. I did a good job, if I say so myself."

"A damn good job, Bud."

This was a big private room that more resembled a hotel suite. There was a divan and a console TV and a dry bar. There was a Picasso lithograph and a walk-in closet and a deck to walk out on. There was a double-sized water bed with enough controls to drive a space ship and a big stereo and a bookcase filled with hardcovers. Most people Parnell knew dreamed of living in such a place. Bud Garrett was dying in it.

"He told you," Garrett said.

"What?" Parnell spun around to face Richard, knowing suddenly the worst truth of all.

"He told you."

"Jesus, Bud, you sent him, didn't you?"

"Yes. Yes, I did."

"Why?"

Parnell looked at Garrett again. How could somebody who used to have a weight problem and who could throw around the toughest drunk the barrio ever produced get to be like this. Nearly every time he talked he winced. And all the time he smelled. Bad.

"I sent for you because none of us is perfect," Bud said.

"I don't understand."

"He's afraid."

"Richard?"

"Yes."

"I don't blame him. I'd be afraid, too." Parnell paused and stared at Bud. "You asked him to kill you, didn't you?"

"Yes. It's his responsibility to do it."

Richard stepped up to his father's bedside and said, "I agree with that, Mr. Parnell. It is my responsibility. I just need a little help is all."

"Doing what?"

"If I buy cyanide, it will eventually be traced to me and I'll be tried for murder. If you buy it, nobody will ever connect you with my father."

Parnell shook his head. "That's bullshit. That isn't what you want me for. There are a million ways you could get cyanide without having it traced back."

Bud Garrett said, "I told him about you. I told him you could help give him strength."

"I don't agree with any of this, Bud. You should die when it's your time to die. I'm a Catholic."

Bud laughed hoarsely. "So am I, you asshole." He coughed and said, "The pain's bad. I'm beyond any help they can give me. But it could go on for a long time." Then, just as his son had an hour ago, Bud Garrett began crying almost imperceptibly. "I'm scared, Parnell. I don't know what's on the other side but it can't be any worse than this." He reached out his hand and for a long time Parnell just stared at it but then he touched it.

"Jesus," Parnell said. "It's pretty fucking confusing, Bud. It's pretty fucking confusing."

Richard took Parnell out to dinner that night. It was a nice place. The table cloths were starchy white and the waiters all wore shiny shoes. Candles glowed inside red glass.

They'd had four drinks apiece, during which Richard told Parnell about his two sons (six and eight respectively) and about the perils and rewards of the rent-a-car business and about how much he liked windsurfing even though he really wasn't much good at it.

Just after the arrival of the fourth drink, Richard took something from his pocket and laid it on the table.

It was a cold capsule.

"You know how the Tylenol Killer in Chicago operated?" Richard asked.

Parnell nodded.

"Same thing," Richard said. "I took the cyanide and put it in a capsule."

"Christ. I don't know about it."

"You're scared, too, aren't you?"

"Yeah, I am."

Richard sipped his whiskey-and-soda. With his regimental

striped tie he might have been sitting in a country club. "May I ask
you something?"

"Maybe."

"Do you believe in God?"

"Sure."

"Then if you believe in God, you must believe in goodness, cor-
rect?"

Parnell frowned. "I'm not much of an intellectual, Richard."

"But if you believe in God, you must believe in goodness,
right?"

"Right."

"Do you think what's happening to my father is good?"

"Of course I don't."

"Then you must also believe that God isn't doing this to him—
right?"

"Right."

Richard held up the capsule. Stared at it. "All I want you to do is
give me a ride to the hospital. Then just wait in the car down in the
parking lot."

"I won't do it."

Richard signaled for another round.

"I won't goddamn do it," Parnell said.

By the time they left the restaurant Richard was too drunk to drive.
Parnell got behind the wheel of the new Audi. "Why don't you tell
me where you live? I'll take you home and take a cab from there."

"I want to go to the hospital."

"No way, Richard."

Richard slammed his fist against the dashboard. "You fucking
owe him that, man!" he screamed.

Parnell was shocked, and a bit impressed, with Richard's violent
side. If nothing else, he saw how much Richard loved his old man.

"Richard, listen."

Richard sat in a heap against the opposite door. His tears were
dry ones, choking ones. "Don't give me any of your speeches." He
wiped snot from his nose on his sleeve. "My dad always told me

what a tough guy Parnell was." He turned to Parnell, anger in him again. "Well, I'm not tough, Parnell, and so I need to borrow some of your toughness so I can get that man out of his pain and grant him his one last fucking wish. DO YOU GODDAMN UNDER-STAND ME?"

He smashed his fist on the dashboard again.

Parnell turned on the ignition and drove them away.

When they reached the hospital, Parnell found a parking spot and pulled in. The mercury vapor lights made him feel as though he were on Mars. Bugs smashed against the windshield.

"I'll wait here for you," Parnell said.

Richard looked over at him. "You won't call the cops?"

"No."

"And you won't come up and try to stop me?"

"No."

Richard studied Parnell's face. "Why did you change your mind?"

"Because I'm like him."

"Like my father?"

"Yeah. A coward. I wouldn't want the pain, either. I'd be just as afraid."

All Richard said, and this he barely whispered, was "Thanks."

While he sat there Parnell listened to country western music and then a serious political call-in show and then a call-in show where a lady talked about Venusians who wanted to pork her and then some salsa music and then a religious minister who sounded like Foghorn Leghorn in the old Warner Brothers cartoons.

By then Richard came back.

He got in the car and slammed the door shut and said, completely sober now, "Let's go."

Parnell got out of there.

They went ten long blocks before Parnell said, "You didn't do it, did you?"

Richard got hysterical. "You sonofabitch! You sonofabitch!"

Parnell had to pull the car over to the curb. He hit Richard once, a fast clean right hand, not enough to make him unconscious but enough to calm him down.

"You didn't do it, did you?"

"He's my father, Parnell. I don't know what to do. I love him so much I don't want to see him suffer. But I love him so much I don't want to see him die, either."

Parnell let the kid sob. He thought of his old friend Bud Garrett and what a good goddamn fun buddy he'd been and then he started crying, too.

When Parnell came down Richard was behind the steering wheel.

Parnell got in the car and looked around the empty parking lot and said, "Drive."

"Any place especially?"

"Out along the East River road. Your old man and I used to fish off that little bridge there."

Richard drove them. From inside his sportcoat Parnell took the pint of Jim Beam.

When they got to the bridge Parnell said, "Give me five minutes alone and then you can come over, OK?"

Richard was starting to sob again.

Parnell got out of the car and went over to the bridge. In the hot night you could hear the hydroelectric dam half a mile downstream and smell the fish and feel the mosquitoes feasting their way through the evening.

He thought of what Bud Garrett had said, "Put it in some whiskey for me, will you?"

So Parnell had obliged.

He stood now on the bridge looking up at the yellow circle of moon thinking about dead people, his wife and many of his WWII friends, the rookie cop who'd died of a sudden tumor, his wife with her rosary-wrapped hands. Hell, there was probably even a chance that nurse from Enid, Oklahoma, was dead.

"What do you think's on the other side?" Bud Garrett had asked just half an hour ago. He'd almost sounded excited. As if he were a farm kid about to ship out with the Merchant Marines.

"I don't know," Parnell had said.

"It scare you, Parnell?"

"Yeah," Parnell had said. "Yeah it does."

Then Bud Garrett had laughed. "Don't tell the kid that. I always told him that nothin' scared you."

Richard came up the bridge after a time. At first he stood maybe a hundred feet away from Parnell. He leaned his elbows on the concrete and looked out at the water and the moon. Parnell watched him, knowing it was all Richard, or anybody, could do.

Look out at the water and the moon and think about dead people and how you yourself would soon enough be dead.

Richard turned to Parnell then and said, his tears gone completely now, sounding for the first time like Parnell's sort of man, "You know, Parnell, my father was right. You're a brave sonofabitch. You really are."

Parnell knew it was important for Richard to believe that—that there were actually people in the world who didn't fear things the way most people did—so Parnell didn't answer him at all.

He just took his pint out and had himself a swig and looked some more at the moon and the water.

SEASONS OF THE HEART

For Charlotte MacLeod

In the mornings now, the fog didn't burn off till much before eight, and the dew stayed silver past nine, and the deeper shadows stayed all morning long in the fine red barn I'd helped build last year. The summer was fleeing.

But that wasn't how I knew autumn was coming.

No, for that all I had to do was look at the freckled face of my granddaughter, Lisa, who would be entering eighth grade this year at the consolidated school ten miles west.

For as much as she read, and when she wasn't doing chores she was always reading something, even when she sat in front of the TV, she hated school. I don't think she'd had her first serious crush yet, and the girlfriends available to her struck her as a little frivolous. They were town girls and they didn't have Lisa's responsibilities.

This particular morning went pretty much as usual.

We had a couple cups of coffee, Lisa and I, and then we hiked down to the barn. It was still dark. You could hear the horses in the hills waking with the dawn, and closer by the chickens. Turn-over day was coming, a frantic day in the life of a farmer. You take the birds to market and then have twenty-four hours to clean out the chicken house before the new shipment of baby chicks arrives. First time I ever did it, I was worn out for three days. That's when my daughter, Emmy, read me the Booker T. Washington quote I'd come to savor: "No race can prosper till it learns that there is as much dignity in tilling a field as writing a poem." Those particular words work just as well as Ben-Gay on sore muscles. For me, anyway.

The barn smelled summer sweet of fresh milk. Lisa liked to lead the animals into the stalls, she had her own reassuring way of talking to them in a language understood only by cows and folk under fourteen years of age. She also liked to hook them up.

The actual milking, I usually did. Lisa always helped me pour the fresh milk into dumping stations. We tried to get a lot of milk per day. We had big payments to make on this barn. The Douglas fir we'd used for the wood hadn't come cheap. Nor had the electricity, the milking machines or the insulation. You've got to take damned good care of dairy cattle.

I worked straight through till Lisa finished cleaning up the east end of the barn. This was one of those days when she wanted to do some of the milking herself. I was happy to let her do it.

Everything went fine till I stepped outside the barn to have a few puffs on my pipe.

Funny thing was, I'd given up both cigarettes and pipe years before. But after Dr. Wharton, back in Chicago when I was still with the flying service, told me about the cancer, I found an old briar pipe of mine and took it up again. I brought it to the farm with me when I came to live with Emmy. I never smoked it in an enclosed area. I didn't want Lisa to pick up any secondhand smoke.

The chestnut mare was on the far hill. She was a beauty and seemed to know it, always prancing about to music no one else seemed to hear, or bucking against the sundown sky when she looked all mythic and ethereal in the darkening day.

And that's just what I was doing, getting my pipe fired up and looking at the roan, when the rifle shot ripped away a large chunk of wood from the door frame no more than three inches to my right.

I wasn't sure what it was. In movies, the would-be target always pitches himself left or right but I just stood there for several long seconds before the echo of the bullet whining past me made me realize what happened.

Only then did I move, running into the barn to warn Lisa but she already knew that something had happened.

Lisa is a tall, slender girl with the dignified appeal of her mother. You wouldn't call either of them beauties but in their fine blond hair and their melancholy brown eyes and their quick and sometimes sad grins, you see the stuff of true heartbreakers, a tradition they inherited from my wife, who broke my heart by leaving me for an advertising man when Emmy was nine years old.

"God, that was a gunshot wasn't it?"

"I'm afraid it was."

"You think it was accidental, Grandad?"

"I don't know. Not yet, anyway. But for now, let's stay in the barn."

"I wonder if Mom heard it."

I smiled. "Not the way she sleeps."

She put her arms around me and gave me a hug. "I was really scared. For you, I mean. I was afraid somebody might have—Well, you know."

I hugged her back. "I'm fine, honey. But I'll tell you what. I want you to go stand in that corner over there while I go up in the loft and see if I can spot anybody."

"It's so weird. Nobody knows you out here."

"Nobody that I know of, anyway."

She broke our hug and looked up at me with those magnificent and often mischievous eyes. "Grandad?"

She always used a certain tone when she was about to ask me something she wasn't sure about.

"Here it is. You've got that tone."

Her bony shoulders shrugged beneath her T-shirt, which depicted a rock-and-roll band I'd never heard of. They were called the Flesh Eaters and she played their tapes a lot.

"I was just wondering if you'd be mad if I wrote it up."

"Wrote what up?"

"You know. Somebody shooting at you."

"Oh."

"Mrs. Price'll make us do one of those dorky how-I-spent-my-summer-vacation deals. It'd be cool if I could write about how a killer was stalking my Grandad."

"Yeah," I said, "that sure sounds cool all right."

She grinned the grin and I saw both her mother and her grandmother in it. "I mean, I might 'enhance' it a little bit. But not a lot."

"Fine by me, pumpkin," I said, leading her over to the corner of the barn where several bales of hay would absorb a gun shot. "I'll be right back."

I figured that the shooter was most likely gone, long gone probably, but I wanted to make sure before I let Lisa stroll back into the barnyard.

I went up the ladder to the hayloft, sneezing all the way. My sinuses act up whenever I get even close to the loft. I used to think it was the hay but then I read a Farm Bulletin item saying it could be the rat droppings. For someone who grew up in the Hyde Park area of Chicago, rat droppings are not something you often consider as a sinus irritant. Farm life was different. I loved it.

I eased the loft door open a few inches. Then stopped.

I waited a full two minutes. No rifle fire.

I pushed the door open several more inches and looked outside. Miles of dark green corn and soybeans and alfalfa. On the hill just about where the mare was, I saw a tree where the gunman might have fired from. Gnarly old oak with branches stout enough for a hanging.

"Grandad?" Lisa called up from below.

"Yeah, hon?"

"Are you all right?"

"I'm fine, hon. How about you?"

"God, I shouldn't have asked you if I could write about this for my class."

"Oh, why not?"

"Because this could be real serious. I mean, maybe it wasn't accidental."

"Now you sound like your grandmother."

"Huh?"

"She'd always do something and then get guilty and start apologizing." I didn't add that despite her apologies, her grandmother generally went right back to doing whatever she'd apologized for in the first place.

"I'm sorry if I hurt your feelings, Grandad."

Lisa never used to treat me like this. So dutifully. Nor did her mother. To them, I was just the biggest kid in the family and was so treated. But the cancer changed all that. Now they'd do something spontaneous and then right away they'd start worrying. There's a grim decorum that goes along with the disease. You become this big sad frail guy who, they seem to think, just can't deal with any of life's daily wear and tear.

That's one of the nice things about my support group. We get to laugh a lot about the delicate way our loved ones treat us sometimes. It's not mean laughter. Hell, we understand that they wouldn't treat us this way if they didn't love us, and love us a lot. But sometimes their dutifulness can be kind of funny in an endearing way.

"You 'enhance' it any way you want to, pumpkin," I said, and started to look around at fields sprawling out in front of me.

I also started sneezing pretty bad again, too.

I spent ten more minutes in the loft, finally deciding it was safe for us to venture out as soon as we finished with the milking for the day.

On the way out of the barn, I said, "Don't tell your mom. You know, about the gunshot."

"How come?"

"You must be crazy, kid. You know how she worries about me."

Lisa smiled. "How about making a bargain?"

"Oh-oh. Here it comes."

"I won't tell Mom and you let me drive the tractor."

Lots of farm kids die in tractor accidents every year. I didn't want Lisa to be one of them. "I'll think about it, how's that?"

"Then I guess I'll just have to think about it, too." But she laughed.

I pulled her closer, my arm around her shoulder. "You think I'm wrong? About not telling your mom?"

She thought for a while. "Nah, I guess not. I mean, Mom really does worry about you a lot already."

We were halfway to the house, a ranch-style home of blond brick with an evergreen windbreak and a white dish antenna east of the trees.

Just as we reached the walk leading to the house, I heard a heavy car come rumbling up the driveway, raising dust and setting both collies to barking. The car was a new baby blue Pontiac with official police insignia decaled on the side.

I stopped, turned around, grinned at Lisa. "Remember now, you've got Friday."

"Yeah, I wish I had Saturday, the way you do."

We'd been betting the last two weeks when Chief of Police Nick Bingham was going to ask Emmy to marry him. They'd been going out for three years, and two weeks ago Nick had said, "I've never said this to you before, Emmy, but you know when I turned forty last year? Well, ever since, I've had this loneliness right in here. A burning." And of course my wiseass daughter had said, "Maybe it's gas." She told this to Lisa and me at breakfast next morning, relishing the punchline.

Because Nick had never said anything like this at all in his three years of courting her, Emmy figured he was just about to pop the question.

So Lisa and I started this little pool. Last week I bet he'd ask her on Friday night and she'd bet he'd ask her on Saturday. But he hadn't asked her either night. Now the weekend was approaching again.

Nick got out of the car in sections. In high school he'd played basketball on a team that had gone three times to state finals and had finished second twice. Nick had played center. He was just over six-five. He went three years to college but dropped out to finish harvest when his father died of a heart attack. He never got the degree. But he did become a good lawman.

"Morning," he said.

"Pink glazed?" Lisa said when she saw the white sack dangling from his left hand.

"Two of 'em are, kiddo."

"Can I have one?"

"No," he said, pulling her to him and giving her a kind of affectionate Dutch rub. "You can have both of 'em."

He wasn't what you'd call handsome but there was a quiet manliness to the broken nose and the intelligent blue eyes that local ladies, including my own daughter, seemed to find attractive, especially when he was in his khaki uniform. They didn't seem to mind that he was balding fast.

Emmy greeted us at the door in a blue sweatshirt and jeans and the kind of white Keds she'd worn ever since she was a tot. No high-priced running shoes for her. With her earnest little face and tortoiseshell glasses, she always reminded me of those quiet, pretty girls I never got to know in my high school class. Her blond hair was cinched in a ponytail that bobbed as she walked.

"Coffee's on," she said, taking the hug Nick offered as he came through the door.

We did this three, four times a week, Nick finishing up his morning meeting with his eight officers then stopping by Donut Dan's and coming out here for breakfast.

Strictly speaking, I was supposed to be eating food a little more nutritional than donuts but this morning I decided to indulge.

The conversation ran its usual course. Lisa and Nick joked with each other, Emmy reminded me about all the vitamins and pills I was supposed to take every morning, and I told them about how hard a time I was having finding a few good extra hands for harvest.

Lisa sounded subdued this morning, which caused Emmy to say, "You feeling all right, hon? You seem sort of quiet."

Lisa faked a grin. "Just all that hard work Grandad made me do. Wore me out."

Lisa was still thinking about the rifle shot. So was I. Several times my eyes strayed to Nick's holster and gun.

Just as we were all starting on our second cup of coffee, Lisa included, a car horn sounded at the far end of our driveway. The mail was here.

Wanting a little time to myself, I said I'd get the mail. Sometimes Lisa walked down to the mailbox with me but this morning she was still working on the second pink glazed donut. The rifle shot had apparently affected her appetite.

After the surgery and the recuperation, I decided to spend whatever time I had left—months maybe or years, the doctors just weren't very sure—living out my Chicago-boy fantasy of being a farmer. Hell hadn't my daughter become a farmer? I inhaled relatively pure fresh air and less than two miles away was a fast-running river where, with the right spoon and plug and sippner, you could catch trout all day long.

I tried to think of that now, as I walked down the rutted road to the mailbox. I was lucky. Few people ever have their fantasies come true. I lived with those I loved, I got to see things grow, and I had for my restive pleasure the sights of beautiful land. And there was a good chance that I was going to kick the cancer I'd been fighting the past two years.

So why did somebody want to go and spoil it for me by shooting at me?

As I neared the mailbox, I admitted to myself that the shot hadn't been accidental. Nor had it been meant to kill me. The shooter was good enough to put a bullet close to my head without doing me any damage. For whatever reason, he'd simply wanted to scare me.

The mailbox held all the usual goodies, circulars from True-Value, Younkers Department Store, Hy-Vee supermarkets, Drug-town and the Ford dealer where I'd bought my prize blue pickup.

The number ten white envelope, the one addressed to me, was the last thing I took from the mailbox.

I knew immediately that the envelope had something to do with the rifle shot this morning. Some kind of telepathic insight allowed me to understand this fact.

There was neither note nor letter inside, simply a photograph, a photo far more expressive than words could ever have been.

I looked away from it at first then slowly came back to it, the edge of it pincered between my thumb and forefinger.

I looked at it for a very long time. I felt hot, sweaty, though it was still early morning. I felt scared and ashamed and sick as I stared at it. So many years ago it had been; something done by a man with my name; but not the same man who bore that name today.

I tucked picture into envelope and went back to the house.

When I was back at the table, a cup of coffee in my hand, I noticed that Emmy was staring at me. "You all right, Dad?"

"I'm fine. Maybe just getting a touch of the flu or something."

While that would normally be a good excuse for looking gray and shaken, to the daughter of a cancer patient those are terrifying words. As if the patient himself doesn't worry about every little ache and pain. But to tell someone who loves you that you suddenly feel sick . . .

I reached across the table and said to Nick, "You mind if I hold hands with your girl?"

Nick smiled. "Not as long as you don't make a habit of it."

I took her hand for perhaps the millionth time in my life, holding in memory all the things this hand had been, child, girl, wife, mother.

"I'm fine, honey. Really."

All she wanted me to see was the love in those blue eyes. But I also saw the fear. I wanted to sit her on my lap as I once had, and rock her on my knees, and tell her that everything was going to be just fine.

"OK?" I said.

"OK," she half whispered.

Nick went back to telling Lisa why her school should have an especially good basketball team this year.

On the wall to the right of the kitchen table, Emmy had hung several framed advertisements from turn-of-the-century magazines, sweet little girls in bonnets and braids, and freckled boys with dogs even cuter than they were, all the faces and poses leading you to believe that theirs was a far more innocent era than ours. But the older I got, the more I realized that the human predicament had always been the same. It had just dressed up in different clothes.

There was one photograph up there. A grimy man in military

fatigues standing with a cigarette dangling from his lips and an M-16 leaning against him. Trying to look tough when all he was was scared. The man was me.

"Well," Nick said about ten minutes later.

Emmy and Lisa giggled.

No matter how many times they kidded Nick about saying "Well" each time he was about to announce his imminent departure, he kept right on saying it.

Emmy walked him out to the car.

I filled the sink with hot soapy water. Lisa piled the breakfast dishes in.

"Grandad?"

"Yes, hon?"

"You sure you don't want to tell Mom about the gunshot?"

"No, hon, I don't. I know it's tempting but she's got enough to worry about." Emmy had had a long and miserable first marriage to a man who had treated adultery like the national pastime. Now, on the small amount of money she got from the farm and from me paying room and board, Emmy had to raise a daughter. She didn't need any more anxiety.

"I'm going into town," I said, as I started to wash the dishes and hand them one by one to Lisa, who was drying.

"How come?"

"Oh, a little business."

"What kind of business?"

"I just want to check out the downtown area."

"For what?"

I laughed. "I'll fill out a written report when I get back."

"I'll go with you."

"Oh, no, hon. This is something I have to do alone."

"Detectives usually have partners."

"I think that's just on TV."

"Huh-uh. In *Weekly Reader* last year there was this article on Chicago police and it said that they usually worked in teams. Team means two. You and me, Grandad."

I guessed I really wasn't going to do much more than nose around. Probably wouldn't hurt for her to ride along.

By the time Emmy got back to the kitchen, looking every bit as happy as I wanted her to be, Lisa and I had finished the dishes and were ready for town.

"When will you be back?"

"Oh, hour or two."

Emmy was suspicious. "Is there something you're not telling me?"

"Nothing, sweetheart," I said, leaning over and kissing her on the cheek. "Honest."

We went out and got in the truck, passing the old cedar chest Lisa had converted into a giant toolbox and placed in the back of the pickup. She had fastened it with strong twine so it wouldn't shift around. It looked kind of funny sitting there like that but Lisa had worked hard at it so I wasn't about to take it out.

Twenty years ago there was hope that the interstate being discussed would run just east of our little town. Unfortunately, it ran north, and twenty miles away. Today the downtown is four two-block streets consisting of dusty redbrick buildings all built before 1930. The post office and the two supermarkets and the five taverns are the busiest places.

I started at the post office, asking for Ev Meader, the man who runs it.

"Gettin' ready for school, Lisa?" Ev said when we came into his office.

She made a face. Ev laughed. "So what can I do for ya today?"

"Wondering if you heard of anybody new moving in around here?" I said. "You know, filling out a new address card."

He scratched his bald head. "Not in the past couple weeks. Least I don't think so. But let me check." He left the office.

I looked down at Lisa. "You going to ask me?"

"Ask you what, Grandad?"

"Ask me how come I'm asking Ev about new people moving into town."

She grinned. "Figured I'd wait till we got back in the truck."

"No new address cards," Ev said when he came back. "I'll keep an eye out for you if you want."

"I'd appreciate it."

In the truck, Lisa said, "Is it all right if I ask you now?"

"I'm wondering if that shot this morning didn't coincide with somebody moving here. Somebody who came here just so they could deal with me."

"You mean, like somebody's after you or something like that?"

"Uh-huh."

"But who'd be after you?"

"I don't know."

The man at the first hotel had a pot belly and merry red suspenders. "Asian, you say?"

"Right."

"Nope. No Asians that I signed in, anyway."

"How about at night?"

"I can check the book."

"I'd appreciate it."

"Two weeks back be all right?"

"That'd been fine."

But two weeks back revealed no Asians. "Sorry," he said, hooking his thumbs in his suspenders.

"How come Asians?" Lisa said after we were back in the truck.

"Just because of something that happened to me once."

We rode in silence for a time.

"Grandad?"

"Yeah."

"You going to tell me? About what happened to you once?"

"Not right now, hon."

"How come?"

"Too hard for me to talk about." And it was. Every time I thought about it for longer than a minute, I could feel my eyes tear up.

The woman at the second motel wore a black T-shirt with a yellow hawk on it. Beneath it said, "I'll do anything for the Hawkeyes." Anything was underlined. The Hawkeyes were the U of Iowa.

"Couple black guys, some kind of salesmen I guess, but no Asians," she said.

"How about at night?"

She laughed. "Bob works at night. He doesn't much like people who aren't white. We had an Asian guy, I'd hear about it, believe me."

The man at the third motel, a hearty man with a farmer's tan and a cheap pair of false teeth said, "No Asian."

"Maybe he came at night?"

"The boy, he works the night shift. Those robberies we had a few months back—that convenience store where that girl got shot?—ever since, he keeps a sharp eye out. Usually tells me all about the guests. He didn't mention any Asian."

"Thanks."

"Sure."

"I'll be happy to ask around," he said.

"Cochran, right?"

"Henry Cochran. Right."

"Thanks for your help, Henry."

"You bet."

"You going to tell me yet?" Lisa said when we were in the pickup and headed back to the farm.

"Not yet."

"Am I bugging you, Grandad?"

I smiled at her. "Maybe a little."

"Then I won't ask you anymore."

She leaned over and gave me a kiss on the cheek, after which she settled back on her side of the seat.

"You know what I forgot to do today?" she said after awhile.

"What?"

"Tell you I loved you."

"Well, I guess you'd better hurry up and do it then."

"I love you, Grandad."

The funny thing was, I'd never been able to cry much till the cancer, which was a few years ago when I turned fifty-two. Not even when my two best soldier friends got killed in Nam did I cry. Not even when my wife left me did I cry. But these days all sorts of things made me cry. And not just about sad things, either. Seeing a horse run free could make me cry; and certain old songs; and my granddaughter's face when she was telling me she loved me.

"I love you, too, Lisa," I said, and gave her hand a squeeze.

That afternoon Lisa and I spent three hours raking corn in a wagon next to the silo, stopping only when the milk truck came. As usual Ken, the driver, took a sample out of the cooling vat where the milk had been stored. He wanted to get a reading on the butter-fat content of the milk. When the truck was just rolling brown dust on the distant road, Lisa and I went back to raking the corn. At five we knocked off. Lisa rode her bike down the road to the creek where she was trying to catch a milk snake for her science class this fall.

I was in scrubbing up for dinner when Emmy called me to the phone. "There's a woman on the line for you. Dad. She's got some kind of accent."

"I'll take it in the TV room," I said.

"This is Mr. Wilson?"

"Yes."

"Mr. Wilson, my name is Nguyn Mai. I am from Vietnam here visiting."

"I see."

"I would like to meet you tonight. I am staying in Iowa City but I would meet you at The Fireplace restaurant. You know where is?"

"Yes, The Fireplace is downtown here."

"Yes. Would seven o'clock be reasonable for you?"

"I have to say eight. There's a meeting I need to go to first."

"I would appreciate it, Mr. Wilson."

She sounded intelligent and probably middle-aged. I got no sense of her mood.

"Eight o'clock," I said.

After dinner, I took a shower and climbed into a newly washed pair of chinos and a white button-down shirt and a blue wind-breaker.

In town, I parked in the Elks lot. Across the cinder alley was the meeting room we used for our support group.

The hour went quickly. There was a new woman there tonight, shy and fresh with fear after her recent operation for breast cancer. At one point, telling us how she was sometimes scared to sleep, she started crying. She was sitting next to me so I put my arm around her and held her till she felt all right again. That was another thing I'd never been too good at till the cancer, showing tenderness.

There were seven of us tonight. We described our respective weeks since the last meeting, exchanged a few low-fat recipes and listened to one of the men discuss some of the problems he was having with his chemotherapy treatments. We finished off with a prayer and then everybody else headed for the coffee pot and the low-fat kolaches one of the women had baked especially for this meeting.

At eight I walked through the door of The Fireplace and got my first look at Nguyn Mai. She was small and fiftyish and pretty in the way of her people. She wore an American dress, dark and simple, a white sweater draped over her shoulders. Her eyes were friendly and sad.

After I ordered my coffee, she said, "I'm sorry I must trouble you, Mr. Wilson."

"Robert is what most people call me."

"Robert, then." She paused, looked down, looked up again. "My brother Ngyun Dang plans to kill you."

I told her about the rifle shot this morning, and the envelope later.

"He was never the same," she said, "after it happened. I am his oldest sister. There was one sister younger, Hong. This is the one who died. She was six years old. Dang, who was twelve at the time, took care of the funeral all by himself, would not even let my parents see her until after he had put her in her casket. Dang always believed in the old religious ways. He buried Hong in our backyard, according to ancient custom. The old ways teach that the head of a virgin girl is very valuable and can be used as a very powerful talisman to bring luck to the family members. Dang was certainly lucky. When he was fourteen, he left our home and went to Saigon. Within ten years, he was a millionaire. He deals in imports. He spent his fortune tracking you down. It was not easy."

"Were you there that day?"

"Yes."

"Did you see what happened?"

She nodded.

"I didn't kill her intentionally. If you saw what happened, you know that's the truth."

"The truth is in the mind's eye, Robert. In my eye, I know you were frightened by a Cong soldier at the other end of our backyard. You turned and fired and accidentally shot Hong. But this is not what my brother saw."

"He saw me kill her in cold blood?"

"Yes."

"But why would I shoot a little girl?"

"It was done, you know, by both sides. Maybe not by you but by others."

"And so now he's here."

"To kill you."

During my second cup of coffee, she said, "I am afraid for him. I do not wish to see you killed but even more I do not wish to see my brother killed. I know that is selfish but those are my feelings."

"I'd have the same feelings." I paused and said, "Do you know where he is?"

"No."

"I looked for him today, after the envelope came."

"And you didn't find him?"

I shook my head. "For what it's worth, Mai, I never forgot what happened that day."

"No?"

"When I got back to the states, I started having nightmares about it. And very bad migraine headaches. I even went to a psychologist for a year or so. Everybody said I shouldn't feel guilty, that those accidents happen in war. Got so bad, it started to take its toll on my marriage. I wasn't much of a husband—or a father, for that matter—and eventually my wife left me. I'd look round at the other guys I'd served with. They'd done ugly things, too, but if it bothered them, they didn't let on. I was even going to go back to Nam and look up your family and tell them I was sorry but my daughter wouldn't let me. At that point, she was ready to put me in a mental hospital. She said that if I seriously tried to go, she'd put me away for sure. I knew she meant it."

"Did you talk to the police today, about his taking a shot at you?"

"You've got to understand something here, Mai. I don't want your brother arrested. I want to find him and talk to him and help him if I can. There hasn't been a day in my life since when I haven't wanted to pick up the phone and talk to your family and tell them how sorry I am."

"If only we could find Dang."

"I'll start looking again tomorrow."

"I feel hopeful for the first time in many years."

I stayed up past midnight because I knew I wouldn't sleep well. There was a Charles Bronson movie on TV, in the course of which he killed four or five people. Before that day in Nam, when I'd been so scared that I'd mistaken a little girl for a VC, I had been all enamored of violence. But no longer. After the war, I gave away all my guns and nearly all my pretensions to machismo. I knew too well where machismo sometimes led.

Ten hours later, coming in from morning chores, I heard the phone ringing. Emmy said it was for me.

It was the motel man with the merry red suspenders. "I heard something you might be interested in."

"Oh?"

"You know where the old Sheldon farm is?"

"I don't think so."

"Well there's a lime quarry due west of the power station. You know where that would be?"

"I can find it."

"There's a house trailer somewhere back in there. Hippie couple lived there for years but they moved to New Mexico last year. Guy in town who owns a tavern—Shelby, maybe you know him— he bought their trailer from them and rents it out sort of like an apartment. Or thought he would, anyway. Hasn't had much luck. Till last week. That's when this Asian guy rented it from him."

The day was ridiculously beautiful, the sweet smoky breath of autumn on the air, the horses in the hills shining the color of saddle leather.

The lime quarry had been closed for years. Some of the equipment had been left behind. Everything was rusted now. The whining wind gave the place the sound of desolation.

I pointed the pickup into the hills where oak and hickory and basswood bloomed, and elm and ash and ironwood leaves caught the bright bouncing beams of the sun.

The trailer was in a grassy valley, buffalo grass knee-deep and waving in the wind, a silver S of creek winding behind the rusted old Airstream.

I pulled off the road in the dusty hills and walked the rest of the way down.

There was a lightning-dead elm thirty yards from the trailer. When I reached it, I got behind it so I could get a better look at the Airstream.

No noise came from the open windows, no smoke from the tin chimney.

I went up to the trailer. Every few feet I expected to hear a bullet cracking from a rifle.

The window screens were badly torn, the three steps tilted rightward, and the two propane tanks to the right of the door leaned forward as if they might fall at any moment.

I reached the steps, tried the door. Locked. Dang was gone. Picking the lock encased in the doorknob was no great trouble.

The interior was a mess. Apparently Dang existed on Godfather's pizza. I counted nine different cartons, all grease-stained, on the kitchen counter. The thrumming little refrigerator smelled vaguely unclean. It contained three sixteen-ounce bottles of Pepsi.

In the back, next to the bed on the wobbly nightstand, I found the framed photos of the little girl. She had been quite pretty, solemn and mischievous at the same time.

The photo Dang had sent me was very different. The girl lay on a table, her bloody clothes wrapped round her. Her chest was a dark and massive hole.

I thought I heard a car coming.

Soon enough I was behind the elm again. But the road was empty. All I'd heard was my own nerves.

During chores two hours later, Lisa said, "You find him?"

"Find who?"

"Find who? Come on, Grandad."

"Yeah, I found him. Or found his trailer, anyway."

"How come you didn't take me with you? I'm supposed to be your partner."

I leaned on my pitchfork. "Hon, from here on out I'll have to handle this alone."

"Oh, darn it, Grandad. I want to help."

There was a sweet afternoon breeze through the barn door, carrying the scents of clover and sunshine.

"All that's going to happen is I'm going to talk to him."

"Gosh, Grandad, he tried to kill you."

"I don't think so."

"But he shot at you."

"He tried to scare me."

"You sure?"

"Pretty sure."

After washing up for the day, I went into the TV room and called Mai and told her that I'd found where her brother was staying.

"You should not go out there," she said. "In my land we say that there are seasons of the heart. The season of my brother's heart is very hot and angry now."

"I just want to talk to him and tell him that I'm sorry. Maybe that will calm him down."

"I will talk to him. You can direct me to this trailer?"

"If you meet me at the restaurant again, I'll lead you out there."

"Then you will go back home?"

"If that's what you want."

She was there right at eight. The full moon, an autumn moon that painted all the pines silver, guided us to the power station and the quarry and finally to the hill above the trailer.

I got out of the car and walked back to hers. "You follow that road straight down."

"Did you see the windows? The lights?"

He was home. Or somebody was.

"I appreciate this, Robert. Perhaps I can reason with my brother."

"I hope so."

She paused, looked around. "It is so beautiful and peaceful here. You are fortunate to live here."

There were owls and jays in the forest trees, and the fast creek silver in the moonlight, and the distant song of a windmill in the breeze. She was right. I was lucky to live here.

She drove on.

I watched her till she reached the trailer, got out, went to the door and knocked.

Even from here, I could see that the man-silhouette held a handgun when he opened the door for her. Mai and I had both assumed we could reason with her brother. Maybe not.

"You up for a game of hearts?" Lisa said awhile later.

"Sure," I said.

"Good. Because I'm going to beat you tonight."

"You sure of that?"

"Uh-huh."

As usual I won. I thought of letting her win but then realized that she wouldn't want that. She was too smart and too honorable for that kind of charity.

When she was in her cotton nightie, her mouth cold and spicy from brushing her teeth, she came down and gave me my good-night kiss.

When Lisa was creaking her way up the stairs, Emmy looked into the TV room and said, "Wondered if I could ask you a question?"

"Sure."

"Are you, uh, all right?"

"Aw, honey. My last tests were fine and I feel great. You've really got to stop worrying."

"I don't mean physically. I mean, you seem preoccupied."

"Everything's fine."

"God, Dad, I love you so much. And I can't help worrying about you."

The full-grown woman in the doorway became my quick little daughter again, rushing to me and sitting on my lap and burying her tear-hot face in my neck so I couldn't see her cry.

We sat that way for a long time and then I started bouncing her on my knee.

She laughed. "I weigh a little more than I used to."

"Not much."

"My bottom's starting to spread a little."

"Nick seems to like it fine."

With her arms still around me, she kissed me on the cheek and then gave me another hug. A few minutes later, she left to finish up in the kitchen.

The call came ten minutes after I fell into a fitful sleep. I'd been expecting Mai. I got Nick.

"Robert, I wondered if you could come down to the station."

"Now? After midnight?"

"I'm afraid so."

"What's up?"

"A Vietnamese woman came into the emergency room over at the hospital tonight. Her arm had been broken. The doc got suspicious and gave me a call. I went over and talked to her. She wouldn't tell me anything at all. Then all of a sudden, she asked if she could see a man named Robert Wilson. You know her, Robert?"

"Yes."

"Who is she?"

"Her name is Nguyn Mai. She's visiting people in the area."

"Which people?"

I hesitated. "Nick, I can't tell you anything more than Mai has."

For the first time in our relationship, Nick sounded cold. "I need you to come down here, Robert. Right away."

Our small town is fortunate enough to have a full-time hospital that doubles as an emergency room.

Mai sat at the end of the long hallway, her arm in a white sling. I sat next to her in a yellow form-curved plastic chair.

"What happened?"

"I was foolish," she said. "We argued and I tried to take one of his guns from him. We struggled and I fell into the wall and I heard my arm snap."

"I don't think Nick believes you."

"He says he knows you."

"He goes out with my daughter."

"Is he a prejudiced man, this Nick?"

"I don't think so. He's just a cop who senses that he's not getting the whole story. Plus you made him very curious when you asked him to call me."

"I knew no one else."

"I understand, Mai. I'm just trying to explain Nick's attitude."

Nick showed up a few minutes later.

"How's the arm? Ready for tennis yet?"

Mai obviously appreciated the way Nick was trying to lighten things up. "Not yet," she said, and smiled like a small shy girl.

"Mind if I borrow your friend a few minutes, Mai?"

She smiled again and shook her head. But there was apprehension in her dark eyes. Would I tell Nick that her brother had taken a shot at me?

In the staff coffee room, I put a lot of sugar and Creamora into my paper cup of coffee. I badly needed to kill the taste.

"You know her in Nam, Robert?"

"No."

"She just showed up?"

"Pretty much."

"Any special reason?"

"Not that I know of."

"Robert, I don't appreciate lies. Especially from my future father-in-law."

"She phoned me last night and we talked. Turns out we knew some of the same people in Nam. That's about all there is to it."

"Right."

"Nick, I can handle this. It doesn't have to involve the law."

"She got her arm broken."

"It was an accident."

"That's what she says."

"She's telling the truth, Nick."

"The same way you're telling the truth, Robert?"

In the hall, Nick said, "She seems like a nice woman."

"She is a nice woman."

When we reached Mai, Nick said, "Robert here tells me you're a nice woman. I'm sorry if my questions upset you."

Mai gave a little half bow of appreciation and good-bye.

In the truck, I turned the heat on. It was 2:00 A.M. of a late August night and it was shivering late October cold.

"Where's your car?"

"The other side of the building," Mai said.

"You'd better not drive back to Iowa City tonight."

"There is a motel?"

After I got her checked in, I pulled the pickup right to her door, Number 17.

Inside, I got the lights on and turned the thermostat up to 80 so it would warm up fast. The room was small and dark. You could hear the ghosts of it crying down the years, a chorus of smiling salesmen and weary vacationers and frantic adulterers.

"I wish I had had better luck with my brother tonight," Mai said. "For everybody's sake."

"Maybe he'll think about it tonight and be more reasonable in the morning."

In the glove compartment I found the old .38 Emmy bought when she moved to the farm. Bucolic as rural Iowa was, it was not without its moments of violence, particularly when drug deals were involved. She kept it in the kitchen cabinet, on the top shelf. I had taken it with me when I left tonight.

In the valley, the trailer was a silhouette outlined in moonsilver. I approached in a crouch, the .38 in my right hand. A white-tailed fawn pranced away to my left; and a raccoon or possum rattled reeds in a long waving patch of bluestem grass.

When I reached the elm, I stopped and listened. No sound whatsoever from the Airstream. The propane tanks stood like sentries.

The doorknob was no more difficult to unlock tonight than it had been earlier.

Tonight the trailer smelled of sleep and wine and rust and ciga-

rette smoke. I stood perfectly still listening to the refrigerator vi-
brate. From the rear of the trailer came the sounds of Dang snor-
ing.

When I stood directly above him, I raised the .38 and pushed it
to within two inches of his forehead.

I spoke his name in the stillness.

His eyes opened but at first they seemed to see nothing. He
seemed to be in a half-waking state.

But then he grunted and something like a sob exploded in his
throat and I said, "If I wanted to, I could kill you right now but I
don't want to. I want you to listen to me."

In the chill prairie night, the coffee Dang put on smelled very good.
We sat at a small table, each drinking from a different 7-Eleven
mug.

He was probably ten years younger than me, slender, with graying hair and a long, intelligent face. He wore good American
clothes and good American glasses. Whenever he looked at me directly, his eyes narrowed with anger. He was likely flashing back to
the frail bloody dead girl in the photo he'd sent me.

"My sister told you why I came here?"

"Yes."

"You came to talk me out of it, that is why you're here?"

"Something like that. The first thing is, I want to tell you how
sorry I am that it happened."

"Words."

"Pardon?"

"Words. In my land there is a saying, 'words only delay the inevitable.' If you do not kill me, Mr. Wilson, I will kill you. No matter
how many words you speak."

"It was an accident."

"I am a believer in Hoa Hao, Mr. Wilson. We do not believe in
accidents. All behavior is willful."

"I willfully murdered a six-year-old girl?"

"In war, there are many atrocities."

Anger came and went in his eyes. When it was gone, he looked
old and sad. Rage seemed to give him a kind of fevered youth.

"You were there, Dang. You saw it happen. I wasn't firing at her. I was firing at a VC. She got in the way."

He stared at me a long time. "Words, Mr. Wilson, words."

I wanted to tell him about my years following the killing, how it shaped and in many respects destroyed my life. I even thought of telling him about my cancer and how the disease had taught me so many important lessons. But I would only sound as if I were begging his pity.

I stood up. "Why don't you leave tomorrow? Your sister is worried about you."

"I'll leave after I've killed you."

"What I did, Dang, I know you can't forgive me for. Maybe I'd be the same way you are. But if you kill me, the police will arrest you. And that will kill Mai. You'll have killed her just as I killed your other sister."

For a time, he kept his head down and said nothing. When he raised his eyes to me, I saw that they were wet with tears. "Before I sleep each night, I play in my head her voice, like a tape. Even at six she had a beautiful voice. I play it over and over again."

He surprised me by putting his head down on the table and weeping.

In bed that night, I thought of how long we'd carried our respective burdens, Dang his hatred of me, and my remorse over Hong's death. I fell asleep thinking of what Dang had said about Hong's voice. I wished I could have heard her sing.

When I got down to the barn in the morning, Lisa was already bottle-feeding the three new calves. I set about the milking operations.

Half an hour later, the calves, the rabbits and the barn cats taken care of, Lisa joined me.

"Mom was worried about you."

"Figured she would be," I said. "You didn't tell her anything, did you?"

"No, but Nick did."

"Nick?"

"Uh-huh. He told her about the Vietnamese woman."

"Oh."

"So Mom asked me if I knew anything about it."

"What'd you say?"

"Said I didn't know anything at all. But I felt kinda weird, Grandad, lying to Mom, I mean."

"I'm sorry, sweetheart."

At lunch, baloney sandwiches and creamed corn and an apple, Emmy said, "Dad, could I talk to you?"

"Sure."

"Lisa, why don't you go on ahead with your chores. Grandad'll be down real soon."

Lisa looked at me. I nodded.

When the screendoor slapped shut, Emmy said, "Nick thinks you're in some kind of trouble, Dad."

"You know how much I like Nick, honey. I also happen to respect him." I held her hand. "But I'm not in any kind of trouble."

"Who's the Vietnamese woman?"

"Nguyn Mai."

"That doesn't tell me much."

"I don't mean for it to tell you much."

"You getting mad?"

"No. Sad, if anything. Sad that I can't have a life of my own without answering a lot of questions."

"Dad, if Nick wasn't concerned, I wouldn't be concerned. But Nick has good instincts about things like this."

"He does indeed."

"So why not tell us the truth?"

I got up from the table, picked up my dishes and carried them over to the sink. "Let me think about it a little while, all right?"

She watched me for a long time, looking both wan and a little bit peeved, and finally said, "Think about it a little while, then."

She got up and left the room.

There were two carts that needed filling with silage. Lisa and I opened the trapdoor in the silo and started digging the silage out. Then we took the first of the carts over and started feeding the cows.

When that was done, I told Lisa to take the rest of the afternoon off. She kept talking about all the school supplies she needed. She'd never find time for them if she was always working.

During the last rain, we'd noticed a few drops plopping down from the area of the living room. The roof was a good ten years old. I put the ladder against the back of the house and went up and looked around. There were some real bad spots.

I called the lumber store and got some prices on roofing materials. I told them what I wanted. They'd have them ready tomorrow afternoon.

There was still some work so after a cup of coffee, I headed for the barn. I hadn't quite reached it before the phone rang.

"For you, Dad," Emmy called.

I picked up.

"Robert?"

"I thought maybe you'd be gone by now, Mai. I went out and visited your brother last night. I don't know if he told you about it. I also don't know if it did any good. But at least I got to tell him I was sorry."

"I need to meet you at the hill above his trailer. Right away, please. Something terrible has happened."

"What're you talking about, Mai?"

"Please. The hill. As soon as possible."

"Can you drive?"

"Yes. I drove a little this morning."

"What's happened, Mai?"

"Your granddaughter. Dang has taken her."

As I was grabbing my jacket, and remembering that I'd left the .38 in the glove compartment, Emmy came into the room.

"I need to go out for a little while."

She touched my arm. "Dad, I don't know what just happened but why don't you get Nick to help you?"

I'd thought about that, too. "Maybe I will."

I drove straight and hard to the hill. All the way there I thought of Dang. One granddaughter for one little sister. Even up. I should have thought of that and protected Lisa.

Mai stood by the dusty rental car.

"How do you know she's down there?"

"An hour ago, I snuck down there and peeked in the window. She is sitting in a chair in the kitchen."

"But she's still alive? You're sure?"

"Yes."

"Did you see if she's bleeding or anything?"

"I don't think he has hurt her. Not yet, anyway."

"I'm going in to get her."

She nodded to the .38 stuffed into my belt. "I am afraid for all of us, now. For Dang and for your granddaughter and for you. And for me."

She fell against me, crying. I was tender as I could be but all I could think of was Lisa.

"I tried to talk him into giving her up. He says that he is only doing the honorable thing." More tears. "Talking won't help, Robert."

I went east, in a wide arc, coming down behind the trailer in a stand of windbreak firs. The back side of the Airstream had only one window. I didn't see anybody watching me.

I bellycrawled from the trees to the front of the trailer. By now, I could hear him shouting in Vietnamese at Lisa. All his anger and all his pain was in those words. The exact meaning made no difference. It was the sounds he made that mattered.

I went to the door and knocked. His words stopped immediately. For a time there was just the soughing silence of the prairie.

"Dang, you let Lisa go and I'll come in and take her place."

"Don't come in, Grandad. He wants to kill you."

"Dang, did you hear me? You let Lisa go and I'll come in. I have a gun now but I'll drop it if you agree."

His first bullet ripped through the glass and screening of the front door.

I pitched left, rolling on the ground to escape the second and third shots.

Lisa yelled at Dang to stop firing, her words echoing inside the trailer.

Prairie silence again; a hawk gliding down the sunbeams.

I scanned the trailer, looking for some way to get closer without getting shot. There wasn't enough room to hide next to the three stairs; nor behind the two silver propane tanks; nor even around the corner. The bedroom window was too high to peek in comfortably.

"He's picking up his rifle, Grandad!" Lisa called.

Two more shots, these more explosive and taking larger chunks of the front door, burst into the afternoon air. I rolled away from them as best I could.

"Grandad, watch out!"

And then a cry came, one so shrill and aggrieved I wasn't sure what it was at first, and then the front door was thrown open and there was Dang, rifle fire coming in bursts as he came out on the front steps, shooting directly at me.

This time I rolled to the right. He was still sobbing out words in Vietnamese and these had the power to mesmerize me. They spoke exactly of how deep his grief ran.

Another burst of rifle fire, Dang standing on the steps of the trailer and having an easy time finding me with his rifle.

There was a long and curious delay before my brain realized that my chest had been wounded. It was as if all time stopped for a long moment, the universe holding its breath; and then came blood and raging blinding pain. Then I felt a bone in my arm crack as a bullet smashed into it.

Lisa screamed again. "Grandad!"

As I lay there, another bullet taking my left leg, I realized I had only moments to do what I needed to. Dang was coming down from the steps, moving in to kill me. I raised the .38 and fired.

The explosion was instant and could probably be heard for miles. I'd been forced to shoot at him at an angle. The bullet had missed and torn into one of the propane tanks. The entire trailer had vanished inside tumbling gritty black smoke and fire at least three different shades of red and yellow. The air reeked of propane and the burning trailer.

I called out for Lisa but I knew I could never get to my feet to help her. I was losing consciousness too fast.

And then Dang was standing over me, rifle pointed directly down at my head.

I knew I didn't have long. "Save her, Dang. She's innocent just the way your sister was. Save her, please. I'm begging you."

The darkness was swift and cold and black, and the sounds of Lisa screaming and fire roaring faded, faded.

The room was small and white and held but one bed and it was mine.

Lisa and Emmy and Nick stood on the left side of the bed while Mai stood on the right.

"I guess I'll have to do some of your chores for a while, Grandad."

"I guess you will, hon."

"That means driving the tractor."

I looked at Emmy, who said, "We'll hire a couple of hands, sweetheart. No tractor for you until Grandad gets back."

Nick looked at his watch. "How about if I take these two beautiful ladies downstairs for some lunch? This is one of the few hospitals that actually serves good food."

But it wasn't just lunch he was suggesting. He wanted to give Mai a chance to speak with me alone.

Lisa and Emmy kissed me then went downstairs with Nick.

I was already developing stiffness from being in bed so long. After being operated on, I'd slept through the night and into this morning.

Mai leaned over and took my hand. "I'm glad you're all right, Mr. Wilson."

"I'm sorry, Mai. How things turned out."

"In the end, he was honorable man."

"He certainly was, Mai. He certainly was."

After I'd passed out, Dang had rushed back into the trailer and rescued Lisa, who had been remarkably unscathed.

Then Dang had run back inside, knowing he would die in the smoke and the flames.

"Tomorrow would have been our little sister's birthday," Mai said, "I do not think he wanted to face that."

She cried for a long time cradled in my good left arm, my right being in a sling like hers.

"He was not a bad man."

"No, he wasn't, Mai. He was a good man."

"I am sorry for your grief."

"And I'm sorry for yours."

She smiled tearily. "Seasons of the heart, Mr. Wilson. Perhaps the season will change now."

"Perhaps they will," I said, and watched her as she leaned over to kiss me on the forehead.

As she was leaving, I pointed to my arm sling and then to hers. "Twins," I said.

"Yes," she said. "Perhaps we are, Robert."

EN FAMILLE

By the time I was eight years old, I'd fallen disconsolately in love with any number of little girls who had absolutely no interest in me. These were little girls I'd met in all the usual places, school, playground, neighborhood.

Only the girl I met at the racetrack took any interest in me. Her name was Wendy and, like me, she was brought to the track three or four times a week by her father, after school in the autumn months, during working hours in the summer.

Ours was one of those impossibly romantic relationships that only a young boy can have (all those nights of kissing pillows while pretending it was her—this accompanied by one of those swelling romantic songs you hear in movies with Ingrid Bergman and Cary Grant—how vulnerable and true and beautiful she always was in my mind's perfect eye). I first saw her the spring of my tenth year, and not until I was fifteen did we even say hello to each other, even though we saw each other at least three times a week. But she was always with me, this girl I thought about constantly, and dreamed of nightly, the melancholy little blonde with the slow sad blue eyes and the quick sad smile.

I knew all about the sadness I saw in her. It was my sadness, too. Our fathers brought us to the track in order to make their gambling more palatable to our mothers. How much of a vice could it be if you took the little one along? The money lost at the track meant rent going unpaid, grocery store credit cut off, the telephone frequently disconnected. It also meant arguing. No matter how deeply I hid in the closet, no matter how many pillows I put over my head, I could still hear them shrieking at each other. Sometimes he hit her. Once he even pushed her down the stairs and she broke her leg. Despite all this, I wanted them to stay together. I was terrified they would split up. I loved them both beyond imagining. Don't ask me why I loved him so much. I have no idea.

The day we first spoke, the little girl and I, that warm May afternoon in my fifteenth year, a black eye spoiled her very pretty, very pale little face. So he'd finally gotten around to hitting her. My father had gotten around to hitting me years ago. They got so frustrated over their gambling, their inability to *stop* their gambling, that they grabbed the first person they found and visited all their despair on him.

She was coming up from the seats in the bottom tier where she and her father always sat. I saw her and stepped out into the aisle.

"Hi," I said after more than six years of us watching each other from afar.

"Hi."

"I'm sorry about your eye."

"He was pretty drunk. He doesn't usually get violent. But it seems to be getting worse lately." She looked back at her seats. Her father was glaring at us. "I'd better hurry. He wants me to get him a hot dog."

"I'd like to see you sometime."

She smiled, sad and sweet with her black eye. "Yeah, me, too."

I saw her the rest of the summer but we never again got the chance to speak. Nor did we make the opportunity. She was my narcotic. I thought of no one else, wanted no one else. The girls at school had no idea what my home life was like, how old and worn my father's gambling had made my mother, how anxious and angry it had made me. Only Wendy understood.

Wendy Wendy Wendy. By now, my needs having evolved, she was no longer just the pure dream of a forlorn boy. I wanted her carnally, too. She'd become a beautiful young woman.

Near the end of that summer an unseasonable rainy grayness filled the skies. People at the track took to wearing winter coats. A few races had to be called off. Wendy and her father suddenly vanished.

I looked for them every day, and every night trudged home feeling betrayed and bereft. "Can't find your little girlfriend?" my father said. He thought it was funny.

Then one night, while I was in my bedroom reading a science fiction magazine, he shouted: "Hey! Get out here! Your girlfriend's on TV!"

And so she was.

"Police announce an arrest in the murder of Myles Larkin, who was found stabbed to death in his car last night. They have taken Larkin's only child, sixteen-year-old Wendy, into custody and formally charged her with the murder of her father."

I went twice to see her but they wouldn't let me in. Finally, I learned the name of her lawyer, lied that I was a shirttail cousin, and he took me up to the cold concrete visitors' room on the top floor of city jail.

Even in the drab uniform the prisoners wore, she looked lovely in her bruised and wan way.

"Did he start beating you up again?" I asked.

"No."

"Did he start beating up your mother?"

"No."

"Did he lose his job or get you evicted?"

She shook her head. "No. It was just that I couldn't take it anymore. I mean, he wasn't losing any more or any less money at the track, it was just I—I snapped. I don't know how else to explain it. It was like I saw what he'd done to our lives and I—I snapped. That's all—I just snapped."

She served seven years in a minimum-security women's prison upstate during which time my parents were killed in an automobile accident, I finished college, got married, had a child and took up the glamorous and adventurous life of a tax consultant. My wife, Donna, knew about my mental and spiritual ups and downs. Her father had been an abusive alcoholic.

I didn't see Wendy until twelve years later, when I was sitting at the track with my seven-year-old son. He didn't always like going to the track with me—my wife didn't like me going to the track at all—so I'd had to fortify him with the usual comic books, candy and a pair of "genuine" Dodgers sunglasses.

Between races, I happened to look down at the seats Wendy and her father usually took, and there she was. Something about the cock of her head told me it was her.

"Can we go, Dad?" my son, Rob, said. "It's so boring here."

Boring? I'd once tried to explain to his mother how good I felt when I was at the track. I was not the miserable, frightened, self-effacing owner of Advent Tax Systems (some system—me and my low-power Radio Shack computer and software). No . . . when I was at the track I felt strong and purposeful and optimistic, and frightened of nothing at all. I was pure potential—potential for winning the easy cash that was the mark of men who were successful with women, and with their competitors, and with their own swaggering dreams.

"Please, Dad. It's really boring here. Honest."

But all I could see, all I could think about, was Wendy. I hadn't seen her since my one visit to jail. Then I noticed that she, too, had a child with her, a very proper-looking little blond girl whose head was cocked at the odd and fetching angle so favored by her mother.

We saw each other a dozen more times before we spoke.

Then: "I knew I'd see you again someday."

Wan smile. "All those years I was in prison, I wasn't so sure." Her daughter came up to her then and Wendy said: "This is Margaret."

"Hello, Margaret. Glad to meet you. This is my son, Rob."

With the great indifference only children can summon, they nodded hellos.

"We just moved back to the city," Wendy explained. "I thought

I'd show Margaret where I used to come with my father." She mentioned her father so casually, one would never have guessed that
she'd murdered the man.

Ten more times we saw each other, children in tow, before our
affair began.

April 6 of that year was the first time we ever made love, this in
a motel where the sunset was the color of blood in the window, and
a woman two rooms away wept inconsolably. I had the brief fantasy
that it was my wife in that room.

"Do you know how long I've loved you?" she said.

"Oh, God, you don't know how good it is to hear that."

"Since I was eight years old."

"For me, since I was nine."

"This would destroy my husband if he ever found out."

"The same with my wife."

"But I have to be honest."

"I want you to be honest."

"I don't care what it does to him. I just want to be with you."

In December of that year, my wife, Donna, discovered a lump
in her right breast. Two weeks later she received a double masec-
tomy and began chemotherapy.

She lived nine years, and my affair with Wendy extended over
the entire time. Early on, both our spouses knew about our relationship. Her husband, an older and primmer man than I might
have expected, stopped by my office one day in his new BMW and
threatened to destroy my business. He claimed to have great influence in the financial community.

My wife threatened to leave me but she was too weak. She had
one of those cancers that did not kill her but that never left her
alone, either. She was weak most of the time, staying for days in the
bedroom that had become hers, as the guest room had become
mine. Whenever she became particularly angry about Wendy, Rob
would fling himself at me, screaming how much he hated me,
pounding me with fists that became more powerful with each passing year. He hated me for many of the same reasons I'd hated my
own father, my ineluctable passion for the track, and the way there
was never any security in our lives, the family bank account wholly

subject to the whims of the horses that ran that day.

Wendy's daughter likewise blamed her mother for the alcoholism that had stricken the husband. There was constant talk of divorce but their finances were such that neither of them could quite afford it. Margaret constantly called Wendy a whore, and only lately did Wendy realize that Margaret sincerely meant it.

Two things happened the next year. My wife was finally dragged off into the darkness, and Wendy's husband crashed his car into a retaining wall and was killed.

Even on the days of the respective funerals, we went to the track.

"He never understood."

"Neither did she," I said.

"I mean why I come here."

"I know."

"I mean how it makes me feel alive."

"I know."

"I mean how nothing else matters."

"I know."

"I should've been nicer to him, I suppose."

"I suppose. But we can't make a life out of blaming ourselves. What's happened, happened. We have to go on from here."

"Do you think Rob hates you as much as Margaret hates me?"

"More, probably," I said. "The way he looks at me sometimes, I think he'll probably kill me someday."

But it wasn't me who was to die.

All during Wendy's funeral, I kept thinking of those words. Margaret had murdered her mother just as Wendy had killed her father. The press made a lot of this.

All the grief I should have visited upon my dead wife I visited upon my dead lover. I went through months of alcoholic stupor. Clients fell away; rent forced me to move from our nice suburban home to a small apartment in a section of the city that always seemed to be on fire. I didn't have to worry about Rob anymore. He got enough loans for college and wanted nothing to do with me.

Years and more years, the track the only constant in my life. Many times I tried to contact Rob through the alumni office of his school but it was no use. He'd left word not to give his current address to his father.

There was the hospital and, several times, the detox clinic. There was the church in which I asked for forgiveness, and the born-again rally at which I proclaimed my happiness in the Lord.

And then there was the shelter. Five years I lived there, keeping the place painted and clean for the other residents. The nuns seemed to like me.

My teeth went entirely, and I had to have dentures. The arthritis in my foot got so bad that I could not wear shoes for days at a time. And my eyesight, beyond even the magic of glasses, got so bad that when I watched the horse races on TV, I couldn't tell which horse was which.

Then one night I got sick and threw up blood and in the morning one of the sisters took me to the hospital where they kept me overnight. In the morning the doctor came in and told me that I had stomach cancer. He gave me five months to live.

There were days when I was happy about my death sentence. Looking back, my life seemed so long and sad, I was glad to have it over with. Then there were days when I sobbed about my death sentence, and hated the God the nuns told me to pray to. I wanted to live to go back to the track again and have a sweet, beautiful winner.

Four months after the doctor's diagnosis, the nuns put me in bed and I knew I'd never walk on my own again. I thought of Donna, and her death, and how I'd made it all the worse with the track and Wendy.

The weaker I got, the more I thought about Rob. I talked about him to the nuns. And then one day he was there.

He wasn't alone, either. With him was a very pretty dark-haired woman and a seven-year-old boy who got the best features of both his mother and father.

"Dad, this is Mae and Stephen."

"Hello, Mae and Stephen. I've very glad to meet you. I wish I was better company."

"Don't worry about that," Mae said. "We're just happy to meet you."

"I need to go to the bathroom," Stephen said.

"Why don't I take him, and give you a few minutes alone with your dad?" Mae said.

And so, after all these years, we were alone and he said, "I still can't forgive you, Dad."

"I don't blame you."

"I want to. But somehow I can't."

I took his hand. "I'm just glad you turned out so well, son. Like your mother and not your father."

"I loved her very much."

"I know you did."

"And you treated her very, very badly."

All his anger. All these years.

"That's a beautiful wife and son you've got."

"They're my whole life, everything that matters to me."

I started crying; I couldn't help it. Here at the end I was glad to know he'd done well for himself and his family.

"I love you, Rob."

"I love you, too, Dad."

And then he leaned down and kissed me on the cheek and I started crying harder and embarrassed both of us.

Mae and Stephen came back.

"My turn," Rob said. He patted me on the shoulder. "I'll be back soon."

I think he wanted to cry but wanted to go somewhere alone to do it.

"So," Mae said, "are you comfortable?"

"Oh, very."

"This seems like a nice place."

"It is."

"And the nuns seem very nice, too."

"Very nice." I smiled. "I'm just so glad I got to see you two."

"Same here. I've wanted to meet you for years."

"Well," I said, smiling. "I'm glad the time finally came."

Stephen, proper in his white shirt and blue trousers and neatly combed dark hair, said, "I just wish you could go to the track with us sometime, Grandpa."

She didn't have to say anything. I saw it all in the quick certain pain that appeared in her lovely gray eyes.

"The race track, you mean?" I said.

"Uh-huh. Dad takes me all the time, doesn't he, Mom?"

"Oh, yes," she said, her voice toneless. "All the time."

She started to say more but then the door opened up and Rob came in and there was no time to talk.

There was no time at all.

MOTHER DARKNESS

The man surprised her. He was black.

Alison had been watching the small filthy house for six mornings now and this was the first time she'd seen him. She hadn't been able to catch him at seven-thirty or even six-thirty. She'd had to try six o'clock. She brought her camera up and began snapping.

She took four pictures of him just to be sure.

Then she put the car in gear and went to get breakfast.

An hour and a half later, in the restaurant where social workers often met, Peter said, "Oh, he's balling her all right."

"God," Alison Cage said. "Can't we talk about something else? Please."

"I know it upsets you. It upsets me. That's why I'm telling you about it."

"Can't you tell somebody else?"

"I've tried and nobody'll listen. Here's a forty-three-year-old man and he's screwing his seven-year-old daughter and nobody'll listen. Jesus."

Peter Forbes loved dramatic moments and incest was about as

dramatic as you could get. Peter was a hold-over hippie. He wore defiantly wrinkled khaki shirts and defiantly torn Lee jeans. He wore his brown hair in a ponytail. In his cubicle back at social services was a faded poster of Robert Kennedy. He still smoked a lot of dope. After six glasses of cheap wine at an office party, he'd once told Alison that he thought she was beautiful. He was forty-one years old and something of a joke and Alison both liked and disliked him.

"Talk to Coughlin," Alison said.

"I've talked to Coughlin."

"Then talk to Friedman."

"I've talked to Friedman, too."

"And what did they say?"

Peter sneered. "He reminded me about the Skeritt case."

"Oh."

"Said I got everybody in the department all bent out of shape about Richard Skeritt and then I couldn't prove anything about him and his little adopted son."

"Maybe Skeritt wasn't molesting him."

"Yeah. Right."

Alison sighed and looked out the winter window. A veil of steam covered most of the glass. Beyond it she could see the parking lot filled with men and women scraping their windows and giving each other pushes. A minor ice storm was in progress. It was seven thirty-five and people were hurrying to work. Everybody looked bundled up, like children trundling to school.

Inside the restaurant the air smelled of cooking grease and cigarettes. Cold wind gusted through the front door when somebody opened it, and people stamped snow from their feet as soon as they reached the tile floor. Because this was several blocks north of the black area, the jukebox ran to Hank Williams Jr. and The Judds. Alison despised country western music.

"So how's it going with you?" Peter said, daubs of egg yolk on his graying bandito mustache.

"Oh. You know." Blond Alison shrugged. "Still trying to find a better apartment for less money. Still trying to lose five pounds. Still trying to convince myself that there's really a God."

"Sounds like you need a Valium."

The remark was so—Peter. Alison smiled. "You think Valium would do it, huh?"

"It picks me up when I get down where you are."

"When you get to be thirty-six and you're alone the way I am, Peter, I think you need more than Valium."

"I'm alone."

"But you're alone in your way. I'm alone in my way."

"What's the difference?"

Suddenly she was tired of him and tired of herself, too. "Oh, I don't know. No difference, I suppose. I was being silly I guess."

"You look tired."

"Haven't been sleeping well."

"That doctor from the medical examiner's office been keeping you out late?"

"Doctor?"

"Oh, come on," Peter said. Sometimes he got possessive in a strange way. Testy. "I know you've been seeing him."

"Doctor Connery, you mean?"

Peter smiled, the egg yolk still on his mustache. "The one with the blue blue eyes, yes."

"It was strictly business. He just wanted to find out about those infants."

"The ones who smothered last year?"

"Yes."

"What's the big deal? Crib death happens all the time."

"Yes, but it still needs to be studied."

Peter smiled his superior smile. "I suppose but—"

"Crib death means that the pathologist couldn't find anything. No reason that the infant should have stopped breathing—no malfunction or anything, I mean. They just die mysteriously. Doctors want to know why."

"So what did your new boyfriend have to say about these deaths? I mean, what's his theory?"

"I'm not going to let you sneak that in there," she said, laughing despite herself. "He's not my boyfriend."

"All right. Then why would he be interested in two deaths that happened a year ago?"

She shrugged and sipped the last of her coffee. "He's exchanging information with other medical data banks. Seeing if they can't find a trend in these deaths."

"Sounds like an excuse to me."

"An excuse for what?" Alison said.

"To take beautiful blondes out to dinner and have them fall under his sway." He bared yellow teeth a dentist could work on for hours. He made claws of his hands. "Dracula; Dracula. That's who Connery really is."

Alison got pregnant her junior year of college. She got an abortion of course but only after spending a month in the elegant home of her rich parents, "moping" as her father characterized that particular period of time. She did not go back to finish school. She went to California. This was in the late seventies just as discos were dying and AIDS was rising. She spent two celibate years working as a secretary in a record company. James Taylor, who'd stopped in to see a friend of his, asked Alison to go have coffee. She was quite silly during their half hour together, juvenile and giggly, and even years later her face would burn when she thought of how foolish she'd been that day. When she returned home, she lived with her parents, a fact that seemed to embarrass all her high school friends. They were busy and noisy with growing families of their own and here was beautiful quiet Alison inexplicably alone and, worse, celebrating her thirty-first birthday while still living at home.

There was so much sorrow in the world and she could tell no one about it. That's why so many handsome and eligible men floated in and out of her life. Because they didn't *understand*. They weren't worth knowing, let alone giving herself to in any respect.

She worked for a year and a half in an art gallery. It was what passed for sophisticated in a midwestern city of this size. Very rich but dull people crowded it constantly, and men both with and without wedding rings pressed her for an hour or two alone.

She would never have known about the income maintenance job if she hadn't been watching a local talk show one day. Here sat two earnest women about her own age, one white, one black, talking about how they acted as liaisons between poor people and the social services agency. Alison knew immediately that she would like a job like this. She'd spent her whole life so spoiled and pampered and useless. And the art gallery—minor traveling art shows and local ad agency artists puffing themselves up as artistes—was simply an extension of this life.

These women, Alison could tell, knew well the sorrow of the world and the sorrow in her heart.

She went down the next morning to the social services agency and applied. The black woman who took her application weighed at least three hundred and fifty pounds which she'd packed into lime green stretch pants and a flowered polyester blouse with white sweat rings under the arms. She smoked Kool filters at a rate Alison hated to see. Hadn't this woman heard of lung cancer?

Four people interviewed Alison that day. The last was a prim but handsome white man in a shabby three-piece suit who had on the wall behind him a photo of himself and his wife and a small child who was in some obvious but undefined way retarded. Alison recognized two things about this man immediately: that here was a man who knew the same sorrow as she; and that here was a man painfully smitten with her already. It took him five and a half months but the man eventually found her a job at the agency.

Not until her third week did she realize that maintenance workers were the lowest of the low in social work, looked down upon by bosses and clients alike. What you did was this: you went out to people—usually women—who received various kinds of assistance from various government agencies and you attempted to prove that they were liars and cheats and scoundrels. The more benefits you could deny the people who made up your caseload, the more your bosses liked you. The people in the state house and the people in Washington, D.C., wanted you to allow your people as little as possible. That was the one and only way to keep taxpayers happy. Of course, your clients had a different version of all this. They needed help. And if you wouldn't give them help, or you tried to take away help you were already giving them, they became vocal. Income maintenance workers were frequently threatened and sometimes punched, stabbed, and shot, men and women alike. The curious thing was that not many of them quit. The pay was slightly better than you got in a factory and the job didn't require a college degree and you could pretty much set your own hours if you wanted to. So, even given the occasional violence, it was still a pretty good job.

Alison had been an income maintenance worker for nearly three years now.

She sincerely wanted to help.

An hour after leaving Peter in the restaurant, Alison pulled her gray Honda Civic up to the small house where earlier this morning she'd snapped photos of the black man. Her father kept trying to buy her a nicer car but she argued that her clients would just resent her nicer car and that she wouldn't blame them.

The name of this particular client was Doreen Hayden. Alison had been trying to do a profile of her but Doreen hadn't exactly cooperated. This was Alison's second appointment with the woman. She hoped it went better than the first.

After getting out of her car, Alison stood for a time in the middle of the cold, slushy street. Snow sometimes had a way of making even rundown things look beautiful. But somehow it only made this block of tiny, aged houses look worse. Brown frozen dog feces covered the sidewalk. Smashed front windows bore masking tape. Rusted-out cars squatted on small front lawns like obscene animals. And factory soot touched everything, everything. It was nineteen days before Christmas—Alison had just heard this on the radio this morning—but this was a neighborhood where Christmas never came.

Doreen answered the door. Through the screen drifted the oppressive odors of breakfast and cigarettes and dirty diapers. In her stained white sweater and tight red skirt, Doreen still showed signs of the attractive woman she'd been a few years ago until bad food and lack of exercise had added thirty pounds to her fine-boned frame.

The infant in her arms was perhaps four months old. She had a sweet little pink face. Her pink blanket was filthy.

"I got all the kids here," Doreen said. "You all comin' in? Gettin' cold with this door open."

All the kids, Alison thought. My God, Doreen was actually going to try that scam.

Inside, the hot odors of food and feces were even more oppressive. Alison sat on the edge of a discount-store couch and looked around the room. Not much had changed since her last visit. The old Zenith color TV set—now blaring Bugs Bunny cartoons—still needed some kind of tube. The floor was still an obstacle course of newspapers and empty Pepsi bottles and dirty baby clothes. There was a crucifix on one wall with a piece of faded, drooping palm stuck behind it. Next to it a photo of Bruce Springsteen had been taped to the soiled wallpaper.

"These kids was off visitin' last time you was here," Doreen said.

She referred to the two small boys standing to the right of the armchair where she sat holding her infant.

"Off visiting where?" Alison said, keeping her voice calm.

"Grandmother's."

"I see."

"They was stayin' there for awhile but now they're back with me so I'm goin' to need more money from the agency. You know."

"Maybe the man you have staying here could help you out." There. She'd said it quickly. With no malice. A plain simple fact.

"Ain't no man livin' here."

"I took a picture of him this morning."

"No way."

Alison sighed. "You know you can't get full payments if you have an adult male staying with you, Doreen."

"He musta been the garbage man or somethin'. No adult male stayin' here. None at all."

Alison had her clipboard out. She noted on the proper lines of the form that a man was staying here. She said, "You borrowed those two boys."

"What?"

"These two boys here, Doreen. You borrowed them. They're not yours."

"No way."

Alison looked at one of the ragged little boys and said, "Is Doreen your mother?"

The little boy, nervous, glanced over at Doreen and then put his head down.

Alison didn't want to embarrass or frighten him anymore.

"If I put these two boys down on the claim form and they send out an investigator, it'll be a lot worse for you, Doreen. They'll try and get you for fraud."

"Goddamn you."

"I'll write them down here if you want me to. But if they get you for fraud—"

"Shit," Doreen said. She shook her head and then she looked at the boys. "You two run on home now, all right?"

"Can we take some cookies, Aunt Doreen?"

She grinned at Alison. "They don't let their Aunt Doreen forget no promises, I'll tell you that." She nodded to the kitchen. "You boys go get your cookies and then go out the back door, all right? Oh, but first say good-bye to Alison here."

Both boys, cute and dear to Alison, smiled at her and then grinned at each other and then ran with heavy feet across the faded linoleum to the kitchen.

"I need more money," Doreen said. "This little one's breakin' me."

"I'm afraid I got you all I could, Doreen."

"You gonna tell them about Ernie?"

"Ernie's the man staying here?"

"Yeah."

"No. Not since you told me the truth."

"He's the father."

"Of your little girl?"

"Yeah."

"You think he'll actually marry you?"

She laughed her cigarette laugh. "Yeah, in about fifty or sixty years."

The house began to become even smaller to Alison then. This

sometimes happened when she was interviewing people. She felt entombed in the anger and despair of the place.

She stared at Doreen and Doreen's beautiful little girl.

"Could I hold her?" Alison said.

"You serious?"

"Yes."

"She maybe needs a change. She poops a lot."

"I don't mind."

Doreen shrugged. "Be my guest."

She got up and brought the infant across to Alison.

Alison perched carefully on the very edge of the couch and received the infant like some sort of divine gift. After a moment the smells of the little girl drifted away and Alison was left holding a very beautiful little child.

Doreen went back and sat in the chair and looked at Alison. "You got any kids?"

"No."

"Wish you did though, huh?"

"Yes."

"You married?"

"Not so far."

"Hell, bet you got guys fallin' all over themselves for you. You're beautiful."

But Alison rarely listened to flattery. Instead she was watching the infant's sweet white face. "Have you ever looked at her eyes, Doreen?"

" 'Course I looked at her eyes. She's my daughter, ain't she?"

"No. I mean looked really deeply."

" 'Course I have."

"She's so sad."

Doreen sighed. "She's got a reason to be sad. Wouldn't you be sad growin' up in a place like this?"

Alison leaned down to the little girl's face and kissed her tenderly on the forehead. They were like sisters, the little girl and Alison. They knew how sad the world was. They knew how sad their hearts were.

When the time came, when the opportunity appeared, Alison would do the same favor for this little girl she'd done for the two other little girls.

Not even the handsome Doctor Connery had suspected anything. He'd just assumed that the other two girls had died from crib death.

On another visit, someday soon, Alison would make sure that she was alone with the little girl for a few minutes. Then it would be done and the little girl would not have to grow up and know the even greater sadness that awaited her.

"You really ain't gonna tell them about Ernie livin' here?"

"I've got a picture of him that I can turn in anytime as evidence. But I'll tell you what, Doreen; you start taking better care of your daughter—changing her diapers more often and feeding her the menu I gave you—and I'll keep Ernie our secret."

"Can't afford to have no more money taken from me," Doreen said.

"Then you take better care of your daughter," Alison said, holding the infant out for Doreen to take now. "Because she's very sad, Doreen. Very very sad."

Alison kissed the little girl on the forehead once more and then gave her up to her mother.

Soon, little one, Alison thought; soon you won't be so sad. I promise.

THE BEAST IN
THE WOODS

By the time I get to the barn tonight, there's already a quarter moon in the September sky, and the barn owl who always sits in the old elm along the creek, he's already hooting into the Iowa darkness.

For the first twenty minutes, I rake out the stalls and scatter hay around the floor. Dairy cows take a lot of work. After that I spread sawdust to eat up some of the dampness and the odors.

Not that I'm paying a whole hell of a lot of attention. All I can think of really is his old army .45. Ordinarily it hangs from a dusty holster on a peg in the spare room upstairs where he moved after Mom died two years ago of the heart disease that's run in her family for years. Dad says he moved in there because whenever he was in their room, lying in their bed, he'd start to cry, and he's a proud man and doesn't think tears are proper. Also, when he was drunk one night, he told me that a few times when he was in her room, he talked to her ghost and that scared him. So now he keeps their bedroom door shut and sleeps in the room down the hall.

I wonder where he is now. I wonder what he's doing.

Three hours ago, he left, saying he'd be back for dinner but he wasn't.

And then when I went in to wash up and heat up some spaghetti, I passed by the spare room and noticed that his .45 was gone from its holster.

When I'm finished with the sawdust, I go outside and stand in the Indian summer dusk, all rolling Iowa hills and bright early stars and the clean fast smell of the nearby creek, and the distant smoky smells of autumn in the piny hills to the east.

All the outbuildings stand in silhouette now against the dusk, the corn wagon parked by the silo reminding me of tomorrow's chores.

There's only one reason he'd take that goddamned gun of his to town. I'm sure glad Mom isn't here. She tended to get real emotional about things. She would've had a real hard time with the past year, Dad's loan going bad at the bank when the flood wiped us out, and the bank being forced to give Dad until three weeks ago to settle up his account or lose the farm. They gave him a little extra time but this morning he got a phone call telling him that the bank'd have to file papers to get the farm back and auction it off. ("It isn't the same anymore, Verne," I heard the banker Ken Ohlers tell him on the porch one afternoon, "we don't own the friggin' bank now—the boys in Minneapolis do, big goddamned banking conglomerate, and frankly they could give a shit about a bunch of Iowa farmers, you know, whether the farmers go out of business or not. They just don't make enough on this kind of farm loan to hassle with it.")

Then he went into town with his gun.

To the north now I see plumes of road dust, inside of which is a gray car that I recognize immediately.

As I expect, he turns right into our long gravel drive and shoots right up to the edge of the outbuildings. He has one of those long whip antennas on the back of his car, Sheriff Mike Rhodes does, giving his car a very official and menacing look.

He jumps out of the car almost before the motor stops running. In his left hand is a shotgun. He's a beefy man of Dad's age, fifty or so. In fact, they served in Nam together, and were the first two Nam vets to be allowed in the local VFW, some of the other vets from WWII and Korea feeling that Vietnam wasn't an actual war. Fifty-nine thousand fucking Americans die there and it isn't actually a war, as my dad used to say all the time.

One more thing about Sheriff Mike. He's my godfather.

"Bobby, is your dad around here?" he says, coming at me like he's going to hit me or something.

"He went into town. How come you got the shotgun, Mike?"

But he doesn't answer my question. He just gets closer. He smells of sweat and aftershave. And he scares me. The same way my dad scares me sometimes when I sense how mad he is and how terrible it's going to be when he lets go of it.

"Bobby, I need to know where your dad is."

"He ain't here. Honest, Mike."

He takes my arm. His fingers hurt me. "Bobby, you listen to me." He is still catching his breath, big man in khaki uniform, wide sweat rings under his arms. "Bobby, you got to think. Think like a normal person. You understand me?"

Sometimes people talk to me like that. They remember when I fell off the tractor when I was seven and how I was never the same. That's what my mom always said. That poor Bobby, he was never the same. In school I didn't read so good and sometimes people would tell me stuff but I couldn't understand them no matter how hard I tried. And that's when I'd always start crying. I guess I must have cried a lot before I quit school in the tenth grade because the kids, they called me "Buckets" and they always made fun of the way I cried.

"I'll listen good, Mike. I promise."

"You know Ken Ohlers down to the bank?"

"Uh-huh."

"Your dad killed him about an hour ago. Shot him with that forty-five of his he used in Song Be that time."

"Oh shit, Mike, I wish you wouldn't've said that."

"I'm sorry, Bobby, I had to tell you."

"It makes me scared. You're gonna hurt my dad now, aren't you?"

"I don't want to, Bobby. That's why I need your help. You see him, you got to convince him to give himself up. There's just you now, Bobby, your ma bein' dead and all. You're the only one he'll listen to."

"I'm scared, Mike. I'm real scared."

And I start crying. Don't want to. But can't stop.

And Mike, he just looks kind of embarrassed for me, the way folks do when I start crying like this.

And then he comes up and slides his arm around me and gives me a little hug. Dad, he'll never do that, not even when I cry. Says it doesn't look right, two grown men hugging each other that way.

He digs in his pocket and takes out his handkerchief. Smells of mint. Mike always carries mints in his right khaki pocket.

"I have a mint, Mike?"

"You bet."

I blow my nose in his handkerchief and try to hand it back to him but he nods for me to keep it and then he digs a mint out and drops it into the palm of my hand.

"You remember what I told you, Bobby?"

"Uh-huh."

"You tell your dad to give himself up."

"Uh-huh."

" 'Cause the mayor, he won't mess around. He never liked your dad, anyway."

"They gonna get the dogs out after him the way they did that time with that black guy?"

"Dogs're already out."

"And the helicopter?"

"Already out, too."

"Scares me, that helicopter."

"Don't like it much myself. Hate ridin' in the friggin' thing." He wipes sweat from his face. "He shows up around here, you give him that message, all right?"

"I will, Mike. I promise."

I'm scared I'm going to start crying again.

He looks at me a long time and then gives me another quick hug. "I'm sorry this happened, Bobby."

"I'll bet he's scared, too. I'm gonna say a prayer for him. Hail Mary. Just like Mom taught me."

"I'll check back later, Bobby."

Then he's trotting back to the big gray car that smells of road dust and oil and gasoline and heat. Inside, he kind of gives me a little wave and then he whips the car around so he can go back out headfirst, and then he's lost again inside heavy rolling dust that's silver now in the moonlight.

I go in the house. Upstairs, I go into their bedroom. Mom always kept a framed picture of Blessed Mother on her nightstand. She always said that Blessed Mother listens to boys like me, you know, boys that don't seem just like other boys. I try not to cry as I pray. Hail Mary full of. Sometimes I get confused. Mom wrote it down for me a lot of times but I have a habit of losing things. Hail Mary full of grace. This time it goes all right. Or mostly all right. And when I'm done praying I light this little votive candle the priest gave her one time he came out here. The match smells of sulphur. The candle smells of wax. Red glow plays across the picture of the Blessed Mother. Hail Mary full of grace. I say a whole nother one. In case she didn't hear it or something.

Then I'm outside, pretty sure where I'll find Dad. There's a line shack up in the hills. Dad and his brother used to play up there. His brother died in Nam. Poor goddamned bastard Dad always says whenever he gets drunk. Poor goddamned bastard. Uncle Win and Mom are buried up to Harrison Cemetery and couple times a month in the warm season, Dad goes up there and puts flowers on their graves. In the winter months he just stands graveside and stares down at their grave markers, leaning over and brushing away the snow so that their names can be read real clear. He even went up there one night when it was ten below and nobody found him till dawn and Doc Hardy said it was a miracle him being exposed like that—should've died for Christ's sake (how old Doc Hardy always talks)—and probably would have if he hadn't been so drunk.

And now I'm running through the long prairie grasses and it feels good. The grasses are up to my waist and it's like running through water, the way the grasses slap at you and tickle you. My mom always read me books about the Iowa Indians and about nature stuff. I liked the names of the flowers especially and always made her read them to me over and over again sort of like singing a song. Rattlesnake master and goldenrod and gay-feather and black-eyed Susans and silverleaf scurf pea and ragwort and shooting star. Some nights I lie in my bed when I can't sleep and just say those names over and over and over again and imagine Mom reading them to me the way she used to, and making me learn new words, too, three "five-dollar words" (as she always called them) each and every week.

A couple times I fall down. I try not to cry. But the second time I fall down I cut my knee on the edge of a rock and I can't help but cry. But then I'm running along the moonsilver creek, ducking below the weeping willows and jumping over a lost little mud frog, and then I'm starting up into the red cedar glade where the cabin lies.

Halfway there I have to stop and pee. Dad always says be proud I don't pee my pants no more. And I am proud. But sometimes I can barely hold it. Like now. And I have to go. The pee is hot and rattles the fallen red leaves. I should wash my hands the way Mom always said but I can't so I run on.

Behind me once, I think I hear something and I stop. I'm scared now, the way I am when monster movies come on TV. You shouldn't watch that crap, Dad always says, snapping off the set when he sees that I'm getting scared. The forest is vast. Dark. Slither and crawl and creep, the things in the forest, possum and snake and wolf. And maybe monsters, the way there are in forests on TV. The Indians always believed there were beasts in the woods.

I start running again. Need to find Dad. Warn him.

Now I think of the things Mom read me about the Indians who used to live here. I like to pretend I'm an Indian. I wish I could wear buffalo masks the way they did when they danced around their campfires. Or the claws of a grizzly bear as a necklace signifying that I am the bravest brave of all. Or paint stripes of blood on my arm, each stripe meaning a different battle. They had to come get me sometimes, Mom and Dad, at suppertime, scared I'd wandered off, but I was always up at the old line shack playing Indian, talking to the prairie sky the way the Indians always had; and watching for the silver wolves to stand in the long grasses and sing and cry and nuzzle their young as the silver moon rose in the pure Iowa night.

I see the shape of the little cabin through the cedars now. It sits all falling down in the middle of a small clearing. No lights; no sound but an owl and the soft soughing of the long grasses; and the smell of rotted wood still wet from the rain last week.

I know he's in there. I sense it.

I crouch down, the way an Indian would, and reach the clearing. And then I start running fast for the cabin.

I am halfway across the clearing when I hear a voice say, "You go back home, Bobby. Right now."

Dad. Inside the cabin.

I am chill with sweat. And shaking. "Mike, he came out to the house, Dad and said—"

"I know what he said."

"He says you killed Mr. Ohler."

"I had to, son. He didn't have no right to take our farm back. He said he was our friend but he wasn't no friend at all."

I don't say anything just then; just the soft soft soughing of the wind, like the breathing of some invisible giant, sleeping.

"Mike, he says he's afraid you'll get killed."

"I don't want to go to prison, Bobby."

"I wish I could see you."

He's in the window, in darkness. He's like Mom now. I can talk to him but I can't see him. It's like death.

"I want to see you, Dad."

"You just go on back, Bobby. You understand me? You just go on back to the farm and wait there."

And then I hear something again, and when I turn I see Mike coming out into the clearing.

He looks all sloppy, his shirt untucked and his graying hair all mussed. He carries his shotgun, cocked in his arm now.

"I figured you'd lead me to him, Bobby."

"He won't let me see him, Mike."

He nods and then says to the cabin. "I want to come in and talk to you."

"Just stay out there, Mike."

"You don't need to make this any worse than it already is. I'm supposed to be your friend."

"Yeah, just the way Ohler was my friend."

"He didn't have nothing to do with taking your farm back. It was those bastards in Minneapolis."

"That's what he liked to say, anyway."

"I'm coming in."

"I'll shoot you if you try."

"Then you'll just have to shoot me, you sonofabitch."

One thing about Mike, he makes up his mind, there's no stopping him. No sir.

I say, "Can I go with you?"

He shakes his head. "You just stay here."

"He's my dad."

"Bobby, goddammit, I got enough on my mind right now, all right? You just stay right here."

"Yes, sir."

"I'm sorry I swore at you like that."

"Yes, sir."

"I won't be long."

From the cabin, my dad shouts, "You just stay out there, Mike. You hear me?"

But Mike walks toward the cabin.

My dad fires.

The shot is loud and flat in the soughing prairie silence.

"Next time I'll hit you."

"You'll just have to hit me, then."

This time, the bullet comes a lot closer. This time it echoes off the hills.

But Mike doesn't slow down.

He walks right up to the one-room cabin and kicks in the front door and then goes inside.

I walk back to the edge of the clearing and look at trees. Mom always used to read me the names of trees, too, white oak and shagbark hickory and basswood and pin oak and green ash and silver maple and honey locusts and big-tooth aspens. Say them over and over and they're like a song, too.

I need to pee again.

I go into the woods.

I wish I could wash my hands. It always makes me feel bad not to do what Mom says, even when she's gone.

In the clearing again, I hear them yelling at each other inside the cabin and I get scared. And they're starting to fight. They slam up against the walls and the whole cabin shakes. I want to run down there but I'm too scared. I don't want to see Dad hurt Mike or Mike hurt Dad. This shouldn't ought to be like this.

And then the shot.

Just one.

And it's louder and the echo is longer and then there is this terrible silence and you can't even hear the wind now.

And then the cabin door opens up and Dad comes out.

He walks to the center of the clearing, his .45 dangling from his right hand. "You get back to the farm, you hear me, Bobby?"

But I can't help myself. I go up to him. And I put my arms around him. And the funny thing is, this time he doesn't push me away or tell me grown men shouldn't hug each other. He holds me real tight and I can feel how raw-boned he is, all sharp shoulders and bony elbows and gaunted ribs.

He holds me tight, too, just as tight as I hold him, and says, "I messed it all up, Bobby. I messed it all up."

And then he starts choking and crying the way he did at Mom's funeral and I hold him and let him cry the way Mom used to hold me and let me cry.

And then he's done.

And standing in the clearing. And staring up at the moon the way Mom told me Indians used to. She said they believed they could read things in the moon, portents for what would happen to them in the future.

Then he looks at me, and he speaks very very softly, and he says, "You get on back now, Bobby. And you call Mr. Sayre, the lawyer, he'll know what to do."

"Is Uncle Mike dead?"

"Yes, he is, Bobby."

"How come you shot him, Dad?"

"I'm not sure why, Bobby. I'm not sure why at all. I just wish I hadn't."

I wanted to say something but I was afraid I would start crying again.

And Dad was already looking back toward the cabin.

"You go on back to the farm now, Bobby, and you call Mr. Sayre."

I reach out gently for his .45 but he pulls it back. "Maybe I should take that from you, Dad."

"You just go on, Bobby."

"I'm scared, Dad, you havin' that .45 and all."

"You just go on. You just hurry and call Mr. Sayre."

"I'm scared, Dad."

"I know you are, Bobby. And I'm scared, too." He nods to the woods and says, very final now, "Git, boy. Git and git fast. You understand?"

"Yessir."

"You run till you get to the farm and then you call Mr. Sayre. You understand?"

"Yessir."

And that is all.

He turns away from me, his face lost in moonshadow, and he goes on back to the cabin.

I know better than to argue or disobey.

I start walking slowly toward the woods again and by the time I reach the front stand of trees, the shot rings out just as I thought it would, and I try to imagine what it must look like, their two bodies there inside the cabin, blood and flies and stink the way it is when any kind of animal is dead like that, and then I get scared, real scared, and I start crying.

I want my dad to hold me again the way he did just a few minutes ago, the way my mom used to hold me anytime I asked her. I want somebody to hold me, and hold me tight, and hold me for a long long time because the night is coming full now, and there is a beast in these woods, just the way the Indians always said, a beast in the dark dark woods.

ONE OF THOSE DAYS,
ONE OF THOSE NIGHTS

The thing you have to understand is that I found it by accident. I was looking for a place to hide the birthday gift I'd bought Laura—a string of pearls she'd been wanting to wear with the new black dress she'd bought for herself—and all I was going to do was lay the gift-wrapped box in the second drawer of her bureau . . .

. . . and there it was.

A plain number ten envelope with her name written across the middle in a big manly scrawl and a canceled Elvis Presley stamp up in the corner. Postmarked two days ago.

Just as I spotted it, Laura called from the living room, "Bye, honey, see you at six." The last two years we've been saving to buy a house so we have only the one car. Laura goes an hour earlier than I do, so she rides with a woman who lives a few blocks over. Then I pick her up at six after somebody relieves me at the computer store where I work. For what it's worth, I have an MA in English Literature but with the economy being what it is, it hasn't done me much good.

I saw a sci-fi movie once where a guy could set something on fire simply by staring at it intently enough. That's what I was trying to do with this letter my wife got. Burn it so that I wouldn't have to read what it said inside and get my heart broken.

I closed the drawer.

Could be completely harmless. Her fifteenth high school re-union was coming up this spring. Maybe it was from one of her old classmates. And maybe the manly scrawl wasn't so manly after all. Maybe it was from a woman who wrote in a rolling dramatic hand.

Laura always said that I was the jealous type and this was cer-tainly proof. A harmless letter tucked harmlessly in a bureau drawer. And here my heart was pounding, and fine cold sweat slicked my face, and my fingers were trembling.

God, wasn't I a pitiful guy? Shouldn't I be ashamed of myself?

I went into the bathroom and lathered up and did my usual re-lentless fifteen-minute morning regimen of shaving, showering and shining up my apple-cheeked Irish face and my thinning Irish hair, if hair follicles can have a nationality, that is.

Then I went back into our bedroom and took down a white shirt, blue necktie, navy blazer and tan slacks. All dressed, I looked just like seventy or eighty million other men getting ready for work this particular sunny April morning.

Then I stood very still in the middle of the bedroom and stared at Laura's bureau. Maybe I wasn't simply going to set the letter on fire. Maybe I was going to ignite the entire bureau.

The grandfather clock in the living room tolled eight-thirty. If I didn't leave now I would be late, and if you were late you inevitably got a chewing out from Ms. Sandstrom, the boss. Anybody who be-lieves that women would run a more benign world than men needs only to spend five minutes with Ms. Sandstrom. Hitler would have used her as a pin-up girl.

The bureau. The letter. The manly scrawl.

What was I going to do?

Only one thing I could think of, since I hadn't made a decision about reading the letter or not. I'd simply take it with me to work. If I decided to read it, I'd give it a quick scan over my lunch hour.

But probably I wouldn't read it at all. I had a lot of faith where Laura was concerned. And I didn't like to think of myself as the sort of possessive guy who snuck around reading his wife's mail.

I reached into the bureau drawer.

My fingers touched the letter.

I was almost certain I wasn't going to read it. Hell, I'd probably get so busy at work that I'd forget all about it.

But just in case I decided to . . .

I grabbed the letter and stuffed it into my blazer pocket, and closed the drawer. In the kitchen I had a final cup of coffee and read my newspaper horoscope. Bad news, as always. I should never read the damn things . . . Then I hurried out of the apartment to the little Toyota parked at the curb.

Six blocks away, it stalled. Our friendly mechanic said that moisture seemed to get in the fuel pump a lot. He's not sure why. We've run it in three times but it still stalls several times a week.

Around ten o'clock, hurrying into a sales meeting that Ms. Sandstrom had decided to call, I dropped my pen. And when I bent over to pick it up, my glasses fell out of my pocket and when I moved to pick them up, I took one step too many and put all 175 pounds of my body directly onto them. I heard something snap.

By the time I retrieved both pen and glasses, Ms. Sandstrom was closing the door and calling the meeting to order. I hurried down the hall trying to see how much damage I'd done. I held the glasses up to the light. A major fissure snaked down the center of the right lens. I slipped them on. The crack was even more difficult to see through than I'd thought.

Ms. Sandstrom, a very attractive fiftyish woman given to sleek gray suits and burning blue gazes, warned us as usual that if sales of our computers didn't pick up, two or three people in this room would likely be looking for jobs. Soon. And just as she finished saying this, her eyes met mine. "For instance, Donaldson, what kind of month are you having?"

"What kind of month am I having?"

"Do I hear a parrot in here?" Ms. Sandstrom said, and several of the salespeople laughed.

"I'm not having too bad a month."

Ms. Sandstrom nodded wearily and looked around the room. "Do we have to ask Donaldson here any more questions? Isn't he telling us everything we need to know when he says 'I'm not having too bad a month?' What're we hearing when Donaldson says that?"

I hadn't noticed till this morning how much Ms. Sandstrom reminded me of Miss Hutchison, my fourth grade teacher. Her favorite weapon had also been humiliation.

Dick Weybright raised his hand. Dick Weybright always raises his hand, especially when he gets to help Ms. Sandstrom humiliate somebody.

"We hear defeatism, when he says that," Dick said. "We hear defeatism and a serious lack of self-esteem."

Twice a week, Ms. Sandstrom made us listen to motivational tapes. You know, "I upped my income, Up yours," that sort of thing. And nobody took those tapes more seriously than Dick Weybright.

"Very good, Dick," Ms. Sandstrom said. "Defeatism and lack of self-esteem. That tells us all we need to know about Donaldson here. Just as the fact that he's got a crack in his glasses tells us something else about him, doesn't it?"

Dick Weybright waggled his hand again. "Lack of self-respect."

"Exactly," Ms. Sandstrom said, smiling coldly at me. "Lack of self-respect."

She didn't address me again until I was leaving the sales room. I'd knocked some of my papers on the floor. By the time I got them picked up, I was alone with Ms. Sandstrom. I heard her come up behind me as I pointed myself toward the door.

"You missed something, Donaldson."

I turned. "Oh?"

She waved Laura's envelope in the air. Then her blue eyes showed curiosity as they read the name on the envelope. "You're not one of those, are you, Donaldson?"

"One of those?"

"Men who read their wives' mail."

"Oh. One of those. I see."

"Are you?"

"No."

"Then what're you doing with this?"

"What am I doing with that?"

"That parrot's in here again."

"I must've picked it up off the table by mistake."

"The table?"

"The little Edwardian table under the mirror in the foyer. Where we always set the mail."

She shook her head again. She shook her head a lot. "You are one of those, aren't you, Donaldson? So were my first three husbands, the bastards."

She handed me the envelope, brushed past me and disappeared down the hall.

There's a park near the river where I usually eat lunch when I'm downtown for the day. I spend most of the time feeding the pigeons.

Today I spent most of my time staring at the envelope laid next to me on the park bench. There was a warm spring breeze and I half hoped it would lift up the envelope and carry it away.

Now I wished I'd left the number ten with the manly scrawl right where I'd found it because it was getting harder and harder to resist lifting the letter from inside and giving it a quick read.

I checked my watch. Twenty minutes to go before I needed to be back at work. Twenty minutes to stare at the letter. Twenty minutes to resist temptation.

Twenty minutes—and how's this for cheap symbolism?—during which the sky went from cloudless blue to dark and ominous.

By now, I'd pretty much decided that the letter had to be from a man. Otherwise, why would Laura have hidden it in her drawer? I'd also decided that it must contain something pretty incriminating.

Had she been having an affair with somebody? Was she thinking of running away with somebody?

On the way back to the office, I carefully slipped the letter from the envelope and read it. Read it four times as a matter of fact. And felt worse every time I did.

So Chris Tomlin, her ridiculously handsome, ridiculously wealthy, ridiculously slick college boyfriend was back in her life.

I can't tell you much about the rest of the afternoon. It's all very vague: voices spoke to me, phones rang at me, computer printers spat things at me—but I didn't respond. I felt as if I were scuttling across the floor of an ocean so deep that neither light nor sound could penetrate it.

Chris Tomlin. My God.

I kept reading the letter, stopping only when I'd memorized it entirely and could keep rerunning it in my mind without any visual aid.

> Dear Laura,
>
> I still haven't forgotten you—or forgiven you for choosing you-know-who over me.
>
> I'm going to be in your fair city this Friday. How about meeting me at the Fairmont right at noon for lunch?
>
> Of course, you could contact me the evening before if you're interested. I'll be staying at the Wallingham. I did a little checking and found that you work nearby.
>
> I can't wait to see you.
>
> Love,
> Chris Tomlin.

Not even good old Ms. Sandstrom could penetrate my stupor. I know she charged into my office a few times and made some nasty threats—something about my not returning the call of one of our most important customers—but I honestly couldn't tell you who she wanted me to call or what she wanted me to say.

About all I can remember is that it got very dark and cold suddenly. The lights blinked on and off a few times. We were having a terrible rainstorm. Somebody came in soaked and said that the storm sewers were backing up and that downtown was a mess.

Not that I paid this information any particular heed.

I was wondering if she'd call him Thursday night. I took it as a foregone conclusion that she would have lunch with him on Friday. But how about Thursday night?

Would she visit him in his hotel room?

And come to think of it, why *had* she chosen me over Chris Tomlin? I mean, while I may not be a nerd, I'm not exactly a movie star, either. And with Chris Tomlin, there wouldn't have been any penny-pinching for a down payment on a house, either.

With his daddy's millions in pharmaceuticals, good ole Chris would have bought her a manse as a wedding present.

The workday ended. The usual number of people peeked into my office to say the usual number of good nights. The usual cleaning crew, high school kids in gray uniforms, appeared to start hauling out trash and run roaring vacuum cleaners. And I went through my usual process of staying at my desk until it was time to pick up Laura.

I was just about to walk out the front door when I noticed in the gloom that Ms. Sandstrom's light was still on.

She had good ears. Even above the vacuum cleaner roaring its way down the hall to her left, she heard me leaving and looked up.

She waved me into her office.

When I reached her desk, she handed me a slip of paper with some typing on it.

"How does that read to you, Donaldson?"

"Uh, what is it?"

"A Help Wanted ad I may be running tomorrow."

That was another thing Miss Hutchison, my fourth grade teacher, had been good at—indirect torture.

Ms. Sandstrom wanted me to read the ad she'd be running for my replacement.

I scanned it and handed it back.

"Nice."

"Is that all you have to say? Nice?"

"I guess so."

"You realize that this means I'm going to fire you?"

"That's what I took it to mean."

"What the hell's wrong with you, Donaldson? Usually you'd be groveling and sniveling by now."

"I've got some—personal problems."

A smirk. "That's what you get for reading your wife's mail." Then a scowl. "When you come in tomorrow morning, you come straight to my office, you understand?"

I nodded. "All right."

"And be prepared to do some groveling and sniveling. You're going to need it."

Why don't I just make a list of the things I found wrong with my Toyota after I slammed the door and belted myself in.

A) The motor wouldn't turn over. Remember what I said about moisture and the fuel pump?

B) The roof had sprung a new leak. This was different from the old leak, which dribbled rain down onto the passenger seat. The new one dribbled rain down onto the driver's seat.

C) The turn signal arm had come loose again and was hanging down from naked wires like a half-amputated limb. Apparently after finding the letter this morning, I was in so much of a fog I hadn't noticed that it was broken again.

I can't tell you how dark and cold and lonely I felt just then. Bereft of wife. Bereft of automobile. Bereft of—dare I say it?—self-esteem and self-respect. And, on top of it, I was a disciple of defeatism. Just ask my co-worker Dick Weybright.

The goddamned car finally started and I drove off to pick up my goddamned wife.

The city was a mess.

Lashing winds and lashing rains—both of which were still lashing merrily along—had uprooted trees in the park, smashed out store windows here and there, and had apparently caused a power outage that shut down all the automatic traffic signals.

I wanted to be home and I wanted to be dry and I wanted to be in my jammies. But most of all I wanted to be loved by the one woman I had ever really and truly loved.

If only I hadn't opened her bureau drawer to hide her pearls . . .

She was standing behind the glass door in the entrance to the art deco building where she works as a market researcher for a mutual fund company. When I saw her, I felt all sorts of things at once—love, anger, shame, terror—and all I wanted to do was park the car and run up to her and take her in my arms and give her the tenderest kiss I was capable of.

But then I remembered the letter and . . .

Well, I'm sure I don't have to tell you about jealousy. There's nothing worse to carry around in your stony little heart. All that rage and self-righteousness and self-pity. It begins to smother you and . . .

By the time Laura climbed into the car, it was smothering me. She smelled of rain and perfume and her sweet tender body.

"Hi," she said. "I was worried about you."

"Yeah. I'll bet."

Then, closing the door, she gave me a long, long look. "Are you all right?"

"Fine."

"Then why did you say, 'Yeah. I'll bet?' "

"Just being funny."

She gave me another stare. I tried to look regular and normal. You know, not on the verge of whipping the letter out and shoving it in her face.

"Oh, God," she said, "you're not starting your period already are you?"

The period thing is one of our little jokes. A few months after we got married, she came home cranky one day and I laid the blame for her mood on her period. She said I was being sexist. I said I was only making an observation. I wrote down the date. For the next four months, on or around the same time each month, she came home crabby. I pointed this out to her. She said, "All right. But men have periods, too."

"They do?"

"You're damned right they do." And so now, whenever I seem inexplicably grouchy, she asks me if my period is starting.

"Maybe so," I said, swinging from outrage to a strange kind of whipped exhaustion.

"Boy, this is really leaking," Laura said.

I just drove. There was a burly traffic cop out in the middle of a busy intersection directing traffic with two flashlights in the rain and gloom.

"Did you hear me, Rich? I said this is really leaking."

"I know it's really leaking."

"What's up with you, anyway? What're you so mad about? Did Sandstrom give you a hard time today?"

"No—other than telling me that she may fire me."

"You're kidding."

"No."

"But why?"

Because while I was going through your bureau, I found a letter from your ex-lover and I know all about the tryst you're planning to set up.

That's what I wanted to say.

What I said was: "I guess I wasn't paying proper attention during another one of her goddamned sales meetings."

"But, Rich, if you get fired—"

She didn't have to finish her sentence. If I got fired, we'd never get the house we'd been saving for.

"She told me that when I came in tomorrow morning, I should be prepared to grovel and snivel. And she wasn't kidding."

"She actually said that?"

"She actually said that."

"What a bitch."

"Boss's daughter. You know how this city is. The last frontier for hard-core nepotism."

We drove on several more blocks, stopping every quarter block or so to pull out around somebody whose car had stalled in the dirty water backing up from the sewers.

"So is that why you're so down?"

"Yeah," I said. "Isn't that reason enough?"

"Usually, about Sandstrom, I mean, you get mad. You don't get depressed."

"Well, Sandstrom chews me out but she doesn't usually threaten to fire me."

"That's true. But—"

"But what?"

"It just seems that there's—something else." Then, "Where're you going?"

My mind had been on the letter tucked inside my blazer. In the meantime, the Toyota had been guiding itself into the most violent neighborhood in the city. Not even the cops wanted to come here.

"God, can you turn around?" Laura said. "I'd sure hate to get stuck here."

"We'll be all right. I'll hang a left at the next corner and then we'll drive back to Marymount Avenue."

"I wondered where you were going. I should have said something." She leaned over and kissed me on the cheek.

That boil of feelings, of profound tenderness and profound rage, churned up inside of me again.

"Things'll work out with Sandstrom," she said, and then smiled. "Maybe she's just starting her period."

And I couldn't help it. The rage was gone, replaced by pure and total love. This was my friend, my bride, my lover. There had to be a reasonable and innocent explanation for the letter. There had to.

I started hanging the left and that's when it happened. The fuel pump. Rain.

The Toyota stopped dead.

"Oh, no," she said, glancing out the windshield at the forbidding blocks of falling-down houses and dark, condemned buildings.

Beyond the wind, beyond the rain, you could hear sirens. There were always sirens in neighborhoods like these.

"Maybe I can fix it," I said.

"But, honey, you don't know anything about cars."

"Well, I watched him make that adjustment last time."

"I don't know," she said skeptically. "Besides, you'll just get wet."

"I'll be fine."

I knew why I was doing this, of course. In addition to being rich, powerful and handsome, Chris Tomlin was also one of those men who could fix practically anything. I remembered her telling me how he'd fixed a refrigerator at an old cabin they'd once stayed in.

I opened the door. A wave of rain washed over me. But I was determined to act like the kind of guy who could walk through a meteor storm and laugh it off. Maybe that's why Laura was considering a rendezvous with Chris. Maybe she was sick of my whining. A macho man, I'm not.

"Just be careful," she said.

"Be right back."

I eased out of the car and then realized I hadn't used the hood latch inside. I leaned in and popped the latch and gave Laura a quick smile.

And then I went back outside into the storm.

I was soaked completely in less than a minute, my shoes soggy, my clothes drenched and cold and clinging. Even my raincoat.

But I figured this would help my image as a take-charge sort of guy. I even gave Laura a little half-salute before I raised the hood. She smiled at me. God, I wanted to forget all about the letter and be happily in love again.

Any vague hopes I'd had of starting the car were soon forgotten as I gaped at the motor and realized that I had absolutely no idea what I was looking at.

The mechanic in the shop had made it look very simple. You raised the hood, you leaned in and snatched off the oil filter and then did a couple of quick things to it and put it back. And *voila*, your car was running again.

I got the hood open all right, and I leaned in just fine, and I even took the oil filter off with no problem.

But when it came to doing a couple of quick things to it, my brain was as dead as the motor. That was the part I hadn't picked up from the mechanic. Those couple of quick things.

I started shaking the oil filter. Don't ask me why. I had it under the protection of the hood to keep it dry and shook it left and shook it right and shook it high and shook it low. I figured that maybe some kind of invisible cosmic forces would come into play here and the engine would start as soon as I gave the ignition key a little turn.

I closed the hood and ran back through the slashing rain, opened the door and crawled inside.

"God, it's incredible out there."

Only then did I get a real good look at Laura and only then did I see that she looked sick, like the time we both picked up a slight case of ptomaine poisoning at her friend Susan's wedding.

Except now she looked a lot sicker.

And then I saw the guy.

In the backseat.

"Who the hell are you?"

But he had questions of his own. "Your wife won't tell me if you've got an ATM card."

So it had finally happened. Our little city turned violent about fifteen years ago, during which time most honest working folks had to take their turns getting mugged, sort of like a rite of passage. But as time wore on, the muggers weren't satisfied with simply robbing their victims. Now they beat them up. And sometimes, for no reason at all, they killed them.

This guy was white, chunky, with a ragged scar on his left cheek, stupid dark eyes, a dark turtleneck sweater and a large and formidable gun. He smelled of sweat, cigarette smoke, beer and a high sweet unclean tang.

"How much can you get with your card?"

"Couple hundred."

"Yeah. Right."

"Couple hundred. I mean, we're not exactly rich people. Look at this car."

He turned to Laura. "How much can he get, babe?"

"He told you. A couple of hundred." She sounded surprisingly calm.

"One more time." He had turned back to me. "How much can you get with that card of yours?"

"I told you," I said.

You know how movie thugs are always slugging people with gun butts? Well, let me tell you something. It hurts. He hit me hard enough to draw blood, hard enough to fill my sight with darkness and blinking stars, like a planetarium ceiling, and hard enough to lay my forehead against the steering wheel.

Laura didn't scream.

She just leaned over and touched my head with her long, gentle fingers. And you know what? Even then, even suffering from what might be a concussion, I had this image of Laura's fingers touching Chris Tomlin's head this way. Ain't jealousy grand?

"Now," said the voice in the backseat, "let's talk."

Neither of us paid him much attention for a minute or so. Laura helped me sit back in the seat. She took her handkerchief and daubed it against the back of my head.

"You didn't have to hit him."

"Now maybe he'll tell me the truth."

"Four or five hundred," she said. "That's how much we can get. And don't hit him again. Don't lay a finger on him."

"The mama lion fights for her little cub. That's nice." He leaned forward and put the end of the gun directly against my ear. "You're gonna have to go back out in that nasty ole rain. There's an ATM machine down at the west end of this block and around the corner. You go down there and get me five hundred dollars and then you haul your ass right back. I'll be waiting right here with your exceedingly good-looking wife. And with my gun."

"Where did you ever learn a word like exceedingly?" I said.

"What the hell's that supposed to mean?"

"I was just curious."

"If it's any of your goddamned business, my cell-mate had one of them improve your vocabulary books."

I glanced at Laura. She still looked scared but she also looked a little bit angry. For us, five hundred dollars was a lot of money.

And now a robber who used the word "exceedingly" was going to take every last dime of it.

"Go get it," he said.

I reached over to touch Laura's hand as reassuringly as possible, and that was when I noticed it.

The white number ten envelope.

The one Chris had sent her.

I stared at it a long moment and then raised my eyes to meet hers.

"I was going to tell you about it."

I shook my head. "I shouldn't have looked in your drawer."

"No, you shouldn't have. But I still owe you an explanation."

"What the hell are you two talking about?"

"Nothing that's exceedingly interesting," I said, and opened the door, and dangled a leg out and then had the rest of my body follow the leg.

"You got five minutes, you understand?" the man said.

I nodded and glanced at Laura. "I love you."

"I'm sorry about the letter."

"You know the funny thing? I was hiding your present, that's how I found it. I was going to tuck it in your underwear drawer and have you find them. You know, the pearls."

"You got me the pearl necklace?"

"Uh-huh."

"Oh, honey, that's so sweet."

"Go get the goddamned money," the man said, "and get it fast."

"I'll be right back," I said to Laura and blew her a little kiss.

If I hadn't been sodden before, I certainly was now.

There were two brick buildings facing each other across a narrow alley. Most people drove up to this particular ATM machine because it was housed in a deep indentation that faced the alley. It could also accommodate foot traffic.

What it didn't do was give you much protection from the storm.

By now, I was sneezing and feeling a scratchiness in my throat. Bad sinuses. My whole family.

I walked up to the oasis of light and technology in this ancient and wild neighborhood, took out my wallet and inserted my ATM card.

It was all very casual, especially considering the fact that Laura was being held hostage.

The card would go in. The money would come out. The thief would get his loot. Laura and I would dash to the nearest phone and call the police.

Except I couldn't remember my secret pin number.

If I had to estimate how many times I'd used this card, I'd put it at probably a thousand or so.

So how, after all those times, could I now forget the pin number?

Panic. That's what was wrong. I was so scared that Laura would be hurt that I couldn't think clearly.

Deep breaths. There.

Now. Think. Clearly.

Just relax and your pin number will come back to you. No problem.

That was when I noticed the slight black man in the rain parka standing just to the left of me. In the rain. With a gun in his hand.

"You wanna die?"

"Oh, shit. You've got to be kidding. You're a goddamned thief?"

"Yes, and I ain't ashamed of it, either, man."

I thought of explaining it to him, explaining that another thief already had first dibs on the proceeds of my bank account—that is, if I could ever remember the pin number but he didn't seem to be the understanding type at all. In fact, he looked even more desperate and crazy than the man who was holding Laura.

"How much can you take out?"

"I can't give it to you."

"You see this gun, man?"

"Yeah. I see it."

"You know what happens if you don't crank some serious money out for me?"

I had to explain after all. ". . . so, you see, I can't give it to you."

"What the hell's that supposed to mean?"

"Somebody's already got dibs on it."

"Dibs? What the hell does 'dibs' mean?"

"It means another robber has already spoken for this money."

He looked at me carefully. "You're crazy, man. You really are. But that don't mean I won't shoot you."

"And there's one more thing."

"What?"

"I can't remember my pin number."

"Bullshit."

"It's true. That's why I've been standing here. My mind's a blank."

"You gotta relax, man."

"I know that. But it's kind of hard. You've got a gun and so does the other guy."

"There's really some other dude holdin' your old lady?"

"Right."

He grinned with exceedingly bad teeth. "You got yourself a real problem, dude."

I closed my eyes.

I must have spent my five minutes already.

Would he really kill Laura?

"You tried deep breathin'?"

"Yeah."

"And that didn't work?"

"Huh-uh."

"You tried makin' your mind go blank for a little bit?"

"That didn't work, either."

He pushed the gun right into my face. "I ain't got much time, man."

"I can't give you the money, anyway."

"You ain't gonna be much use to your old lady if you got six or seven bullet holes in you."

"God!"

"What's wrong?"

My pin number had popped into my head.

Nothing like a gun in your face to jog your memory.

I dove for the ATM machine.

And started punching buttons.

The right buttons.

"Listen," I said as I cranked away, "I really can't give you this money."

"Right."

"I mean, I would if I could but the guy would never believe me if I told him some other crook had taken it. No offense, 'crook' I mean."

"Here it comes."

"I'm serious. You can't have it."

"Pretty, pretty Yankee dollars. Praise the Lord."

The plastic cover opened and the machine began spitting out green Yankee dollars.

And that's when he slugged me on the back of the head.

The guy back in the car had hit me but it had been nothing like this.

This time, the field of black floating in front of my eyes didn't even have stars. This time, hot shooting pain traveled from the point of impact near the top of my skull all the way down into my neck and shoulders. This time, my knees gave out immediately.

Pavement. Hard. Wet. Smelling of cold rain. And still the darkness. Total darkness. I had a moment of panic. Had I been blinded for life? I wanted to be angry but I was too disoriented. Pain. Cold. Darkness.

And then I felt his hands tearing the money from mine.

I had to hold on to it. Had to. Otherwise Laura would be injured. Or killed.

The kick landed hard just above my sternum. Stars suddenly appeared in the field of black. His foot seemed to have jarred them loose.

More pain. But now there was anger. I blindly lashed out and grabbed his trouser leg, clung to it, forcing him to drag me down the sidewalk as he tried to get away. I don't know how many names I called him, some of them probably didn't even make sense, I just clung to his leg, exulting in his rage, in his inability to get rid of me.

Then he leaned down and grabbed a handful of my hair and pulled so hard I screamed. And inadvertently let go of his leg.

And then I heard his footsteps, retreating, retreating, and felt the rain start slashing at me again. He had dragged me out from beneath the protection of the ATM overhang.

I struggled to get up. It wasn't easy. I still couldn't see. And every time I tried to stand, I was overcome by dizziness and a faint nausea.

But I kept thinking of Laura. And kept pushing myself to my feet, no matter how much pain pounded in my head, no matter how I started to pitch forward and collapse again.

By the time I got to my feet, and fell against the rough brick of the building for support, my eyesight was back. Funny how much you take it for granted. It's terrifying when it's gone.

I looked at the oasis of light in the gloom. At the foot of the

ATM was my bank card. I wobbled over and picked it up. I knew that I'd taken out my allotted amount for the day but I decided to try and see if the cosmic forces were with me for once.

They weren't.

The only thing I got from the machine was a snotty little note saying that I'd have to contact my personal banker if I wanted to receive more money.

A) I had no idea who this personal banker was, and

B) I doubted if he would be happy if I called him at home on such a rainy night even if I did have his name and number.

Then I did what any red-blooded American would do. I started kicking the machine. Kicking hard. Kicking obsessively. Until my toes started to hurt.

I stood for a long moment in the rain, letting it pour down on me, feeling as if I were melting like a wax statue in the hot sun. I became one with the drumming and thrumming and pounding of it all.

There was only one thing I could do now.

I took off running back to the car. To Laura. And the man with the gun.

I broke into a crazy grin when I saw the car. I could see Laura's profile in the gloom. She was still alive.

I reached the driver's door, opened it up and pitched myself inside.

"My God, what happened to you?" Laura said. "Did somebody beat you up?"

The man with the gun was a little less sympathetic. "Where the hell's the money?"

I decided to answer both questions at once. "I couldn't remember my pin number so I had to stand there for a while. And then this guy—this black guy—he came out of nowhere and he had a gun and then he made me give him the money." I looked back at the man with the gun. "I couldn't help it. I told him that you had first dibs on the money but he didn't care."

"You expect me to believe that crap?"

"Honest to God. That's what happened."

He looked at me and smiled. And then put the gun right up

against Laura's head. "You want me to show you what's gonna happen here if you're not back in five minutes with the money?"

I looked at Laura. "God, honey, I'm telling the truth. About the guy with the gun."

"I know."

"I'm sorry." I glanced forlornly out the window at the rain filling the curbs. "I'll get the money. Somehow."

I opened the door again. And then noticed the white envelope still sitting on her lap. "I'm sorry I didn't trust you, sweetheart."

She was scared, that was easy enough to see, but she forced herself to focus and smile at me. "I love you, honey."

"Get the hell out of here and get that money," said the man with the gun.

"I knew you wouldn't believe me."

"You heard what I said. Get going."

I reached over and took Laura's hand gently. "I'll get the money, sweetheart. I promise."

I got out of the car and started walking again. Then trotting. Then flat-out running. My head was still pounding with pain but I didn't care. I had to get the money. Somehow. Somewhere.

I didn't even know where I was going. I was just running. It was better than standing still and contemplating what the guy with the gun might do.

I reached the corner and looked down the block where the ATM was located.

A car came from behind me, its headlights stabbing through the silver sheets of night rain. It moved on past me. When it came even with the lights of the ATM machine, it turned an abrupt left and headed for the machine.

Guy inside his car. Nice and warm and dry. Inserts his card, gets all the money he wants, and then drives on to do a lot of fun things with his nice and warm and dry evening.

While I stood out here in the soaking rain and—

Of course, I thought.

Of course.

There was only one thing I could do.

I started running, really running, splashing through puddles and tripping and nearly falling down. But nothing could stop me.

The bald man had parked too far away from the ATM to do his banking from the car. He backed up and gave it another try. He was concentrating on backing up so I didn't have much trouble opening the passenger door and slipping in.

"What the—" he started to say as he became aware of me.

"Stick up."

"What?"

"I'm robbing you."

"Oh, man, that's all I need. I've had a really crummy day today, mister," he said. "I knew I never should've come in this neighborhood but I was in a hurry and—"

"You want to hear about my bad day, mister? Huh?"

I raised the coat of my raincoat, hoping that he would think that I was pointing a gun at him.

He looked down at my coat-draped fist and said, "You can't get a whole hell of a lot of money out of these ATM machines."

"You can get three hundred and that's good enough."

"What if I don't have three hundred?"

"New car. Nice new suit. Maybe twenty CDs in that box there. You've got three hundred. Easy."

"I work hard for my money."

"So do I."

"What if I told you I don't believe you've got a gun in there?"

"Then I'd say fine. And then I'd kill you."

"You don't look like a stick-up guy."

"And you don't look like a guy who's stupid enough to get himself shot over three hundred dollars."

"I have to back up again. So I can get close."

"Back up. But go easy."

"Some goddamned birthday this is."

"It's your birthday?"

"Yeah. Ain't that a bitch?"

He backed up, pulled forward again, got right up next to the ATM, pulled out his card and went to work.

The money came out with no problem. He handed it over to me.

"You have a pencil and paper?"

"What?"

"Something you can write with?"

"Oh. Yeah. Why?"

"I want you to write down your name and address."

"For what?"

"Because tomorrow morning I'm going to put three hundred dollars in an envelope and mail it to you."

"Are you some kind of crazy drug addict or what?"

"Just write down your name and address."

He shook his head. "Not only do I get robbed, I get robbed by some goddamned fruitcake."

But he wrote down his name and address, probably thinking I'd shoot him if he didn't.

"I appreciate the loan," I said, getting out of his car.

"Loan? You tell the cops it was a 'loan' and see what they say."

"Hope the rest of your day goes better," I said, and slammed the door.

And I hope the rest of my day goes better, too, I thought.

"Good thing you got back here when you did," the man with the gun said. "I was just about to waste her."

"Spare me the macho crap, all right?" I said. I was getting cranky. The rain. The cold. The fear. And then having to commit a felony to get the cash I needed—and putting fear into a perfectly decent citizen who'd been having a very bad day himself.

I handed the money over to him. "Now you can go," I said.

He counted it in hard, harsh grunts, like a pig rutting in the mud.

"Three goddamned hundred. It was supposed to be four. Or five."

"I guess you'll just have to shoot us, then, huh?"

Laura gave me a frantic look and then dug her nails into my hands. Obviously, like the man I'd just left at the ATM, she thought I had lost what little of my senses I had left.

"I wouldn't push it, punk," the man with the gun said. "Because I just might shoot you yet."

He leaned forward from the backseat and said, "Lemme see your purse, babe."

Laura looked at me. I nodded. She handed him her purse.

More rutting sounds as he went through it.

"Twenty-six bucks?"

"I'm sorry," Laura said.

"Where're your credit cards?"

"We don't have credit cards. It's too tempting to use them. We're saving for a house."

"Ain't that sweet!"

He pitched the purse over the front seat and opened the back door.

Chill. Fog. Rain.

"You got a jerk for a husband, babe, I mean, just in case you haven't figured that out already."

Then he slammed the door and was gone.

"You were really going to tear it up?"

"Or let you tear it up. Whichever you preferred. I mean, I know you think I still have this thing for Chris but I really don't. I was going to prove it to you by showing you the letter tonight and letting you do whatever you wanted with it."

We were in bed, three hours after getting our car towed to a station, the tow truck giving us a ride home.

The rain had quit an hour ago. Now there were just icy winds. But it was snug and warm in the bed of my one true love and icy winds didn't bother me at all.

"I'm sorry," I said, "about being so jealous."

"And I'm sorry about hiding the letter. It made you think I was going to take him up on his offer. But I really don't have any desire to see him at all."

Then we kind of just lay back and listened to the wind for a time.

And she started getting affectionate, her foot rubbing my foot, her hand taking my hand.

And then in the darkness, she said, "Would you like to make love?"

"Would I?" I laughed. "Would I?"

And then I rolled over and we began kissing and then I began running my fingers through her long dark hair and then I suddenly realized that—

"What's wrong?" she said, as I rolled away from her, flat on my back, staring at the ceiling.

"Let's just go to sleep."

"God, honey, I want to know what's going on. Here we are making out and then all of a sudden you stop."

"Oh God," I said. "What a day this has been." I sighed and prepared myself for the ultimate in manly humiliation. "Remember that time when Rick's sister got married?"

"Uh-huh."

"And I got real drunk?"

"Uh-huh."

"And that night we tried—well, we tried to make love but I couldn't?"

"Uh-huh." She was silent a long moment. Then, "Oh, God, you mean, the same thing happened to you just now?"

"Uh-huh," I said.

"Oh, honey, I'm sorry."

"The perfect ending to the perfect day," I said.

"First you find that letter from Chris—"

"And then I can't concentrate on my job—"

"And then Ms. Sandstrom threatens to fire you—"

"And then a man sticks us up—"

"And then you have to stick up another man—"

"And then we come home and go to bed and—" I sighed. "I think I'll just roll over and go to sleep."

"Good idea, honey. That's what we both need. A good night's sleep."

"I love you, sweetheart," I said. "I'm sorry I wasn't able to . . . well, you know."

"It's fine, sweetie. It happens to every man once in a while."

"It's just one of those days," I said.

"And one of those nights," she said.

✿　✿　✿

But you know what? Some time later, the grandfather clock in the living room woke me as it tolled twelve midnight, and when I rolled over to see how Laura was doing, she was wide awake and took me in her sweet warm arms, and I didn't have any trouble at all showing her how grateful I was.

It was a brand-new day . . . and when I finally got around to breakfast, the first thing I did was lift the horoscope section from the paper . . . and drop it, unread, into the wastebasket.

No more snooping in drawers . . . and no more bad-luck horoscopes.

SURROGATE

That spring I began following fourteen-year-old David Mallory home from school.

I always borrowed a car from one of the other lawyers in the firm, and I always wore a hat with the brim low over my face.

With all the talk of child molesters in the news, I knew what people would think if I ever got caught trailing him. To make things worse, his father, Stephen, was my racquetball partner three days a week. We lived on the same upwardly mobile street, attended the same upwardly mobile church, and drove the same kind of upwardly mobile car. Their family BMW was blue; ours was red.

Most days, David went straight home from school, a ten-block walk that skirted a shaggy wooded area where the neighborhood kids liked to play.

After a week of tailing him, I was about to give up. Then came the rainy day when he met the tall boy at the south end of the woods and handed him what appeared to be a white number ten business envelope.

I used my binoculars so I could get a better look at the other boy. He was blond, freckled and thin, though it was a sinewy thinness that suggested both strength and speed. He looked to be about fourteen but there was an anger and cunning in his face that you don't often see in kids, not in our kind of neighborhood anyway.

He opened the envelope, peeked inside and gave David an angry shove. I couldn't hear their words but I didn't need to. The tall boy was disappointed by what he'd found inside and was obviously making this clear to David.

He lashed out and grabbed David by the jacket and hoisted him half a foot off the ground. He flung the envelope to the ground and then slapped David twice hard across the mouth.

Then he let David fall in a heap to the ground.

The only sounds were the light rain thrumming on my borrowed car and the faint irregular pulse of an engine badly in need of a tune-up. In the rain and the faint fog, the tall boy stood over fallen David, still cursing him.

He brought a leg up and kicked David in the stomach.

David went backwards, splayed face up on the winter brown grass.

The other boy bent over him, shaking the white envelope in David's face.

The tall boy left abruptly, with no further words, with no warning of any sort. He turned and ran at a trot into the woods, and then vanished, seeming to be as much a creature of the forest as a fox.

David lay in the rain for a long time. I doubted he was badly hurt. Even the kick couldn't have done all that much damage. But he was probably embarrassed and afraid, the way I'd always been at his age when bullies had taken their turn with me. Even with nobody around to witness your beating, you still felt humiliated.

Eventually, he struggled to his feet. He was soaked. He took a few tentative steps and then fell into his regular pace. He was all right.

He reached the sidewalk and then finished the rest of the walk home.

In the next three weeks, he met the blond boy three more times. Always on Wednesdays. All three times, David handed over a white number ten business envelope and the blond boy quickly peered inside. David had obviously done what the other boy had demanded. The boy accepted the envelope, said a few words I couldn't hear of course, and then went back into the same dark woods he'd come from.

Who was he? Where did he live? What was in the envelopes David was giving him?

A week later, I got to the site where they met and hid myself in the woods, far to the right of the narrow dirt path the blond boy always used. I got there half an hour early.

He came up from the wide creek that wound through the center of the woods. He moved as usual at a trot, showing no signs of exertion at all. On a sunny spring day like this one, he wore only a T-shirt and a pair of jeans.

He reached the mouth of the woods, stopped, and within a minute or so, David was there, looking nervous as usual, handing over the white envelope as if in appeasement to a dark god who might smite him dead at any moment.

As I hunched down behind the low-hanging branches of a jack pine, I saw an American Copper butterfly light on a green bush, and I felt a terrible and sudden melancholy, thinking of what had happened in the past and how my wife still woke up sobbing at night, and what surely lay before us in the days ahead. I wanted the peace and wisdom of the butterfly for my own, to know the succor of sunlight and release from my rage.

But all I could do was follow the boy back into the woods, into the shifting shadows and ripe spring scents in which squirrels and stray kittens and birds slept and romped and luxuriated.

The boy went back into his trot, indifferent to the branches slapping him on face and arms.

He came to a fork and went west, toward the wide muddy creek.

After a few more minutes, I lost him completely. I couldn't even hear him disturb the undergrowth.

I was just inching my way to the clearing on the bank above the creek when he reappeared.

He climbed without pause to the very top of the railroad truss bridge that lay across the fast-moving creek. He scurried up to the top chord, which rose twenty feet above the tracks below, and stood there gaping at the countryside.

He was king-of-the-hill up there, taking a package of cigarettes from his jeans pocket and lighting up, looking over the world below with his customary sneer.

A train came soon enough, twenty-six swaying rattling boxcars pulled by an engine car running hard and fast and invincible.

This was the nightmare shared by every parent in our neighborhood—that one of our children (even though strictly forbidden to play anywhere near the bridge) would fall into the path of the pitiless engine and be killed instantly.

The train roared through.

The entire bridge swayed.

But the boy, still enjoying his cigarette, rode the top span of the bridge as if he were aboard a bucking bronc. He stood upright, swaying with the power beneath him, becoming one with its rhythm.

And then the train was gone, taking its furious sounds with it, till all you could hear in the silence after was the incomprehensible chitter and chatter of birds.

From my hiding place, I watched the boy a few more minutes, trying to make some sense of that sullen, angry face and insolent stance. But I could make no sense of him at all.

Soon after, I left.

Next afternoon, it rained again. I parked two blocks down from school.

When I saw David I honked my horn. Today I was in my own car, and without hat, so he recognized me right away.

He came over and opened the door.

"Hi, Mr. Rhodes."

"Hi, David. Get in and I'll give you a ride home."

He looked confused for a moment. What was I doing parked along the street this way? he had to be wondering.

"Really, Mr. Rhodes, I can walk."

"C'mon, David, get in. It's going to start raining again anytime now."

He still seemed apprehensive but he reluctantly got in and closed the door.

I pulled away from the curb, out into traffic.

"So how've you been, David?"

"Oh, you know, fine, I guess."

"Your dad tells me you're getting good grades."

"Yeah, well, you know." He half smiled, embarrassed.

"Makes me think about Jeff. You know, how he'd be doing in school these days."

I looked over at David. I knew he'd get uncomfortable and start squirming. Which is just what he did.

"He'd be doing just great, Jeff would," David said. "He really would," David added, as if he needed to convince me of it.

"You ever think about him?"

"Sure. He was my best friend."

"He felt the same way about you."

David was getting uncomfortable again. Staring out the window.

His house was approaching. I sped up.

"Hey, Mr. Rhodes, we're goin' right past my house."

"Yeah, I guess we are."

"Mr. Rhodes, I'm gettin' kind of nervous, I mean, I wish you'd just let me out right here."

I stared at him a long moment and said, "David, you're going to tell me what happened to Jeff or I'm going to hurt you. Hurt you very badly. Do you understand?"

He got pale. He was just a kid.

I said, "I want to know what's in that envelope you're giving that blond kid every Wednesday, and I want to know who the blond kid is. Though I think I've got a pretty good idea."

I made it as pleasant as possible. I took him to a Pizza Hut in a nearby mall. We had a double-cheese and two large Cokes and eventually he told me all about it.

He didn't show up Sunday, Monday or Tuesday, the blond kid, but Wednesday, just as I reached my hiding place back of the clearing, I saw him climb the bridge and stand on top in that swaggering way of his.

I watched him for a few moments and then I walked into the clearing and through the buffalo grass to the bridge.

I wasn't nearly as good at it as the kid, of course. He was younger; the monkey in him hadn't yet fled.

He watched me. He watched me very carefully and very curiously.

He wasn't afraid. If he had been, he'd have walked down the other side and run into the woods.

No. He just stood there smoking his cigarette watching me as I finally reached the top chord and started across to him.

For the first time, he showed some anxiety as to who I might be. "Nice up here, ain't it?" he said.

But I didn't hear him. I heard only the approaching train.

"Don't usually see guys your age up here," he said, smirking a little about my thirty-eight years.

The train, right on time according to what I'd been able to observe over the past week, rumbled toward us. You could feel its power shuddering through the iron box of bridge.

The blond kid looked behind him. At the other end of the bridge. The free end. He looked as if he wanted to turn and run now.

The big bass horn of the train set the forest animals to scurrying. And then the engine came hurtling around the bend into the straightaway across the bridge.

The kid finally figured out what I was going to do but he was too late.

I grabbed him by the hair, jerked him to me and then held him till the train was twenty yards from crossing the bridge. We were up too high for anybody in the train to see us. He smelled of sweat and heat and dirt and cigarette smoke.

His mouth swore at me but I couldn't hear in all the noise. He fought but he was no match for me, not at all.

I shoved him downward just at the right moment.

I suppose I should have looked away but I didn't. I watched every moment of it.

How he hit the tracks on his back, legs flung across one track, head and arms across the opposite track.

He screamed but he was in pantomime. He tried to scramble to his feet but it was too late.

The train lifted him and punted him into one side of the bridge. When his body collided with the iron, he splattered. That's the only way to describe it. Splattered.

Then the train was gone, receding, receding, and there was just birdsong and sunlight and the fast muddy movement of the creek far below, and the ragged bloody remains of what had once been a human boy. The animals would come soon, and feast on it.

Just as I was getting in bed that night, my wife came in and said, "My God, Charlie, on the news."

She was ashen.

"What about the news?" I said, sliding between the covers.

"A boy. Fourteen years old. Playing on that railroad bridge. He—was killed just the way Jeff was."

She started sobbing so I held her. She was a good true woman and good true mother and good true wife. Nothing bad should have happened to her. Not ever.

I suppose that was why I never quit looking into our son's "accidental" death. Going through his things one day up in the attic, I'd come across a note he'd written to David Mallory, saying that even though David was mad at Jeff because Jeff kissed his girlfriend . . . Jeff didn't think it was fair that David would hire Lon McKenzie to beat him up.

David had finally told me all about it that afternoon at the Pizza Hut. The blond kid was one Lon McKenzie from the steeltown section of the city, a bully who not only took pride in his work but charged for it. If you wanted somebody taken care of, you hired Lon to do it and if the price was right, your enemy would receive a beating that he would remember for a long, long time.

A hit man for the junior high set.

❀ ❀ ❀

Lon had probably followed Jeff to the bridge, where Jeff—despite our constant complaints—frequently played. Jeff loved to sit up on the top span and look out at the woods.

Afterward, McKenzie had bragged to David that he'd killed Jeff on purpose. He'd never seen anybody die before and he was curious. Then he'd started blackmailing David. Twenty-five dollars a week—or McKenzie would go to the police and implicate David in Jeff's death. David had been scared and guilty enough to go along, saving every bit of his allowance to pay McKenzie.

Now it was all done. I suppose I should have hated David but I couldn't quite. Foolish as he'd been, he hadn't wanted to see Jeff die.

My wife turned off the light and got in next to me and clung to me in the darkness the way she would cling to a life preserver.

"I just keep thinking of that boy's poor parents," she said, starting to cry again. "It must be terrible for them."

"Yeah," I said there in the darkness, seeing again the train lift Lon McKenzie's body and boot it against the bridge, "yeah, it must be awful for them."

THE REASON WHY

I'm scared."
"This was your idea, Karen."
"You scared?"
"No."
"You bastard."
"Because I'm not scared I'm a bastard?"
"You not being scared means you don't believe me."
"Well."
"See. I knew it."
"What?"
"Just the way you said 'Well.' You bastard."

I sighed and looked out at the big redbrick building that sprawled over a quarter mile of spring grass turned silver by a fat June moon. Twenty-five years ago a 1950 Ford fastback had sat in the adjacent parking lot. Mine for two summers of grocery store work.

We were sitting in her car, a Volvo she'd cadged from her last marriage settlement, number four if you're interested, and sharing a pint of bourbon the way we used to in high school when we'd been more than friends but never quite lovers.

The occasion tonight was our twenty-fifth class reunion. But there was another occasion, too. In our senior year a boy named Michael Brandon had jumped off a steep clay cliff called Pierce Point to his death on the winding river road below. Suicide. That, anyway, had been the official version.

A month ago Karen Lane (she had gone back to her maiden name these days, the Karen Lane-Cummings-Todd-Brown-LeMay getting a tad too long) had called to see if I wanted to go to dinner and I said yes, if I could bring Donna along, but then Donna surprised me by saying she didn't care to go along, that by now we should be at a point in our relationship where we trusted each other ("God, Dwyer, I don't even look at other men, not for very long anyway, you know?"), and Karen and I had had dinner and she'd had many drinks, enough that I saw she had a problem, and then she'd told me about something that had troubled her for a long time. . . .

In senior year she'd gone to a party and gotten sick on wine and stumbled out to somebody's backyard to throw up and it was there she'd overheard the three boys talking. They were earnestly discussing what happened to Michael Brandon the previous week and they were even more earnestly discussing what would happen to them if "anybody ever really found out the truth."

"It's bothered me all these years," she'd said over dinner a month earlier. "They murdered him and they got away with it."

"Why didn't you tell the police?"

"I didn't think they'd believe me."

"Why not?"

She shrugged and put her lovely little face down, dark hair covering her features. Whenever she put her face down that way it meant that she didn't want to tell you a lie so she'd just as soon talk about something else.

"Why not, Karen?"

"Because of where we came from. The Highlands."

The Highlands is an area that used to ring the iron foundries and factories of this city. Way before pollution became a fashionable concern, you could stand on your front porch and see a peculiarly beautiful orange haze on the sky every dusk. The Highlands had bars where men lost ears, eyes, and fingers in just garden-variety fights, and streets where nobody sane ever walked after dark, not even cops unless they were in pairs. But it wasn't the phys-ical violence you remembered so much as the emotional violence of poverty. You get tired of hearing your mother scream because there isn't enough money for food and hearing your father scream back because there's nothing he can do about it. Nothing.

Karen Lane and I had come from the Highlands, but we were smarter and, in her case, better looking than most of the people from the area, so when we went to Wilson High School—one of those nightmare conglomerates that shoves the poorest kids in a city in with the richest—we didn't do badly for ourselves. By senior year we found ourselves hanging out with the sons and daughters of bankers and doctors and city officials and lawyers and riding around in new Impala convertibles and attending an occasional party where you saw an actual maid. But wherever we went, we'd manage for at least a few minutes to get away from our dates and talk to each other. What we were doing, of course, was trying to comfort ourselves. We shared terrible and confusing feelings—pride that we were acceptable to those we saw as glamorous, shame that we felt disgrace for being from the Highlands and having fathers who worked in factories and mothers who went to Mass as often as nuns and brothers and sisters who were doomed to punching the clock and yelling at ragged kids in the cold factory dusk. (You never real-ize what a toll such shame takes till you see your father's waxen face there in the years-later casket.)

That was the big secret we shared, of course, Karen and I, that we were going to get out, leave the place once and for all. And her brown eyes never sparkled more Christmas-morning bright than at those moments when it all was ahead of us, money, sex, endless thrills, immortality. She had the kind of clean good looks brought out best by a blue cardigan with a line of white button-down shirt at the top and a brown suede car coat over her slender shoulders and moderately tight jeans displaying her quietly artful ass. Nothing splashy about her. She had the sort of face that snuck up on you. You had the impression you were talking to a pretty but in no way spectacular girl, and then all of a sudden you saw how the eyes burned with sad humor and how wry the mouth got at certain times and how the freckles enhanced rather than detracted from her beauty and by then of course you were hopelessly entangled. Hopelessly.

This wasn't just my opinion, either. I mentioned four divorce settlements. True facts. Karen was one of those prizes that powerful and rich men like to collect with the understanding that it's only something you hold in trust, like a yachting cup. So, in her time, she'd been an ornament for a professional football player (her college beau), an orthodontist ("I think he used to have sexual fantasies about Barry Goldwater"), the owner of a large commuter airline ("I slept with half his pilots; it was kind of a company benefit"), and a sixty-nine-year-old millionaire who was dying of heart disease ("He used to have me sit next to his bedside and just hold his hand—the weird thing was that of all of them, I loved him, I really did—and his eyes would be closed and then every once in a while tears would start streaming down his cheeks as if he was remembering something that really filled him with remorse; he was really a sweetie, but then cancer got him before the heart disease and I never did find out what he regretted so much, I mean if it was about his son or his wife or what"), and now she was comfortably fixed for the rest of her life and if the crow's feet were a little more pronounced around eyes and mouth and if the slenderness was just a trifle too slender (she weighed, at five-three, maybe ninety pounds and kept a variety of diet books in her big sunny kitchen), she was a damn good-looking woman nonetheless, the world's absurdity catalogued and evaluated in a gaze that managed to be both weary and impish, with a laugh that was knowing without being cynical.

So now she wanted to play detective.

I had some more bourbon from the pint—it burned beautifully—and said, "If I had your money, you know what I'd do?"

"Buy yourself a new shirt?"

"You don't like my shirt?"

"I didn't know you had this thing about Hawaii."

"If I had your money I'd just forget about all of this."

"I thought cops were sworn to uphold the right and the true."

"I'm an ex-cop."

"You wear a uniform."

"That's for the American Security Agency."

She sighed. "So I shouldn't have sent the letters?"

"No."

"Well, if they're guilty, they'll show up at Pierce Point tonight."

"Not necessarily."

"Why?"

"Maybe they'll know it's a trap. And not do anything."

She nodded to the school. "You hear that?"

"What?"

"The song?"

It was Bobby Vinton's "Roses Are Red."

"I remember one party when we both hated our dates and we ended up dancing to that over and over again. Somebody's basement. You remember?"

"Sort of, I guess," I said.

"Good. Let's go in the gym and then we can dance to it again."

Donna, my lady friend, was out of town attending an advertising convention. I hoped she wasn't going to dance with anybody else because it would sure make me mad.

I started to open the door and she said, "I want to ask you a question."

"What?" I sensed what it was going to be so I kept my eyes on the parking lot.

"Turn around and look at me."

I turned around and looked at her. "Okay."

"Since the time we had dinner a month or so ago I've started receiving brochures from Alcoholics Anonymous in the mail. If you were having them sent to me, would you be honest enough to tell me?"

"Yes, I would."

"Are you having them sent to me?"

"Yes, I am."

"You think I'm a lush?"

"Don't you?"

"I asked you first."

So we went into the gym and danced.

Crepe of red and white, the school colors, draped the ceiling; the stage was a cave of white light on which stood four balding fat guys with spit curls and shimmery gold lamé dinner jackets (could these be the illegitimate sons of Bill Haley?) playing guitars, drum, and saxophone; on the dance floor couples who'd lost hair, teeth, jaw lines, courage and energy (everything, it seemed, but weight) danced to lame cover versions of "Breaking up Is Hard to Do" and "Sheila," "Run-around Sue" and "Running Scared" (tonight's lead singer sensibly not even trying Roy Orbison's beautiful falsetto) and then, they broke into a medley of dance tunes—everything from "Locomotion" to "The Peppermint Twist"—and the place went a little crazy, and I went right along with it.

"Come on," I said.

"Great."

We went out there and we burned ass. We'd both agreed not to dress up for the occasion so we were ready for this. I wore the Hawaiian shirt she found so despicable plus a blue blazer, white socks and cordovan penny-loafers. She wore a salmon-colored Merikani shirt belted at the waist and tan cotton fatigue pants and, sweet Christ, she was so adorable half the guys in the place did the kind of double takes usually reserved for somebody outrageous or famous.

Over the blasting music, I shouted, "Everybody's watching you!"

She shouted right back, "I know! Isn't it wonderful?"

The medley went twenty minutes and could easily have been confused with an aerobics session. By the end I was sopping and wishing I was carrying ten or fifteen pounds less and sometimes feeling guilty because I was having too much fun (I just hoped Donna, probably having too much fun, too, was feeling guilty), and then finally it ended and mate fell into the arms of mate, hanging on to stave off sheer collapse.

Then the head Bill Haley clone said, "Okay, now we're going to do a ballad medley," so then we got everybody from Johnny Mathis to Connie Francis and we couldn't resist that, so I moved her around the floor with clumsy pleasure and she moved me right back with equally clumsy pleasure. "You know something?" I said.

"We're both shitty dancers?"

"Right."

But we kept on, of course, laughing and whirling a few times, and then coming tighter together and just holding each other silently for a time, two human beings getting older and scared about getting older, remembering some things and trying to forget others and trying to make sense of an existence that ultimately made sense to nobody, and then she said, "There's one of them."

I didn't have to ask her what "them" referred to. Until now she'd refused to identify any of the three people she'd sent the letters to.

At first I didn't recognize him. He had almost white hair and a tan so dark it looked fake. He wore a black dinner jacket with a lacy shirt and a black bow tie. He didn't seem to have put on a pound in the quarter century since I'd last seen him.

"Ted Forester?"

"Forester," she said. "He's president of the same savings and loan his father was president of."

"Who are the other two?"

"Why don't we get some punch?"

"The kiddie kind?"

"You could really make me mad with all this lecturing about alcoholism."

"If you're really not a lush then you won't mind getting the kiddie kind."

"My friend, Sigmund Fraud."

We had a couple of pink punches and caught our respective breaths and squinted in the gloom at name tags to see who we were saying hello to and realized all the terrible things you realize at high school reunions, namely that people who thought they were better than you still think that way, and that all the sad people you feared for—the ones with blackheads and low IQs and lame left legs and walleyes and lisps and every other sort of unfair infirmity people get stuck with—generally turned out to be deserving of your fear, for there was melancholy in their eyes tonight that spoke of failures of every sort, and you wanted to go up and say something to them (I wanted to go up to nervous Karl Carberry, who used to twitch—his whole body twitched—and throw my arm around him and tell him what a neat guy he was, tell him there was no reason whatsoever for his twitching, grant him peace and self-esteem and at least a modicum of hope; if he needed a woman, get him a woman, too), but of course you didn't do that, you didn't go up, you just made edgy jokes and nodded a lot and drifted on to the next piece of human carnage.

"There's number two," Karen whispered.

This one I remembered. And despised. The six-three blond movie-star looks had grown only slightly older. His blue dinner jacket just seemed to enhance his air of malicious superiority. Larry Price. His wife, Sally, was still perfect, too, though you could see in the lacquered blond hair and maybe a hint of face-lift that she'd had to work at it a little harder. A year out of high school, at a bar that took teenage IDs checked by a guy who must have been legally blind, I'd gotten drunk and told Larry that he was essentially an asshole for beating up a friend of mine who hadn't had a chance against him. I had the street boy's secret belief that I could take anybody whose father was a surgeon and whose house included a swimming pool. I had hatred, bitterness and rage going, right? Well, Larry and I went out into the parking lot, ringed by a lot of drunken spectators, and before I got off a single punch, Larry hit me with a shot that stood me straight up, giving him a great opportunity to hit me again. He hit me three times before I found his face and sent him a shot hard enough to push him back for a time. Before we could go at it again, the guy who checked IDs got himself between us. He was madder than either Larry or me. He ended the fight by taking us both by the ears (he must have trained with nuns) and dragging us out to the curb and telling neither of us to come back.

"You remember the night you fought him?"

"Yeah."

"You could have taken him, Dwyer. Those three punches he got in were just lucky."

"Yeah, that was my impression, too. Lucky."

She laughed. "I was afraid he was going to kill you."

I was going to say something smart, but then a new group of people came up and we gushed through a little social dance of nostalgia and lies and self-justifications. We talked success (at high school reunions, everybody sounds like Amway representatives at a pep rally) and the old days (nobody seems to remember all of the kids who got treated like shit for reasons they had no control over) and didn't so-and-so look great (usually this meant they'd managed to keep their toupees on straight) and introducing new spouses (we all had to explain what happened to our original mates; I said mine had been eaten by alligators in the Amazon, but nobody seemed to find that especially believable) and in the midst of all this, Karen tugged my sleeve and said, "There's the third one."

Him I recognized, too. David Haskins. He didn't look any happier than he ever had. Parent trouble was always the explanation you got for his grief back in high school. His parents had been rich, truly so, his father an importer of some kind, and their arguments so violent that they were as eagerly discussed as who was or was not pregnant. Apparently David's parents weren't getting along any better today because although the features of his face were open and friendly enough, there was still the sense of some terrible secret stooping his shoulders and keeping his smiles to furtive wretched imitations. He was a paunchy balding little man who might have been a church usher with a sour stomach.

"The Duke of Earl" started up then and there was no way we were going to let that pass so we got out on the floor; but by now, of course, we both watched the three people she'd sent letters to. Her instructions had been to meet the anonymous letter writer at nine-thirty at Pierce Point. If they were going to be there on time, they'd be leaving soon.

"You think they're going to go?"

"I doubt it, Karen."

"You still don't believe that's what I heard them say that night?"

"It was a long time ago and you were drunk."

"It's a good thing I like you because otherwise you'd be a distinct pain in the ass."

Which is when I saw all three of them go stand under one of the

glowing red Exit signs and open a fire door that led to the parking
lot.

"They're going!" she said.

"Maybe they're just having a cigarette."

"You know better, Dwyer. You know better."

Her car was in the lot on the opposite side of the gym.

"Well, it's worth the drive even if they don't show up. Pierce
Point should be nice tonight."

She squeezed against me and said, "Thanks, Dwyer. Really."

So we went and got her Volvo and went out to Pierce Point
where twenty-five years ago a shy kid named Michael Brandon had
fallen or been pushed to his death.

Apparently we were about to find out which.

The river road wound along a high wall of clay cliffs on the left and
a wide expanse of water on the right. The spring night was impossibly beautiful, one of those moments so rich with sweet odor and
even sweeter sight you wanted to take your clothes off and run
around in some kind of crazed animal circles out of sheer joy.

"You still like jazz," she said, nodding to the radio.

"I hope you didn't mind my turning the station."

"I'm kind of into country."

"I didn't get the impression you were listening."

She looked over at me. "Actually, I wasn't. I was thinking about
you sending me all of those AA pamphlets."

"It was arrogant and presumptuous and I apologize."

"No, it wasn't. It was sweet and I appreciate it."

The rest of the ride, I leaned my head back and smelled flowers
and grass and river water and watched moonglow through the elms
and oaks and birches of this new spring. There was a Dakota Staton
song, "Street of Dreams," and I wondered as always where she was
and what she was doing, she'd been so fine, maybe the most unap-
preciated jazz singer of the entire fifties.

Then we were going up a long, twisting gravel road. We pulled
up next to a big park pavilion and got out and stood in the wet grass,
and she came over and slid her arm around my waist and sort of
hugged me in a half-serious way. "This is probably crazy, isn't it?"

I sort of hugged her back in a half-serious way. "Yeah, but it's a nice night for a walk so what the hell."

"You ready?"

"Yep."

"Let's go then."

So we went up the hill to the Point itself, and first we looked out at the far side of the river where white birches glowed in the gloom and where beyond you could see the horseshoe shape of the city lights. Then we looked down, straight down the drop of two hundred feet, to the road where Michael Brandon had died.

When I heard the car starting up the road to the east, I said, "Let's get in those bushes over there."

A thick line of shrubs and second-growth timber would give us a place to hide, to watch them.

By the time we were in place, ducked down behind a wide elm and a mulberry bush, a new yellow Mercedes sedan swung into sight and stopped several yards from the edge of the Point.

A car radio played loud in the night. A Top 40 song. Three men got out. Dignified Forester, matinee-idol Price, anxiety-tight Haskins.

Forester leaned back into the car and snapped the radio off. But he left the headlights on. Forester and Price each had cans of beer. Haskins bit his nails.

They looked around in the gloom. The headlights made the darkness beyond seem much darker and the grass in its illumination much greener. Price said harshly, "I told you this was just some kind of goddamn prank. Nobody knows squat."

"He's right. He's probably right," Haskins said to Forester. Obviously he was hoping that was the case.

Forester said, "If somebody didn't know something, we would never have gotten those letters."

She moved then and I hadn't expected her to move at all. I'd been under the impression we would just sit there and listen and let them ramble and maybe in so doing reveal something useful.

But she had other ideas.

She pushed through the undergrowth and stumbled a little and got to her feet again and then walked right up to them.

"Karen!" Haskins said.

"So you did kill Michael," she said.

Price moved toward her abruptly, his hand raised. He was drunk and apparently hitting women was something he did without much trouble.

Then I stepped out from our hiding place and said, "Put your hand down, Price."

Forester said, "Dwyer."

"So," Price said, lowering his hand, "I was right, wasn't I?" He was speaking to Forester.

Forester shook his silver head. He seemed genuinely saddened. "Yes, Price, for once your cynicism is justified."

Price said, "Well, you two aren't getting a goddamned penny, do you know that?"

He lunged toward me, still a bully. But I was ready for him, wanted it. I also had the advantage of being sober. When he was two steps away, I hit him just once and very hard in the solar plexus. He backed away, eyes startled, and then he turned abruptly away.

We all stood looking at one another, pretending not to hear the sounds of violent vomiting on the other side of the splendid new Mercedes.

Forester said, "When I saw you there, Karen, I wondered if you could do it alone."

"Do what?"

"What?" Forester said. "What? Let's at least stop the games. You two want money."

"Christ," I said to Karen, who looked perplexed, "they think we're trying to shake them down."

"Shake them down?"

"Blackmail them."

"Exactly," Forester said.

Price had come back around. He was wiping his mouth with the back of his hand. In his other hand he carried a silver-plated .45, the sort of weapon professional gamblers favor.

Haskins said, "Larry, Jesus, what is that?"

"What does it look like?"

"Larry, that's how people get killed." Haskins sounded like Price's mother.

Price's eyes were on me. "Yeah, it would be terrible if Dwyer here got killed, wouldn't it?" He waved the gun at me. I didn't really think he'd shoot, but I sure was afraid he'd trip and the damn thing would go off accidentally. "You've been waiting since senior year to do that to me, haven't you, Dwyer?"

I shrugged. "I guess so, yeah."

"Well, why don't I give Forester here the gun and then you and I can try it again."

"Fine with me."

He handed Forester the .45. Forester took it all right, but what he did was toss it somewhere into the gloom surrounding the car. "Larry, if you don't straighten up here, I'll fight you myself. Do you understand me?" Forester had a certain dignity and when he spoke, his voice carried an easy authority. "There will be no more fighting, do you both understand that?"

"I agree with Ted," Karen said.

Forester, like a teacher tired of naughty children, decided to get on with the real business. "You wrote those letters, Dwyer?"

"No."

"No?"

"No. Karen wrote them."

A curious glance was exchanged by Forester and Karen.

"I guess I should have known that," Forester said.

"Jesus, Ted," Karen said, "I'm not trying to blackmail you, no matter what you think."

"Then just exactly what are you trying to do?"

She shook her lovely little head. I sensed she regretted ever writing the letters, stirring it all up again. "I just want the truth to come out about what really happened to Michael Brandon that night."

"The truth," Price said. "Isn't that goddamn touching?"

"Shut up, Larry," Haskins said.

Forester said, "You know what happened to Michael Brandon?"

"I've got a good idea," Karen said. "I overheard you three talking at a party one night."

"What did we say?"

"What?"

"What did you overhear us say?"

Karen said, "You said that you hoped nobody looked into what really happened to Michael that night."

A smile touched Forester's lips. "So on that basis you concluded that we murdered him?"

"There wasn't much else to conclude."

Price said, weaving still, leaning on the fender for support, "I don't goddamn believe this."

Forester nodded to me. "Dwyer, I'd like to have a talk with Price and Haskins here, if you don't mind. Just a few minutes." He pointed to the darkness beyond the car. "We'll walk over there. You know we won't try to get away because you'll have our car. All right?"

I looked at Karen.

She shrugged.

They left, back into the gloom, voices receding and fading into the sounds of crickets and a barn owl and a distant roaring train.

"You think they're up to something?"

"I don't know," I said.

We stood with our shoes getting soaked and looked at the green green grass in the headlights.

"What do you think they're doing?" Karen asked.

"Deciding what they want to tell us."

"You're used to this kind of thing, aren't you?"

"I guess."

"It's sort of sad, isn't it?"

"Yeah, it is."

"Except for you getting the chance to punch out Larry Price after all these years."

"Christ, you really think I'm that petty?"

"I know you are. I know you are."

Then we both turned to look back to where they were. There'd been a cry and Forester shouted, "You hit him again, Larry, and I'll

THE REASON WHY   223

break your goddamn jaw." They were arguing about something and it had turned vicious.

I leaned back against the car. She leaned back against me. "You think we'll ever go to bed?"

"I'd sure like to, Karen, but I can't."

"Donna?"

"Yeah. I'm really trying to learn how to be faithful."

"That been a problem?"

"It cost me a marriage."

"Maybe I'll learn how someday, too."

Then they were back. Somebody, presumably Forester, had torn Price's nice lacy shirt into shreds. Haskins looked miserable.

Forester said, "I'm going to tell you what happened that night." I nodded.

"I've got some beer in the backseat. Would either of you like one?"

Karen said, "Yes, we would."

So he went and got a six-pack of Michelob and we all had a beer and just before he started talking he and Karen shared another one of those peculiar glances and then he said, "The four of us—myself, Price, Haskins, and Michael Brandon—had done something we were very ashamed of."

"Afraid of," Haskins said.

"Afraid that if it came out, our lives would be ruined. Forever," Forester said.

Price said, "Just say it, Forester." He glared at me.

"We raped a girl, the four of us."

"Brandon spent two months afterward seeing the girl, bringing her flowers, apologizing to her over and over again, telling her how sorry we were, that we'd been drunk and it wasn't like us to do that and—" Forester sighed, put his eyes to the ground. "In fact we had been drunk; in fact it wasn't like us to do such a thing—"

Haskins said, "It really wasn't. It really wasn't."

For a time there was just the barn owl and the crickets again, no talk, and then gently I said, "What happened to Brandon that night?"

"We were out as we usually were, drinking beer, talking about it, afraid the girl would finally turn us in to the police, still trying to figure out why we'd ever done such a thing—"

The hatred was gone from Price's eyes. For the first time the matinee idol looked as melancholy as his friends. "No matter what you think of me, Dwyer, I don't rape women. But that night—" He shrugged, looked away.

"Brandon," I said. "You were going to tell me about Brandon."

"We came up here, had a case of beer or something, and talked about it some more, and that night," Forester said, "that night Brandon just snapped. He couldn't handle how ashamed he was or how afraid he was of being turned in. Right in the middle of talking—"

Haskins took over. "Right in the middle, he just got up and ran out to the Point." He indicated the cliff behind us. "And before we could stop him, he jumped."

"Jesus," Price said, "I can't forget his screaming on the way down. I can't ever forget it."

I looked at Karen. "So what she heard you three talking about outside the party that night wasn't that you'd killed Brandon but that you were afraid a serious investigation into his suicide might turn up the rape?"

Forester said, "Exactly." He stared at Karen. "We didn't kill Michael, Karen. We loved him. He was our friend."

But by then, completely without warning, she had started to cry and then she began literally sobbing, her entire body shaking with some grief I could neither understand nor assuage.

I nodded to Forester to get back in his car and leave. They stood and watched us a moment and then they got into the Mercedes and went away, taking the burden of years and guilt with them.

This time I drove. I went far out the river road, miles out, where you pick up the piney hills and the deer standing by the side of the road.

From the glove compartment she took a pint of J&B, and I knew better than to try and stop her.

I said, "You were the girl they raped, weren't you?"

"Yes."

"Why didn't you tell the police?"

She smiled at me. "The police weren't exactly going to believe a girl from the Highlands about the sons of rich men."

I sighed. She was right.

"Then Michael started coming around to see me. I can't say I ever forgave him, but I started to feel sorry for him. His fear—" She shook her head, looked out the window. She said, almost to herself, "But I had to write those letters, get them there tonight, know for sure if they killed him." She paused. "You believe them?"

"That they didn't kill him?"

"Right."

"Yes, I believe them."

"So do I."

Then she went back to staring out the window, her small face childlike there in silhouette against the moonsilver river. "Can I ask you a question, Dwyer?"

"Sure."

"You think we're ever going to get out of the Highlands?"

"No," I said, and drove on faster in her fine new expensive car. "No, I don't."

THE UGLY FILE

The cold rain didn't improve the looks of the housing development, one of those sprawling valleys of pastel-colored tract
houses that had sprung from the loins of greedy contractors right at
the end of WWII, fresh as flowers during that exultant time but
now dead and faded.

I spent fifteen minutes trying to find the right address. Houses
and streets formed a blinding maze of sameness.

I got lucky by taking what I feared was a wrong turn. A few minutes later I pulled my new station wagon up to the curb, got out,
tugged my hat and raincoat on snugly, and then started unloading.

Usually, Merle, my assistant, is on most shoots. He unloads and
sets up all the lighting, unloads and sets up all the photographic
umbrellas, and unloads and sets up all the electric sensors that trip
the strobe lights. But Merle went on this kind of shoot once before
and he said never again, "not even if you fire my ass." He was too
good an assistant to give up so now I did these particular jobs alone.

My name is Roy Hubbard. I picked up my profession of photography in Nam, where I was on the staff of a captain whose greatest
thrill was taking photos of bloody and dismembered bodies. He

didn't care if the bodies belonged to us or them just as long as they had been somehow disfigured or dismembered.

In an odd way, I suppose, being the captain's assistant prepared me for the client I was working for today, and had been working for, on and off, for the past two months. The best-paying client I've ever had, I should mention here. I don't want you to think that I take any special pleasure, or get any special kick, out of gigs like this. I don't. But when you've got a family to feed, and you live in a city with as many competing photography firms as this one has, you pretty much take what's offered you.

The air smelled of wet dark earth turning from winter to spring. Another four or five weeks and you'd see cardinals and jays sitting on the blooming green branches of trees.

The house was shabby even by the standards of the neighborhood, the brown grass littered with bright cheap forgotten plastic toys and empty Diet Pepsi cans and wild rain-sodden scraps of newspaper inserts. The small picture window to the right of the front door was taped lengthwise from some long-ago crack, and the white siding ran with rust from the drain spouts. The front door was missing its top glass panel. Cardboard had been set in there.

I knocked, ducking beneath the slight overhang of the roof to escape the rain.

The woman who answered was probably no older than twenty-five but her eyes and the sag of her shoulders said that her age should not be measured by calendar years alone.

"Mrs. Cunningham?"

"Hi," she said, and her tiny white hands fluttered about like doves. "I didn't get to clean the place up very good."

"That's fine."

"And the two oldest kids have the flu so they're still in their pajamas and—"

"Everything'll be fine, Mrs. Cunningham." When you're a photographer who deals a lot with mothers and children, you have to learn a certain calm, doctorly manner.

She opened the door and I went inside.

The living room, and what I could see of the dining room, was basically a continuation of the front yard—a mine field of cheap toys scattered everywhere, and inexpensive furniture of the sort you buy by the room instead of the piece, strewn with magazines and pieces of the newspaper and the odd piece of children's clothing.

Over all was a sour smell, one part the rain-sodden wood of the exterior house, one part the lunch she had just fixed, one part the house cleaning this place hadn't had in a good long while.

The two kids with the flu, boy and girl respectively, were parked in a corner of the long, stained couch. Even from here I knew that one of them had diapers in need of changing. They showed no interest in me or my equipment. Out of dirty faces and dead blue eyes they watched one cartoon character beat another with a hammer on a TV whose sound dial was turned very near the top.

"Cindy's in her room," Mrs. Cunningham explained.

Her dark hair was in a pert little ponytail. The rest of her chunky self was packed into a faded blue sweatshirt and sweatpants. In high school she had probably been nice and trim. But high school was an eternity behind her now.

I carried my gear and followed her down a short hallway. We passed two messy bedrooms and a bathroom and finally we came to a door that was closed.

"Have you ever seen anybody like Cindy before?"

"I guess not, Mrs. Cunningham."

"Well, it's kind of shocking. Some people can't really look at her at all. They just sort of glance at her and look away real quick. You know?"

"I'll be fine."

"I mean, it doesn't offend me when people don't want to look at her. If she wasn't my daughter, I probably wouldn't want to look at her, either. Being perfectly honest, I mean."

"I'm ready, Mrs. Cunningham."

She watched me a moment and said, "You have kids?"

"Two little girls."

"And they're both fine?"

"We were lucky."

For a moment, I thought she might cry. "You don't know how lucky, Mr. Hubbard."

She opened the door and we went into the bedroom.

It was a small room, painted a fresh, lively pink. The furnishings in here—the bassinet, the bureau, the rocking horse in the corner—were more expensive than the stuff in the rest of the house. And the smell was better. Johnson's Baby Oil and Johnson's Baby Powder are always pleasant on the nose. There was a reverence in the appointments of this room, as if the Cunninghams had consciously decided to let the yard and the rest of the house go to hell. But this room—

Mrs. Cunningham led me over to the bassinet and then said, "Are you ready?"

"I'll be fine, Mrs. Cunningham. Really."

"Well," she said, "here you are then."

I went over and peered into the bassinet. The first look is always rough. But I didn't want to upset the lady so I smiled down at her baby as if Cindy looked just like every other baby girl I'd ever seen.

I even touched my finger to the baby's belly and tickled her a little. "Hi, Cindy."

After I had finished my first three or four assignments for this particular client, I went to the library one day and spent an hour or so reading about birth defects. The ones most of us are familiar with are clubfoots and cleft palates and harelips and things like that. The treatable problems, that is. From there you work up to spina bifida and cretinism. And from there—

What I didn't know until that day in the library is that there are literally hundreds of ways in which infants can be deformed, right up to and including the genetic curse of The Elephant Man. As soon as I started running into words such as achondroplastic dwarfism and supernumerary chromosomes, I quit reading. I had no idea what those words meant.

Nor did I have any idea of what exactly you would call Cindy's malformation. She had only one tiny arm and that was so short that her three fingers did not quite reach her rib cage. It put me in mind of a flipper on an otter. She had two legs but only one foot and only three digits on that. But her face was the most terrible part of it all, a tiny little slit of a mouth and virtually no nose and only one good eye. The other was almond-shaped and in the right position but the eyeball itself was the deep, startling color of blood.

"We been tryin' to keep her at home here," Mrs. Cunningham said, "but she can be a lot of trouble. The other two kids make fun of her all the time and my husband can't sleep right because he keeps havin' these dreams of her smotherin' because she don't have much of a nose. And the neighbor kids are always tryin' to sneak in and get a look at her."

All the time she talked, I kept staring down at poor Cindy. My reaction was always the same when I saw these children. I wanted to find out who was in charge of a universe that would permit something like this and then tear his fucking throat out.

"You ready to start now?"

"Ready," I said.

She was nice enough to help me get my equipment set up. The pictures went quickly. I shot Cindy from several angles, including several straight-on. For some reason, that's the one the client seems to like best. Straight-on. So you can see everything.

I used VPS large format professional film and a Pentax camera because what I was doing here was essentially making many portraits of Cindy, just the way I do when I make a portrait of an important community leader.

Half an hour later, I was packed up and moving through Mrs. Cunningham's front door.

"You tell that man—that Mr. Byerly who called—that we sure do appreciate that $2000 check he sent."

"I'll be sure to tell him," I said, walking out into the rain.

"You're gonna get wet."

"I'll be fine. Goodbye, Mrs. Cunningham."

Back at the shop, I asked Merle if there had been any calls and he said nothing important. Then, "How'd it go?"

"No problems," I said.

"Another addition to the ugly file, huh?" Then he nodded to the three filing cabinets I'd bought years back at a government auction. The top drawer of the center cabinet contained the photos and negatives of all the deformed children I'd been shooting for Byerly.

"I still don't think that's funny, Merle."

"The ugly file?" He'd been calling it that for a couple weeks now and I'd warned him that I wasn't amused. I have one of those tempers that it's not smart to push on too hard or too long.

"Uh-huh," I said.

"If you can't laugh about it then you have to cry about it."

"That's a cop-out. People always say that when they want to say something nasty and get away with it. I don't want you to call it that anymore, you fucking understand me, Merle?"

I could feel the anger coming. I guess I've got more of it than I know what to do with, especially after I've been around some poor goddamned kid like Cindy.

"Hey, boss, lighten up. Shit, man, I won't say it anymore, OK?"

"I'm going to hold you to that."

I took the film of Cindy into the darkroom. It took six hours to process it all through the chemicals and get the good, clear proofs I wanted.

At some point during the process, Merle knocked on the door and said, "I'm goin' home now, all right?"

"See you tomorrow," I said through the closed door.

"Hey, I'm sorry I pissed you off. You know, about those pictures."

"Forget about it, Merle. It's over. Everything's fine."

"Thanks. See you tomorrow."

"Right."

When I came out of the darkroom, the windows were filled with night. I put the proofs in a manila envelope with my logo and return address on it and then went out the door and down the stairs to the parking lot and my station wagon.

The night was like October now, raw and windy. I drove over to the freeway and took it straight out to Mannion Springs, the wealthiest of all the wealthy local suburbs.

On sunny afternoons, Mary and I pack up the girls sometimes and drive through Mannion Springs and look at all the houses and daydream aloud of what it would be like to live in a place where you had honest-to-God maids and honest-to-God butlers the way some of these places do.

I thought of Mary now, and how much I loved her, more the longer we were married, and suddenly I felt this terrible, almost oppressive loneliness, and then I thought of little Cindy in that bassinet this afternoon and I just wanted to start crying and I couldn't even tell you why for sure.

The Byerly place is what they call a shingle Victorian. It has dormers of every kind and description—hipped, eyebrow and gabled. The place is huge but has far fewer windows than you'd expect to find in a house this size. You wonder if sunlight can ever get into it.

I'd called Byerly before leaving the office. He was expecting me.

I parked in the wide asphalt drive that swept around the grounds. By the time I reached the front porch, Byerly was in the arched doorway, dressed in a good dark suit.

I walked right up to him and handed him the envelope with the photos in it.

"Thank you," he said. "You'll send me a bill?"

"Sure," I said. I was going to add "That's my favorite part of the job, sending out the bill" but he wasn't the kind of guy you joke with. And if you ever saw him, you'd know why.

Everything about him tells you he's one of those men who used to be called aristocratic. He's handsome, he's slim, he's athletic, and he seems to be very, very confident in everything he does—until you look at his eyes, at the sorrow and weariness of them, at the trapped gaze of a small and broken boy hiding in there.

Of course, on my last trip out here I learned why he looks this way. Byerly was out and the maid answered the door and we started talking and then she told me all about it, in whispers of course, because Byerly's wife was upstairs and would not have appreciated being discussed this way.

Four years ago, Mrs. Byerly gave birth to their only child, a son. The family physician said that he had never seen a deformity of this magnitude. The child had a head only slightly larger than an apple and no eyes and no arms whatsoever. And it made noises that sickened even the most doctorly of doctors. . . .

The physician even hinted that the baby might be destroyed, for the sake of the entire family. . . .

Mrs. Byerly had a nervous breakdown and went into a mental

hospital for nearly a year. She refused to let her baby be taken to a state institution. Mr. Byerly and three shifts of nurses took care of the boy.

When Mrs. Byerly got out of the hospital everybody pretended that she was doing just fine and wasn't really crazy at all. But then Mrs. Byerly got her husband to hire me to take pictures of deformed babies for her. She seemed to draw courage from knowing that she and her son were not alone in their terrible grief. . . .

All I could think of was those signals we send deep into outer space to see if some other species will hear them and let us know that we're not alone, that this isn't just some frigging joke, this nowhere planet spinning in the darkness. . . .

When the maid told me all this, it broke my heart for Mrs. Byerly and then I didn't feel so awkward about taking the pictures anymore. Her husband had his personal physician check out the area for the kind of babies we were looking for and Byerly would call the mother and offer to pay her a lot of money . . . and then I'd go over there and take the pictures of the kid. . . .

Now, just as I was about to turn around and walk off the porch, Byerly said, "I understand that you spent some time here two weeks ago talking to one of the maids."

"Yes."

"I'd prefer that you never do that again. My wife is very uncomfortable about our personal affairs being made public."

He sounded as I had sounded with Merle earlier today. Right on the verge of being very angry. The thing was, I didn't blame him. I wouldn't want people whispering about me and my wife, either.

"I apologize, Mr. Byerly. I shouldn't have done that."

"My wife has suffered enough." The anger had left him. He sounded drained. "She's suffered way too much, in fact."

And with that, I heard a child cry out from upstairs.

A child—yet not a child—a strangled, mournful cry that shook me to hear.

"Good night," he said.

He shut the door very quickly, leaving me to the wind and rain and night.

After awhile, I walked down the wide steps to my car and got inside and drove straight home.

As soon as I was inside, I kissed my wife and then took her by the hand and led her upstairs to the room our two little girls share.

We stood in the doorway, looking at Jenny and Sara. They were asleep.

Each was possessed of two eyes, two arms, two legs; and each was possessed of song and delight and wonderment and tenderness and glee.

And I held my wife tighter than I ever had, and felt an almost giddy gratitude for the health of our little family.

Not until much later, near midnight it was, my wife asleep next to me in the warmth of our bed—not until much later did I think again of Mrs. Byerly and her photos in the upstairs bedroom of that dark and shunned Victorian house, up there with her child trying to make frantic sense of the silent and eternal universe that makes no sense at all.

FRIENDS

i

I saw a small child twisted with cerebral palsy. I saw an even smaller child, stomach-bloated with malnutrition, flies walking his face. And a man who had ruined his life with cocaine. And a forlorn, whispery woman dying of AIDS.

I almost couldn't finish the late-night dinner I'd brought back to my motel room from a nearby McDonald's.

I don't mean to be sarcastic. I felt all the things those television commercials begged me to feel—guilt, sadness, rage at injustice, and utter helplessness. You know the commercials I mean and you know the time I mean—late-night TV in between commercials for Boxcar Willie and Slim Whitman albums and forthcoming professional wrestling matches.

The trouble is, being a sixty-plus retired sheriff's deputy, I don't exactly have a lot of money to contribute to charities, worthy or not, and even if I did have money, I'd be confused as to which one needed my funding most. How do you decide between a kid with cerebral palsy and a kid with Down's syndrome?

Finishing my cheeseburger that was by now cold, finishing my Coke that was by now warm, I rolled up the grease-stained sack and hook-shot it for two points into a tiny brown plastic wastebasket next to the bureau. The wastebasket was one of the few things not chained down in this small motel room right on the edge of a Chicago ghetto. I'd been here three days. It seemed more like sixty.

I was starting to think about Faith and Hoyt again—Faith being my thirty-one-year-old lady-friend and Hoyt the child we inadvertently produced—when the phone rang.

I had hopes, of course, that it would be Faith herself, even though I'd given her all sorts of stern reasons not to phone me and run up the bill, reasons that seemed inane this lonely time of night.

I grabbed the phone.

"Mr. Parnell?"

The voice was young, black.

"We probably should talk."

"I'm listening."

"You was in the neighborhood today."

"Yes."

"Looking for somebody who knows somethin' about a certain woman."

"Right."

"You still interested?"

"Very much."

"You was lookin' in the wrong places. Ask for Charlene."

"Charlene."

"She works at a restaurant called Charlie's. She's cashier there."

"OK. You mind if I ask who I'm speaking with?"

"Why you want to know?"

I looked at my Bulova. "It's nearly midnight. You wouldn't be suspicious about a call like this?"

"I guess."

"Plus, if this leads somewhere, there might be some money in it."

"I'll call you tomorrow night. If there's some money in it, tell me then."

Even though I was alone, I shrugged. "Maybe we could accomplish more if we could sit down and talk. Face to face."

"No reason for that."

"Up to you."

"Charlene can tell you some things."

"I appreciate the advice."

"Tomorrow night, then."

He hung up.

I replaced the receiver, stretched my legs and set them between the cigarette burns somebody had decorously put in the bedspread, and leaned back to watch an episode of "Andy Griffith," the one where Gomer proves to be a better singer than Barney.

About halfway through the show, two men in the room next door came back from some sort of close and prolonged association with alcohol and turned on their TV to some kind of country-western hoedown that lead them to stomp their feet and say every few minutes, "Lookit the pair on that babe, will ya?" and then giggle and giggle.

About the time Andy was figuring out a solution to Barney's dilemma (if you watch the show often enough, you'll see how Andy evolved over the years into a genuinely wise and compassionate man) and about the time I was sneaking my fifth cigarette for the day (but sneaking from whom? I was alone), the phone rang.

I decided to be bold and not even say hello. "I'm sure glad you don't do what old farts tell you to."

Faith laughed. "I'm glad I don't, either. Otherwise I never would have called tonight."

"How's Hoyt's cold?"

"A lot better."

"How're you?"

"Feeling wonderful. I took Hoyt to Immaculate Conception tonight. I've always liked Lenten services for some reason. Maybe it's the bare altar and all the incense and the monks chanting." A little more than a year ago, Faith had had a mastectomy. You sure wouldn't know it now.

I laughed. "There were monks there tonight?"

"No, but when I was a girl they'd come up from New Mallory, the monks, and the Gregorian chant was beautiful. Really. You still depressed?"

"It's just the weather. You know how November is. Rainy and damp."

"Anything turn up on Carla DiMonte yet?"

"Maybe. Just had a phone call about twenty minutes ago."

"I miss you."

"I miss you," I said. I hesitated.

"You're doing it, aren't you?"

"What?"

"Looking at your wristwatch."

"Clairvoyance."

"No; it's just something I've picked up on since you've been in Chicago. How you start noting the minutes."

"We're coming up on three minutes."

She laughed. "God, I wish you were here."

"Kiss Hoyt for me."

Ten minutes later, I lay in bed afraid I'd have to go and confront the guests next door. But there was a crash, leaden weight smashing into an end table it sounded like, and then a male voice laughing said, "Man, you're really soused. You better lay down." Then the TV went off and then later there was just the sound of the toilet flushing.

Then there was just the darkness of the room and the way the bloodred light of the neon outside climbed along the edge of the curtain like a luminous snake.

Always late at night, and particularly when I was alone, the fear came about Faith. Everything seemed to be all right. Seemed to.

I fell asleep saying earnest grade school Hail Marys. I woke up twice, the second time to hear one of the men next door barfing on the other side of the wall.

ii

I came to Chicago at the request of Sal Carlucci, a Brooklyn private investigator with whom I served in World War II. Sal had been hired by no less a mobster than Don DiMonte to check into the activities of Carla DiMonte, the mobster's twenty-one-year-old daughter who had a penchant for trouble. At sixteen, for example,

DiMonte had had to ease her out of a murder charge. A few weeks ago DiMonte had received a blackmail letter saying that his daughter had killed somebody else—and that if one million dollars wasn't turned over to the letter writer, said letter writer would go to the police with evidence that would convict Carla.

As if Mr. DiMonte's troubles weren't already plentiful, there was yet one more problem. A private detective he'd hired showed him that over the past year Carla had traveled with a rock band, spending decent amounts of time in five major cities. The murder, if it had actually taken place, most likely occurred in one of these cities.

Now, as good a private investigator as Sal Carlucci is, there's no way he could visit five cities in a week—the amount of time DiMonte figures he had to hold the blackmailer off. So Carlucci hired four other private investigators, including me, to help. Since I'm closest to Chicago, and since Carla spent time there, that's where I headed.

I spent the first day in the new library on North Franklin, checking out all the local murders for the past twelve months. It was Carlucci's idea that we first try to ascertain if the blackmailer really had something on Carla—was there an unsolved murder that sounded as if Carla might have been involved?

I found nothing that looked even promising until late in the day when I found an item about the slaying of a prominent drug dealer near a housing project. Several witnesses said that he had been shot dead by a white woman who seemed to resemble very much the description I'd been given of Carla DiMonte.

I spent yesterday walking off the blocks around the development where the killing had taken place. I had interviewed a few dozen people but learned precisely nothing. Nobody, it seemed, had ever heard of John Wade, the drug dealer who'd been murdered, nor had anybody seen a well-dressed white woman down here. "She wouldn't'a stayed white for long, man" one man told me around a silver-toothed grin.

Around nine the next morning I walked into "Charlie's," the restaurant I'd been told about by my mysterious late-night caller.

Neither black nor white faces looked up at me as I came inside out of the raw gray cold and stood in the entranceway watching a chunky black cashier in a pink uniform stab out numbers on a cash register with deadly efficiency. Presumably, this was Charlene.

I stood there ten minutes. It took that long for the line to disperse. Then I went inside.

"Charlene," I said over the Phil Collins record assaulting the smoke-hazed air.

She looked up at me from under aqua eyebrows that seemed to be the texture of lizard skin. "Yes."

"My name's Parnell."

"So?"

"I just wondered if I could ask you some questions?"

"You law?"

"Indirectly. I'm a private investigator."

"Then I don't have to answer?"

"Right. You don't have to answer."

She shrugged meaty shoulders. "Then get lost."

"You mind?" a white guy said to me. "Jesus." He pushed into place at the cash register and handed over a green ticket. He only glared at me maybe three times while Charlene did her killer routine with his receipt. "You have a nice day, Charlene," he said to her when she handed him back his change but he was staring at me. He was no more than thirty and obviously he could see that I was about twice his age. He had the energy of a pit bull. Energy wasn't something I had in plentiful supply these days. He made sure to push against me as he went out the door.

Two more guys came up and handed her tickets. During her business, she glanced up at me twice and scowled.

When the guys were gone. I said, "Did you know a man named John Wade?"

Her eyes revealed nothing but her full, sensuous mouth gave an unpleasant little tug. She was maybe forty and twenty pounds overweight but she was an appealing woman nonetheless, one of those women of fleshy charms men seem to appreciate the older they get, when the ideal of femininity has given way to simple need. You no longer worry about physical beauty so much; you want companionship in and out of bed. Charlene looked as if she'd be a pretty good companion. "You know what I do when I get off this ten-hour shift?"

"No. What?"

"I go home and take care of my two kids."

"Hard work?"

"Real hard."

"But I'm afraid I don't get your point."

A black guy came over. He was little and seemed nervous. He kept coughing as if an invisible doctor were giving him an invisible hernia checkup.

"You have a nice day, Benny," Charlene said to the little man as he pushed out the door. She looked at me again. "What I'm saying is that I'm too busy for trouble. I work here and then I go home. I don't have time to get involved in whatever it is you're pushing."

"You get a break?"

She sighed. "Nine forty-five Belinda comes out from the book-keeping office and spells me for fifteen minutes."

I nodded to the long row of red-covered seats that ran along the counter. But it was a booth I wanted. "I'll go have some breakfast over there. By nine forty-five I should have gotten us a booth. All right?"

"I get anything for this?"

"Fifty dollars if you tell me anything useful."

She shrugged again. It was the gesture of a weary woman who had long ago been beaten past pain into sullen submission. "Guess that'll pay a few doctor bills."

The food—bacon, two eggs over easy, a big piece of wheat toast spread with something that managed to taste neither like butter nor margarine—was better than I had expected.

Afterward, I read the *Tribune,* all about Richard Daley Jr.'s new administration, and drank three cups of hot coffee and was naughty and smoked two cigarettes.

Charlene appeared right on time.

She had brought a black plastic purse the size of a shopping bag with her. She slipped into the other side of the booth and said,

"He's been dead several months. Why're you interested in him now?"

"You knew him?"

"You're not going to answer my question?"

"Not now. But I need you to tell me about him."

She tamped a cigarette from a black-and-white Generi pack and said, "What's to know? In this neighborhood, he was an important man."

"A pusher."

Anger filled her chocolate eyes. "Maybe, being a black man, that's the only thing he knew how to do."

"You really believe that?"

She cooled down, exhaled smoke, looked out the window. "No." She looked back at me. "He was the father of my two boys."

"Did you live with him?"

"A long time ago. Not since the youngest was born." She smiled her full, erotic smile. "That's the funny thing about some men. You have a kid for them and all of a sudden they start to treat you like you're some kind of old lady. Right after Ornette was born, John started up with very young girls. Nineteen seemed to be the right age for him."

"Was he pushing then?"

"Not so much. Actually, he still had his job at the A&P as an assistant manager. Then he started doing drugs himself and—" The shrug again. "It changed him. He'd always had a good mind, one of the best in the neighborhood. He decided to put it to use, I guess."

"Pushing?"

"Uh-huh."

"The newspaper accounts said that several eyewitnesses saw him being shot to death by a white woman. You know anything about that?"

She hesitated. "I was one of the eyewitnesses."

"You saw him being shot?"

"Right."

"He was getting out of his car—"

"He was getting out of his car when this other car pulled up and a white woman got out and said something to him and then shot him. She got back in the car and took off before any of us could do anything about it."

"Would you describe the woman?"

The description she gave matched that in the newspaper. While it could fit a lot of women, it could also fit Carla DiMonte.

"You'd never seen her before?" I asked.

"No."

"So you wouldn't have any idea why she shot him?"

"No."

"How'd your boys deal with it?"

"I don't want to talk about my boys."

"They don't know he was their father?"

"Why is that important?"

"Just curious, I guess."

"My boys didn't have nothing to do with this."

"So John was a big man in the neighborhood?"

She looked relieved that I'd changed the subject. "Very big."

"Feared or respected?"

"Both. In the ghetto, nobody respects you unless they fear you, too."

I laughed. "I don't think that applies to just the ghetto."

"Well, you know what I mean."

"Sure."

"He had a big blue Mercedes and he had a reputation for having never been busted and he lived over near Lake Shore in this fabulous condo and when he'd come back to the neighborhood the kids would flock around like some rock star had shown up or something."

"That's one of the things I don't understand."

"What's that?"

"Why he'd come back to the neighborhood. He didn't need to."

"His ego."

"How so?"

"He wasn't an especially strong man, you know. Growing up, he'd had to take a lot of pushing around by other kids in the neighborhood. I don't think he ever got over the thrill of coming back here and kind of rubbing their faces in it."

She glanced at her wristwatch. "Time's up. I told you. I wouldn't be much help."

"You see him much?"

"Not much."

"He pay you child support?"

"Not much."

"With all his money?"

"With all his money."

"He sees the kids much?"

"When it suited him."

"He have a lot of enemies?"

She looked at me as if I were hopelessly naive. "You know much about dealing drugs? All you got is enemies."

"The white woman—you think she killed him because of drugs?"

"I wouldn't know."

"And you don't care?"

"I quit caring about him a long time ago."

"You give me the names of the other witnesses?"

Again, she hesitated. "I guess you could find out anyway."

She gave me the names. I wrote them down in my little notebook.

"What're you lookin' for, mister?" she said.

I sighed. "I wish I knew, Charlene. I wish I knew."

iii

Two blocks after leaving the restaurant, I was joined by a jaunty little black man in a coat of blue vinyl that tried with great and sad difficulty to be leather. It would probably have even settled for being leatherette.

He was my age and he walked with a slight limp and he knew nothing whatsoever about tailing anybody. It had not taken Charlene long to get to the phone.

I thought about this as I reached the neighborhood proper, five square blocks where rats crouched in living room corners and where there wasn't enough water pressure to flush a toilet. Given the flow of human traffic, the neighborhood seemed to huddle, as if for warmth and inspiration, around a ma and pa corner grocery store with rusting forty-year-old "PEPSI-COLA . . . in the big bottle!" signs on either side of the door. People came and went bearing groceries bought with food stamps and the quick sad last of paychecks, shuffling shambling stumbling away if they were into hootch or cough syrup or street drugs, moving briskly and soberly if they had some sort of purpose, kids to feed, jobs to get to. In the cold drizzle, the dark faces staring at me held distrust and anger and curiosity; only a few smiled. I wouldn't have smiled at me, either.

For a time, I stood out on the corner looking at the place, in front of the laundromat that also rented videos, where John Wade had been shot to death and where a woman who had looked not unlike Carla DiMonte had been seen fleeing.

The jaunty little man in the blue vinyl coat stood maybe thirty yards away, leaning into a doorway and hacking harshly around his cigarette. Twice we made eye contact. I doubted I'd be hiring him in the near future to do any legwork.

Inside, the grocery store smelled of spices, overripe fruit, and blooded meat.

A tiny bald black man in a proud white apron stood behind a counter dispatching people with all the efficiency and courtesy of a supply sergeant dispatching recruits. His plastic name badge read Phil Warren. He was one of the people I was looking for.

One woman was stupid enough to question a certain odor about the bundled hamburger she laid on the counter and the little black man said, "You want to talk about your bill now, Bertha?"

The woman dropped her gaze. He wrote up her ticket and jammed it into a large manila envelope taped to the wall next to endless rows of cigarettes. In Magic Marker the envelope was labeled Credit.

When my turn came, I said, "I'd like to ask you some questions about John Wade." I'd waited until the place was empty except for a chunky woman sweeping up in back. The only real noise in the place was the thrumming of cooler motors too old to work efficiently.

The little man, who looked to be about forty and who wore a

snappy red bow tie across the collar of his white shirt, said, "I can tell you exactly two things about John Wade. One is that he's dead; two is that he deserves to be dead."

"I understand you were an eyewitness?"

"Yes, I happen to be." He looked at me carefully. "You're not the law, are you?"

"Not the official law."

"You couldn't be a friend of his because drug dealers don't have friends."

"I suspect that's true."

"So you're trying to find out exactly what?"

"If you saw this woman kill him."

"Oh, I saw it all right."

I described the woman to him.

"That's her, all right," he said.

"And you actually saw her shoot him?"

"I actually saw her shoot him."

"And then get into a Mercedes-Benz and leave?"

He nodded. "Umm-hmm. Why would you be interested now? He's been dead some time.

"A client is interested."

"Oh," he said. "A client. Must be an interesting business you're in."

I smiled. "Sometimes."

For the first time, he smiled, too. "This used to be a nice neighborhood. Oh, I don't mean like your white neighborhoods. But nice. If you lived here, you were reasonably safe." He shook his head. "And there were drugs. I mean, I can't deny that. Why, I can remember after coming back from Korea, all the marijuana I suddenly saw here. But the past ten years, it's different. They'll kill you to get drug money and the pushers are gods and that's maybe the saddest thing of all. How the youngsters look up to the pushers."

"So John Wade was—"

"—was just one less pusher to worry about."

"Exactly."

I was reaching over to take a book of matches from a small white plastic box that said Free when I saw something familiar written on a notepad next to the black dial telephone.

"Charlene called you."

"Pardon me?" he said, suddenly snappy as his bow tie.

"Your notepad there."

He saw the problem and grabbed the notepad.

"You had my name written on it. So, unless you're a psychic, Charlene called ahead about me and told you my name."

He decided to give up the ruse. "You know how it is in a neighborhood. People take care of each other."

Just then, from the back, a tall, good-looking woman of perhaps twenty-five came through curtains and walked up to the register. She had the kind of coffee-colored beauty that lends itself to genuine grace. She said to Phil Warren, "Here's a list of everything I took, Phil. Just put it on the Friends House account." She glanced at me dismissively and went out the door, toting a large square cardboard box heavy with groceries.

"Would that be Karen Dooley?"

"I suppose," he said.

I nodded. "Thank you." Then I went out the door quickly. She was already halfway down the block by the time I reached her. She walked with her head down to avoid the stinging drizzle.

"I'd be happy to carry that for you," I said.

"It's fine just the way it is."

"My name's Parnell."

"Hello, Mr. Parnell."

"I take it Charlene has called you about me."

She surprised me by laughing. "Charlene is very fast on the phone. That's why the local political machine always tries to recruit her at election time. She can call five people in the time it takes others to call two."

"You work at Friends House?"

"I'm the director there."

"And you were an eyewitness to John Wade being murdered?"

She stopped. Stared at me. "Charlene said you were going to ask me that. What is it you want, Mr. Parnell?"

"I'm just looking into some things for a client."

"I see."

Her beautiful eyes held mine for a long time. Then we were walking again.

Behind us, the man in the blue vinyl coat was limping along.

She said, "These are getting heavy, Mr. Parnell. Maybe I'll take you up on your offer to carry them, after all."

I felt almost idiotically blessed by her decision to let me help her in some small way.

The first thing you noticed about Friends House was the new paint job. A two-story frame house with a long front porch and a steep, sloping roof, Friends House looked as if it had been lifted out of a very nice middle-class neighborhood and set down here, in the middle of this bombed-out neighborhood, to serve as a reminder of the lifestyle that awaited those plucky and lucky enough to seize it.

The new casement windows sported smart black trim, the roof vivid new red tiles, and the new aluminum front door a dignified gray that complemented perfectly the new white paint.

Inside, the marvels continued, each room I saw a model of middle-class decorum. Nothing fancy, you understand; nothing ostentatious, just plain good furniture, just plain good taste, including a redbrick fireplace with an oak mantle in the living room and country-style decor throughout.

Here and there along the trim, or in a slightly crooked line of wallpaper, you could see that the refurbishment had not been perfect but it was easy to see that what had probably been a run-down house had been transformed, despite a few flaws, into a real beauty.

In the kitchen, I set the groceries on a butcher-block table and turned to see two young women watching me.

"Dora, Janie, this is Mr. Parnell, the man Charlene told us would be coming." She looked at me and smiled. "And Mr. Parnell, we're the three eyewitnesses you wanted to interview. Along with Phil Warren, we're the ones who went to the police." She nodded to a silver coffee urn on the white stove and said, "Would you care for a cup?"

"I'd appreciate it."

After the coffee came in a hefty brown mug, the four of us sat at the kitchen table. Steam had collected on one of the kitchen windows and was now dripping down; beyond the pane you could see the hard gray November sky. In the oven a coffee cake was baking, filling the air with sweet smells. I felt warm for the first time in an hour, and pleasantly dulled.

Dora was a white girl of perhaps twenty. She wore a blue jumper and a white turtleneck sweater and her blond hair was caught back in a leather catch. She said, "Charlene says you wouldn't tell her why you were asking questions, Mr. Parnell."

I smiled. "Nothing all that mysterious. I'm trying to find out a few things about the woman who shot John Wade."

"About the woman?" Janie said. She was Dora's black counterpart—almost prim in her starched aqua blouse and V-neck sweater and fitted gray skirt. "About the woman?" she repeated, glancing at Karen.

Karen said, "I'm afraid we don't know much about the woman, Mr. Parnell."

From my pocket, I took out the newspaper clipping and read to them the gospel according to the *Tribune*, from the account of the shooting itself, to the description of the murderess.

"Is that about the way it happened?" I asked when I'd finished reading.

"Exactly," Karen Dooley said.

"She didn't say anything?"

"Say anything?" Karen asked, obviously the official spokesperson for the three of them.

"The woman. The killer. She didn't shout anything at Wade?"

"Not that I heard," Karen said. "Do either of you two girls remember hearing anything?"

They shook their heads.

"And then she just got in her car and sped away, right?"

"Right."

"The same kind of car as described in the newspaper account, right?"

"Right."

"And that's about it?"

"That's about it."

"You never saw her previously; you've never seen her since?"

"Right."

Dora put her pert nose into the air. "I'd say that coffee cake's about done." She smiled her lopsided smile. "Mrs. Weiderman upstairs will sure be glad to hear about that."

She got up and went over to the stove, grabbing a wide red oven mitt on the way. "You'll want some of this, Mr. Parnell."

I looked back at Karen. "So all you saw—"

"—was exactly what it said we saw. In the paper, I mean." She laughed. "We're kind of frustrating, aren't we? We had the same effect on the police. They went over and over our story but this is about all they could get from us."

Janie put down her coffee cup and said, "We were scared, Mr. Parnell. I know that people who live outside the neighborhood think that we get used to all the violence but we don't. We get scared just like everybody else."

Dora opened the oven door. Billows of warm air tumbled toward us bearing the wonderful scent of coffee cake. "The truth is, we don't know what happened, Mr. Parnell, because we were so frightened we tried to duck behind a light pole. I know that sounds pathetic but that's what we did." She grinned. "Three of us behind the same light pole."

"And anyway," Karen said, "it happened very quickly. It was over in no more than half a minute or so. She just stepped from her car and shot him."

"And then got back in and drove away," Janie said.

"And we never saw her again," Dora said.

"Honest," Karen said.

The cake cut and cooled slightly, Janie served me a formidable wedge. She also gave me more coffee.

While I was eating, two very old people came into the kitchen, one with a chrome walker, the other with a cane. Both were men. Karen introduced us. We all nodded. She told them about the cake they'd have in their rooms. They smiled like children. Dora led them away.

When I was nearly finished, a young man came into the kitchen and stood watching me eat. I tried not to be self-conscious. He was probably Janie's age, of mixed blood, and wore a Bears sweatshirt and jeans. He twitched very badly and in the course of a minute or so, teared up twice, as if overcome by terrible emotion.

Karen, who had excused herself to go to the bathroom, came back, saw him and said, "Kenny, this is Mr. Parnell."

Kenny bobbed his head in my direction. He looked both suspicious and exhausted.

Just then Dora appeared. Karen gave her Kenny's elbow as if she were passing off a baton. "Why don't you go back to your room, Kenny, and Dora will give you some coffee cake."

"Jackie Gleason's on," Kenny said. "Pretty soon."

"I forgot," Karen said tenderly, "how much you like Jackie Gleason."

"I like Ed Norton more," Kenny said.

"Good," Karen said and glanced at Dora, who led Kenny away.

Karen came back to the table and sat across from me. "Would you like some more coffee cake, Mr. Parnell?"

"It's tempting but I think I've had enough." I looked around the kitchen. "You've got a nice place here. What is it—a shelter of some kind?"

"I guess that's a fair way to put it. Friends House is a place where anybody in the neighborhood can come and stay for awhile when things get too bad on the street. Those two older gentlemen, for instance, they're staying here because the landlord of their apartment house didn't pay the gas bill—and they're too old to freeze. Soon as the gas goes back on, we'll take them back. And Kenny—well, he's trying to kick heroin. Right now, he's very afraid of going to a clinic. His brother died there of some complications with methadone. We had a doctor check Kenny and the doctor said Kenny was fine to stay here for a few days."

"So no permanent solution but at least a temporary one?"

"Exactly."

"How many guest rooms do you have?"

"With the four new ones in the basement, we've got fourteen. That's nowhere near enough to help everybody in the neighborhood who's hurting very badly but at least it's something."

"It must be pretty expensive, running a place like this. Does the city contribute?"

"Yes, the city." She made a clucking noise and glanced down at the slender gold watch on her slender brown wrist. "Oops, I'm sorry, Mr. Parnell. I'm afraid I've got a meeting upstairs. Have we helped you?"

I stood up. "As much as you could, I guess."

She put out her hand and we shook.

"I hope you find whatever you're looking for, Mr. Parnell," she said.

In less than a minute, I was standing on the sidewalk again. The coffee cake kept me full and warm.

I decided to find out who was following me and why.

iv

We went two blocks. A hard wind came and chafed my cheeks and nose, a mumbling drunken black man bounced off a building and nearly fell into me, a cop ticketed a rusted weary VW that looked as if it had not been moved in weeks, and the man tailing me got all worked up when I took two steps into an alley.

Pressed against the wall, I waited, making a fist of my gloved hand.

But he was in no shape to swing on me when he came trotting into the alley, a small man the color of hickory, his chest heaving from a long lifetime of cigarettes.

He ran right into me and I grabbed him.

I didn't put him against the wall with any special force but even so he looked afraid. His nose was running in the cold and he hadn't cleaned his eyes so well this morning.

"Make it easy on yourself," I said. "Who put you onto me?"

"Tommy," he said between gasps.

"Who?"

"Tommy, man."

"I don't know any Tommy."

His brown eyes narrowed. "Her son. Charlene's."

I thought of last night, the late phone call, the young black voice. "Why'd he put you onto me?"

"Don't know."

"Bull."

"Don't, man. Honest. He's jes' a good kid so I tol' him I'd help him."

"Why didn't he tail me himself?"

"Aw, I guess 'cause he believes some of mah stories. Been tellin' them stories for years and years, ever since he was a little kid."

"What stories?"

"You know, man, how I was an MP in Korea. That whole gig."

"And you weren't?"

He shrugged. "Had a buddy who was, I guess."

"How did Tommy know about me?"

"He heard about you bein' in the neighborhood yesterday then he saw you with his ma this morning."

"He isn't in school?"

"Dropped out."

"Where do I find him?"

He told me.

V

Steam rolled from the front end of the car wash like smoke from an angry dragon. Inside the smoke you could see a shiny new red Buick struggling like some metal monster to be born. As soon as the Buick reached the park area, the smoke evaporating now against the gray sky, four black boys descended on it with dirty white rags and dirtier white wiping mitts, shouting things to each other over the top of the car as rap music played above the roar of the cleaning and buffing machinery inside. One of the boys, I suspected, was Tommy.

Inside, the plump dark woman in the lime green blast jacket put down her Kool filter-tip and said, "Tommy's a good kid."

All I'd asked was where I'd find him. Nothing else.

"Not all the kids who work here are good kids, if you know what

I mean," she went on. "But Tommy is. Most definitely."

"I'm not going to hurt him."

"He ain't done nothin', if that's what you're about."

"I'd just like to ask him some questions."

"He's straight. In every sense. No fightin', no drugs, nothin'. He's the one I leave in charge when I got to go to the doctor or somethin'. You can trust him."

Feeling eyes on me, I turned at an angle. Through the glass separating the wind tunnel of the wash itself from the shabby waiting area, I saw a tall, lean young man, gray in the shadows now, watching me.

I nodded in his direction. "Tommy?"

She saw him, too. "Yes."

"Thanks."

I went out the door and into the wind tunnel. The roar was deafening. Customers waved white tickets at the cleaning kids and then piled in their cars. It reminded me of working around fighter planes in WWII, the ceaseless and overwhelming noise that you got lost inside of.

For a moment, Tommy looked afraid, and I had the sense that he might run.

Then he surprised me by tossing his rag to another kid and coming toward me.

"I'm Tommy," he shouted over the roar.

"Yes."

"Let's go in the back where we can have a cup of coffee."

"Fine."

I followed him down a narrow concrete path that paralleled the cleaning equipment. Sudsy spray flicked at us. It was freezing in here. The kids probably had headcolds all winter long.

In a small room with two vending machines and a long, scarred table Tommy got two cups of black coffee in paper cups and set them down on either side of the table.

He sat down and I did likewise.

"I figured you'd come looking for me," he said.

"You were the one who called me last night, right?"

"Right."

I watched him. He had a good, high, intelligent forehead and somber, intelligent eyes. Even dressed in a sweatshirt and a dirty blastjacket, he carried himself with poise and dignity.

He had long but very masculine hands the undersides of which were tan in contrast to the dark uppers. He was one of those kids who would have been mature around age ten. He said, "I want you to find out who killed my father."

"From the police and press reports, I gather it was an unidentified white woman."

"No."

"You know something they don't?"

"I just know it wasn't an 'unidentified white woman.' "

"How do you know that?"

"Because of what Phil Warren did to me."

"The guy who runs the grocery store?"

"Right."

"What did he do to you?"

"Slapped me. Real hard."

"For what?"

"For eavesdropping."

"When?"

"The night my father was killed. I went looking for my mother—my little brother told me she was over at Warren's—and I heard them in the back room there. Phil's got a little room where some of the neighborhood people meet when something bad happens or when they want to get some neighborhood project going. At least, they used his little room till they got Friends House."

"So what did you hear?"

"When I was eavesdropping?"

"Right."

"Nothing. I was just there a minute or two, you know, kind of pressed up against the door and I stumbled against something and Phil came out and—"

"Why didn't you just go inside the room or knock? Why were you eavesdropping?"

He shrugged. "I don't know. I guess I heard voices and I didn't want to interrupt. So I kind of started listening and—"

In the silence I could hear the distant roar of the car wash. It was like the distant sound of war.

"Why aren't you in school?"

"My father didn't get much education. He did pretty well."

"Yeah, he did pretty well all right, Tommy. Somebody shot him to death in the street."

Tommy's eyes dropped to his coffee. "Maybe I'll go back sometime. You know, to school."

"The longer you're out, the harder it'll be to go back."

"You sound like my mother."

"She seems like a decent woman."

He didn't say anything, which I found odd. Most boys agree with nice things said about their mothers.

I said, "Who do you think killed him?"

"I don't know."

"You want to try and look me in the eye and tell me that?"

He raised his gaze. "I don't know."

"C'mon, Tommy. There's something you're not saying."

"Some white chick killed him!"

"You believe that, do you?"

"That's what the papers said, right?" He glanced down at a battered Timex on his right wrist. "Mr. Franklin don't like us taking long breaks. I better get back."

"You heard something, didn't you? When you were eavesdropping."

He took his soggy paper coffee cup and tossed it for three points into a wastebasket to our right. "I didn't hear anything," he said. He stood up. "I better get back, man."

When we reached the roar of the cleaning machines, he shouted a good-bye and disappeared into the chill rolling steam.

vi

"When did Tommy drop out of school?" I said.

"I don't know. A while back."

"Right after his father was murdered, maybe?"

Charlene looked at me with growing impatience. "I already told you, Parnell, I'm busy."

She wasn't kidding about that. The restaurant was packed with suppertime customers. Smoke and grease were heavy.

"Tommy dropped out of school because he found out who really killed his father," I said. "He figured being a good boy wasn't worth it anymore."

"Is that right?" she said, reaching past me to take a green ticket from a customer.

She punched it up with her usual formidable efficiency.

"He also called me in my room last night so I'd be sure to do some investigating," I said.

"Have a nice night," she said to the customer, a man who looked at me with equal degrees of malice and pity, bothering the pretty woman as I was.

"He knows who killed his father but he won't tell me," I said.

This time it was a chunky woman bundled up inside a threadbare brown coat. She looked like a nearsighted bear.

"Don't forget, your favorite show's on TV tonight, Emma," Charlene said, as she handed her back her change.

The old woman, nearsighted, tromped on my foot as she moved past the register.

"If your son knows who killed his father, that means you do, too," I said.

Only at the last did I see the flick of her eyes, a preordained signal of some kind that brought a dusky fellow too young, too angry and too big for me to do anything about.

"He's hassling me, Roland," Charlene said.

"I'm leaving," I said.

Down the block was an old-fashioned glass phone booth whose dim light was like a forlorn beacon in the gathering gloom. Though it was not yet four-thirty in the afternoon, night was here.

Inside, a drunken kid with a mean facial scar stood bounding on his feet as if he had to go to the bathroom very badly and trying to explain in a whining voice why he'd been unfaithful to the woman he was attempting to sweet-talk on the other end of the phone.

Finally—she must have known telepathically how cold I was getting waiting my turn—she hung up on him. For the next minute silver breath poured from his mouth as he shouted at the phone he'd just slammed.

Tearing open the door, he came out onto the sidewalk, seeing me for the first time.

"She's a bitch," he said, and vanished into the shadows.

There wasn't, of course, anything left of the phone book except the black plastic covers. I had to call information for the general number and then I had to ask the operator who answered the general number to whom I might speak about funding for halfway houses.

In all, I talked to four people at some length before I got my answer.

By then, I was very cold and not just physically. Now, I understood why an otherwise all right kid like Tommy would drop out of school.

Down by the restaurant, I waited next to a tree, smoking cigarettes eight, nine, and ten for the day, until Charlene came walking fast out of the restaurant.

vii

"I'd like to talk with you," I said, trying to match her quick steps.

Turning, seeing who I was, her pace only increased. "I've had enough of you, Parnell. Now, I want you to leave me alone."

People appeared and disappeared in the darkness like phantoms. I caught up with her and took her arm and slowed her down.

"He knows," I said.

"I don't know what you're talking about, Parnell."

"Your son. Tommy. He knows what happened."

Only for a moment did her eyes allow the possibility that she was afraid. Then she tried to cover everything in anger again. "Leave me alone."

"It isn't too hard to figure out, when you think about it," I said.

"A drug dealer making a drop is going to have a lot of money on him. Did he have it in a suitcase?"

Ahead, in the faint streetlight, I could see the new, clean shape of Friends House, obviously her destination. Knowing what I knew now, that did not surprise me.

Silhouetted on the front steps, the open door pouring warm yellow light into the chill night, stood Phil Warren. He held his hand out to her, as if to a drowning victim.

She went up the steps two at a time, huddling next to him like a girl to her father when the neighborhood bully came round.

"You don't have no call to be here, Mr. Parnell. Now, you go on back to where you belong," Warren said. In his cardigan sweater, white shirt and gray slacks, he looked relaxed and composed. Not even his voice betrayed the panic he must have been feeling. "Out of this neighborhood," he said, in case I didn't get the point.

"There wasn't any white woman who shot John Wade, was there? She was somebody you made up and told the police about."

"You heard me, Mr. Parnell. You get away from us and stay away."

He took Charlene's arm and turned to guide her inside.

"There's a sixteen-year-old boy who wants to know why the four of you murdered his father," I said, there in the glow of the porch light, my breath cold. Down the street a dog barked angrily at the quarter-moon.

Warren had the grace and good sense to let that one stop him. To Charlene, he said, "You go on inside. I'll talk to him."

She glanced down at me and said, "Maybe you don't understand everything you *think* you do, Parnell."

"Hand me my coat, would you, Charlene?" Warren asked, going to the threshold and putting his hand out. He bundled up inside a dark topcoat and then came down the stairs.

We walked two blocks before saying anything. In the soft moonlight the ugliness of the neighborhood, the buildings half-toppled, the rusted deserted automobiles, the brothers standing loud and boastful in the red-lit roaring mouths of bars—in the moonlight and shadows none of this looked so forlorn and menacing. There was even a lurid beauty about it, one only a tourist like myself could appreciate. The practiced eye of the resident would see far different things.

"You know what it's like to need help and have nowhere to turn?" Warren asked.

"Not really. I've been lucky."

"It's about the most terrible feeling there is."

"And that's what Friends House is all about?"

"We've helped more than three hundred people in less than a year. That's a lot of people."

"What happens when the money runs out? You going to kill another dealer?"

He kept walking but looked over at me. "If we have to."

"What happens if I tell the police what I know?"

"Somehow, I think you're a better man than that."

We walked another block. Babies cried. Couples argued. Music played too loud. In front of us a homeless man crouched with a bottle of wine in a doorway. Warren knelt down to him and said, "You know where you should be, Clinton. Now, you git, hear me?"

"Charlene there?" the man asked, his face buried somewhere in a dusty dark stocking cap and several days growth of beard.

Warren grinned. "She's waiting for you, Clinton. You're her favorite."

Clinton grinned back. He had no teeth.

"Now, git. It's suppertime," Warren said.

Clinton struggled to his feet and moved off in the direction of the shelter.

After another block of silent walking, Warren said, "You know how this neighborhood has changed over the past fifteen years?" He was being rhetorical, of course. "Back then, we were poor and were angry and we had a lot of resentment toward white people—but we didn't prey on each other. Not very much, anyway. Then the drug dealers appeared in our midst and—" He shook his head. His rage was visible. "Now in the neighborhood, we have two kinds of slavery—we've got black skin and half our children are hooked on crack cocaine."

"So you killed him?"

"He was a sonofabitch, Mr. Parnell. He took some of his drug money downtown and bribed a judge into helping him get custody of his two kids. Charlene's a hardworking, decent woman and she's raised those boys well. You know the kind of lifestyle they would have seen with their father? All his thugs and whores? Charlene came to me and I knew then that was the only way to stop him."

"Where did the money come in?"

He shrugged. "Well, when you've lived in the neighborhood as long as I have, you see just how many people need help. I have to turn them away in my store. I can't give everybody credit or I'd go broke myself. So I had the idea for a place like Friends House for a long time, even went to talk to some politicians about it but got nowhere. So then I thought—Well, we waited until a night when John Wade was making a drug deal and we shot him. He had a lot of money in his car."

We had reached the steps of a massive stone Catholic church whose spires seemed tall enough to snag the passing silver clouds.

"I'm sorry Tommy found out," Warren said. "When I saw him that night, standing by the door while we were counting the money—you know, Charlene and me and the two girls you met—I knew he'd heard what happened."

"Making it right with him is going to be difficult. Killing his father and all."

"Maybe when he's a little older, he'll understand why we had to kill him. What kind of parasite his father and all drug dealers are. How they prey on their own, how they take the last ounce of hope and dignity from people who have very little hope and dignity to begin with."

"You're going to kill more so you can keep Friends House going?"

"As the need arises, Mr. Parnell; as the need arises. And as far as I'm concerned, we'll be doing the neighborhood and our society a favor." He put his hand out.

He had a firm grip.

"You know what you're asking me to do?" I said.

"I know."

"Conceal evidence from the police."

"Maybe if you lived in the neighborhood, you'd understand my point of view a little bit more."

"I'm going to have to think about it. I'll call you later tonight and let you know. I really don't feel right about this. I spent my life as a law officer."

"It's not easy for any of us, Mr. Parnell. But it's something that needs to be done."

The two guys in the next room were watching a country-western cable channel and remarking on how big the women's breasts were. The guys seemed almost appealing right then, juvenile and naive and clean-cut. A long way from a neighborhood where you had to make judgments on predators so that others could live.

I called Faith and she put Hoyt up to the phone and he babbled a few of those squeaky wet two-year-old noises that can break your heart when you're alone and far away and then I told Faith how much I loved her and how much I missed her and that I would be coming home tomorrow.

"So how did it work out?" she said. "Was Carla DiMonte involved in the murder?"

"Huh-uh. I'll call Carlucci tomorrow and tell him."

"You sound tired."

"Yeah, I guess so, hon. Long day."

"Well, maybe you'll get a good night's sleep for once."

"Hope so. Love you, hon. Very much."

I sat five minutes in the room with two quick cigarettes and a can of beer and then I looked up Warren's number in the plump red Chicago phone book and called him.

"I'm kind of nervous, Mr. Parnell," he said. "I mean, a lot's riding on your answer."

"Some of these dealers may catch on to what you're doing and come after you."

"I'm willing to take that chance."

"Then I wish you luck, Mr. Warren. I wish you a lot of luck."

"You're going to keep our secret?"

"I am."

"God bless you, Mr. Parnell."

"I just hope Tommy can understand someday."

"We'll all say prayers for that, Mr. Parnell. We'll all say prayers."

Afterwards, I went over to the set and cranked up *The Honeymooners*. It was the episode where Ralph confuses a dog's terminal diagnosis with his own.

There's an especially moving scene where the great Gleason sits at the shabby table in the shabby little apartment and tries to make sense of the things that composed his life. And can't.

I thought of Phil Warren and what he was doing and how wrong it was yet how right it was, too.

Some things you can't make sense of, I guess; some things you just can't.

BLESS US O LORD

I usually think of Midwestern Thanksgivings as cold, snowy days. But as we gathered around the table this afternoon, my parents and my wife, Laura, and our two children, Rob and Kate, I noticed that the blue sky and sunlight in the window looked more like an April day than one in late November.

"Would you like to say grace today?" my mother said to four-year-old Kate.

Kate of the coppery hair and slow secretive smile nodded and started in immediately. She got the usual number of words wrong and everybody smiled the usual number of times and then the meal began.

Dad is a retired steelworker. I remember, as a boy, watching fascinated as he'd quickly work his way through a plate heaped with turkey, sweet potatoes, dressing, cranberry sauce and two big chunks of the honey wheat bread Mom always makes for Thanksgiving and Christmas. And then go right back for seconds of everything and eat all that up right away, too.

He's sixty-seven now and probably thirty pounds over what he should be and his eyesight is fading and the only exercise he gets is taking out the garbage once a day—but he hasn't, unfortunately, lost that steelworker's appetite.

Mom on the other hand, thin as she was in her wedding pictures, eats a small helping of everything and then announces, in a sort of official way, "I'm stuffed."

"So how goes the lawyer business?" Dad asked after everybody had finished passing everything around.

Dad never tires of reminding everybody that his youngest son did something very few young men in our working-class neighborhood did—went on to become a lawyer, and a reasonably successful one, too, with downtown quarters in one of the shiny new office buildings right on the river, and two BMWs in the family, even if one of them is fourteen years old.

"Pretty well, I guess," I said.

Laura smiled and laid her fingers gently on my wrist. "Someday this son of yours has to start speaking up for himself. He's doing very well. In fact, Bill Grier—one of the three partners—told your son here that within two years he'll be asked to be a partner, too."

"Did you hear that, Margaret?" Dad said to Mom.

"I heard," she said, grinning because Dad was grinning.

Dad's folks were Czechs. His father and mother landed in a ship in Galveston and trekked all the way up to Michigan on the whispered rumor of steel mill work. Dad was the first one in his family to learn English well. So I understood his pride in me.

Laura patted me again and went back to her food. I felt one of those odd gleeful moments that married people get when they realize, every once in a while, that they're more in love with their mates now than they were even back when things were all backseat passion and spring flowers.

Of course, back then, I'd been a little nervous about bringing Laura around the house. Mom and Dad are very nice people, you understand, but Laura's father is a very wealthy investment banker and I wasn't sure how she'd respond to the icons and mores of the working class—you know, the lurid and oversweet paintings of Jesus in the living room and the big booming excitement Dad brings to his pro wrestling matches on the tube.

But she did just fine. She fell in love with my mom right away and if she was at first a little intimidated by the hard Slav passions of my father, she was still able to see the decent and gentle man abiding in his heart.

As I thought of all this, I looked around the table and felt almost tearful. God, I loved these people, they gave my life meaning and worth and dignity, every single one of them.

And then Mom said it, as I knew she inevitably would. "It's a little funny without Davey here, isn't it?"

Laura glanced across the table at me then quickly went back to her cranberry sauce.

Dad touched Mom's hand right away and said, "Now, Mom, Davey would want us to enjoy ourselves and you know it."

Mom was already starting to cry. She got up from the table and whispered, "Excuse me," and left the dining room for the tiny bathroom off the kitchen.

Dad put his fork down and said, "She'll be all right in a minute or two."

"I know," I said.

My six-year-old son, Rob, said, "Is Gramma sad about Uncle Davey, Grandpa?"

And Dad, looking pretty sad himself, nodded and said, "Yes, she is, honey. Now you go ahead and finish your meal."

Rob didn't need much urging to do that.

A minute later, Mom was back at the table. "Sorry," she said.

Laura leaned over and kissed Mom on the cheek.

We went back to eating our Thanksgiving meal.

Davey was my younger brother. Five years younger. He was everything I was not—socially poised, talented in the arts, a heartbreaker with the ladies. I was plodding, unimaginative and no Robert Redford, believe me.

I had only one advantage over Davey. I never became a heroin addict. This happened sometime during his twenty-first year, back at the time the last strident chords of all those sixties protest guitars could be heard fading into the dusk.

He never recovered from this addiction. I don't know if you've ever known any family that's gone through addiction but in some ways the person who suffers least is the person who is addicted. He or she can hide behind the drugs or the alcohol. He doesn't have to watch himself slowly die, nor watch his loved ones die right along with him, or watch them go through their meager life savings trying to help him.

Davey was a heroin addict for fourteen years. During that time he was arrested a total of sixteen times, served three long stretches in county jail (he avoided prison only because I called in a few favors), went through six different drug rehab programs, got into two car accidents—one that nearly killed him, one that nearly killed a six-year-old girl—and went through two marriages and countless clamorous relationships, usually with women who were also heroin addicts (a certain primness keeps me from calling my brother a "junkie," I suppose).

And most of the time, despite the marriages, despite the relationships, despite the occasional rehab programs, he stayed at home with my folks.

Those happy retirement years they'd long dreamed of never came because Davey gave them no rest. One night a strange and exotic creature came to the front door and informed Dad that if Davey didn't pay him the drug money he owed him in the next twenty-four hours, Davey would be a dead man. Another night Davey pounded another man nearly to death on the front lawn.

Too many times, Dad had to go down to the city jail late at night to bail Davey out. Too many times, Mom had to go to the doctor to get increased dosages of tranquilizers and sleeping pills.

Davey was six months shy of age forty and it appeared that given his steely Czech constitution, he was going to live a lot longer—not forgo the heroin, you understand—live maybe another full decade, a full decade of watching him grind Mom and Dad down with all his hopeless grief.

Then a few months ago, early September, a hotel clerk found him in this shabby room frequently used as a "shooting gallery." He was dead. He'd overdosed.

Mom and Dad were still working through the shock.

"Is there pink ice cream, Grandma?" Kate asked.

Grandma smiled at me. Baskin-Robbins has a bubble-gum-flavored ice cream and Mom has made it Kate's special treat whenever she visits.

"There's plenty of pink ice cream," Grandma said. "Especially for good girls like you."

And right then, seeing Kate and my mother beaming at each other, I knew I'd done the right thing sneaking up to the hotel room where Davey sometimes went with other junkies, and then giving him another shot when he was still in delirium and blind ecstasy from the first. He was still my brother, lying there dying before me, but I was doing my whole family a favor. I wanted Mom and Dad to have a few good years anyway.

"Hey, Mr. Counselor," Dad said, getting my attention again. "Looks like you could use some more turkey."

I laughed and patted my burgeoning little middle-class belly. "Correction," I said. "I could use a lot more turkey."

STALKER

i

Eleven years, two months, and five days later, we caught him. In an apartment house on the west edge of Des Moines. The man who had raped and murdered my daughter.

Inside the rental Pontiac, Slocum said, "I can fix it so we have to kill him." The dramatic effect of his words was lost somewhat when he waggled a bag of Dunkin' Donuts at me.

I shook my head. "No."

"No to the doughnuts. Or no to killing him?"

"Both."

"You're the boss."

I suppose I should tell you about Slocum. At least two hundred pounds overweight, given to western clothes too large for even his bulk (trying to hide that slope of belly, I suppose), Slocum is thirty-nine, wears a beard the angriest of Old Testament prophets would have envied, and carries at all times in his shoulder holster a Colt King Cobra, one of the most repellent-looking weapons I've ever seen. I don't suppose someone like me—former economics professor at the state university and antigun activist of the first form—

ever quite gets used to the look and feel and smell of such weapons. Never quite.

I had been riding shotgun in an endless caravan of rented cars, charter airplanes, Greyhound buses, Amtrak passenger cars and even a few motorboats for the past seven months, ever since that day in Chicago when I turned my life over to Slocum the way others turned their lives over to Jesus or Republicanism.

I entered his office, put twenty-five thousand dollars in cash on his desk, and said, "Everybody tells me you're the best. I hope that's true, Mr. Slocum."

He grinned at me with teeth that Red Man had turned the color of peach wine. "Fortunately for you, it is true. Now, what is it you'd like me to do?" He turned down the Hank Williams Jr. tape he'd been listening to and waved to me, with a massive beefy hand bearing two faded blue tattoos, to start talking.

I had worked with innumerable police departments, innumerable private investigators, two soldiers of fortune, and a psychic over the past eleven years in an effort to find the man who killed my daughter.

That cold, bright January day seven months ago, and as something of a last resort, I had turned to a man whose occupation sounded far too romantic to be any good to me: Slocum was a bounty hunter.

"Maybe you should wait here."

"Why?" I said.

"You know why."

"Because I don't like guns? Because I don't want to arrange it so we have to kill him?"

"It could be dangerous."

"You really think I care about that?"

He studied my face. "No, I guess you don't."

"I just want to see him when he gets caught. I just want to see his expression when he realizes he's going to go to prison for the rest of his life."

He grinned at me with his stained teeth. "I'd rather see him when he's been gut-shot. Still afraid to die but at the same time wanting to. You know? I gut-shot a gook in Nam once and watched him the whole time. It took him an hour. It was one long hour, believe me."

Staring at the three-story apartment house, I sighed. "Eleven years."

"I'm sorry for all you've gone through."

"I know you are, Slocum. That's one of the things a good liberal like me can't figure out about a man like you."

"What's that?"

"How you can enjoy killing people and still feel so much compassion for the human race in general."

He shrugged. "I'm not killing humanity in general, Robert. I'm killing animals." He took out the Cobra, grim gray metal almost glowing in the late June sunlight, checked it, and put it back. His eyes scanned the upper part of the redbrick apartment house. Many of the screens were torn and a few shattered windows had been taped up. The lawn needed mowing and a tiny black baby walked around wearing a filthy too-small T-shirt and nothing else. Twenty years ago this had probably been a very nice middle-class place. Now it had the feel of an inner-city housing project.

"One thing," he said, as I started to open the door. He put a meaty hand on my shoulder for emphasis.

"Yes?"

"When this is all over—however it turns out—you're going to feel let down."

"You maybe; not me. All I've wanted for the past eleven years was finding Dexter. Now we have found him. Now I can start my life again."

"That's the thing," he said. "That's what you don't understand."

"What don't I understand?"

"This has changed you, Robert. You start hunting people—even when you've got a personal stake in it—and it changes you."

I laughed. "Right. I think this afternoon I'll go down to my friendly neighborhood recruiting office and sign up for Green Beret school."

Occasionally, he got irritated with me. Now seemed to be one of those times. "I'm just some big dumb redneck, right, Robert? What would I know about the subtleties of human psychology, right?"

"Look, Slocum, I'm sorry if—"
He patted his Cobra. "Let's go."

ii

They found her in a grave that was really more of a wide hole up in High Ridge forest where the scrub pines run heavy down to the river. My daughter, Debbie. The coroner estimated she had been there at least thirty days. At the time of her death she'd been seventeen.

This is the way the official version ran: Debbie, leaving her job at the Baskin-Robbins, was dragged into a car, taken into the forest, raped, and killed. Only when I pressed him on the subject did the coroner tell me the extent to which she had been mutilated, the mutilation coming, so far as could be determined, after she had died. At the funeral the coffin was closed.

At the time I had a wife—small, tanned, intelligent in a hard sensible way I often envied, quick to laugh, equally quick to cry—and a son. Jeff was twelve the year his sister died. He was seventeen when he died five years later.

When you're sitting home watching the sullen parade of faceless murders flicker and die on your screen—the weeping mother of the victim, the carefully spoken detective in charge, the sexless doll-like face of the reporter signing off on the story—you don't take into account the impact that the violent death of a loved one has on a family. I do; after Debbie's death, I made a study of the subject. Like so many things I've studied in my life, I ended up with facts that neither enlightened nor comforted. They were just facts.

My family's loss was measured in two ways—my wife's depression (she came from a family that suffered mental illness the way some families suffered freckles) and my son's wildness.

Not that I was aware of either of these problems as they began to play out. When it became apparent to me that the local police were never going to solve the murder—their entire investigation centered on an elusive 1986 red Chevrolet—I virtually left home. Using a generous inheritance left to me by an uncle, I began—in tandem with the private eyes and soldiers of fortune and psychics

I've already mentioned—to pursue my daughter's killer. I have no doubt that my pursuit was obsessive, and clinically so. Nights I would lie on the strange, cold, lonely bed of a strange, cold, lonely motel room thinking of tomorrow, always tomorrow, and how we were only hours away from a man we now knew to be one William K. Dexter, age thirty-seven, twice incarcerated for violent crimes, unduly attached to a very aged mother, perhaps guilty of two similar killings in two other midwestern states. I thought of nothing else—so much so that sometimes, lying there in the motel room, I wanted to take a butcher knife and cut into my brain until I found the place where memory dwelt—and cut it away. William K. Dexter was my only thought.

During this time, me gone, my wife began a series of affairs (I learned all this later) that only served to increase the senseless rage she felt (she seemed to resent the men because they could not give her peace)—she still woke up screaming Debbie's name. Her drinking increased also and she began shopping around for new shrinks the way you might shop around for a new car. A few times during her last two months we made love when I came home on the weekend from pursuing Dexter in one fashion or another—but afterward it was always the same. "You weren't a good father to her, Robert." "I know." "And I wasn't a good mother. We're such goddamned selfish people." And then the sobbing, sobbing to the point of passing out (always drunk of course) in a little-girl pile in the bathroom or the center of the hardwood bedroom floor.

Jeff found her. Just home from school, calling her name, not really expecting her to be there, he went upstairs to the TV room for the afternoon ritual of a dance show and there he found her. The last images of a soap opera flickering on the screen. A drink of bourbon in the Smurf glass she always found so inexplicably amusing. A cigarette guttering out in the ashtray. Dressed in one of Jeff's T-shirts with the rock-and-roll slogan on its front and a pair of designer jeans that pointed up the teenage sleekness of her body. Dead. Heart attack.

On the day of her funeral, up in the TV room where she'd died, I was having drinks of my own, wishing I had some facts to tell me what I should be feeling now . . . when Jeff came in and sat down next to me and put his arm around my neck the way he used to when he was three or four. "You can't cry, can you, Dad?" All I could do was sigh. He'd been watching me. "You should cry, Dad. You really should. You didn't even cry when Debbie was killed. Mom told me." He said all this in the young man's voice I still couldn't quite get used to—the voice he used so successfully with ninth-grade girls on the phone. He wasn't quite a man yet but he wasn't a kid, either. In a moment of panic I felt he was an imposter, that this was a joke; where was my little boy? "That's all I do, Dad. Is cry, I mean. I think it helps me. I really do."

So I'd tried, first there with Jeff in the TV room, later alone in my bedroom. But there were just dry choking sounds and no tears at all. At all. I would think of Debbie, her sweet soft radiance; and of my wife, the years when it had been good for us, her so tender and kind in the shadows of our hours together; and I wanted to cry for the loss I felt. But all I could see was the face of William K. Dexter. In some way, he had become more important to me even than the two people he'd taken from me.

Jeff died three years later, wrapped around a light pole on the edge of a country park, drugs and vodka found in the front seat of the car I'd bought him six months earlier.

Left alone at the wake, kneeling before his waxen corpse, an Our Father faint on my lips, I'd felt certain I could cry. It would be a tribute to Jeff; one he'd understand; some part of the process by which he'd forgive me for being gone so much, for pursuing William K. Dexter while Jeff was discovering drugs and alcohol and girls too young to know about nurturing. I put out my hand and touched his cheek, his cold waxen cheek, and I felt something die in me. It was the opposite of crying, of bursting forth with poisons that needed to be purged. Something was dead in me and would never be reborn.

It was not too long after this that I met Frank Slocum and it was not long after Slocum took the case that we began to close inexorably in on William K. Dexter.

And soon enough we were here, at the apartment house just outside Des Moines.

Eleven years, two months, and five days later.

iii

The name on the hallway mailbox said Severn, George Severn. We knew better, of course.

Up carpeted stairs threadbare and stained, down a hallway thick with dusty sunlight, to a door marked 4-A.

"Behind me," Slocum whispered, waving me to the wall.

For a moment, the only noises belonged to the apartment building; the thrum of electricity snaking through the walls; the creak of roof in summer wind; a toilet exploding somewhere on the floor below us.

Slocum put a hefty finger to his thick mouth, stabbing through a thistle of beard to do so. Sssh.

Slocum stood back from the door himself. His Cobra was in his hand, ready. He reached around the long way and set big knuckles against the cheap faded pine of the door.

On the other side of the door, I heard chair legs scrape against tile.

Somebody in there.

William K. Dexter.

Chair legs scraped again; footsteps. They did not come all the way to the door, however, rather stopped at what I imagined was probably the center of the living room.

"Yeah?"

Slocum put his finger to his lips again. Reached around once more and knocked.

"I said 'Yeah.' Who the hell is it?"

He was curious about who was in the hall, this George Severn was, but not curious enough to open the door and find out.

One more knock. Quick rap really; nothing more.

Inside, you could sense Severn's aggravation.

"Goddammit," he said and took a few loud steps toward the door but then stopped.

Creak of floor; flutter of robin wings as bird settled on hallway window; creak of floor again from inside the apartment.

Slocum held up a halting hand. Then he pantomimed Don't Move with his lips. He waited for my reaction. I nodded.

He looked funny, a man as big as he was, doing a very broad, cartoon version of a man walking away. Huge noisy steps so that it sounded as if he were very quickly retreating. But he did all this in place. He did it for thirty seconds and then he eased himself flat back against the wall. He took his Cobra and put it man-high on the edge of the door frame.

Severn didn't come out in thirty seconds but he did come out in about a minute.

For eleven years I'd wondered what he'd look like. Photos deceive. I always pictured him as formidable. He would have to be, I'd reasoned; the savage way he'd mutilated her . . . He was a skinny fortyish man in a stained white T-shirt and Levis that looked a little too big. He wore the wide sideburns of a hillbilly trucker and the scowl of a mean drunk. He stank of sleep and whiskey. He carried a butcher knife that appeared to be new. It still had the lime green price sticker on the black handle.

When he came out of his apartment, he made the mistake of looking straight ahead.

Slocum did two things at the same time: slammed the Cobra's nose hard against Severn's temple and yanked a handful of hair so hard, Severn's knees buckled. "You're dead, man, in case you haven't figured it out already," Slocum said. He seemed enraged; he was a little frightening to watch.

He grabbed some more hair and then he pushed Severn all the way back into his apartment.

iv

Slocum got him on a straight-backed chair, hit him so hard in the mouth that you could hear teeth go, and then handcuffed him, still in the chair, to the aged Formica dining-room table.

Slocum then cocked his foot back and kicked Severn clean and hard in the ribs. Almost immediately, Severn's mouth started boiling with red mucus that didn't seem quite thick enough to be blood.

Slocum next went over to Severn and ripped his T-shirt away from his shoulder. Without a word, Slocum motioned me over.

With his Cobra, Slocum pointed to a faded tattoo on Severn's right shoulder. It read: *Mindy* with a rose next to it. Not many men had such a tattoo on their right shoulder. It was identical to the one listed in all of Severn's police records.

Slocum slapped him with stunning ferocity directly across the mouth, so hard that both Severn and his chair were lifted from the floor.

For the first time, I moved. Not to hit Severn myself but to put a halting hand on Slocum's arm. "That's enough."

"We've got the right guy!" It was easy to see he was crazed in some profound animal way I'd never seen in anybody before.

"I know we do."

"The guy who killed your daughter!"

"I know," I said, "but—"

"But what?"

I sighed. "But I don't want to be like him and if we sat here and beat him, that's exactly what we'd be. Animals—just like him."

Slocum's expression was a mixture of contempt and disbelief. I could see whatever respect he'd had for me—or perhaps it had been nothing more than mere pity—was gone now. He looked at me the same way I looked at him—as some alien species.

"Please, Slocum," I said.

He got one more in, a good solid right hand to the left side of Severn's head. Severn's eyes rolled and he went out. From the smell, you could tell he'd wet his pants.

I kept calling him Severn. But of course he wasn't Severn. He was William K. Dexter.

Slocum went over to the ancient Kelvinator, took out a can of Hamms and opened it with a great deal of violence, and then slammed the refrigerator door.

"You think he's all right?" I said.

"What the hell's that supposed to mean?"

"It means did you kill him?"

"Kill him?" He laughed. The contempt was back in his voice. "Kill him? No, but I should have. I keep thinking of your daughter, man. All the things you've told me about her. Not a perfect kid—no kid is—but a real gentle little girl. A girl you supposedly loved. Your frigging daughter, man. Your frigging daughter." He sloshed his

beer in the general direction of Dexter. "I should get out my hunting knife and cut his balls off. That's what I should do. And that's
just for openers. Just for openers."

He started pacing around, then, Slocum did, and I could gauge
his rage. I suppose at that moment he wanted to kill us both—Dexter for being an animal, me for being a weakling—neither of us the
type of person Slocum wanted in his universe.

The apartment was small and crammed with threadbare and
wobbly furniture. Everything had been burned with cigarettes and
disfigured with beer-can rings. The sour smell of bad cooking lay on
the air; sunlight poured through filthy windows; and even from
here you could smell the rancid odors of the bathroom. On the bureau lay two photographs, one of a plump woman in a shabby
housedress standing with her arm around Dexter, obviously his
mother; and a much younger Dexter squinting into the sun outside
a gray metal barracks where he had served briefly as an army private before being pushed out on a mental.

Peeking into the bedroom, I found the centerfolds he'd pinned
up. They weren't the centerfolds of the quality men's magazines
where the women were beautiful to begin with and made even
more so with careful lighting and gauzy effects; no, these were the
women of the street, hard-eyed, flabby-bodied, some even tattooed
like Dexter himself. They covered the walls on either side of his sad
little cot where he slept in a room littered with empty beer cans and
hard-crusted pizza boxes. Many of the centerfolds he'd defaced,
drawing penises in black ballpoint aimed at their vaginas or their
mouths, or putting huge blood-dripping knives into their breasts or
eyes or even their vaginas. All I could think of was Debbie and what
he'd done to her that long-ago night. . . .

A terrible, oppressive nausea filled me as I backed out of the
bedroom and groped for the couch so I could sit down.

"What's the matter?" Slocum said.

"Shut up."

"What?"

"Shut the fuck up!"

I sank to the couch—the sunlight through the greasy window

making me ever warmer—and cupped my hands in my face and swallowed again and again until I felt the vomit in my throat and esophagus and stomach recede.

I was shaking, chilled now with sweat.

"Can you wake him up?"

"What?"

"Can you wake him up?"

"Sure," Slocum said. "Why?"

"Because I want to talk to him."

Slocum gulped the last of his beer, tossed the can into a garbage sack overflowing with coffee grounds and tomato rinds, and then went over to the sink. He took down a big glass with the Flintstones on it and filled it with water, then took the glass over to where he had Dexter handcuffed. With a certain degree of obvious pleasure, he threw the water across Dexter's head. He threw the glass—as if it were now contaminated—into the corner where it shattered into three large jagged pieces.

He grabbed Dexter by the hair and jerked his head back.

Groaning, Dexter came awake.

"Now what?" Slocum said, turning to me.

"Now I want to talk to him."

"Talk to him," Slocum said. "Right."

He pointed a large hand at Dexter as if he were a master of ceremonies introducing the next act.

It wasn't easy, getting up off that couch and going over to him. In a curious way, I was terrified of him. If I pushed him hard enough, he would tell me the exact truth about the night. The truth in detail. What she had looked like and sounded like—her screams as he raped her; her screams as she died—and then I would have my facts . . . but facts so horrible I would not be able to live with them. How many times—despite myself—I had tried to recreate that night. But there would be no solace in this particular truth; no solace at all.

I stood over him. "Have you figured out who I am yet?"

He stared up at me. He started crying. "Hey, man, I never did nothing to you."

"You raped and killed a girl named Debbie eleven years ago."

"I don't know what you're talking about, man. Honest. You got the wrong guy."

I knew that by the way I studied his face—every piece of beard stubble, the green matter collected in the corners of his eyes, the dandruff flaked off at the front of his receding hairline—that I was trying to learn something about him, something that would grant me peace after all these years.

A madman, this Dexter, and so not quite responsible for what he'd done and perhaps even deserving of pity in my good liberal soul.

But he didn't seem insane, at least not insane enough to move me in any way. He was just a cheap trapped frightened animal.

"Really, man; really I don't know what the hell you're talking about."

"I've been tracking you for eleven years now—"

"Jesus, man; listen—"

"You're going to hate prison, Dexter. Or maybe they'll even execute you. Did you ever read anything about the injections they give? They make it sound so humane but it's the waiting, Dexter. It's the waiting—"

"Please," he said, "please," and he writhed against his handcuffs, scraping the table across the floor in the process.

"Eleven years, Dexter," I said.

I could hear my voice, what was happening to it—all my feelings about Dexter were merging into my memories of those defaced centerfolds in his bedroom—and Slocum must have known it, too, with his animal wisdom, known at just what moment I would be right for it

because just then and just so

the Cobra came into my hands and I

shot Dexter once in the face and once in the

chest and I

V

Slocum explained to me—though I really wasn't listening—that they were called by various names (toss guns or throwaway guns) but they were carried by police officers in case they wanted to show that the person they'd just killed had been armed.

From a holster strapped to his ankle, Slocum took a .38, wiped it clean of prints, and set it next to Dexter's hand.

Below and to the side of us the apartment house was a frenzy of shouts and cries—fear and panic—and already in the distance sirens exploded red on the soft blue air of the summer day.

vi

That evening I cried.

I sat in a good room in a good hotel with the air-conditioning going strong, a fine dinner and many fine drinks in my belly, and I cried.

Wept, really.

Whatever had kept me from crying for my daughter and then my wife and then my son was gone now and so I could love and mourn them in a way I'd never been able to. I thought of each of them—their particular ways of laughing, their particular sets of pleasures and dreams, their particular fears and apprehensions— and it was as if they joined me there in that chill antiseptic hotel room, Debbie in her blue sweater and jeans, my wife in her white linen sheath, Jeff in his Kiss T-shirt and chinos—came round in the way the medieval church taught that angels gathered around the bed of a dying person . . . only I wasn't dying.

My family was there to tell me that I was to live again. To seek some sort of peace and normalcy after the forced march of these past eleven years.

"I love you so much," I said aloud to each of them, and wept all the more; "I love you so much."

And then I slept.

vii

"I talked to the district attorney," Slocum said in the coffee shop the following morning. "He says it's very unlikely there will be any charges."

"He really thought Dexter was armed?"

"Wouldn't you? A piece of trash like Dexter?"

I stared at him. "You know something terrible?"

"What?"

"I don't feel guilty."

He let go with one of those cigarette-raspy laughs of his. "Good."

Then it was his turn to stare at me, there in the hubbub of clattering dishes and good sweet coffee smells and bacon sizzling on the grill. "So what now?"

"See if I can get my job back."

"At the university?"

"Umm-hmm."

He kept staring. "You don't feel any guilt, do you?"

"No. I mean, I know I should. Whatever else, he was a human being. But—"

He smiled his hard Old Testament smile. "Now, don't you go giving me any of those mousy little liberal 'buts,' all right?"

"All right."

"You just go back and live your life and make it a good one."

"I owe you one hell of a lot, Slocum."

He put forth a slab of hand and a genuine look of affection in his eyes. "Just make it a good one," he said. "Promise?"

"Promise."

"And no guilt?"

"No guilt."

He grinned. "I knew I could make a man out of you."

viii

Her name was Anne Stevens and she was to dominate my first year back at the university. Having met at the faculty picnic—hot August giving way to the fierce melancholy of Indian summer—we began what we both hoped (her divorced; me not quite human yet) would be a pleasant but slow-moving relationship. We were careful to not introduce real passion, for instance, until we both felt certain we could handle it, about the time the first of the Christmas decorations blew in the gray wind of Harcourt Square.

School itself took some adjusting. First, there was the fact that the students seemed less bright and inquisitive, more conservative than the students I remembered. Second, the faculty had some doubts about me; given my experiences over the past eleven years, they wondered how I would fit into a setting whose goals were at best abstract. I wondered, too. . . .

After the first time we made love—Anne's place, unplanned, satisfying if slightly embarrassing—I went home and stared at the photograph of my wife I keep on my bureau. In whispers, I apologized for what I'd done. If I'd been a better husband I would have no guilt now. But I had not, alas, been a better husband at all. . . .

In the spring, a magazine took a piece on inflation I wrote and the academic dean made a considerable fuss over this fact. Also in the spring Anne and I told each other that we loved each other in a variety of ways, emotionally, sexually, spiritually. We set June 23 as our wedding day.

It was on May 5 that I saw the item in the state newspaper. For the following three weeks I did my best to forget it, troubling as it was. Anne began to notice a difference in my behavior, and to talk about it. I just kept thinking of the newspaper item and of something Slocum had said that day when I killed Dexter.

In the middle of a May night—the breeze sweet with the newly blooming world—I typed out a six-page letter to Anne, packed two bags, stopped by a 7-Eleven and filled the Volvo and dropped Anne's letter in a mailbox, and then set out on the interstate.

Two mornings later, I walked up a dusty flight of stairs inside an apartment house. A Hank Williams Jr. record filled the air.

To be heard above the music, I had to pound.

I half expected what would happen, that when the door finally opened a gun would be shoved in my face. It was.

A Cobra.

I didn't say anything. I just handed him the news clipping. He waved me in—he lived in a place not dissimilar from the one Dexter had lived in—read the clipping as he opened an 8:48 A.M. beer.

Finished reading it, he let it glide to the coffee table that was covered with gun magazines.

"So?"

"So I want to help him. I don't want him to go through what I did."

"You know him or something?"

"No."

"Just some guy whose daughter was raped and killed and the suspect hasn't been apprehended."

"Right."

"And you want what?"

"I've got money and I've got time. I quit my job."

"But what do you want?"

"I want us to go after him. Remember how you said that I'd changed and that I didn't even know it?"

"Yeah, I remember."

"Well, you were right. I have changed."

He stood up and started laughing, his considerable belly shaking beneath his Valvoline T-shirt. "Well, I'll be goddamned, Robert. I'll be goddamned. I did make a man out of you, after all. So how about having a beer with me?"

At first—it not being 9:00 A.M. yet—I hesitated. But then I nodded my head and said, "Yeah, Slocum. That sounds good. That really sounds good."

THE WIND FROM MIDNIGHT

For Ray Bradbury

E ven with the windows open, the Greyhound bus was hot inside as it roared through the rural California night.

Plump ladies in sweat-soaked summer dresses furiously worked paper fans that bore the names of funeral parlors. Plump men in sleeveless T-shirts sat talking of disappointing baseball scores ("Them goddamn Red Sox just don't have it this year; nossir they don't") and the Republican convention that had just nominated Dwight Eisenhower. Most of the men aboard liked Ike and liked him quite a bit. These men smoked Lucky Strikes and Chesterfields and Fatimas and more than a few of them snuck quick silver flasks from their hip pockets.

In the middle of the bus was a slender, pretty woman who inexplicably burst into tears every twenty miles or so. It was assumed by all who watched her that she was having man trouble of some sort. A woman this pretty wouldn't carry on so otherwise. She'd been deserted and was heading home to Mama was the consensus aboard the Greyhound.

Traveling with the pretty woman was a sweet-faced little girl who was obviously the daughter. She was maybe five or six and wore a faded white dress that reminded some of First Communion, and patent-leather shoes that reminded others of Shirley Temple. For the most part she was well-behaved, the little girl, stroking and petting her mama when she cried, and sitting prim and obedient when Mama was just looking sadly out the window.

But fifty miles ago the little girl had gone back to use the rest-room—she'd had a big nickel Pepsi and it had gone right through her—and there she'd seen the tiny woman sitting all by herself in one corner of the vast backseat.

All the little girl could think of—and this was what she whispered to her mama later—was a doll that had come to life.

Before the bus pulled into the oceanside town for a rest stop, the little girl found exactly four excuses to run back there and get another good peek at the tiny woman.

She just couldn't believe what she was seeing.

A lot of passengers hurried to get off the bus so they could stand around the front of the depot and get a good look at her. In the rolling darkness of the Greyhound, they hadn't really gotten much of a glimpse and they were just naturally curious, this kind of people.

She didn't disappoint them.

She was just as tiny as she'd seemed and in her plain white blouse and her navy linen skirt and her dark seamed hose and her cute little pumps with the two-inch heels she looked like a five-year-old who was all dressed up in her mama's clothes.

Back on the bus they'd argued in whispers whether she was a dwarf or a midget. There was some scientific difference between the two but damned if anybody could remember exactly what that was.

From inside the depot came smells of hamburgers and onions and french fries and cigar smoke, all stale on the still summer air. Also from inside came the sounds of Miss Kay Starr singing "The Wheel of Fortune." Skinny white cowboys clung like moths to the lights of the depot entrance as did old black men the color of soot and snappy young sailors in their dress whites and hayseed grins.

This was the scene the tiny woman confronted. And in moments she was gone from it.

The cabbie knew where the carnival was, of course. There would be only one in a burg like this.

He drove his rattling '47 Plymouth out to the pier where the midway and all the rides looked like the toys of a baby giant.

He drove her right up to the entrance and said, "That'll be eighty-five cents, miss."

She opened her purse and sank a tiny hand into its deep waiting darkness.

She gave him a dollar's worth of quarters and said, "That's for you."

"Why, thank you."

She opened the door. The dome light came on. He noticed for the first time that she was nice-looking. Not gorgeous or anything like that. But nice-looking. Silken dark hair in a pageboy. Blue eyes that would have been beautiful if they weren't tainted with sorrow. And a full mouth so erotic it made him uncomfortable. Why if a normal-sized man was to try anything with a tiny woman like this—

He put the thought from his mind.

As she started to leave the cab, he just blurted it out. "I suppose you know what happened here a month ago. About the—little guy, I mean."

She just looked at him.

"He stole a gun from one of the carnies here and raced back to his hotel room and killed himself." The cabbie figured that the tiny woman would want to know about it, her being just like the little guy and all. To show he was friendly, the cabbie always told colored people stories about colored people in just the same way.

The cabbie's head was turned in profile, waiting for the woman to respond.

But the only sound, faint among the *crack* of air rifles and the roar of the rollercoaster and the high piping pitch of the calliope, was the cab door being quietly closed.

❖   ❖   ❖

A lady with a beard, a man with a vagina. A chance to get your fortune told by a gypsy woman with a knife scar on her left cheek. A sobbing little blond boy looking frantically for his lost mother. A man just off the midway slapping hard a woman he called a fucking whore bitch. An old man in a straw hat gaping fixedly at a chunky stripper the barker kept pointing to with a long wooden cane.

Linnette saw all these things and realized why her brother had always liked carnivals. She liked them for the same reason. Because in all the spectacle—beautiful and ugly, happy and sad alike—tiny people tended to get overlooked. There was so much to see and do and feel and desire that normal people barely gave tiny people a glance.

And that's why, for many of his thirty-one years, her brother had been drawn to midways.

He told her about this one, of course, many times. How he came here after a long day at the typewriter. How he liked to sit on a bench up near the shooting gallery and watch the women go by and try and imagine what they'd be like if he had had the chance to meet them. He was such a romantic, her brother, in his heart a matinee idol worthy of Valentino and Gable.

She'd learned all this from his infrequent phone calls. He always called at dinner time on Sunday evening because of the rates and he always talked nine minutes exactly. He always asked her how things were going at the library where she worked and she always asked him if he was ever going to write that important novel she knew he had in him.

They were brother and sister, and more, of course, which was why, when he'd put that gun to his head there in the dim little coffin of a room where he lived and wrote—

She tried not to think of these things now.

She worked her way through the crowd, moving slowly toward the steady *cracking* sounds of the shooting gallery. A Mr. Kelly was who she was looking for.

A woman given to worry and anxiety, she kept checking the new white number ten envelope in her purse. One hundred dollars in crisp green currency. Certainly that should be enough for Mr. Kelly.

*   *   *

Aimee was taking a cigarette break when she happened to see Linnette. She'd spent the last month trying to forget about the dwarf and the part Ralph Banghart, the man who ran the Mirror Maze, had played in the death of the dwarf.

And the part Aimee had played, too.

Maybe if she'd never gotten involved, never tried to help the poor little guy—

Aimee lit her next Cavalier with the dying ember of her previous Cavalier.

Standing next to the tent she worked, Aimee reached down to retrieve the Coke she'd set in the grass.

And just as she bent over, she felt big male hands slip over her slender hips. "Booo!"

She jerked away from him immediately. She saw him now as this diseased person. Whatever ugliness he had inside him, she didn't want to catch.

"I told you, Ralph, I don't ever want you touching me again."

"Aw, babe, I just—"

She slapped him. And hard enough that his head jerked back and a grunt of pain sounded in his throat.

"Hey—"

"You still don't give a damn that little guy killed himself, do you?"

Ralph rubbed his sore cheek. "I didn't kill him."

"Sure you did. You're just not man enough to admit it. If you hadn't played that practical joke on him—"

"If the little bastard couldn't take a joke—"

She raised her hand to slap him again. Grinning, he started to duck away.

She spit at him. This, he didn't have time to duck away from. She got him right on the nose.

"I don't want you to come anywhere goddamn near me, do you understand?" Aimee said, knowing she was shrieking and not caring.

Ralph looked around, embarrassed now that people were starting to watch, shook his head and muttered some curses, and left, daubing off the spittle with his white soiled handkerchief.

Aimee tossed her cigarette into the summer dry grass and started looking around for the dwarf woman again.

She just had this sense that the woman had somehow known the little guy who'd killed himself.

Aimee just had to find her and talk to her. Just had to.

She started searching.

Mr. Kelly turned out to be a big man with an anchor tattoo on his right forearm and beads of silver sweat standing in rows on his pink bald pate.

At the moment he was showing a woman with huge breasts how to operate an air rifle. Mr. Kelly kept nudging her accidentally-on-purpose with his elbow. If the woman minded, she didn't complain. But then the woman's boyfriend came back from somewhere and he looked to be about the same size but younger and trimmer than Mr. Kelly so Mr. Kelly withdrew his elbow and let the boyfriend take over the shooting lessons.

Then Mr. Kelly turned to Linnette. "What can I do for ya, small fry?"

Linnette always told herself that insults didn't matter. Sticks and stones and all that. And most of the time they didn't. But every once in a while, as right now for instance, they pierced the heart like a fatal sliver of glass.

"My name is Linnette Dobbins."

"So? My name is Frank Kelly."

"A month or so ago my brother stole a gun from you and—"

Smiles made most people look pleasant. But Mr. Kelly's smile only served to make him look knowing and dirty. "Oh, the dwarf." He looked her up and down. "Sure. I should've figured that out for myself."

"The police informed me that they've given you the gun back."

"Yeah. What about it?"

"I'd like to buy it from you."

"Buy it from me? What the hell're you talkin' about, small fry?"

Mr. Kelly was just about to go on when a new pair of lovers bellied up to the gallery counter and waited for instructions.

Without excusing himself, Mr. Kelly went over to the lovers, picked up an air rifle and started demonstrating how to win the gal here a nice little teddy bear.

"A dwarf, you say?"

Aimee nodded.

"Jeeze, Aimee, I think I'd remember if I'd seen a dwarf woman wanderin' around the midway."

"Thanks, Hank."

Hank then got kind of flustered and said, "You think we're ever gonna go to a movie sometime Aimee, like I asked you that time?"

She touched his shoulder tenderly and gave him a sweet quick smile. "I'm sure thinking about it, Hank. I really am." Hank was such a nice guy. She just wished he were her type.

And then she was off again, moving frantically around the midway, asking various carnies if they'd seen a woman who was a dwarf.

Hank's was the tenth booth she'd stopped at.

Nobody had seen the woman. Nobody.

"So why would you want the gun your brother killed himself with, small fry?"

From her purse, Linnette took the plain white number ten envelope and handed it up to Mr. Kelly.

"What's this?" he said.

"Look inside."

He opened the envelope flap and peeked in. He ran a pudgy finger through the bills. He whistled. "Hundred bucks."

"Right."

"For a beat-up old service revolver. Hell, small fry, you don't know much about guns. You could buy a gun like that in a pawn shop for five bucks."

"The money's all yours."

"Just for this one gun?"

"That's right, Mr. Kelly. Just for this one gun."

He whistled again. The money had made him friendlier. This time his smile lacked malevolence. "Boy, small fry, I almost hate to take your money."

"But you will?"

He gave her a big cornball grin now and she saw in it the fact that he was just as much a hayseed as the rubes he bilked every night. The difference was, he didn't know he was a hayseed.

"You damn bet ya I will," he said, and trotted to the back of the tent to get the gun.

"I'll need some bullets for it, too," Linnette called after him.

He turned around and looked at her. "Bullets? What for?"

"Given the price I'm paying, Mr. Kelly, I'd say that was my business."

He looked at her for a long time and then his cornball grin opened his face up again. "Well, small fry, I guess I can't argue with you on that one now, can I? Bullets it is."

The carnival employed a security man named Bulicek. It was said that he was a former cop who'd gotten caught running a penny ante protection racket on his beat and had been summarily discharged. Here, he always smelled of whiskey and Sen-Sen to cut the stink of the whiskey. He strutted around in his blue uniform with big half-moons of sweat under each arm and a creaking leather holster riding around his considerable girth. His best friend in the carny was Kelly at the shooting gallery, which figured.

Aimee avoided Bulicek because he always managed to put his hands on her in some way whenever they talked. But now she had no choice.

She'd visited seven more carnies since Hank and nobody had seen a woman dwarf.

Bulicek was just coming out of the big whitewashed building that was half men's and half women's.

He smiled when he saw her. She could feel his paws on her already.

"I'm looking for somebody," she said.

"So am I. And I found her." Bulicek knew every bad movie line in the world.

"A woman who's a dwarf. She's somewhere on the midway. Have you seen her?"

Bulicek shrugged. "What do I get if I tell ya?"

"You get the privilege of doing your job." She tried to keep the anger from her voice. She needed his cooperation.

"And nothing else?" His eyes found a nice place on her body to settle momentarily.

"Nothing else."

He raised his eyes and shook his head and took out a package of cigarettes.

Some teenagers with ducks ass haircuts and black leather jackets—even in this kind of heat for crissakes—wandered by and Bulicek, he-man that he was, gave them the bad eye.

When he turned back to Aimee, she was shocked by his sudden anger. "You think you could talk to me one time, Miss High and Mighty, without making me feel I'm a piece of dog shit?"

"You think you could talk to me one time without copping a cheap feel?"

He surprised her by saying, "I shouldn't do that, Aimee, and I'm sorry. You wanna try and get along?"

She laughed from embarrassment. "God, you're really serious aren't you?"

"Yeah, I am." He put out a hand. "You wanna be friends, Aimee?"

This time the laugh was pure pleasure. "Sure, Bulicek. I'd like to be friends. I really would. You show me some respect and I'll show you some, too."

They shook hands.

"Now, about the dwarf you was askin' about?"

"Yeah? You saw her?" Aimee couldn't keep the excitement from her voice.

Bulicek pointed down the midway. "Seen her 'bout fifteen minutes ago at Kelly's."

Aimee thanked him and started running.

Linnette had a different taxi driver this time.

This guy was heavy and Mexican. The radio played low, Mexican songs from a station across the border. The guy sure wore a lot of aftershave.

Linnette sat with the gun inside her purse and her purse on her lap.

She looked out the window at the passing streets. Easy to imagine her brother walking across these streets, always the focus of the curious stare and the cold quick smirk. Maybe it was harder for men, she thought. They were expected to be big and strong and—

She opened her purse. The sound was loud in the taxi. She saw the driver's eyes flick up to his rearview and study her. Then his eyes flicked away.

She rode the rest of the way with her hand inside her purse, gripping the gun.

She closed her eyes and tried to imagine her brother's hand on the handle, on the trigger.

She hoped that there was a God somewhere and that all of this made sense somehow, that some people should be born of normal height and others, freaks, be born with no arms or legs or eyes.

Or be born dwarfs.

"Here you are, lady."

He pulled over to the curb and told her the fare.

Once again, she found her money swiftly and paid him off.

He reached over and opened the door for her, studying her all the time. Did it ever occur to him—fat and Mexican and not very well educated—that he looked just as strange to her as she did to him? But no, he wouldn't be the kind of man who'd have an insight like that.

She got out of the cab and he drove away.

Even in a bleak little town like this one, the Ganges Arms was grim. Fireproof was much larger than Ganges on the neon sign outside, and the drunk throwing up over by the curb told her more than she wanted to know about the type of man who lived up there.

She couldn't imagine how her brother had managed to survive here six years.

She went inside. The lobby was small and filled with ancient couches that dust rose from like shabby ghosts. A long-dead potted plant filled one corner while a cigarette vending machine filled the other. In the back somewhere a toilet flushed with the roar of an avalanche. A black-and-white TV screen flickered with images of Milton Berle in a dress.

A big woman in a faded housedress that revealed fleshy arms and some kind of terrible rash on her elbows was behind the desk. The woman had a beauty mark that was huge and hairy, like a little animal clinging to her cheek.

She grinned when she saw Linnette.

"You don't have to tell me, sweetie."

"Tell you?"

"Sure. Who you are."

"You know who I am?"

"Sure. You're the little guy's sister. He talked about you all the time."

She leaned over the counter, coughing a cigarette hack that sounded sickeningly phlegmy, and said, "Linnette, right?"

"Right."

The woman grimaced. "Sorry about the little guy."

"Thank you."

"I was the one who found him. He wasn't pretty, believe me."

"Oh."

"And I was the first one who read the note." She shook her head again and put a cigarette in her mouth. "He was pretty gimped up inside, poor little guy."

"Yes; yes he was."

The woman stared at her, not as if Linnette were a freak, but rather curious about why she might be here.

"I was just traveling through," Linnette said quietly. "I thought I might stay here tonight." She hesitated. "Sleep in my brother's room, perhaps."

Now the woman really stared at her. "You sure, hon?"

"Sure?"

"About wantin' to take his room and all? Frankly, it'd give me the creeps."

Linnette opened her purse, reached in for her bills. "I'd just like to see where he lived and worked is all. I'm sure it will be a nice experience."

The woman shrugged beefy shoulders. "You're the boss, hon. You're the boss."

Kelly was arguing with a drunk who claimed that the shooting gallery was rigged. The drunk had been bragging to his girl about what a marksman he'd become in Korea and wanted to do a little showing off. All he'd managed to do was humiliate himself.

Aimee waited as patiently as she could for a few minutes and then she interrupted the drunk—whose girlfriend was now trying to tug him away from making any more of a scene—and said, "Kelly, I'm looking for a woman who's a dwarf. Bulicek said he saw her here."

The drunk turned and looked at Aimee as if she'd just said she'd seen a Martian.

Aimee's remark unsettled the drunk enough that his girlfriend was now able to draw him away, and get themselves lost on the midway.

"Yeah. She was here. So what?"

"Did you talk to her?"

"Yeah."

"About what?"

"What the hell's your interest, Aimee?"

"Kelly, I don't have time to explain. Just please help me, all right?"

Kelly sighed. "Okay, kid, what do you want?"

"What'd she say to you?"

"She said she wanted to buy a gun."

"A gun? What kind of gun?"

"The gun her brother stole from me."

"My God."

"What's wrong?"

"Don't you see?"

"See what, kid? Calm down."

"If she wanted to buy the gun her brother stole from you then maybe she plans to use it on herself just the way her brother did."

Kelly said, "Shit. You know, I never thought of that."

"So you gave her the gun?"

Kelly seemed a little embarrassed now. "Yeah. Gave it to her for a hundred bucks."

"A hundred? But Kelly that isn't worth more than—"

"That's what she offered me for it. So that's what I took, kid. I never said I was no saint."

"Where did she go?"

"Hell, how would I know?"

"God, Kelly, didn't you notice the direction she was going?"

He shrugged. "Down near the entrance, I guess." He looked chastened that he hadn't paid attention.

"Thanks, Kelly. I appreciate it."

And before he could say another word, she was gone, running fast toward the front of the midway.

There was a card table sitting next to the room's only window. It had the uncertain legs of a young colt. He'd put his portable type-writer on it—the one she'd bought him for his birthday ten years ago—and worked long into the night.

The room had a bureau with somebody's initials knifed into the top, a mirror mottled with age, wallpaper stained with moisture, a double bed with a paint-chipped metal headboard, and linoleum so old it was worn to wood in patches.

She tried not to think of all the sad lives that had been lived out here. Men without women; men without hope.

She made sure the door was locked behind her and then came into the room.

She could feel him here, now. She had always believed in ghosts—were ghosts any more unlikely than men and women who only grew to be three-and-a-half feet tall?—and so she spoke out loud to him for the first time since being told of his suicide.

"I hope you know how much I love you, brother," she said, moving across the small, box-like room to the card table, running her fingers across the small indentations the Smith-Corona had made on the surface.

She decided against turning the overhead light on.

The on-and-off red of the neon was good enough.

"I miss you, brother. I hope you know that, too."

She heard the *clack* of a ghostly typewriter; saw her brother's sweet round face smiling up at her after he'd finished a particularly good sentence; listened to the soft sad laughter that only she'd been able to elicit from him.

"I wish you would have called me, brother. I wish you would have told me what you had in mind. You know why?"

She said nothing for a time.

Distant ragged traffic sounds from the highway; the even fainter music of the midway further away in the darkness.

"Because I would have joined you, brother. I would have joined you."

She set her purse on the card table. She unclasped the leather halves and then reached in.

The gun waited there.

She brought out the gun with the reverence of a priest bringing forth something that has been consecrated to God.

She brought out the gun and held it for a time, in silhouette, against the window with the flashing red neon.

And then, slowly, inevitably, she brought the gun to her temple.

And eased the hammer back.

At the entrance, Aimee asked fourteen people if they'd seen the woman. None had. But the fifteenth did, and pointed to a rusted beast of a taxi cab just now pulling in.

Aimee ran to the cab and pushed her head in the front window before the driver even stopped completely.

"The dwarf woman. Where did you take her?"

"Who the hell are you?"

"The woman, where did you take her?" Aimee knew she was screaming. She didn't care.

"Goddamn, lady. You're fucking nuts." But despite his tough words, the cab driver saw that she was going to stay here until she had her answer. He said, "I took her to the Ganges Arms. Why the hell're you so interested, anyway?"

"Then take me there, too," Aimee said, flinging open the back door and diving in. "Take me there, too!"

✧   ✧   ✧

She went over and sat on the bed.

That would make it easier for everybody. The mess would be confined to the mattress. A mattress you could just throw out.

She lay back on the bed.

Her shoes fell off, one at a time, making sharp noises as they struck the floor.

Two-inch heels, she thought. How pathetic of me. Wanting so desperately to be like other people.

She closed her eyes and let the sorrow come over her. Sorrow for her brother and herself; sorrow for their lives.

She saw him again at his typewriter; heard keys striking the eternal silence.

"I wish you would have told me, brother. I wish you would have. It would have been easier for you. We could have comforted each other."

She raised the hand carrying the gun, brought the gun to her temple once again.

The hammer was still back.

"Can't you go any faster?"

"Maybe you think this is an Indy race car or somethin', huh, lady?"

"God, please; please just go as fast as you can."

"Jes-uz," the cab driver said. "Jes-uz."

She said a prayer, nothing formal, just words that said she hoped there was a God and that he or she or it or whatever form it took would understand why she was doing this and how much she longed to be with her brother again and that both God and her brother would receive her with open arms.

She tightened her finger on the trigger and then—

—the knock came.

"Hon?"

Oh, my Lord.

"Hon, you awake in there?"

Finding her voice. Clearing her throat. "Yes?"

"Brought you some Kool-Aid. That's what I drink all summer.

Raspberry Kool-Aid. Quenches my thirst a lot better than regular pop, you know? Anyway, I brought you a glass. You wanna come get it?"

Did she have any choice?

Linnette lay the gun down on the bed and pulled the purse over the gun.

She got up and straightened her skirt and went to the door.

A long angle of dirty yellow light fell across her from the hallway.

The woman was a lot heavier than she'd looked downstairs. Linnette liked her.

The woman bore a large glass of Kool-Aid in her right hand and a cigarette in her left. She kept flicking her ashes on the hallway floor.

"You like raspberry?"

"Thank you very much."

"Sometimes I like cherry but tonight I'm just in a kind of raspberry mood. You know?"

"I really appreciate this."

The woman nodded to the stairs. "You get lonely, you can always come down and keep me company."

"I think I'll try and get some sleep first but if I don't doze off, I'll probably be down."

The woman looked past Linnette into the room. "You got everything you need?"

"I'm fine."

"If your brother's room starts to bother you, just let me know. You can always change rooms for no extra cost."

"Thanks."

The woman smiled. "Enjoy the Kool-Aid." She checked the man's wristwatch she wore on her thick wrist. "Hey, time for Blackie."

"Blackie?"

"Boston Blackie. You ever watch him?"

"I guess not."

"Great show; really, great show."

"Well, thank you."

"You're welcome. And remember about keeping me company."

"Oh, I will. I promise."

"Well, good night."

"Good night," Linnette said, and then quietly closed the door.

Ten minutes later, the cabbie pulled up in front of the hotel.

As always, the street reminded Aimee of a painting by Thomas Hart Benton she'd once seen in a Chicago gallery, a street where even the street lamps looked twisted and grotesque.

Aimee flung a five-dollar bill in the front seat and said, "I appreciate you speeding."

The cabbie picked up the fin, examined it as if he suspected it might be counterfeit, and then said, "Good luck with whatever your problem is, lady."

Aimee was out of the cab, hurrying into the lobby.

She went right to the desk and to the heavyset clerk who was leaning on her elbows and watching Kent Taylor as "Boston Blackie."

The woman sighed bitterly, as if she'd just been forced to give up her firstborn, and said, "Help you?"

"I'm looking for a woman who just came in here."

"What kind of woman?"

"A dwarf."

The desk clerk looked Aimee over more carefully. "What about her?"

"It's important that I talk to her right away."

"Why?"

"Because—because she's a friend of mine and I think she's going to do something very foolish."

"Like what?"

"For God's sake," Aimee said. "I know she's here. Tell me what room's she in before it's too late."

The desk clerk was just about to respond when the gunshot sounded on the floor above.

Aimee had never heard anything so loud in her life.

The echo seemed to go on for hours.

"What room is she in?" Aimee screamed.

"208!" the woman said.

Aimee reached the staircase in moments, and started running up the steps two at a time.

An old man in boxer shorts and a sunken, hairy chest stood in the hallway in front of 208 looking sleepy and scared.

"What the Sam hell's going on?"

Aimee said nothing, just pushed past him to the door. She turned the knob. Locked.

Aimee heard the desk clerk lumbering up the stairs behind her.

Aimee turned and ran toward the steps again. She pushed out her hand and laid the palm up and open.

"The key. Hurry."

The desk clerk, her entire body heaving from her exertion, dropped the key in Aimee's hand. The desk clerk tried to say something but she had no wind.

Aimee ran back to 208, inserted the key. Pushed the door open.

The first thing was the darkness; the second, the acrid odor of gunpowder. The third was the hellish neon red that shone through the dirty sheer curtains.

Aimee was afraid of what she was going to see.

Could she really handle seeing somebody who'd shot herself at point-blank range?

Aimee took two steps over the threshold.

And then heard the noise.

At first, she wasn't sure what it was. Only after she took a few more steps into the dark tiny room did she recognize what she was hearing.

A woman lying face down in the bed, the sound of her sobbing muffled into the mattress.

Just now the desk clerk came panting into the yellow frame of the door and said, "She dead?"

"No," Aimee said quietly to the woman. "No, she's not dead."

And then Aimee silently closed the door behind her and went to sit with Linnette on the bed.

✿   ✿   ✿

Aimee had been with carnivals since she was fourteen years old, when she'd run off from a Kentucky farm and from a pa who saw nothing wrong with doing with her what he'd done with her other two sisters. She was now twenty-eight. In the intervening years she'd wondered many times what it would be like to have a child of her own and tonight she thought she was finding out, at least in a curious sort of way.

It was not respectful, she was sure, to think of Linnette as a child just because Linnette was so little, but as Aimee sat there for three and a half hours in the dark, breathless from holding Linnette in her lap and rocking her as she would an infant, the thought was inevitable. And then the wind from midnight came, and things cooled off at least a little bit.

Aimee didn't say much, really—what could she say?—she just hugged Linnette and let her cry and let her talk and let her cry some more and it was so sad that Aimee herself started crying sometimes, thinking of how cruel people could be to anybody who was different in any way, and thinking of that sonofabitch Ralph Banghart spying on the little guy in the house of mirrors, and thinking of how terrified the little guy had been when he fell prey to Ralph's practical joke. Life was just so sad sometimes when you saw what happened to people, and usually to innocent people at that, people that life had been cruel enough to already.

So that's why she mostly listened, Aimee, because when something was as overwhelming as the little guy's life had been—

Sometimes the desk clerk made the long and taxing trip up the stairs and knocked with a single knuckle and said, "You okay in there, hon?"

And Aimee would say, "We're fine, we're fine," not knowing exactly who "you" meant.

And then the desk clerk would go away and Aimee would start rocking Linnette again and listening to her and wanting to tell Linnette that she felt terrible about the little guy's death.

And then it occurred to Aimee that maybe by sitting here like this and listening to Linnette and rocking her, maybe she was in some way making up for playing a small part in the little guy's suicide.

"Sometimes I just get so scared," Linnette said just as dawn was breaking coral-colored across the sky.

And Aimee knew just what Linnette was talking about because Aimee got scared like that, too, sometimes.

The Greyhound arrived twenty-three minutes late that afternoon.

Aimee and Linnette stood in the depot entrance with a group of other people. There was a farm girl who kept saying how excited she was to be going to Fresno and a marine who kept saying it was going to be good to see Iowa again and an old woman who kept saying she hoped they kept the windows closed because even on a ninety-two-degree day like this one she'd get a chill.

"You ever get up to Sacramento?" Linnette asked.

"Sometimes."

"You could always call me at the library and we could have lunch."

"That sounds like fun, Linnette. It really does."

Linnette took Aimee's hand and gave it a squeeze. "You really helped me last night. I'll never forget it, Aimee. I really won't."

Just then the bus pulled in with a *whoosh* of air brakes and a puff of black diesel smoke.

In one of the front windows a five-year-old boy was looking out and when he saw Linnette, he started jumping up and down and pointing, and then a couple of moments later another five-year-old face appeared in the same window and now there were two boys looking and pointing and laughing at Linnette.

Maybe the worst part of it all, Aimee thought, was that they didn't even really mean to be cruel.

And then the bus door was flung open and a Greyhound driver looking dapper in a newly starched uniform stepped down and helped several old ladies off the bus.

"I wish he could have known you, Aimee," Linnette said. "He sure would have liked you. He sure would've."

And then, for once, it was Aimee who started the crying and she wasn't even sure why. It just seemed right somehow, she thought, as she helped the little woman take the first big step up into the bus.

A minute later, Linnette was sitting in the middle of the bus, next to a window seat. Her eyes barely reached the window ledge.

Behind Aimee, the door burst open and the two five-year-olds came running out of the depot, carrying cups of Pepsi.

They looked up and saw Linnette in the window. They started pointing and giggling immediately.

Aimee grabbed the closest one by the ear, giving it enough of a twist to inflict some real pain.

"That's one fine lady aboard that bus there, you hear me? And you treat her like a fine lady, too, or you're going to get your butts spanked! Do you understand me?" Aimee said.

Then she let go of the boy's ear.

"You understand me?" she repeated.

The boys looked at each other and then back to Aimee. They seemed scared of her, which was what she wanted them to be.

"Yes, ma'm," both boys said in unison. "We understand."

"Good. Now you get up there on that bus and behave yourselves."

"Yes, ma'am," the boys said again, and climbed aboard the bus, not looking back at her even once.

Aimee waited till the Greyhound pulled out with a roar of engine and a poof of sooty smoke.

She waved at Linnette and Linnette waved back. "Good-bye," Aimee said, and was afraid she was going to start crying.

When the bus was gone, Aimee walked over to the taxi stand. A young man who looked like a child was driving.

Aimee told him to take her to the carnival and then she settled back in the seat and looked out the window.

After a time, it began to rain, a hot summer rain, and the rest of the day and all the next long night, Aimee tried to keep herself from thinking about certain things. She tried so very hard.

PRISONERS

For Gail Cross

I am in my sister's small room with its posters of Madonna and Tiffany. Sis is fourteen. Already tall, already pretty. Dressed in jeans and a blue T-shirt. Boys call and come over constantly. She wants nothing to do with boys.

Her back is to me. She will not turn around. I sit on the edge of her bed, touching my hand to her shoulder. She smells warm, of sleep. I say, "Sis listen to me."

She says nothing. She almost always says nothing.

"He wants to see you Sis."

Nothing.

"When he called last weekend—you were all he talked about. He even started crying when you wouldn't come to the phone Sis. He really did."

Nothing.

"Please, Sis. Please put on some good clothes and get ready 'cause we've got to leave in ten minutes. We've got to get there on time and you know it." I lean over so I can see her face.

She tucks her face into her pillow.

She doesn't want me to see that she is crying.

"Now you go and get ready Sis. You go and get ready, all right?"

"I don't know who she thinks she is," Ma says when I go downstairs. "Too good to go and see her own father."

As she talks Ma is packing a big brown grocery sack. Into it go a cornucopia of goodies—three cartons of Lucky Strike filters, three packages of Hershey bars, two bottles of Ban roll-on deodorant, three Louis L'Amour paperbacks as well as all the stuff that's there already.

Ma looks up at me. I've seen pictures of her when she was a young woman. She was a beauty. But that was before she started putting on weight and her hair started thinning and she stopped caring about how she dressed and all. "She going to go with us?"

"She says not."

"Just who does she think she is?"

"Calm down Ma. If she doesn't want to go, we'll just go ahead without her."

"What do we tell your dad?"

"Tell him she's got the flu?"

"The way she had the flu the last six times?"

"She's gone a few times."

"Yeah twice out of the whole year he's been there."

"Well."

"How do you think he feels? He gets all excited thinking he's going to see her and then she doesn't show up. How do you think he feels? She's his own flesh and blood."

I sigh. Ma's none too healthy and getting worked up this way doesn't do her any good. "I better go and call Riley."

"That's it. Go call Riley. Leave me here alone to worry about what we're going to tell your dad."

"You know how Riley is. He appreciates a call."

"You don't care about me no more than your selfish sister does."

I go out to the living room where the phone sits on the end table I picked up at Goodwill last Christmastime. A lot of people don't like to shop at Goodwill, embarrassed about going in there and all.

The only thing I don't like is the smell. All those old clothes hanging. Sometimes I wonder if you opened up a grave if it wouldn't
smell like Goodwill.

I call Kmart, which is where I work as a manager trainee while
I'm finishing off my retail degree at the junior college. My girlfriend Karen works at Kmart too. "Riley?"

"Hey, Tom."

"How're things going in my department?" A couple months ago
Riley, who is the assistant manager over the whole store, put me in
charge of the automotive department.

"Good great."

"Good. I was worried." Karen always says she's proud 'cause I
worry so much about my job. Karen says it proves I'm responsible.
Karen says one of the reasons she loves me so much is 'cause I'm
responsible. I guess I'd rather have her love me for my blue eyes or
something but of course I don't say anything because Karen can get
crabby about strange things sometimes.

"You go and see your old man today, huh?" Riley says.

"Yeah."

"Hell of a way to spend your day off."

"It's not so bad. You get used to it."

"Any word on when he gets out?"

"Be a year or so yet. Being his second time in and all."

"You're a hell of a kid Tom, I ever tell you that before?"

"Yeah you did Riley and I appreciate it." Riley is a year older
than me but sometimes he likes to pretend he's my uncle or something. But he means well and, like I told him, I appreciate it. Like
when Dad's name was in the paper for the burglary and everything.
The people at Kmart all saw it and started treating me funny. But
not Riley. He'd walk up and down the aisles with me and even put
his arm on my shoulder like we were the best buddies in the whole
world or something. In the coffee room this fat woman made a
crack about it and Riley got mad and said, "Why don't you shut your
fucking mouth, Shirley?" Nobody said anything more about my dad
after that. Of course poor Sis had it a lot worse than me at Catholic
school. She had it real bad. Some of those kids really got vicious. A

lot of nights I'd lay awake thinking of all the things I wanted to do to those kids. I'd do it with my hands, too, wouldn't even use weapons.

"Well say hi to your mom."

"Thanks Riley. I'll be sure to."

"She's a hell of a nice lady." Riley and his girl came over one night when Ma'd had about three beers and was in a really good mood. They got along really well. He had her laughing at his jokes all night. Riley knows a lot of jokes. A lot of them.

"I sure hope we make our goal today."

"You just relax Tom and forget about the store. OK?"

"I'll try."

"Don't try Tom. Do it." He laughs, being my uncle again. "That's an order."

In the kitchen, done with packing her paper bag, Ma says, "I shouldn't have said that."

"Said what?" I say.

"About you being like your sister."

"Aw Ma. I didn't take that seriously."

"We couldn't have afforded to stay in this house if you hadn't been promoted to assistant manager. Not many boys would turn over their whole paychecks to their mas." She doesn't mention her sister who is married to a banker who is what bankers aren't supposed to be, generous. I help but he helps a lot.

She starts crying.

I take her to me, hold her. Ma needs to cry a lot. Like she fills up with tears and will drown if she can't get rid of them. When I hold her I always think of the pictures of her as a young woman, of all the terrible things that have cost her her beauty.

When she's settled down some I say, "I'll go talk to Sis."

But just as I say that I hear the old boards of the house creak and there in the doorway, dressed in a white blouse and a blue skirt and blue hose and the blue flats I bought her for her last birthday, is Sis.

Ma sees her, too, and starts crying all over again. "Oh God hon thanks so much for changing your mind."

Then Ma puts her arms out wide and she goes over to Sis and throws her arms around her and gets her locked inside this big hug.

I can see Sis's blue eyes staring at me over Ma's shoulder.

In the soft fog of the April morning I see watercolor brown cows on the curve of the green hills and red barns faint in the rain. I used to want to be a farmer till I took a two-week job summer of junior year where I cleaned out dairy barns and it took me weeks to get the odor of wet hay and cowshit and hot pissy milk from my nostrils and then I didn't want to be a farmer ever again.

"You all right hon?" Ma asks Sis.

But Sis doesn't answer. Just stares out the window at the watercolor brown cows.

"Ungrateful little brat," Ma says under her breath.

If Sis hears this she doesn't let on. She just stares out the window.

"Hon slow down," Ma says to me. "This road's got a lot of curves in it."

And so it does.

Twenty-three curves—I've counted them many times—and you're on top of a hill looking down into a valley where the prison lies.

Curious, I once went to the library and read up on the prison. According to the historical society it's the oldest prison still standing in the Midwest, built of limestone dragged by prisoners from a nearby quarry. In 1948 the west wing had a fire that killed eighteen blacks (they were segregated in those days) and in 1957 there was a riot that got a guard castrated with a busted pop bottle and two inmates shot dead in the back by other guards who were never brought to trial.

From the two-lane asphalt road that winds into the prison you see the steep limestone walls and the towers where uniformed guards toting riot guns look down at you as you sweep west to park in the visitors' parking lot.

      ✿   ✿   ✿

As we walk through the rain to the prison, hurrying as the fat drops splatter on our heads, Ma says, "I forgot. Don't say anything about your cousin Bessie."

"Oh. Right."

"Stuff about cancer always makes your dad depressed. You know it runs in his family a lot."

She glances over her shoulder at Sis shambling along. Sis had not worn a coat. The rain doesn't seem to bother her. She is staring out at something still as if her face was nothing more than a mask which hides her real self. "You hear me?" Ma asks Sis.

If Sis hears she doesn't say anything.

"How're you doing this morning Jimmy?" Ma asks the fat guard who lets us into the waiting room.

His stomach wriggles beneath his threadbare uniform shirt like something troubled struggling to be born.

He grunts something none of us can understand. He obviously doesn't believe in being nice to Ma no matter how nice Ma is to him. Would break prison decorum apparently, the sonofabitch. But if you think he is cold to us—and most people in the prison are— you should see how they are to the families of queers or with men who did things to children.

The cold is in my bones already. Except for July and August prison is always cold to me. The bars are cold. The walls are cold. When you go into the bathroom and run the water your fingers tingle. The prisoners are always sneezing and coughing. Ma always brings Dad lots of Contac and Listerine even though I told her about this article that said Listerine isn't anything except a mouthwash.

In the waiting room—which is nothing more than the yellow-painted room with battered old wooden chairs—a turnkey named Stan comes in and leads you right up to the visiting room, the only problem being that separating you from the visiting room is a set of bars. Stan turns the key that raises these bars and then you get inside and he lowers the bars behind you. For a minute or so you're locked in between two walls and two sets of bars. You get a sense of what it's like to be in a cell. The first couple times this happened I got scared. My chest started heaving and I couldn't catch my breath, sort of like the nightmares I have sometimes.

Stan then raises the second set of bars and you're one room away from the visiting room or VR as the prisoners call it. In prison you always lower the first set of bars before you raise the next one. That way nobody escapes.

In this second room, not much bigger than a closet with a stand-up clumsy metal detector near the door leading to the VR, Stan asks Ma and Sis for their purses and me for my wallet. He asks if any of us have got any open packs of cigarettes and if so to hand them over. Prisoners and visitors alike can carry only full packs of cigarettes into the VR. Open packs are easy to hide stuff in.

You pass through the metal detector and straight into the VR room.

The first thing you notice is how all of the furniture is in color-coded sets—loungers and vinyl molded chairs makes up a set—orange green blue or red. Like that. This is so Mona the guard in here can tell you where to sit just by saying a color such as "Blue" which means you go sit in the blue seat. Mona makes Stan look like a really friendly guy. She's fat with hair cut man short and a voice man deep. She wears her holster and gun with real obvious pleasure. One time Ma didn't understand what color she said and Mona's hand dropped to her service revolver like she was going to whip it out or something. Mona doesn't like to repeat herself. Mona is the one the black prisoner knocked unconscious a year ago. The black guy is married to this white girl which right away you can imagine Mona not liking at all so she's looking for any excuse to hassle him so the black guy one time gets down on his hands and knees to play with his little baby and Mona comes over and says you can only play with the kids in the Toy Room (TR) and he says can't you make an exception and Mona sly-like bumps him hard on the shoulder and he just flashes the way prisoners sometimes do and jumps up from the floor and not caring that she's a woman or not just drops her with a right hand and the way the story is told now anyway by pris-

oners and their families, everybody in VR instead of rushing to help
her break out into applause just like it's a movie or something.
Standing ovation. The black guy was in the hole for six months but
was quoted afterward as saying it was worth it.

Most of the time it's not like that at all. Nothing exciting I mean.
Most of the time it's just depressing.

Mostly it's women here to see husbands. They usually bring
their kids so there's a lot of noise. Crying laughing chasing around.
You can tell if there's trouble with a parole—the guy not getting out
when he's supposed to—because that's when the arguments always
start, the wife having built her hopes up and then the husband saying there's nothing he can do I'm sorry honey nothing I can do and
sometimes the woman will really start crying or arguing. I even saw
a woman slap her husband once, the worst being of course when
some little kid starts crying and says, "Daddy I want you to come
home!" That's usually when the prisoner himself starts crying.

As for touching or fondling, there's none of it. You can kiss your
husband for thirty seconds and most guards will hassle you even
before your time's up if you try it open mouth or anything. Mona in
particular is a real bitch about something like this. Apparently
Mona doesn't like the idea of men and women kissing.

Another story you hear a lot up here is how this one prisoner cut
a hole in his pocket so he could stand by the Coke machine and
have his wife put her hand down his pocket and jack him off while
they just appeared to be innocently standing there, though that may
be one of those stories the prisoners just like to tell.

The people who really have it worst are those who are in the
hole or some other kind of solitary. On the west wall there's this
long screen for them. They have to sit behind the screen the whole
time. They can't touch their kids or anything. All they can do is look.

I can hear Ma's breath take up sharp when they bring Dad in.

He's still a handsome man—thin, dark curly hair with no gray,
and more solid than ever since he works out in the prison weight
room all the time. He always walks jaunty as if to say that wearing a
gray uniform and living in an interlocking set of cages has not yet

broken him. But you can see in his blue eyes that they broke him a long time ago.

"Hiya everybody," he says trying to sound real happy.

Ma throws her arms around him and they hold each other. Sis and I sit down on the two chairs. I look at Sis. She stares at the floor.

Dad comes over then and says, "You two sure look great."

"So do you," I say. "You must be still lifting those weights."

"Bench pressed two-twenty-five this week."

"Man," I say and look at Sis again. I nudge her with my elbow. She won't look up.

Dad stares at her. You can see how sad he is about her not looking up. Soft he says, "It's all right."

Ma and Dad sit down then and we go through the usual stuff, how things are going at home and at my job and in junior college, and how things are going in prison. When he first got there, they put Dad in with this colored guy—he was Jamaican—but then they found out he had AIDS so they moved Dad out right away. Now he's with this guy who was in Vietnam and got one side of his face burned. Dad says once you get used to looking at him he's a nice guy with two kids of his own and not queer in any way or into drugs at all. In prison the drugs get pretty bad.

We talk a half hour before Dad looks at Sis again. "So how's my little girl."

She still won't look up.

"Ellen," Ma says, "you talk to your dad and right now."

Sis raises her head. She looks right at Dad but doesn't seem to see him at all. Ellen can do that. It's really spooky.

Dad puts his hand out and touches her.

Sis jerks her hand away. It's the most animated I've seen her in weeks.

"You give your dad a hug and you give him a hug right now," Ma says to Sis.

Sis, still staring at Dad, shakes her head.

"It's all right," Dad says. "It's all right. She just doesn't like to come up here and I don't blame her at all. This isn't a nice place to visit at all." He smiles. "Believe me I wouldn't be here if they didn't make me."

Ma asks, "Any word on your parole?"

"My lawyer says two years away. Maybe three, 'cause it's a second offense and all." Dad sighs and takes Ma's hand. "I know it's hard for you to believe hon—I mean practically every guy in here says the same thing—but I didn't break into that store that night. I really didn't. I was just walking along the river."

"I do believe you hon," Ma says, "and so does Tom and so does Sis. Right kids?"

I nod. Sis has gone back to staring at the floor.

" 'Cause I served time before for breaking and entering the cops just automatically assumed it was me," Dad says. He shakes his head. The sadness is back in his eyes. "I don't have no idea how my billfold got on the floor of that place." He sounds miserable and now he doesn't look jaunty or young. He looks old and gray.

He looks back at Sis. "You still gettin' straight A's hon?"

She looks up at him. But doesn't nod or anything.

"She sure is," Ma says. "Sister Rosemary says Ellen is the best student she's got. Imagine that."

Dad starts to reach out to Sis again but then takes his hand back.

Over in the red section this couple start arguing. The woman is crying and this little girl maybe six is holding real tight to her dad who looks like he's going to start crying, too. That bitch Mona has put on her mirror sunglasses again so you can't tell what she's thinking but you can see from the angle of her face that she's watching the three of them in the red section. Probably enjoying herself.

"Your lawyer sure it'll be two years?" Ma says.

"Or three."

"I sure do miss you hon," Ma says.

"I sure do miss you too hon."

"Don't know what I'd do without Tom to lean on." She makes a point of not mentioning Sis who she's obviously still mad at because Sis won't speak to Dad.

"He's sure a fine young man," Dad says. "Wish I woulda been that responsible when I was his age. Wouldn't be in here today if I'da been."

Sis gets up and leaves the room. Says nothing. Doesn't even

look at anybody exactly. Just leaves. Mona directs her to the ladies room.

"I'm sorry she treats you this way hon," Ma says. "She thinks she's too good to come see her dad in prison."

"It's all right," Dad says looking sad again. He watches Sis leave the visiting room.

"I'm gonna have a good talk with her when we leave here hon," Ma says.

"Oh don't be too hard on her. Tough for a proud girl her age to come up here."

"Not too hard for Tom."

"Tom's different. Tom's mature. Tom's responsible. When Ellen gets Tom's age I'm sure she'll be mature and responsible too."

Half hour goes by before Sis comes back. Almost time to leave. She walks over and sits down.

"You give your dad a hug now," Ma says.

Sis looks at Dad. She stands up then and goes over and puts her arms out. Dad stands up grinning and takes her to him and hugs her tighter than I've ever seen him hug anybody. It's funny because right then and there he starts crying. Just holding Sis so tight. Crying.

"I love you hon," Dad says to her. "I love you hon and I'm sorry for all the mistakes I've made and I'll never make them again I promise you."

Ma starts crying, too.

Sis says nothing.

When Dad lets her go I look at her eyes. They're the same as they were before. She's staring right at him but she doesn't seem to see him somehow.

Mona picks up the microphone that blasts through the speakers hung from the ceiling. She doesn't need a speaker in a room this size but she obviously likes how loud it is and how it hurts your ears.

"Visiting hours are over. You've got fifteen seconds to say good-bye and then inmates have to start filing over to the door."

"I miss you so much hon," Ma says and throws her arms around Dad.

He hugs Ma but over his shoulder he's looking at Sis. She is standing up. She has her head down again.

Dad looks so sad, so sad.

"I'd like to know just who the hell you think you are treatin' your own father that way," Ma says on the way back to town.

The rain and the fog are real bad now so I have to concentrate on my driving. On the opposite side of the road cars appear quickly in the fog and then vanish. It's almost unreal.

The wipers are slapping loud and everything smells damp—the rubber of the car and the vinyl seat covers and the ashtray from Ma's menthol cigarettes. Damp.

"You hear me young lady?" Ma says.

Sis is in the backseat again alone. Staring out the window. At the fog I guess.

"Come on Ma, she hugged him," I say.

"Yeah when I practically had to twist her arm to do it." Ma shakes her head. "Her own flesh and blood."

Sometimes I want to get really mad and let it out but I know it would just hurt Ma to remind her what Dad was doing to Ellen those years after he came out of prison the first time. I know for a fact he was doing it because I walked in on them one day little eleven-year-old Ellen was there on the bed underneath my naked dad, staring off as he grunted and moved around inside her, staring off just the way she does now.

Staring off.

Ma knew about it all along of course but she wouldn't do anything about it. Wouldn't admit it probably not even to herself. In psychology, which I took last year at the junior college, that's called denial. I even brought it up a couple times but she just said I had a filthy mind and don't ever say nothing like that again.

Which is why I broke into that store that night and left Dad's billfold behind. Because I knew they'd arrest him and then he couldn't force Ellen into the bed anymore. Not that I blame Dad entirely. Prison makes you crazy no doubt about it and he was in there four years the first time. But even so I love Sis too much.

"Own flesh and blood," Ma says again lighting up one of her menthols and shaking her head.

I look into the rearview mirror at Sis's eyes. "Wish I could make you smile," I say to her. "Wish I could make you smile."

But she just stares out the window.

She hasn't smiled for a long time of course.

Not for a long time.

RENDER UNTO CAESAR

I never paid much attention to their arguments until the night he hit her.

The summer I was twenty-one I worked construction upstate. This was 1963. The money was good enough to float my final year and a half at college. If I didn't blow it the way some of the other kids working construction did, that is, on too many nights at the tavern, and too many weekends trying to impress city girls.

The crew was three weeks in Cedar Rapids and so I looked for an inexpensive sleeping room. The one I found was in a neighborhood my middle-class parents wouldn't have approved of but I wasn't going to be here long enough for them to know exactly where I was living.

The house was a faded frail Victorian. Upstairs lived an old man named Murchison. He'd worked forty years on the Crandic as a brakeman and was retired now to sunny days out at Ellis park watching the softball games, and nights on the front porch with his quarts of cheap Canadian Ace beer and the high sweet smell of his Prince Albert pipe tobacco and his memories of WWII. Oh, yes, and his cat, Caesar. You never saw Murch without that hefty gray cat of his, usually sleeping in his lap when Murch sat in his front porch rocking chair.

And Murch's fondness for cats didn't stop there. But I'll tell you about that later.

Downstairs lived the Brineys. Pete Briney was in his early twenties, handsome in a roughneck kind of way. He sold new Mercurys for a living. He came home in a different car nearly every night, just at dusk, just at the time you could smell the dinner his wife, Kelly, had set out for him.

According to Murch, who seemed to know everything about them, Kelly had just turned nineteen and had already suffered two miscarriages. She was pretty in a sweet, already tired way. She seemed to spend most of her time cleaning the apartment and taking out the garbage and walking up to Dlask's grocery, two blocks away. One day a plump young woman came over to visit but this led to an argument later that night. Pete Briney did not want his wife to have friends. He seemed to feel that if Kelly had concentrated on her pregnancy, she would not have miscarried.

Briney did not look happy about me staying in the back room on the second floor. The usual tenants were retired men like Murch. I had a tan and was in good shape and while I wasn't handsome girls didn't find me repulsive, either. Murch laughed one day and said that Briney had come up and said, "How long is that guy going to be staying here, anyway?" Murch, who felt sorry for Kelly and liked Briney not at all, lied and said I'd probably be here a couple of years.

A few nights later Murch and I were on the front porch. All we had upstairs were two window fans that churned the ninety-three-degree air without cooling it at all. So, after walking up to Dlask's for a couple of quarts of Canadian Ace and two packs of Pall Malls, I sat down on the front porch and prepared myself to be dazzled by Murch's tales of WWII in the Pacific theater. (And Murch knew lots of good ones, at least a few of which I strongly suspected were true.)

Between stories we watched the street. Around nine, dusk dying, mothers called their children in. There's something about the sound of working-class mothers gathering their children—their voices weary, almost melancholy, at the end of another grinding day, the girls they used to be still alive somewhere in their voices, all that early hope and vitality vanishing like the faint echoes of tender music.

And there were the punks in their hot rods picking up the meaty young teenage girls who lived on the block. And the sad factory drunks weaving their way home late from the taverns to cold meals and broken-hearted children. And the furtive lonely single men getting off the huge glowing insect of the city bus, and going upstairs to sleeping rooms and hot plates and lonesome letters from girlfriends in far and distant cities.

And in the midst of all this came a brand-new red Mercury convertible, one far too resplendent for the neighborhood. And it was pulling up to the curb and—

The radio was booming "Surf City" with Jan and Dean—and—

Before the car even stopped, Kelly jerked open her door and jumped out, nearly stumbling in the process.

Briney slammed on the brakes, killed the headlights and then bolted from the car.

Before he reached the curb, he was running.

"You whore!" he screamed.

He was too fast for her. He tackled her even before she reached the sidewalk.

Tackled her and turned her over. And started smashing his fists into her face, holding her down on the ground with his knees on her slender arms, and smashing and smashing and smashing her face—

By then I was off the porch. I was next to him in moments. Given that his victim was a woman, I wasted no time on fair play. I kicked him hard twice in the ribs and then I slammed two punches into the side of his head. She screamed and cried and tried rolling left to escape his punches, and then tried rolling right. I didn't seem to have fazed him. I slammed two more punches into the side of his head. I could feel these punches working. He pitched sideways, momentarily unconscious, off his wife.

He slumped over on the sidewalk next to Kelly. I got her up right away and held her and let her sob and twist and moan and jerk in my arms. All I could think of were those times when I'd seen my otherwise respectable accountant father beat up my mother, and how I'd cry and run between them terrified and try to stop him with my own small and useless fists. . . .

Murch saw to Briney. "Sonofabitch's alive, anyway," he said looking up at me from the sidewalk. "More than he deserves."

By that time, a small crowd stood on the sidewalk, gawkers in equal parts thrilled and sickened by what they'd just seen Briney do to Kelly. . . .

I got her upstairs to Murch's apartment and started taking care of her cuts and bruises. . . .

I mentioned that Murch's affection for cats wasn't limited to Caesar. I also mentioned that Murch was retired, which meant that he had plenty of time for his chosen calling.

The first Saturday I had off, a week before the incident with Pete and Kelly Briney, I sat on the front porch reading a John D. MacDonald paperback and drinking a Pepsi and smoking Pall Malls. I was glad for a respite from the baking, bone-cracking work of summer road construction.

Around three that afternoon, I saw Murch coming down the sidewalk carrying a shoebox. He walked toward the porch, nodded hello, then walked to the backyard. I wondered if something was wrong. He was a talker, Murch was, and to see him so quiet bothered me.

I put down my Pepsi and put down my book and followed him, a seventy-one-year-old man with a stooped back and liver-spotted hands and white hair that almost glowed in the sunlight and that ineluctable dignity that comes to people who've spent a life at hard honorable work others consider menial.

He went into the age-worn garage and came out with a garden spade. The wide backyard was burned stubby grass and a line of rusted silver garbage cans. The picket fence sagged with age and the walk was all busted and jagged. To the right of white flapping sheets drying on the clothesline was a small plot of earth that looked like a garden.

He set the shoebox down on the ground and went to work with

the shovel. He was finished in three or four minutes. A nice fresh
hole had been dug in the dark rich earth.

He bent down and took the lid from the shoebox. From inside
he lifted something with great and reverent care. At first I couldn't
see what it was. I moved closer. Lying across his palms was the dead
body of a small calico cat. The blood on the scruffy white fur indicated that death had been violent, probably by car.

He knelt down and lowered the cat into the freshly dug earth.
He remained kneeling and then closed his eyes and made the sign
of the cross.

And then he scooped the earth in his hands and filled in the
grave.

I walked over to him just as he was standing up.

"You're some guy, Murch," I said.

He looked startled. "Where the hell did you come from?"

"I was watching." I nodded to the ground. "The cat, I mean."

"They've been damn good friends to me—cats have—figure it's
the least I can do for them."

I felt I'd intruded; embarrassed him. He picked up the spade
and started over to the garage.

"Nobody gives a damn about cats," he said. "A lot of people
even hate 'em. That's why I walk around every few days with my
shoebox and if I see a dead one, I pick it up and bring it back here
and bury it. They're nice little animals." He grinned. "Especially
Caesar. He's the only good friend I've made since my wife died ten
years ago."

Murch put the shovel in the garage. When he came back out, he
said, "You in any kind of mood for a game of checkers?"

I grinned. "I hate to pick on old farts like you."

He grinned back. "We'll see who's the old fart here."

When I got home the night following the incident with Kelly and
Briney, several people along the block stopped to ask me about the
beating. They'd heard this and they'd heard that but since I lived in
the house, they figured I could set them right. I couldn't, or at least

I said I couldn't, because I didn't like the quiet glee in their eyes, and the subtle thrill in their voices.

Murch was on the porch. I went up and sat down and he put Caesar in my lap the way he usually did. I petted the big fellow till he purred so hard he sounded like a plane about to take off. Too bad most humans weren't as appreciative of kindness as good old Caesar.

When I spoke, I sort of whispered. I didn't want the Brineys to hear.

"You don't have to whisper, Todd," Murch said, sucking on his pipe. "They're both gone. Don't know where he is, and don't care. She left about three this afternoon. Carrying a suitcase."

"You really think she's leaving him?"

"Way he treats her, I hope so. Nobody should be treated like that, especially a nice young woman like her." He reached over and petted Caesar who was sleeping in my lap. Then he sat back and drew on his pipe again and said, "I told her to go. Told her what happens to women who let their men beat them. It keeps on getting worse and worse until—" He shook his head. "The missus and I knew a woman whose husband beat her to death one night. Right in front of her two little girls."

"Briney isn't going to like it, you telling her to leave him."

"To hell with Briney. I'm not afraid of him." He smiled. "I've got Caesar here to protect me."

Briney didn't get home till late. By that time we were up off the porch and in our respective beds. Around nine a cool rain had started falling. I was getting some good sleep when I heard him down there.

The way he yelled and the way he smashed things, I knew he was drunk. He'd obviously discovered that his compliant little wife had left him. Then there was an abrupt and anxious silence. And then there was his crying. He wasn't any better at it than I was, didn't really know how, and so his tears came out in violent bursts that resembled throwing up. But even though I was tempted to feel sorry for him, he soon enough made me hate him again. Between bursts of tears he'd start calling his wife names, terrible names that should never have been put to a woman like Kelly.

I wasn't sure of the time when he finally gave it all up and went to bed. Late, with just the sounds of the trains rushing through the night in the hills, and the hoot of a barn owl lost somewhere in leafy midnight trees.

The next couple days I worked overtime. The road project had fallen behind. In the early weeks of the job there'd been an easy camaraderie on the work site. But that was gone for good now. The supervisors no longer took the time to joke, and looked you over skeptically every time you walked back to the wagon for a drink of water.

Kelly came back at dusk on Friday night. She stepped out of a brand-new blue Mercury sedan, Pete Briney at the wheel. She carried a lone suitcase. When she reached the porch steps and saw Murch and me, she looked away and walked quickly toward the door. Briney was right behind her. Obviously he'd told her not to speak to us.

That night, Murch and I spoke in whispers, both of us naturally wondering what had happened. Briney had gone over to her mother's, where Murch had suggested she go, and somehow convinced Kelly to come back.

They kept the curtains closed, the TV low and if they spoke, it was so quietly we couldn't hear them.

I spent an hour with Caesar on my lap and Murch in my ear about politicians. He was a John Kennedy supporter and tried to convince me I should be, too.

For the next two days and nights, I didn't see or hear either of the Brineys. On Saturday afternoon, Murch returned from one of his patrols with his shoebox. He went in the back and buried a cat he'd found and then came out on the porch to smoke a pipe. "Poor little thing," he said. "Wasn't any bigger than this." With his hands, he indicated how tiny the kitten had been.

Kelly came out on the porch a few minutes later. She wore a white blouse and jeans and had her auburn hair swept back into a loose ponytail. She looked neat and clean. And nervous.

She muttered a hello and started down the stairs.

"Ain't you ever going to talk to us again, Kelly?" Murch said.

There was no sarcasm in his voice, just an obvious sadness.

She stopped halfway toward the sidewalk. Her back was to us. For long moments she just stood there.

When she turned around and looked at us, she said, "Pete don't want me to talk to either of you." Then, gently, "I miss sitting out on the porch."

"He's your husband, honey. You shouldn't let him be your jailer," Murch said.

"He said he was sorry about the other night. About hitting me." She paused. "He came over to my mother's house and he told my whole family he was sorry. He even started crying."

Murch didn't say anything.

"I know you don't like him, Murch, but I'm his wife and like the priest said, I owe him another chance."

"You be careful of him, especially when he's drinking."

"He promised he wouldn't hit me no more, Murch. He gave his solemn word."

She looked first at him and then at me, and then was gone down the block to the grocery store. From a distance she looked fifteen years old.

He went two more nights, Briney did, before coming home drunk and loud.

I knew just how drunk he was because I was sitting on the porch around ten o'clock when a new pink Mercury came up and scraped the edge of its right bumper long and hard against the curbing.

The headlights died. Briney sat in the dark car smoking a cigarette. I could tell he was staring at us.

Murch just sat there with Caesar on his lap. I just sat there waiting for trouble. I could sense it coming and I wanted it over with.

Briney got out of the car and tried hard to walk straight up the walk to the porch. He wasn't a comic drunk, doing an alcoholic rhumba, but he certainly could not have passed a sobriety test.

He came up on the porch and stopped. His chest was heaving from anger. He smelled of whiskey and sweat and Old Spice.

"You think I don't fucking know the shit you're putting in my old lady's mind?" he said to Murch. "Huh?"

Murch didn't say anything.

"I asked you a fucking question, old man."

Murch said, softly, "Why don't you go in and sleep it off, kid?"

"You're the goddamned reason she went to her mother's last week. You told her to!"

And then he lunged at Murch and I was up out of my chair. He was too drunk to swing with any grace or precision but he caught me on the side of the head with the punch he'd intended for Murch, and for a dizzy moment I felt my knees go. He could hit. No doubt about that.

And then he was on me, having given up on Murch, and I had to take four or five more punches while I tried to gather myself and bring some focus to my fear and rage.

I finally got him in the ribs with a good hooking right, and I felt real exhilaration when I heard the air *whoof* out of him, and then I banged another one just to the right off his jaw and backed him up several inches and then—

Then Kelly was on the porch crying and screaming and putting herself between us, a child trying to separate two mindless mastodons from killing each other and—

"You promised you wouldn't drink no more!" she kept screaming over and over at Briney.

All he could do was stand head hung and shamed like some whipped giant there in the dirty porch light she'd turned on. "But honey . . ." he'd mumble. Or "But sweetheart . . ." Or "But Kelly, jeez I . . ."

"Now you get inside there, and right now!" she said, no longer his wife but his mother. And she sternly pointed to the door. And he shambled toward it, not looking back at any of us, just shuffling and shambling, drunk and dazed and sweaty, depleted of rage and pride, and no longer fierce at all.

When he was inside, the apartment door closed, she said, "I'm real sorry, Todd. I heard everything from inside."

"It's all right."

"You hurt?"

"I'm fine."

"I'm real sorry."

"I know."

She went over to Murch and touched him tenderly on the shoulder. He was standing up, this tired and suddenly very old-looking man, and he had good gray Caesar in his arms. Kelly leaned over and petted Caesar and said, "I wish I had a husband like you, Caesar."

She went back inside. The rest of our time on the porch, the Brineys spoke again in whispers.

Just before he went up to bed, Murch said, "He's going to kill her someday. You know that, don't you, Todd?"

This time I was ready for it. Six hours had gone by. I'd watched the late movie and then lay on the bed smoking a cigarette in the darkness and just staring at the play of streetlight and tree shadow on the ceiling.

The first sound from below was very, very low and I wasn't even sure what it was. But I threw my legs off the bed and sat up, grabbing for my cigarettes as I did so.

When the sound came again, I recognized it immediately for what it was. A soft sobbing. Kelly.

Voices. Muffled. Bedsprings squeaking. A curse—Briney.

And then, sharp and unmistakable, a slap.

And then two, three slaps.

Kelly screaming. Furniture being shoved around.

I was up from the sweaty bed and into my jeans, not bothering with a shirt, and down the stairs two at a time.

By now, Kelly's screams filled the entire house. Behind me, at the top of the stairs, I could hear Murch shouting down, "You gotta stop him, son! You gotta stop him!"

More slaps; the muffled thud of closed fists pounding into human flesh and bone.

I stood back from the door and raised my foot and kicked with the flat of my heel four times before shattering the wood into jagged splinters.

Briney had Kelly pinned on the floor as he had last week, and he was putting punches into her at will. Even at a glance, I could see that her nose was broken. Ominously, blood leaked from her ear.

I got him by the hair and yanked him to his feet. He still wasn't completely sober so he couldn't put up the resistance he might have at another time.

I meant to make him unconscious and that was exactly what I did. I dragged him over to the door. He kept swinging at me and occasionally landing hard punches to my ribs and kidney but at the moment I didn't care. He smelled of sweat and pure animal rage and Kelly's fresh blood. I got him to the door frame and held him high by his hair and then slammed his temple against the edge of the frame.

It only took once. He went straight down to the floor in an unmoving heap.

Murch came running through the door. "I called the cops!"

He went immediately to Kelly, knelt by her. She was over on her side, crying crazily and throwing up in gasps that shook her entire body. Her face was a mask of blood. He had ripped her nightgown and dug fierce raking fingers over her breasts. She just kept crying.

Even this late at night, the neighbors were up for a good show, maybe two dozen of them standing in the middle of the street as the whipping red lights of police cars and ambulance gave the crumbling neighborhood a nervous new life.

Kelly had slipped into unconsciousness and was brought out strapped to a stretcher.

Two uniformed cops questioned Briney on the porch. He kept pointing to me and Murch, who stood holding Caesar and stroking him gently.

There was an abrupt scuffle as Briney bolted and took a punch at one of the cops. He was a big man, this cop, and he brought Briney down with two punches. Then he cuffed him and took him to the car.

From inside the police vehicle, Briney glared at me and kept glaring until the car disappeared into the shadows at the end of the block.

Kelly was a week in the hospital. Murch and I visited her twice. In addition to a broken nose, she'd also suffered a broken rib and two broken teeth. She had a hard time talking. She just kept crying softly and shaking her head and patting the hands we both held out to her.

Her brother, a burly man in his twenties, came over to the house two days later with a big U-Haul and three friends and cleaned out the Briney apartment. Murch and I gave him a hand loading.

The newspaper said that Peter James Briney had posted a $2500 bond and had been released on bail. He obviously wasn't going to live downstairs. Kelly's brother hadn't left so much as a fork behind, and the landlord had already nailed a Day-Glo For Rent sign on one of the front porch pillars.

As for me, the crew was getting ready to move on. In two more days, we'd pack and head up the highway toward Des Moines.

I tried to make my last two nights with Murch especially good. There was a pizza and beer restaurant over on Ellis Boulevard and on the second to last night, I took him there for dinner. I even co-erced him into telling me some of those good old WWII stories of his.

The next night, the last night in Cedar Rapids, we had to work over-time again.

I got home after nine, when it was full and starry dark.

I was walking up the street when one of the neighbors came down from his porch and said, "They took him away."

I stopped. My body temperature dropped several degrees. I knew what was coming. "Took who off?"

"Murch. You know, that guy where you live."

"The cops?"

The man shook his head. "Ambulance. Murch had a heart at-tack."

I ran home. Up the stairs. Murch's place was locked. I had a key for his apartment in my room. I got it and opened the place up.

I got the lights on and went through each of the four small rooms. Murch was an orderly man. Though all the furnishings were old, from the ancient horsehair couch to the scarred chest of drawers, there was an obstinate if shabby dignity about them, much like Murch himself.

I found what I was looking for in the bathtub. Apparently the ambulance attendants hadn't had time to do anything more than rush Murch to the hospital.

Caesar, or what was left of him anyway, they'd left behind.

He lay in the center of the old claw-footed bathtub. He had been stabbed dozens of times. His gray fur was matted and stiff with his own blood. He'd died in the midst of human frenzy.

I didn't have to wonder who'd done this or what had given Murch his heart attack.

I went over to the phone and called both hospitals. Murch was at Mercy. The nurse I spoke with said that he had suffered a massive stroke and was unconscious. The prognosis was not good.

After I hung up, I went through the phone book looking for Brineys. It took me six calls to get the right one but finally I found Pete Briney's father. I convinced him that I was a good friend of Pete's and that I was just in town for the night and that I really wanted to see the old sonofagun. "Well," he said, "he hangs out at the Log Cabin a lot."

The Log Cabin was a tavern not far away. I was there within fifteen minutes.

The moment I stepped through the bar, into a working-class atmosphere of clacking pool balls and whiney country western music, I saw him.

He was in a booth near the back, laughing about something with a girl with a beehive hairdo and a quick beery smile.

When he saw me, he got scared. He left the booth and ran toward the back door. By now, several people were watching. I didn't care.

I went out the back door after him. I stood beneath a window-unit air conditioner that sounded like a B-52 starting up and bled water like a wound. The air was hot and pasty and I slapped at two mosquitos biting my neck.

Ahead of me was a gravel parking lot. The only light was spill from the back windows of the tavern. The lot was about half full.

Briney hadn't had time to get into that nice golden Mercury convertible at the end of the lot. He was hiding somewhere behind one of the cars.

I walked down the lot, my heels adjusting to the loose and wobbly feel of the gravel beneath.

He came lunging out from behind a pickup truck. Because I'd been expecting him, I was able to duck without much problem.

I turned and faced him. He was crouched down, ready to jump at me.

"I'd still have a wife if it wasn't for you two bastards," he said.

"You're a pretty brave guy, Briney. You wait till Murch goes somewhere and then you sneak in and kill his cat. And then Murch comes home and finds Caesar dead and—"

But I was through talking.

I kicked him clean and sharp. I broke his nose. He gagged and screamed and started puking—he must have had way too much to drink that night—and sank to his knees and then I went over and kicked him several times in the ribs.

I kicked him until I heard the sharp brittle sound of bones breaking, and until he pitched forward, still screaming and crying, to the gravel. Then I went up and kicked him in the back of the head.

A couple of his friends from the tavern came out and started toward me but I was big enough and angry enough that they were wary.

"Personal dispute," I said. "Nothing to do with you boys at all."

Then they went over and tried to help their friend to his feet. It wasn't easy. He was a mess.

Murch died an hour and ten minutes after I got to the hospital. I went into his room and looked at all the alien tentacles stretching from beeping cold metal boxes to his warm but failing body. I stood next to his bed until a doctor came in and asked very softly and politely if I'd mind waiting in the hall while they did some work.

It was while the doctor was in there that Murch died. He had never regained consciousness and so we'd never even said proper good-byes.

At the house, I went into Murch's apartment and found the shoebox and took it into the bathroom and gathered up the remains of poor Caesar.

I took the box down the stairs and out to the garage where I got the garden spade. Then I went over and in the starry prairie night, buried Caesar properly. I even blessed myself, though I wasn't a Catholic, and then knelt down and took the rich damp earth and covered Caesar's grave.

I didn't sleep that night. I just sat up in my little room with my last quart of Canadian Ace and my last pack of Pall Malls and thought about Kelly and thought about Caesar and especially I thought about Murch.

Just at dawn, it started to rain, a hot dirty city rain that would neither cool nor cleanse, and I packed my bags and left.

OUT THERE IN
THE DARKNESS

For Richard Matheson

i

The night it all started, the whole strange spiral, we were having our usual midweek poker game—four fortyish men who work in the financial business getting together for beer and bawdy jokes and straight poker. No wild card games. We hate them.

This was summer, and vacation time, and so it happened that the game was held two weeks in a row at my house. Jan had taken the kids to see her Aunt Wendy and Uncle Verne at their fishing cabin, and so I offered to have the game at my house this week, too. With nobody there to supervise, the beer could be laced with a little bourbon, and the jokes could get even bawdier. With the wife and kids in the house, you're always at least a little bit intimidated.

Mike and Bob came together, bearing gifts, which in this case meant the kind of sexy magazines our wives did not want in the house in case the kids might stumble across them. At least that's what they say. I think they sense, and rightly, that the magazines might give their spouses bad ideas about taking the secretary out for a few after-work drinks, or stopping by a singles bar some night.

We got the chips and cards set up at the table, we got the first beers open (Mike chasing a shot of bourbon with his beer), and we started passing the dirty magazines around with tenth-grade glee. The magazines compensated, I suppose, for the balding head, the bloating belly, the stooping shoulders. Deep in the heart of every hundred-year-old man is a horny fourteen-year-old boy.

All this, by the way, took place up in the attic. The four of us got to know each other when we all moved into what city planners called a "transitional neighborhood." There were some grand old houses that could be renovated with enough money and real care. The city designated a ten-square-block area as one it wanted to restore to shiny new luster. Jan and I chose a crumbling Victorian. You wouldn't recognize it today. And that includes the attic, which I've turned into a very nice den.

"Pisses me off," Mike O'Brien said. "He's always late."

And that was true. Neil Solomon *was* always late. Never by that much but always late nonetheless.

"At least tonight he has a good excuse," Bob Genter said.

"He does?" Mike said. "He's probably swimming in his pool." Neil recently got a bonus that made him the first owner of a full-size outdoor pool in our neighborhood.

"No, he's got Patrol. But he's stopping at nine. He's got somebody trading with him for next week."

"Oh, hell," Mike said, obviously sorry that he'd complained. "I didn't know that."

Bob Genter's handsome black head nodded solemnly.

Patrol is something we all take very seriously in this newly restored "transitional neighborhood." Eight months ago, the burglaries started, and they've gotten pretty bad. My house has been burglarized once and vandalized once. Bob and Mike have had curb-sitting cars stolen. Neil's wife, Sheila, was surprised in her own kitchen by a burglar. And then there was the killing four months ago, man and wife who'd just moved into the neighborhood, savagely stabbed to death in their own bed. The police caught the guy a few days later trying to cash some of the traveler's checks he'd stolen after killing his prey. He was typical of the kind of man who infested this neighborhood after sundown: a twentyish junkie stoned to the point of psychosis on various street drugs, and not at all averse to murdering people he envied and despised. He also knew a whole hell of a lot about fooling burglar alarms.

After the murders there was a neighborhood meeting and that's when we came up with the Patrol, something somebody'd read about being popular back East. People think that a nice middle-sized Midwestern city like ours doesn't have major crime problems. I invite them to walk many of these streets after dark. They'll quickly be disabused of that notion. Anyway, the Patrol worked this way: each night, two neighborhood people got in the family van and patrolled the ten-block area that had been restored. If they saw anything suspicious, they use their cellular phones and called the police. We jokingly called it the Baby Boomer Brigade. The Patrol had one strict rule: you were never to take direct action unless somebody's life was at stake. Always, always use the cellular phone and call the police.

Neil had Patrol tonight. He'd be rolling in here in another half hour. The Patrol had two shifts: early, 8:00–10:00; late, 10:00–12:00.

Bob said, "You hear what Evans suggested?"

"About guns?" I said.

"Yeah."

"Makes me a little nervous," I said.

"Me, too," Bob said. For somebody who'd grown up in the worst area of the city, Bob Genter was a very polished guy. Whenever he joked that he was the token black, Neil always countered with the fact that he was the token Jew, just as Mike was the token Catholic, and I was the token Methodist. We were friends of convenience, I suppose, but we all really did like each other, something that was demonstrated when Neil had a cancer scare a few years back. Bob, Mike and I were in his hospital room twice a day, all eight days running.

"I think it's time," Mike said. "The bad guys have guns, so the good guys should have guns."

"The good guys are the cops," I said. "Not us."

"People start bringing guns on Patrol," Bob said, "somebody innocent is going to get shot."

"So some night one of us here is on Patrol and we see a bad guy and he sees us and before the cops get there, the bad guy shoots us? You don't think that's going to happen?"

"It *could* happen, Mike," I said, "but I just don't think that justifies carrying guns."

The argument gave us something to do while we waited for Neil.

"Sorry I'm late," Neil Solomon said after he followed me up to the attic and came inside.

"We already drank all the beer," Mike O'Brien said loudly.

Neil smiled. "That gut you're carrying lately, I can believe that *you* drank all the beer."

Mike always enjoyed being put down by Neil, possibly because most people were a bit intimidated by him—he had that angry Irish edge—and he seemed to enjoy Neil's skilled and fearless handling of him. He laughed with real pleasure.

Neil sat down, I got him a beer from the tiny fridge I keep up here, cards were dealt, seven card stud was played.

Bob said, "How'd Patrol go tonight?"

Neil shrugged. "No problems."

"I still say we should carry guns," Mike said.

"You're not going to believe this but I agree with you," Neil said.

"Seriously?" Mike said.

"Oh, great," I said to Bob Genter, "another beer-commercial cowboy."

Bob smiled. "Where I come from we didn't have cowboys, we had 'mothas.'" He laughed. "Mean mothas, let me tell you. And practically *all* of them carried guns."

"That mean you're siding with them?" I said.

Bob looked at his cards again then shrugged. "Haven't decided yet, I guess."

I didn't think the antigun people were going to lose this round. But I worried about the round after it, a few months down the line when the subject of carrying guns came up again. All the TV coverage violence gets in this city, people are more and more developing a siege mentality.

"Play cards," Mike said, "and leave the debate society crap till later."

Good idea.

We played cards.

In forty-five minutes, I lost $63.82. Mike and Neil always played as if their lives were at stake. All you had to do was watch their faces. Gunfighters couldn't have looked more serious or determined.

The first pit stop came just after ten o'clock and Neil took it. There was a john on the second floor between the bedrooms, and another john on the first floor.

Neil said, "The good Doctor Gottesfeld had to give me a finger-wave this afternoon, gents, so this may take a while."

"You should trade that prostate of yours in for a new one," Mike said.

"Believe me, I'd like to."

While Neil was gone, the three of us started talking about the Patrol again, and whether we should go armed.

We made the same old arguments. The passion was gone. We were just marking time waiting for Neil and we knew it.

Finally, Mike said, "Let me see some of those magazines again."

"You got some identification?" I said.

"I'll show you some identification," Mike said.

"Spare me," I said, "I'll just give you the magazines."

"You mind if I use the john on the first floor?" Bob said.

"Yeah, it would really piss me off," I said.

"Really?"

That was one thing about Bob. He always fell for deadpan humor.

"No, not 'really,' " I said. "Why would I care if you used the john on the first floor?"

He grinned. "Thought maybe they were segregated facilities or something."

He left.

Mike said, "We're lucky, you know that?"

"You mean me and you?"

"Yeah."

"Lucky how?"

"Those two guys. They're great guys. I wish I had them at work." He shook his head. "Treacherous bastards. That's all I'm around all day long."

"No offense, but I'll bet you can be pretty treacherous yourself."

He smiled. "Look who's talking."

The first time I heard it, I thought it was some kind of animal noise from outside, a dog or a cat in some kind of discomfort maybe. Mike, who was dealing himself a hand of solitaire, didn't even look up from his cards.

But the second time I heard the sound, Mike and I both looked up. And then we heard the exploding sound of breaking glass.

"What the hell is that?" Mike said.

"Let's go find out."

Just about the time we reached the bottom of the attic steps, we saw Neil coming out of the second-floor john. "You hear that?"

"Sure as hell did," I said.

We reached the staircase leading to the first floor. Everything was dark. Mike reached for the light switch but I brushed his hand away.

I put a *ssshing* finger to my lips and then showed him that Louisville Slugger I'd grabbed from Tim's room. He's my nine-year-old and his most devout wish is to be a good baseball player. His mother has convinced him that just because I went to college on a baseball scholarship, I was a good player. I wasn't. I was a lucky player.

I led the way downstairs, keeping the bat ready at all times.

"You sonofabitch!"

The voice belonged to Bob.

More smashing glass.

I listened to the passage of the sound. Kitchen. Had to be the kitchen.

In the shadowy light from the street, I saw their faces, Mike and Neil's. They looked scared.

I hefted the bat some more and then started moving fast to the kitchen.

Just as we passed through the dining room, I heard something heavy hit the kitchen floor. Something human and heavy.

I got the kitchen light on.

He was at the back door. White. Tall. Blond shoulder-length hair. Filthy tan T-shirt. Greasy jeans. He had grabbed one of Jan's carving knives from the huge iron rack that sits atop the butcher-block island. The one curious thing about him was the eyes: there was a malevolent iridescence to the blue pupils, an angry but somehow alien intelligence, a silver glow.

Bob was sprawled facedown on the tile floor. His arms were spread wide on either side of him. He didn't seem to be moving. Chunks and fragments of glass were strewn everywhere across the floor. My uninvited guest had smashed two or three of the colorful pitchers we'd bought the winter before in Mexico.

"Run!" the burglar cried to somebody on the back porch.

He turned, waving the butcher knife back and forth to keep us at bay.

Footsteps out the back door.

The burglar held us off a few more moments but then I gave him a little bit of tempered Louisville Slugger wood right across the wrist. The knife went clattering.

By this time, Mike and Neil were pretty crazed. They jumped him, hurled him back against the door, and then started putting in punches wherever they'd fit.

"Hey!" I said, and tossed Neil the bat. "Just hold this. If he makes a move, open up his head. Otherwise leave him alone."

They really were crazed, like pit bulls who'd been pulled back just as a fight was starting to get good.

"Mike, call the cops and tell them to send a car."

I got Bob up and walking. I took him into the bathroom and sat him down on the toilet lid. I found a lump the size of an egg on the back of his head. I soaked a clean washcloth with cold water and pressed it against the lump. Bob took it from there.

"You want an ambulance?" I said.

"An ambulance? Are you kidding? You must think I'm a ballet dancer or something."

I shook my head. "No, I know better than that. I've got a male cousin who's a ballet dancer and he's one tough sonofabitch, believe me. You—" I smiled. "You aren't that tough, Bob."

"I don't need an ambulance. I'm fine."

He winced and tamped the rag tighter against his head. "Just a little headache is all." He looked young suddenly, the aftershock of fear in his brown eyes. "Scared the hell out of me. Heard something when I was leaving the john. Went out to the kitchen to check it out. He jumped me."

"What'd he hit you with?"

"No idea."

"I'll go get you some whiskey. Just sit tight."

"I love sitting in bathrooms, man."

I laughed. "I don't blame you."

When I got back to the kitchen, they were gone. All three of them. Then I saw the basement door. It stood open a few inches. I could see dusty light in the space between door and frame. The basement was our wilderness. We hadn't had the time or money to really fix it up yet. We were counting on this year's Christmas bonus from the Winsdor Financial Group to help us set it right.

I went down the stairs. The basement is one big, mostly unused room except for the washer and drier in the corner. All the boxes and odds and ends that should have gone to the attic instead went down here. It smells damp most of the time. The idea is to turn it into a family room for when the boys are older. These days it's mostly inhabited by stray waterbugs.

When I reached the bottom step, I saw them. There are four metal support poles in the basement, near each corner. They had him lashed to a pole in the east quadrant, lashed his wrists behind him with rope found in the tool room. They also had him gagged with what looked like a pillowcase. His eyes were big and wide. He looked scared and I didn't blame him. I was scared, too.

"What the hell are you guys doing?"

"Just calm down, Papa Bear," Mike said. That's his name for me whenever he wants to convey to people that I'm kind of this old fuddy-duddy. It so happens that Mike is two years older than I am and it also happens that I'm not a fuddy-duddy. Jan has assured me of that, and she's completely impartial.

"Knock off the Papa Bear bullshit. Did you call the cops?"

"Not yet," Neil said. "Just calm down a little, all right?"

"You haven't called the cops. You've got some guy tied up and gagged in my basement. You haven't even asked how Bob is. And you want me to calm down."

Mike came up to me, then. He still had that air of pit-bull craziness about him, frantic, uncontrollable, alien.

"We're going to do what the cops *can't* do, man," he said. "We're going to sweat this son of a bitch. We're going to make him tell us who he was with tonight, and then we're going to make him give us every single name of every single bad guy who works this neighborhood. And then we'll turn all the names over to the cops."

"It's just an extension of the Patrol," Neil said. "Just keeping our neighborhood safe is all."

"You guys are nuts," I said, and turned back toward the steps. "I'm going up and calling the cops."

That's when I realized just how crazed Mike was. "You aren't going anywhere, man. You're going to stay here and help us break this bastard down. You're going to do your goddamned neighborhood *duty.*"

He'd grabbed my sleeve so hard that he'd torn it at the shoulder. We both discovered this at the same time.

I expected him to look sorry. He didn't. In fact, he was smirking at me. "Don't be such a wimp, Aaron," he said.

ii

Mike led the charge getting the kitchen cleaned up. I think he was feeling guilty about calling me a wimp with such angry exuberance. Now I understood how lynch mobs got formed. One guy like Mike stirring people up by alternately insulting them and urging them on.

After the kitchen was put back in order, and after I'd taken in-

ventory to find that nothing had been stolen, I went to the refrigerator and got beers for everybody. Bob had drifted back to the
kitchen, too.

"All right," I said, "now that we've all calmed down, I want to
walk over to that yellow kitchen wall phone there and call the police. Any objections?"

"I think blue would look better in here than yellow," Neil said.

"Funny," I said.

They looked themselves now, no feral madness on the faces of
Mike or Neil, no winces on Bob's.

I started across the floor to the phone.

Neil grabbed my arm. Not with the same insulting force Mike
had used on me. But enough to get the job done.

"I think Mike's right," Neil said. "I think we should grill that
bastard a little bit."

I shook my head, politely removed his hand from my forearm,
and proceeded to the phone.

"This isn't just your decision alone," Mike said.

He'd finally had his way. He'd succeeded in making me angry. I
turned around and looked at him. "This is my house, Mike. If you
don't like my decisions, then I'd suggest you leave."

We both took steps toward each other. Mike would no doubt
win any battle we had but I'd at least be able to inflict a little damage and right now that's all I was thinking about.

Neil got between us.

"Hey," he said. "For God's sake you two, c'mon. We're friends,
remember?"

"This is my house," I said, my words childish in my ears.

"Yeah, but we live in the same neighborhood, Aaron," Mike
said, "which makes this 'our' problem."

"He's right, Aaron," Bob said from the breakfast nook. There's a
window there where I sometimes sit to watch all the animals on
sunny days. I saw a mother raccoon and four baby raccoons one
day, marching single file across the grass. My grandparents were
the last generation to live on the farm. My father came to town here
and ended up working at a ball bearing company. Raccoons are a lot
more pleasant to gaze upon than people.

"He's not right," I said to Bob. "He's wrong. We're not cops, we're not bounty hunters, we're not trackers. We're a bunch of god-damned guys who peddle stocks and bonds. Mike and Neil shouldn't have tied him up downstairs—that happens to be illegal, at least the way they went about it—and now I'm going to call the cops."

"Yes, that poor thing," Mike said, "aren't we just picking on him, though? Tell you what, why don't we make him something to eat?"

"Just make sure we have the right wine to go with it," Neil said. "Properly chilled, of course."

"Maybe we could get him a chick," Bob said.

"With bombers out to here," Mike said, indicating with his hands where "here" was.

I couldn't help it. I smiled. They were all being ridiculous. A kind of fever had caught them.

"You really want to go down there and question him?" I said to Neil.

"Yes. We can ask him things the cops can't."

"Scare the bastard a little," Mike said. "So he'll tell us who was with him tonight, and who else works this neighborhood." He came over and put his hand out. "God, man, you're one of my best friends. I don't want you mad at me."

Then he hugged me, which is something I've never been comfortable with men doing, but to the extent I could, I hugged him back.

"Friends?" he said.

"Friends," I said. "But I still want to call the cops."

"And spoil our fun?" Neil said.

"And spoil your fun."

"I say we take it to a vote," Bob said.

"This isn't a democracy," I said. "It's my house and I'm the king. I don't want to have a vote."

"Can we ask him one question?" Bob said.

I sighed. They weren't going to let go. "One question?"

"The name of the guy he was with tonight."

"And that's it?"

"That's it. That way we get him and one other guy off the street."

"And then I call the cops?"

"Then," Mike said, "you call the cops."

"One question," Neil said.

While we finished our beers, we argued a little more, but they had a lot more spirit left than I did. I was tired now and missing Jan and the kids and feeling lonely. These three guys had become strangers to me tonight. Very old boys eager to play at boy games once again.

"One question," I said. "Then I call the cops."

I led the way down, sneezing as I did so.

There's always enough dust floating around in the basement to play hell with my sinuses.

The guy was his same sullen self, glaring at us as we descended the stairs and then walked over to him. He smelled of heat and sweat and city grime. The long bare arms sticking out of his filthy T-shirt told tattoo tales of writhing snakes and leaping panthers. The arms were joined in the back with rope. His jaw still flexed, trying to accommodate the intrusion of the gag.

"Maybe we should castrate him," Mike said, walking up close to the guy. "You like that, scumbag? If we castrated you?"

If the guy felt any fear, it wasn't evident in his eyes. All you could see there was the usual contempt.

"I'll bet this is the jerk who broke into the Donaldson's house a couple weeks ago," Neil said.

Now he walked up to the guy. But he was more ambitious than Mike had been. Neil spat in the guy's face.

"Hey," I said, "cool it."

Neil glared at me. "Yeah, I wouldn't want to hurt his feelings, would I?"

Then he suddenly turned back on the guy, raised his fist and started to swing. All I could do was shove him. That sent his punch angling off to the right, missing our burglar by about half a foot.

"You asshole," Neil said, turning back on me now.

But Mike was there, between us.

"You know what we're doing? We're making this jerk happy.

He's gonna have some nice stories to tell all his criminal friends."

He was right. The burglar was the one who got to look all cool and composed. We looked like squabbling brats. As if to confirm this, a hint of amusement played in the burglar's blue eyes.

"Oh, hell, Aaron, I'm sorry," Neil said, putting his hand out. This was like a political convention, all the handshaking going on.

"So am I, Neil," I said. "That's why I want to call the cops and get this over with."

And that's when he chose to make his move, the burglar. As soon as I mentioned the cops, he probably realized that this was going to be his last opportunity.

He waited until we were just finishing up with the handshake, when we were all focused on each other. Then he took off running. We could see that he'd slipped the rope. He went straight for the stairs, angling out around us like a running back seeing daylight. He even stuck his long, tattooed arm out as if he was trying to repel a tackle.

"Hey," Bob shouted. "He's getting away."

He was at the stairs by the time we could gather ourselves enough to go after him. But when we moved, we moved fast, and in virtual unison.

By the time I got my hand on the cuff of his left jean, he was close enough to the basement door to open it.

I yanked hard and ducked out of the way of his kicking foot. By now I was as crazy as Mike and Neil had been earlier. There was adrenaline and great anger. He wasn't just a burglar, he was all burglars, intent not merely on stealing things from me, but hurting my family, too. He hadn't had time to take the gag from his mouth.

This time, I grabbed booted foot and leg and started hauling him back down the stairs. At first he was able to hold on to the door but when I wrenched his foot rightward, he tried to scream behind the gag. He let go of the doorknob.

The next half minute is still unclear in my mind. I started running down the stairs, dragging him with me. All I wanted to do was get him on the basement floor again, turn him over to the others to watch, and then go call the cops.

But somewhere in those few seconds when I was hauling him back down the steps, I heard edge of stair meeting back of skull. The others heard it, too, because their shouts and curses died in their throats.

When I turned around, I saw the blood running fast and red from his nose. The blue eyes no longer held contempt. They were starting to roll up white in the back of his head.

"God," I said. "He's hurt."

"I think he's a lot more than hurt," Mike said.

"Help me carry him upstairs."

We got him on the kitchen floor. Mike and Neil rushed around soaking paper towels. We tried to revive him. Bob, who kept wincing from his headache, tried the guy's wrist, ankle and throat for a pulse. None. His nose and mouth were bloody. Very bloody.

"No way you could *die* from hitting your head like that," Neil said.

"Sure you could," Mike said. "You hit it just the right way."

"He can't be dead," Neil said. "I'm going to try his pulse again."

Bob, who obviously took Neil's second opinion personally, frowned and rolled his eyes. "He's dead, man. He really is."

"Bullshit."

"You a doctor or something?" Bob said.

Neil smiled nervously. "No, but I play one on TV."

So Neil tried the pulse points. His reading was exactly what Bob's reading had been.

"See," Bob said.

I guess none of us were destined to ever quite be adults.

"Man," Neil said, looking down at the long, cold unmoving form of the burglar. "He's really dead."

"What the hell're we gonna do?" Mike said.

"We're going to call the police," I said, and started for the phone.

"The hell we are," Mike said. "The hell we are."

iii

Maybe half an hour after we laid him on the kitchen floor, he started to smell. We'd looked for identification and found none. He was just the Burglar.

We sat at the kitchen table, sharing a fifth of Old Grandad and innumerable beers.

We'd taken two votes and they'd come up ties. Two for calling the police, Bob and I; two for not calling the police, Mike and Neil.

"All we have to tell them," I said, "is that we tied him up so he wouldn't get away."

"And then they say," Mike said, "so why didn't you call us before now?"

"We just lie about the time a little," I said. "Tell them we called them within twenty minutes."

"Won't work," Neil said.

"Why not?" Bob said.

"Medical examiner can fix the time of death," Neil said.

"Not that close."

"Close enough so that the cops might question our story," Neil said. "By the time they get here, he'll have been dead at least an hour, hour and a half."

"And then we get our names in the paper for not reporting the burglary or the death right away," Mike said. "Brokerages just love publicity like that."

"I'm calling the cops right now," I said, and started up from the table."

"Think about Tomlinson a minute," Neil said.

Tomlinson was my boss at the brokerage. "What about him?"

"Remember how he canned Dennis Bryce when Bryce's ex-wife took out a restraining order on him?"

"This is different," I said.

"The hell it is," Mike said. "Neil's right, none of our bosses will like publicity like this. We'll all sound a little—crazy—you know, keeping him tied up in the basement. And then killing him when he tried to get away."

They all looked at me.

"You bastards," I said. "I was the one who wanted to call the police in the first place. And I sure as hell didn't try to kill him on purpose."

"Looking back on it," Neil said, "I guess you were right, Aaron. We should've called the cops right away."

"Now's a great time to realize that," I said.

"Maybe they've got a point," Bob said softly, glancing at me, then glancing nervously away.

"Oh, great. You, too?" I said.

"They just might kick my black ass out of there if I had any publicity that involved somebody getting killed," Bob said.

"He was a frigging burglar," I said.

"But he's dead," Neil said.

"And we killed him," Mike said.

"I appreciate you saying 'we,' " I said.

"I know a good place," Bob said.

I looked at him carefully, afraid of what he was going to say next.

"Forget it," I said.

"A good place for what?" Neil said.

"Dumping the body," Bob said.

"No way," I said.

This time when I got up, nobody tried to stop me. I walked over to the yellow wall telephone.

I wondered if the cozy kitchen would ever feel the same to me now that a dead body had been laid upon its floor.

I had to step over him to reach the phone. The smell was even more sour now.

"You know how many bodies get dumped in the river that never wash up?" Bob said.

"No," I said, "and you don't, either."

"Lots," he said.

"There's a scientific appraisal for you. 'Lots.' "

"Lots and lots, probably," Neil said, taking up Bob's argument.

Mike grinned. "Lots and lots and *lots*."

"Thank you, Professor," I said.

I lifted the receiver and dialed 0.

"Operator."

"The police department, please."

"Is this an emergency?" asked the young woman. Usually I would have spent more time wondering if the sweetness of her voice was matched by the sweetness of her face and body. I'm still a face man. I suppose it's my romantic side. "Is this an emergency?" she repeated.

"No; no, it isn't."

"I'll connect you," she said.

"You think your kids'll be able to handle it?" Neil said.

"No mind games," I said.

"No mind games at all," he said. "I'm asking you a very realistic question. The police have some doubts about our story and then the press gets ahold of it and bam. We're the lead story on all three channels. 'Did four middle-class men murder the burglar they captured?' The press even goes after the kids these days. 'Do *you* think your daddy murdered that burglar, son?'"

"Good evening. Police Department."

I started to speak but I couldn't somehow. My voice wouldn't work. That's the only way I can explain it.

"The six o'clock news five nights running," Neil said softly behind me. "And the DA can't endorse any kind of vigilante activity so he nails us on involuntary manslaughter."

"Hello? This is the Police Department," said the black female voice on the phone.

Neil was there then, reaching me as if by magic.

He took the receiver gently from my hand and hung it back up on the phone again.

"Let's go have another drink and see what Bob's got in mind, all right?"

He led me, as if I were a hospital patient, slowly and carefully back to the table where Bob, over more whiskey, slowly and gently laid out his plan.

The next morning, three of us phoned in sick. Bob went to work because he had an important meeting.

Around noon—a sunny day when a softball game and a cold six-pack of beer sounded good—Neil and Mike came over. They looked as bad as I felt, and no doubt looked myself.

We sat out on the patio eating the Hardee's lunch they'd bought. I'd need to play softball to work off some of the calories I was eating.

Birdsong and soft breezes and the smell of fresh cut grass should have made our patio time enjoyable. But I had to wonder if we'd ever enjoy anything again. I just kept seeing the body momentarily arced above the roaring waters of the dam; and dropping into white churning turbulence.

"You think we did the right thing?" Neil said.

"Now's a hell of a time to ask that," I said.

"Of course we did the right thing," Mike said. "What choice did we have? It was either that or get our asses arrested."

"So you don't have any regrets?" Neil said.

Mike sighed. "I didn't say that. I mean, I wish it hadn't happened in the first place."

"Maybe Aaron was right all along," Neil said.

"About what?"

"About going to the cops."

"Goddamn," Mike said, sitting up from his slouch. We all wore button-down shirts without ties and with the sleeves rolled up. Somehow there was something profane about wearing shorts and T-shirts on a workday. We even wore pretty good slacks. We were that kind of people. "Goddamn."

"Here he goes," Neil said.

"I can't believe you two," Mike said. "We should be happy that everything went so well last night—and what are we doing? Sitting around here pissing and moaning."

"That doesn't mean it's over," I said.

"Why the hell not?" Mike said.

"Because there's still one left."

"One what?"

"One burglar."

"So?"

"So you don't think he's going to get curious about what the hell happened to his partner?"

"What's he gonna do?" Mike said. "Go to the cops?"

"Maybe."

"Maybe? You're crazy. He goes to the cops, he'd be setting himself up for a robbery conviction."

"Not if he tells them we murdered his pal."

Neil said, "Aaron's got a point. What if this guy goes to the cops?"

"He's not going to the cops," Mike said. "No way he's going to the cops at all."

iv

I was dozing on the couch, a Cubs game on the TV set, when the phone rang around nine that evening. I hadn't heard from Jan yet so I expected it would be her. Whenever we're apart, we call each other at least once a day.

The phone machine picks up on the fourth ring so I had to scramble to beat it.

"Hello?"

Nothing. But somebody was on the line. Listening.

"Hello?"

I never play games with silent callers. I just hang up. I did so now.

Two innings later, having talked to Jan, having made myself a tuna fish sandwich on rye, found a package of potato chips I thought we'd finished off at the poker game, and gotten myself a new can of beer, I sat down to watch the last inning. The Cubs had a chance of winning. I said a silent prayer to the God of Baseball.

The phone rang.

I mouthed several curses around my mouthful of tuna sandwich and went to the phone.

"Hello?" I said, trying to swallow the last of the bite.

My silent friend again.

I slammed the phone.

The Cubs got two more singles, I started on the chips and I had polished off the beer and was thinking of getting another one when the phone rang again.

I had a suspicion of who was calling and then saying nothing—
but I didn't really want to think about it.

Then I decided there was an easy way to handle this situation.
I'd just let the phone machine take it. If my anonymous friend
wanted to talk to a phone machine, good for him.

Four rings. The phone machine took over, Jan's pleasant voice
saying that we weren't home but would be happy to call you back if
you'd just leave your number.

I waited to hear dead air then a click.

Instead a familiar female voice said: "Aaron, it's Louise. Bob—"
Louise was Bob's wife. She was crying. I ran from the couch to the
phone machine in the hall.

"Hello, Louise. It's Aaron."

"Oh, Aaron. It's terrible."

"What happened, Louise?"

"Bob—" More tears. "He electrocuted himself tonight out in
the garage." She said that a plug had accidentally fallen into a bowl
of water, according to the fire captain on the scene, and Bob hadn't
noticed this and put the plug into the outlet and—

Bob had a wood craft workshop in his garage, a large and sophisticated one. He knew what he was doing.

"He's dead, Aaron. He's dead."

"Oh, God, Louise. I'm sorry."

"He was so careful with electricity, too. It's just so hard to believe—"

Yes, I thought. Yes, it was hard to believe. I thought of last
night. Of the burglars—one who'd died. One who'd gotten away.

"Why don't I come over?"

"Oh, thank you, Aaron, but I need to be alone with the children.
But if you could call Neil and Mike—"

"Of course."

"Thanks for being such good friends, you and Jan."

"Don't be silly, Louise. The pleasure's ours."

"I'll talk to you tomorrow. When I'm—you know."

"Good night, Louise."

* * *

Mike and Neil were at my place within twenty minutes. We sat in the kitchen again, where we were last night.

I said, "Either of you get any weird phone calls tonight?"

"You mean just silence?" Neil said.

"Right."

"I did," Mike said. "Carrie was afraid it was that pervert who called all last winter."

"I did, too," Neil said. "Three of them."

"Then a little while ago, Bob dies out in his garage," I said. "Some coincidence."

"Hey, Aaron," Mike said. "Is that why you got us over here? Because you don't think it was an accident?"

"I'm sure it wasn't an accident," I said. "Bob knew what he was doing with his tools. He didn't notice a plug that had fallen into a bowl of water?"

"He's coming after us," Neil said.

"Oh, God," Mike said. "Not you, too."

"He calls us, gets us on edge," I said. "And then he kills Bob. Making it look like an accident."

"These are pretty bright people," Mike said sarcastically.

"You notice the burglar's eyes?" Neil said.

"I did," I said. "He looked very bright."

"And spooky," Neil said. "Never saw eyes like that before."

"I can shoot your theory right in the butt," Mike said.

"How?" I said.

He leaned forward, sipped his beer. I'd thought about putting out some munchies but somehow that seemed wrong given poor Bob's death and the phone calls. The beers we had to have. The munchies were too festive.

"Here's how. There are two burglars, right? One gets caught, the other runs. And given the nature of burglars, keeps on running. He wouldn't even know who was in the house last night, except for Aaron, and that's only because he's the owner and his name would be in the phone book. But he wouldn't know anything about Bob or Neil or me. No way he'd have been able to track down Bob."

I shook my head. "You're overlooking the obvious."

"Like what?"

"Like he runs off last night, gets his car and then parks in the alley to see what's going to happen."

"Right," Neil said. "Then he sees us bringing his friend out wrapped in a blanket. He follows us to the dam and watches us throw his friend in."

"And," I said, "everybody had his car here last night. Very easy for him to write down all the license numbers."

"So he kills Bob," Neil said. "And starts making the phone calls to shake us up."

"Why Bob?"

"Maybe he hates black people," I said.

Mike looked first at me and then at Neil. "You know what this is?"

"Here he goes," Neil said.

"No; no, I'm serious here. This is Catholic guilt."

"How can it be Catholic guilt when I'm Jewish?" Neil said.

"In a culture like ours, everybody is a little bit Jewish and a little bit Catholic, anyway," Mike said. "So you guys are in the throes of Catholic guilt. You feel bad about what we had to do last night— and we did have to do it, we really didn't have any choice—and the guilt starts to play on your mind. So poor Bob electrocutes himself accidentally and you immediately think it's the second burglar."

"He followed him," Neil said.

"What?" Mike said.

"That's what he did, I bet. The burglar. Followed Bob around all day trying to figure out what was the best way to kill him. You know, the best way that would look like an accident. So then he finds out about the workshop and decides it's perfect."

"That presumes," Mike said, "that one of us is going to be next."

"Hell, yes," Neil said. "That's why he's calling us. Shake us up. Sweat us out. Let us know that he's out there somewhere, just waiting. And that we're next."

"I'm going to follow you to work tomorrow, Neil," I said. "And Mike's going to be with me."

"You guys are having breakdowns. You really are," Mike said.

"We'll follow Neil tomorrow," I said. "And then on Saturday you and Neil can follow me. If he's following *us* around, then we'll see it. And then we can start following him. We'll at least find out who he is."

"And then what?" Mike said. "Suppose we do find out where he lives? Then what the hell do we do?"

Neil said, "I guess we worry about that when we get there, don't we?"

In the morning, I picked Mike up early. We stopped off for doughnuts and coffee. He's like my brother, not a morning person. Crabby. Our conversation was at a minimum, though he did say, "I could've used the extra hour's sleep this morning. Instead of this crap, I mean."

As agreed, we parked half a block from Neil's house. Also as agreed, Neil emerged exactly at 7:35. Kids were already in the wide suburban streets on skateboards and rollerblades. No other car could be seen, except for a lone silver BMW in a driveway far down the block.

We followed him all the way to work. Nobody followed him. Nobody.

When I dropped Mike off at his office, he said, "You owe me an hour's sleep."

"Two hours," I said.

"Huh?"

"Tomorrow, you and Neil follow me around."

"No way," he said.

There are times when only blunt anger will work with Mike. "It was your idea not to call the police, remember? I'm not up for any of your sulking, Mike. I'm really not."

He sighed: "I guess you're right."

I drove for two and a half hours Saturday morning. I hit a hardware store, a lumberyard, and a Kmart. At noon, I pulled into a McDonald's. The three of us had some lunch.

"You didn't see anybody even suspicious?"

"Not even suspicious, Aaron," Neil said. "I'm sorry."

"This is all bullshit. He's not going to follow us around."

"I want to give it one more chance," I said.

Mike made a face. "I'm not going to get up early, if that's what you've got in mind."

I got angry again. "Bob's dead, or have you forgotten?"

"Yeah, Aaron," Mike said, "Bob *is* dead. He got electrocuted. Accidentally."

I said, "You really think it was an accident?"

"Of course I do," Mike said. "When do you want to try it again?"

"Tonight. I'll do a little bowling."

"There's a fight on I want to watch," Mike said.

"Tape it," I said.

" 'Tape it,' " he mocked. "Since when did you start giving us orders?"

"Oh, for God's sake, Mike, grow up," Neil said. "There's no way that Bob's electrocution was an accident or a coincidence. He's probably not going to stop with Bob, either."

The bowling alley was mostly teenagers on Saturday night. There was a time when bowling was mostly a working-class sport. Now it's come to the suburbs and the white-collar people. Now the bowling lane is a good place for teenage boys to meet teenage girls.

I bowled two games, drank three beers, and walked back outside an hour later.

Summer night. Smell of dying heat, car exhaust, cigarette smoke, perfume. Sound of jukebox, distant loud mufflers, even more distant rushing train, lonely baying dogs.

Mike and Neil were gone.

I went home and opened myself a beer.

The phone rang. Once again, I was expecting Jan.

"Found the bastard," Neil said. "He followed you from your house to the bowling alley. Then he got tired of waiting and took off again. This time we followed *him.*"

"Where?"

He gave me an address. It wasn't a good one.

"We're waiting for you to get here. Then we're going up to pay him a little visit."

"I need twenty minutes."

"Hurry."

Not even the silver touch of moonlight lent these blocks of crumbling stucco apartment houses any majesty or beauty. The rats didn't even bother to hide. They squatted red-eyed on the unmown lawns, amidst beer cans, and broken bottles, and wrappers from Taco John's, and used condoms that looked like deflated mushrooms.

Mike stood behind a tree.

"I followed him around back," Mike said. "He went up the fire escape on the back. Then he jumped on this veranda. He's in the back apartment on the right side. Neil's in the backyard, watching for him."

Mike looked down at my ball bat. "That's a nice complement," he said. Then he showed me his handgun. "To this."

"Why the hell did you bring that?"

"Are you kidding? You're the one who said he killed Bob."

That, I couldn't argue with.

"All right," I said, "but what happens when we catch him?"

"We tell him to lay off us," Mike said.

"We need to go to the cops."

"Oh, sure. Sure we do." He shook his head. He looked as if he were dealing with a child. A very slow one. "Aaron, going to the cops now won't bring Bob back. And it's only going to get us in trouble."

That's when we heard the shout. It sounded like Neil.

Maybe five feet of rust-colored grass separated yard from the alley that ran along the west side of the apartment house.

We ran down the alley, having to hop over an ancient drooping picket fence to reach the backyard where Neil lay sprawled, face down, next to a twenty-year-old Chevrolet that was tireless and up on blocks. Through the windshield, you could see the huge gouges in the seats where the rats had eaten their fill.

The backyard smelled of dog shit and car oil.

Neil was moaning. At least we knew he was alive.

"The sonofabitch," he said, when we got him to his feet. "I moved over to the other side, back of the car there, so he wouldn't see me if he tried to come down that fire escape. I didn't figure there was another fire escape on the side of the building. He must've come around there and snuck up on me. He tried to kill me but I had this—"

In the moonlight, his wrist and the switchblade knife he held in his fingers were wet and dark with blood. "I got him a couple of times in the arm. Otherwise, I'd be dead."

"We're going up there," Mike said.

"How about checking Neil first?" I said.

"I'm fine," Neil said. "A little headache from where he caught me on the back of the neck." He waved his bloody blade. "Good thing I had this."

The landlord was on the first floor. He wore Bermuda shorts and no shirt. He looked eleven or twelve months pregnant with little male titties and enough coarse black hair to knit a sweater with. He had a plastic-tipped cigarillo in the left corner of his mouth.

"Yeah?"

"Two-F," I said.

"What about it?"

"Who lives there?"

"Nobody."

"Nobody?"

"If you were the law, you'd show me a badge."

"I'll show you a badge," Mike said, making a fist.

"Hey," I said, playing good cop to his bad cop. "You just let me speak to this gentleman."

The guy seemed to like my reference to him as a gentleman. It was probably the only name he'd never been called.

"Sir, we saw somebody go up there."

"Oh," he said, "the vampires."

"Vampires?"

He sucked down some cigarillo smoke. "That's what we call 'em, the missus and me. They're street people, winos and homeless and all like that. They know that sometimes some of these apartments ain't rented for a while, so they sneak up there and spend the night."

"You don't stop them?"

"You think I'd get my head split open for something like that?"

"I guess that makes sense." Then: "So nobody's renting it now?"

"Nope, it ain't been rented for three months. This fat broad lived there then. Man, did she smell. You know how fat people can smell sometimes? *She* sure smelled." He wasn't svelte.

Back on the front lawn, trying to wend my way between the mounds of dog shit, I said, " 'Vampires.' Good name for them."

"Yeah it is," Neil said. "I just keep thinking of the one who died. His weird eyes."

"Here we go again," Mike said. "You two guys love to scare the shit out of each other, don't you? They're a couple of nickel-dime crooks, and that's *all* they are."

"All right if Mike and I stop and get some beer and then swing by your place?"

"Sure," I said. "Just as long as Mike buys Bud and none of that generic crap."

"Oh, I forgot," Neil laughed. "He does do that when it's his turn to buy, doesn't he?"

"Yeah," I said, "he certainly does."

I was never sure what time the call came. Darkness. The ringing phone seemed part of a dream from which I couldn't escape. Somehow I managed to lift the receiver before the phone machine kicked in.

Silence. That special *kind* of silence.

Him. I had no doubt about it. The vampire, as the landlord had called him. The one who'd killed Bob. I didn't say so much as hello. Just listened, angry, afraid, confused.

After a few minutes, he hung up.

Darkness again; deep darkness, the quarter moon in the sky a cold golden scimitar that could cleave a head from a neck.

V

About noon on Sunday, Jan called to tell me that she was staying a few days extra. The kids had discovered archery and there was a course at the Y they were taking and wouldn't she please please *please* ask good old Dad if they could stay. I said sure.

I called Neil and Mike to remind them that at nine tonight we were going to pay a visit to that crumbling stucco apartment house again.

I spent an hour on the lawn. My neighbors shame me into it. Lawns aren't anything I get excited about. But they sort of shame you into it. About halfway through, Byrnes, the chunky advertising man who lives next door, came over and clapped me on the back. He was apparently pleased that I was a real human being and taking a real human being's interest in my lawn. As usual he wore an expensive T-shirt with one of his client products on it and a pair of Bermuda shorts. As usual he tried hard to be the kind of winsome neighbor you always had in sitcoms of the fifties. But I knew somebody who knew him. Byrnes had fired his number two man so he wouldn't have to keep paying the man's insurance. The man was unfortunately dying of cancer. Byrnes was typical of all the ad people I'd met. Pretty treacherous people who spent most of their time cheating clients out of their money and putting on awards banquets so they could convince themselves that advertising was actually an endeavor that was of consequence.

Around four *Hombre* was on one of the cable channels so I had a few beers and watched Paul Newman doing the best acting of his career. At least that was my opinion.

I was just getting ready for the shower when the phone rang.

He didn't say hello. He didn't identify himself. "Tracy call you?"

It was Neil. Tracy was Mike's wife. "Why should she call me?"

"He's dead. Mike."

"What?"

"You remember how he was always bitching about that elevator at work?"

Mike worked in a very old building. He made jokes about the antiquated elevators. But you could always tell the joke simply hid his fears. He'd gotten stuck innumerable times, and it was always stopping several feet short of the upcoming floor.

"He opened the door and the car wasn't there. He fell eight floors."

"Oh, God."

"I don't have to tell you who did it, do I?"

"Maybe it's time—"

"I'm way ahead of you, Aaron. I'll pick you up in half an hour. Then we go to the police. You agree?"

"I agree."

Late Sunday afternoon, the second precinct parking lot is pretty empty. We'd missed the shift change. Nobody came or went.

"We ask for a detective," Neil said. He was dark sportcoat–white shirt–necktie earnest. I'd settled for an expensive blue sport-shirt Jan had bought me for my last birthday.

"You know one thing we haven't considered?"

"You're not going to change my mind."

"I'm not *trying* to change your mind, Neil, I'm just saying that there's one thing we haven't considered."

He sat behind his steering wheel, his head resting on the back of his seat.

"A lawyer."

"What for?"

"Because we may go in there and say something that gets us in very deep shit."

"No lawyers," he said. "We'd just look like we were trying to hide something from the cops."

"You sure about that?"

"I'm sure."

"You ready?" I said.

"Ready."

The interior of the police station was quiet. A muscular bald man in a dark uniform sat behind a desk that read Information.

He said, "Help you?"

"We'd like to see a detective," I said.

"Are you reporting a crime?"

"Uh, yes," I said.

"What sort of crime?" he said.

I started to speak but once again lost my voice. I thought about all the reporters, about how Jan and the kids would be affected by it all. How my job would be affected. Taking a guy down to the basement and tying him up and then accidentally killing him—

Neil said: "Vandalism."

"Vandalism?" the cop said. "You don't need a detective, then. I can just give you a form." Then he gave us a leery look, as if he sensed we'd just changed our minds about something.

"In that case, could I just take it home with me and fill it out there?" Neil said.

"Yeah, I guess." The cop still watched as carefully now.

"Great."

"You sure that's what you wanted to report? Vandalism?"

"Yeah; yeah, that's exactly what we wanted to report," Neil said. "Exactly."

"Vandalism?" I said, when we were back in the car.

"I don't want to talk right now."

"Well, maybe *I* want to talk."

"I just couldn't do it."

"No kidding."

He looked over at me. "You could've told him the truth. Nobody was stopping you."

I looked out the window. "Yeah, I guess I could've."

"We're going over there tonight. To the vampire's place."

"And do what?"

"Ask him how much he wants."

"How much he wants for what?" I said.

"How much he wants to forget everything. He goes on with his life, we go on with ours."

I had to admit, I'd had a similar thought myself. Neil and I didn't know how to do any of this. But the vampire did. He was good at stalking, good at harassing, good at violence.

"We don't have a lot of money to throw around."

"Maybe he won't *want* a lot of money. I mean, this guy isn't exactly sophisticated."

"He's sophisticated enough to make two murders look like accidents."

"I guess that's a point."

"I'm just not sure we should pay him anything, Neil."

"You got any better ideas?"

I didn't, actually; I didn't have any better ideas at all.

vi

I spent an hour on the phone with Jan that afternoon. The last few days I'd been pretty anxious and she'd sensed it and now she was making sure that everything was all right with me. In addition to being wife and lover, Jan's also my best friend. I can't kid her. She always knows when something's wrong. I'd put off telling her about Bob and Mike dying. I'd been afraid that I might accidentally say more than I should and make her suspicious. But now I had to tell her about their deaths. It was the only way I could explain my tense mood.

"That's awful," she said. "Their poor families."

"They're handling it better than you might think."

"Maybe I should bring the kids home early."

"No reason to, hon. I mean, realistically there isn't anything any of us can do."

"Two accidents in that short a time. It's pretty strange."

"Yeah, I guess it is. But that's how it happens sometimes."

"Are you going to be all right?"

"Just need to adjust is all." I sighed. "I guess we won't be having our poker games anymore."

Then I did something I hadn't intended. I started crying and the tears caught in my throat.

"Oh, honey," Jan said. "I wish I was there so I could give you a big hug."

"I'll be OK."

"Two of your best friends."

"Yeah." The tears were starting to dry up now.

"Oh, did I tell you about Tommy?" Tommy was our six-year-old.

"No, what?"

"Remember how he used to be so afraid of horses?"

"Uh-huh."

"Well, we took him out to this horse ranch where you can rent horses?"

"Uh-huh."

"And they found him a little Shetland pony and let him ride it and he loved it. He wasn't afraid at all." She laughed. "In fact, we could barely drag him home." She paused. "You're probably not in the mood for this, are you? I'm sorry, hon. Maybe you should go do something to take your mind off things. Is there a good movie on?"

"I guess I could check."

"Something light, that's what you need."

"Sounds good," I said. "I'll go get the newspaper and see what's on."

"Love you."

"Love you, too, sweetheart," I said.

I spent the rest of the afternoon going through my various savings accounts and investments. I had no idea what the creep would want to leave us alone. We could always threaten him with going to the police, though he might rightly point out that if we really wanted to do that, we would already have done it.

I settled in the five-thousand-dollar range. That was the maximum cash I had to play with. And even then I'd have to borrow a little from one of the mutual funds we had earmarked for the kids and college.

Five thousand dollars. To me, it sounded like an enormous amount of money, probably because I knew how hard I'd had to work to get it.

But would it be enough for our friend the vampire?

Neil was there just at dark. He parked in the drive and came in. Meaning he wanted to talk.

We went in the kitchen. I made us a couple of highballs and we sat there and discussed finances.

"I came up with six thousand," he said.

"I got five."

"That's eleven grand," he said. "It's got to be more cash than this creep has ever seen."

"What if he takes it and comes back for more?"

"We make it absolutely clear," Neil said, "that there is no more. That this is it. Period."

"And if not?"

Neil nodded. "I've thought this through. You know the kind of lowlife we're dealing with? A) He's a burglar which means, these days, that he's a junkie. B) If he's a junkie then that means he's very susceptible to AIDS. So between being a burglar and shooting up, this guy is probably going to have a very short lifespan."

"I guess I'd agree."

"Even if he wants to make our lives miserable, he probably won't live long enough to do it. So I think we'll be making just the one payment. We'll buy enough time to let nature take its course— his nature."

"What if he wants more than the eleven grand?"

"He won't. His eyes'll pop out when he sees this."

I looked at the kitchen clock. It was going on nine now.

"I guess we could drive over there."

"It may be a long night," Neil said.

"I know."

"But I guess we don't have a hell of a lot of choice, do we?"

As we'd done the last time we'd been here, we split up the duties. I took the backyard, Neil the apartment door. We'd waited until midnight. The rap music had died by now. Babies cried and mothers screamed; couples fought. TV screens flickered in dark windows.

I went up the fire escape slowly and carefully. We'd talked about bringing guns then decided against it. We weren't exactly marksmen and if a cop stopped us for some reason, we could be arrested for carrying unlicensed firearms. All I carried was a flashlight in my back pocket.

As I grabbed the rungs of the ladder, powdery rust dusted my hands. I was chilly with sweat. My bowels felt sick. I was scared. I just wanted it to be over with. I wanted him to say yes he'd take the money and then that would be the end of it.

The stucco veranda was filled with discarded toys—a tricycle, innumerable games, a space helmet, a Wiffle bat and ball. The floor was crunchy with dried animal feces. At least I hoped the feces belonged to animals and not human children.

The door between veranda and apartment was open. Fingers of moonlight revealed an overstuffed couch and chair and a floor covered with the debris of fast food, McDonald's sacks, Pizza Hut wrappers and cardboards, Arby's wrappers, and what seemed to be five or six dozen empty beer cans. Far toward the hall that led to the front door I saw four red eyes watching me; a pair of curious rats.

I stood still and listened. Nothing. No sign of life. I went inside. Tiptoeing.

I went to the front door and let Neil in. There in the murky light of the hallway, he made a face. The smell *was* pretty bad.

Over the next ten minutes, we searched the apartment. And found nobody.

"We could wait here for him," I said.

"No way."

"The smell?"

"The smell, the rats, God; don't you just feel unclean?"

"Yeah, guess I do."

"There's an empty garage about halfway down the alley. We'd have a good view of the back of this building."

"Sounds pretty good."

"Sounds better than this place, anyway."

This time, we both went out the front door and down the stairway. Now the smells were getting to me as they'd earlier gotten to Neil. Unclean. He was right.

We got in Neil's Buick, drove down the alley that ran along the west side of the apartment house, backed up to the dark garage, and whipped inside.

"There's a sack in back," Neil said. "It's on your side."

"A sack?"

"Brewskis. Quart for you, quart for me."

"That's how my old man used to drink them," I said. I was the only blue-collar member of the poker game club. "Get off work at the plant and stop by and pick up two quart bottles of Hamms. Never missed."

"Sometimes I wish I would've been born into the working class," Neil said.

I was the blue-collar guy and Neil was the dreamer, always inventing alternate realities for himself.

"No, you don't," I said, leaning over the seat and picking up the sack damp from the quart bottles. "You had a damned nice life in Boston."

"Yeah, but I didn't learn anything. You know I was eighteen before I learned about cunnilingus?"

"Talk about cultural deprivation," I said.

"Well, every girl I went out with probably looks back on me as a pretty lame lover. They went down on me but I never went down on them. How old were you when you learned about cunnilingus?"

"Maybe thirteen."

"See?"

"I learned about it but I didn't do anything about it."

"I was twenty years old before I lost my cherry," Neil said.

"I was seventeen."

"Bullshit."

"Bullshit what? I was seventeen."

"In sociology, they always taught us that blue-collar kids always lost their virginity a lot earlier than white-collar kids."

"That's the trouble with sociology. It tries to particularize from generalities."

"Huh?" He grinned. "Yeah, I always thought sociology was full of shit, too, actually. But you were really seventeen?"

"I was really seventeen."

I wish I could tell you that I knew what it was right away, the missile that hit the windshield and shattered and starred it, and then kept right on tearing through the car until the back window was also shattered and starred.

But all I knew was that Neil was screaming and I was screaming and my quart bottle of Miller's was spilling all over my crotch as I tried to hunch down behind the dashboard. It was a tight fit because Neil was trying to hunch down behind the steering wheel.

The second time, I knew what was going on: somebody was

shooting at us. Given the trajectory of the bullet, he had to be right in front of us, probably behind the two dumpsters that sat on the other side of the alley.

"Can you keep down and drive this sonofabitch at the same time?"

"I can try," Neil said.

"If we sit here much longer, he's going to figure out we don't have guns. Then he's gonna come for us for sure."

Neil leaned over and turned on the ignition. "I'm going to turn left when we get out of here."

"Fine. Just get moving."

"Hold on."

What he did was kind of slump over the bottom half of the wheel, just enough so he could sneak a peek at where the car was headed.

There were no more shots.

All I could hear was the smooth-running Buick motor.

He eased out of the garage, ducking down all the time.

When he got a chance, he bore left.

He kept the lights off.

Through the bullet hole in the windshield I could see an inch or so of starry sky.

It was a long alley and we must have gone a quarter block before he said, "I'm going to sit up. I think we lost him."

"So do I."

"Look at that frigging windshield."

Not only was the windshield a mess, the car reeked of spilled beer.

"You think I should turn on the headlights?"

"Sure," I said. "We're safe now."

We were still crawling at maybe ten miles per hour when he pulled the headlights on.

That's when we saw him, silver of eye, dark of hair, crouching in the middle of the alley waiting for us. He was a good fifty yards ahead of us but we were still within range.

There was no place we could turn around.

He fired.

This bullet shattered whatever had been left untouched of the windshield. Neil slammed on the brakes.

Then he fired a second time.

By now, both Neil and I were screaming and cursing again.

A third bullet.

"Run him over!" I yelled, ducking behind the dashboard.

"What?" Neil yelled back.

"Floor it!"

He floored it. He wasn't even sitting up straight. We might have gone careening into one of the garages or Dumpsters. But somehow the Buick stayed in the alley. And very soon it was traveling eighty-five miles per hour. I watched the speedometer peg it.

More shots, a lot of them now, side windows shattering, bullets ripping into fender and hood and top.

I didn't see us hit him but I *felt* us hit him, the car traveling that fast, the creep so intent on killing us he hadn't bothered to get out of the way in time.

The front of the car picked him up and hurled him into a garage near the head of the alley.

We both sat up, watched as his entire body was broken against the edge of the garage, and he then fell smashed and unmoving to the grass.

"Kill the lights," I said.

"What?"

"Kill the lights and let's go look at him."

Neil punched off the headlights.

We left the car and ran over to him.

A white rib stuck bloody and brazen from his side. Blood poured from his ears, nose, mouth. One leg had been crushed and also showed white bone. His arms had been broken, too.

I played my flashlight beam over him.

He was dead, all right.

"Looks like we can save our money," I said. "It's all over now."

"I want to get the hell out of here."

"Yeah," I said. "So do I."

We got the hell out of there.

vii

A month later, just as you could smell autumn on the summer winds, Jan and I celebrated our twelfth wedding anniversary. We drove up to Lake Geneva, in Wisconsin, and stayed at a very nice hotel and rented a Chris-Craft for a couple of days. This was the first time I'd been able to relax since the thing with the burglar had started.

One night when Jan was asleep, I went up on the deck of the boat and just watched the stars. I used to read a lot of Edgar Rice Burroughs when I was a boy. I always remembered how John Carter felt—that the stars had a very special destiny for him—and would someday summon him to that destiny. My destiny, I decided that night there on the deck, was to be a good family man, a good stockbroker, and a good neighbor. The bad things were all behind me now. I imagined Neil was feeling pretty much the same way. Hot bitter July seemed a long ways behind us now. Fall was coming, bringing with it football and Thanksgiving and Christmas. July would recede even more with snow on the ground.

The funny thing was, I didn't see Neil much anymore. It was as if the sight of each other brought back a lot of bad memories. It was a mutual feeling, too. I didn't want to see him any more than he wanted to see me. Our wives thought this was pretty strange. They'd meet at the supermarket or shopping center and wonder why "the boys" didn't get together anymore. Neil's wife, Sarah, kept inviting us over to "sit around the pool and watch Neil pretend he knows how to swim." September was summer hot. The pool was still the centerpiece of their life.

Not that I made any new friends. The notion of a midweek poker game had lost all its appeal. There was work and my family and little else.

Then one sunny Indian summer afternoon, Neil called and said, "Maybe we should get together again."

"Maybe."

"It's over, Aaron. It really is."

"I know."

"Will you at least think about it?"

I felt embarrassed. "Oh, hell, Neil. Is that swimming pool of yours open Saturday afternoon?"

"As a matter of fact, it is. And as a matter of fact, Sarah and the girls are going to be gone to a fashion show at the club."

"Perfect. We'll have a couple of beers."

"You know how to swim?"

"No," I said, laughing. "And from what Sarah says, you don't, either."

I got there about three, pulled into the drive, walked to the back where the gate in the wooden fence led to the swimming pool. It was eighty degrees and even from here I could smell the chlorine.

I opened the gate and went inside and saw him right away. The funny thing was, I didn't have much of a reaction at all. I just watched him. He was floating. Facedown. He looked pale in his red trunks. This, like the others, would be judged an accidental death. Of that I had no doubt at all.

I used the cellular phone in my car to call 911.

I didn't want Sarah and the girls coming back to see an ambulance and police cars in the drive and them not knowing what was going on.

I called the club and had her paged.

I told her what I'd found. I let her cry. I didn't know what to say. I never do.

In the distance, I could hear the ambulance working its way toward the Neil Solomon residence.

I was just about to get out of the car when my cellular phone rang. I picked up. "Hello?"

"There were three of us that night at your house, Mr. Bellini. You killed two of us. I recovered from when your friend stabbed me, remember? Now I'm ready for action. I really am, Mr. Bellini."

Then the emergency people were there, and neighbors, too, and then wan, trembling Sarah. I just let her cry some more. Gave her whiskey and let her cry.

viii

He knows how to do it, whoever he is.

He lets a long time go between late-night calls. He lets me start to think that maybe he changed his mind and left town. And then he calls.

Oh, yes, he knows just how to play this little game.

He never says anything, of course. He doesn't need to. He just listens. And then hangs up.

I've considered going to the police, of course, but it's way too late for that. Way too late.

Or I could ask Jan and the kids to move away to a different city with me. But he knows who I am and he'd find me again.

So all I can do is wait and hope that I get lucky, the way Neil and I got lucky the night we killed the second of them.

Tonight I can't sleep.

It's after midnight.

Jan and I wrapped presents until well after eleven. She asked me again if anything was wrong. We don't make love as much as we used to, she said; and then there are the nightmares. Please tell me if something's wrong, Aaron. Please.

I stand at the window watching the snow come down. Soft and beautiful snow. In the morning, a Saturday, the kids will make a snowman and then go sledding and then have themselves a good old-fashioned snowball fight, which invariably means that one of them will come rushing in at some point and accuse the other of some terrible misdeed.

I see all this from the attic window.

Then I turn back and look around the poker table. Four empty chairs. Three of them belong to dead men.

I look at the empty chairs and think back to summer.

I look at the empty chairs and wait for the phone to ring.

I wait for the phone to ring.

AFTERWORD
DEAN KOONTZ

1. The Origins of the Relationship

Ed Gorman and I met on the telephone and spent scores of hours in conversation spread over almost two years before we finally met face to face. No, it wasn't one of those sleazy pay-by-the-minute "party-line" dating services gone awry. It started as an interview for his magazine, *Mystery Scene*, but we spent so much time laughing that we began having bull sessions on a regular basis.

He has a marvelous sense of humor and a dry wit. Oh, sure, he can produce faux flatulence with his hand in his armpit every bit as convincingly as Princess Di can, and like the Pope he never goes anywhere without plastic vomit and a dribble glass, but it's the more *refined* side of Ed that I find the most amusing.

2. How I Wound Up in Cedar Rapids

In 1989, my wife, Gerda, and I drove across country to do some book research, to visit some relatives and old friends, to receive an honorary doctorate at my alma mater in Pennsylvania—and to give a proper test to our new radar detector. The detector worked swell: we left the Los Angeles area at eight o'clock on a Thursday morning and were in eastern Arkansas in time for dinner. We ate at our motel, and the food wasn't all that good, but everyone thought we were enjoying the hell out of ourselves because crossing six states under four Gs of acceleration contorts your face muscles into a wide grin that remains fixed for eight to ten hours after you get out of the car.

The research was conducted successfully. The visits with friends and relatives were a delight. The address I delivered to the graduating class was well received. I was awarded the honorary doctorate—whereafter I had to decide whether to be a podiatrist or cardiovascular surgeon, a very difficult choice in a world where heart disease and sore feet tragically afflict millions.

Soon we were driving west from Pennsylvania, on our way home, our tasks completed and our lofty goals fulfilled. Our radar detector was clipped to the sun visor, Ohio and Illinois and Indiana were passing in a pretty blur rather like that of the star swarms beyond the portals of the Enterprise when Captain Kirk tells Scotty to put the ship up to warp speed, and we were proud to be participating in that great American pastime—Avoiding Police Detection. Driving in opposition to the direction of Earth's rotation, therefore having to set the car clock back an hour every once in a while, we might have made it to California before we left for the journey east, in time to warn ourselves against that damn salad-bar restaurant outside of Memphis—except we planned to take a side trip to Cedar Rapids, Iowa, to meet Ed and his wife, Carol.

3. The First Night of That Historic Visit
After leaving Interstate 80, we passed through gently rising plains and rich farmland, all of it so bland that we began to be afraid that we had died and gone to the twenty-third circle of hell (Dante had it wrong; he undercounted), where the punishment for the sinner is terminal boredom. We couldn't get anything on the radio but Merle Haggard tunes.

Late in the afternoon, we reached Cedar Rapids, which proved to be a surprisingly pleasant place, attractive to more than the eye. As we crossed the city line, the air was redolent of brown sugar, raisins, coconut and other delicious aromas, because one of the giant food-processing companies was evidently cooking up a few hundred thousand granola bars. How pleasant, we thought, to live in a place where the air was daily perfumed with such delicious scents. It would be like living in the witch's fragrant gingerbread house after Hansel and Gretel had disposed of her and there was no longer a danger of becoming a human popover in the crone's oven.

That evening we went to dinner with Ed and Carol at a lovely restaurant in our hotel. We had a great good time. Carol, who is also a writer—primarily of young-adult fiction—is an attractive blonde with delicate features, very personable and very much a lady. Ed surprised us by wearing shoes. Not to say that shoes were the only thing he was wearing. He had socks, too, and a nice suit, and I think he was also wearing a shirt, though my memory might well be faulty regarding that detail.

There was almost *too* much conviviality for one evening. Ed started telling jokes about Zoroastrianism, involving the god Ahura Mazda, of which he has an infinite store—always a sure sign that he is having too good a time and might begin to hyperventilate or even pass a kidney stone out of sheer exuberance. They usually begin, "Ahura Mazda, Jehova and Buddha were all in a rowboat together," or something like that. For his sake, we decided to call it an evening and meet again first thing in the morning. Carol asked if there was anything special we'd like to do or see around town (like watch corn growing), and we said that we had heard there was a large Czecho-slovakian community in Cedar Rapids; as this was an ethnic group about which we knew little, we thought it might be interesting to visit any shops that dealt in Czech arts, crafts, foods, assault weap-ons imported from the East Bloc, and that sort of thing. We all hugged, and after Ed told one more Zoroastrianism joke—"Ahura Mazda was having lunch with two attorneys and a proctologist"—we parted for the night.

4. On the Edge of Sleep

Lying in our hotel-room bed that night, on the edge of sleep, Gerda and I spoke of what a lovely evening it had been.

"They're both so nice," Gerda said.

"It's so nice that someone you like on the phone turns out to be someone you also like in person," I said.

"I had such a nice time," Gerda said.

"That's nice," I said.

"Those Zoroastrianism jokes were hilarious."

"He was wearing shoes," I noted.

"I was a little worried when he hyperventilated."

"Yeah, I was afraid it was going to build up to a kidney-stone expulsion," I said.

"But it didn't," Gerda said, "and that's nice."

"Yes, that's very nice," I agreed.

"Tomorrow is going to be a very nice day."

"Very nice," I agreed, anticipating the morning with enormous pleasure.

5. A Very Nice Day

Overnight, Ed and Carol discovered a museum of Czechoslovakian arts and crafts in Cedar Rapids, and in the morning we happily embarked on a cultural expedition. The museum proved to be on a—how shall I say this as nicely as possible?—on a rather *frayed* edge of town. When we got out of Ed's car, I was hit by the most powerful stench I'd ever encountered in more than forty years of varied experience. This was a stink so profound that it not only brought tears to my eyes and forced me to clamp a handkerchief over my nose but brought me instantly to the brink of regurgitation that would have made the explosively vomiting girl in *The Exorcist* seem like a mere dribbler. When I looked at Gerda, I saw she had also resorted to a handkerchief over the nose. Though you might have noticed that comic hyperbole is an element of the style in which I've chosen to write this piece, you must understand that as regards this odor, I am not exaggerating in the least. This vile miasma was capable of searing the paint off a car and blinding small animals, yet Ed and Carol led us toward the museum, chatting and laughing, apparently oblivious of the hellish fetor that had nearly rendered us unconscious.

Finally, after I had clawed desperately at Ed's arm for ten or fifteen unsteady steps, I caught his attention. Choking and wheezing in disgust, I said, "Ed, for the love of God, man, what is that horrible odor?"

"Odor?" Ed said. Puzzled he stopped, turned, sniffing delicately at the air, as if seeking the elusive scent of a frail tropical flower.

"Surely you smell it," I protested. "It's so bad I'm beginning to bleed from the ears!"

"Oh, *that*," Ed said. He pointed toward some huge buildings fully five hundred yards away. "That's a slaughterhouse. They must be in the middle of a hog kill, judging by the smell. It's the stink of blood, feces, urine, internal organs, all mixed up together."

"It doesn't bother you?"

"Not really. When you've smelled it often enough over the years, you get used to it."

Gagging but determined to be manly about this, I managed to follow them into the Czech museum, where the odor miraculously did not penetrate. The museum turned out to be one of the most fascinating we'd ever toured, humble quarters but a spectacular and charming collection of all things Czech.

We spent longer there than we had anticipated, and when we stepped outside again, the air was clean, the stench gone without a trace. All the paint had melted off the Gormans' car, and a couple of hundred birds had perished in flight and now littered the ground, but otherwise there was no indication that the air had ever been anything but sweet.

I thought of the delicious aroma of granola-bar manufacturing, which had marked our arrival. That was at the front door. The steaming malodor of the slaughterhouse indicated what went on at the back door. Suddenly Cedar Rapids seemed less innocent, even sinister, and I began to understand for the first time how Ed could live in such sunny, bucolic environs with the gracious and lovely Carol always nearby—and nevertheless be inspired to write about the dark side of the human heart.

6. Ed Gorman, Writer

Aside from being a great guy, Ed Gorman can write circles around a whole slew of authors who are more famous than he is. Hell, he could write hexagons around them if he wanted.

He has a knack for creating dialogue that sounds natural and true. His metaphors and similes are spare and elegant. His characters are multifaceted and often too human for their own good. His style is so clean and sharp you could almost perform surgery with it; *he* does, using it like a scalpel to lay bare the inner workings of the human mind and heart.

His Jack Dwyer mysteries—especially *The Autumn Dead* and the beautifully moody and poignant *A Cry of Shadows*—are as compelling and stylistically sophisticated as any detective stories I've ever read.

If Ed has a shortcoming as a writer, it is that he wants to do *everything*. He likes Westerns, so periodically he writes an oater— always a damned good oater, too. He likes horror stories, so now and then, writing as Daniel Ransom, he produces a horror story. He likes totally serious, almost somber detective fiction but also lighter-hearted detective fiction; he has written both types well. He likes suspense, science fiction . . . well, you get the idea. Having such a catholic taste is healthy; it contributes to his freshness of viewpoint. But when a writer actually produces work in multiple genres, he dilutes his impact with readers and has more difficulty building a reputation. I know too well. Over the years, always looking for a different challenge, I've written in virtually every genre *except* the Western. Finally I discovered a way to combine many of my favorite categories of fiction into one novel, which is when I started to develop a larger audience. In time, I suspect, Ed will find his own way to make his wide-ranging interests more a marketing asset than a liability. I, for one, can't wait to see what he'll give us in the years ahead.

One warning: considering how powerful Ed's prose can be, if he ever writes about a hog kill, his personal experience should lead to such pungent olfactory descriptions that readers all over the world will be hard-pressed not to void their most recent meals into the pages of that book. Don't worry, you'll be warned in advance if one of his novels has a hog-kill scene in it because, being the reader's friend, I will be sure to have an endorsement on the jacket, alerting you in language something like this: "A brilliant, dazzling, breath-taking novel, a work of sheer genius. Everyone should read Gorman—but in this case, only while wearing a protective rubber sheet or while sitting naked in a bathtub."

7. *The Lovely Gorman Home*

That fine spring day in Cedar Rapids, after visiting the Czech museum adjacent to the hog kill, we went to lunch at an all-you-can-eat buffet restaurant with as lavish a spread as I had ever seen. I ate a soda cracker.

After lunch we went to Ed and Carol's house, which was most tastefully furnished. The place was spotless, with beautiful polished-wood floors, and suffused with a friendly atmosphere.

A couple of minutes after we arrived, my eyes began to sting, then burn, then flood with tears. For a moment I thought I was overcome with emotion at being welcomed into my friends' home. Then my sinuses suddenly felt as if they had been filled with cement, my face began to swell, and my lips itched. I realized that I had either been caught in the beam of an extraterrestrial death ray—or was in a house where a cat resided. As I had never previously encountered monsters from far worlds but *had* encountered cats to which I was allergic, I decided I could believe the Gormans when they repeatedly insisted that they were not harboring fiendish extraterrestrials but merely felines.

I wish I could tell you that their house was positively crawling with scores of cats; an eccentricity like that would make them even more fun to write about. However, as I remember, there were only two. For some reason I am not allergic to every cat who crosses my path, only to about half those I meet, but I seemed to be allergic to both the Gorman cats. Neither creature looked like a feline from hell, though they had a demonic effect on me, and in less than half an hour we had to move on.

When I stumbled out of the Gorman house, I was shockingly pale, sweating and gasping for breath. My watering eyes were so bloodshot they appeared to be on fire, and the only sound I could squeeze out of my irritated vocal cords and swollen throat was a wretched gurgle rather like that issued by a nauseated wombat.

(I realized much later, the oddest thing about that moment was the reaction of the neighbors to my near-death paroxysms on the Gormans' front lawn. None of them exhibited the least surprise or concern. It was as if they had seen scores—perhaps hundreds—of people erupting from that house in far worse condition and had become enured to the drama. Maybe they *were* cats from hell . . . which might explain why sometimes, instead of purring, they spoke rapid, intricately cadenced Latin.)

The Gormans, being two of the nicest people I've ever known, were excessively apologetic, as if somehow they were responsible for my stupid allergy. When I could breathe again, and when my eyes had stopped spurting blood, I found myself repeatedly assuring them that none of it was their fault, that they are *allowed* to have cats in the United States of America regardless of my allergy, and that they would not rot in hell because of their choice of pets.

(Ed has a tendency to feel responsible for the world and to blame himself for things beyond his control—like floods in Sri Lanka and train wrecks in Uzbekistan. Like any good Catholic boy, he knows that he is guilty for all the sins of the world, a vile repository of shameless want and need and lust, who deserves far worse punishment than any plague God could deliver upon him. In his mind, having cats to which a guest has an allergy is just one small step below taking an Uzi out to the mall and blowing away a hundred Christmas shoppers.)

8. A Thankfully Uneventful Trip to Iowa City, Iowa

Anxious to get me away from his cats and to atone for what they had done to me, Ed suggested we take a ride from Cedar Rapids to Iowa City, where we could have a pleasant stroll through Prairie Lights, a large and nationally known bookstore, then have an early-ish dinner (as Gerda and I had to rise at dawn to resume our journey to California). He assured us that Iowa City also boasted a feline slaughterhouse where we could go to compare the stink of cat kill to that of a hog kill.

Aside from a hair-raising ride due to the sheer contempt in which Ed holds those lane-dividing lines on public highways, our sidetrip to Iowa City was uneventful. Just good conversation—

much of it book talk—and a nice dinner. I had another soda cracker. I was able to keep it down with little trouble. I was quite sure that, in a month or so, the memory of the hog-kill stench would have faded sufficiently to allow me to eat normally again, certainly before my weight had slipped much lower than ninety pounds.

9. *Ed Gorman, the Phone Company, and Me*

As I write this, it is nearly three years since our stay in Cedar Rapids and our two days with Ed and Carol. As both of us are to some degree workaholics and as neither of us, therefore, is much of a traveler, Ed and I have not yet managed to get together again face to face. We stay in touch by reading each other's books—and with the help of the telephone. Our conversations continue to be punctuated with a lot of laughter—a precious, vital medicine in this madhouse world. Here's a cute anecdote: sometimes at three in the morning, Ed calls up and, with a couple of handkerchiefs over the mouthpiece of his phone, distorts his voice and makes obscene threats, apparently because he's concerned about keeping my life interesting and full of color, and I am always touched by his genuine concern that I never become bored, by the fact that he would take the time and trouble to entertain me in such a fashion. He doesn't realize that I know the identity of the obscene caller, and he would surely be embarrassed to know that I am aware of his thoughtfulness. But you see, no matter how much he distorts his voice, those cats are in his study with him, and even long-distance my lips go numb and my eyes begin to bleed.